p R e s e n c e

GEORGIA REVIEW BOOKS
EDITED BY Gerald Maa

PReS

BReNDa

ence

a novel

IIJIMA

THE UNIVERSITY OF GEORGIA PRESS *ATHENS*

Published by the University of Georgia Press
Athens, Georgia 30602
www.ugapress.org
© 2024 by Brenda Iijima
All rights reserved
Designed by Kaelin Chappell Broaddus
Set in 10.25/13.5 Alegreya Regular by Kaelin Chappell Broaddus

Most University of Georgia Press titles are
available from popular e-book vendors.

Printed digitally

Library of Congress Cataloging-in-Publication Data

Names: Iijima, Brenda, author.
Title: Presence : a novel / Brenda Iijima.
Description: Athens : The University of Georgia Press, [2024] |
    Includes
bibliographical references. |
Identifiers: LCCN 2023025314 (print) | LCCN 2023025315 (ebook)
    | ISBN 9780820365299 (hardback) | ISBN 9780820365305
    (paperback) | ISBN 9780820365312 (epub)
Subjects: LCGFT: Novels.
Classification: LCC PS3559.I35 P74 2024 (print) | LCC PS3559.I35
    (ebook) | DDC 813/.6—dc23/eng/20230607
LC record available at https://lccn.loc.gov/2023025314
LC ebook record available at https://lccn.loc.gov/2023025315

Presence is for my planetary mother, Earth, and my human mother, Erika Uchman. With gratitude to Cindy Schneider, wonderful person, tremendous caregiver.

contents

earth science

P R e s e n c e

PROLOGUe

a catalyst for adaptability yet written in a script that used terms like eden to refute endless change. we were inhabitants who survived the catastrophes for the meantime, back in time.

We had a history of genocide, slavery, and appropriation of all personhood and earth material as possession. We forged a nation nefariously, handing out gifts in the form of woolen blankets saturated in lethal germs. The doctrine of discovery was one such instrument used as a legal, political, and spiritual justification for the seizure and control of Indigenous lands by settler colonialists who after arrival immediately thought of the land as theirs. A violent superiority was a narcissism that pervaded all relations between the settler colonialists and people who did not have the identical skin tone as them or did not share their religious affiliation. A fear of "wilderness" influenced their actions. Nature had to be tamed, land made productive. Property acquisition was the priority. Vying colonial interests fought for territory. The environment was divided into parcels for sale. Dispossession occurred. With ownership came individualized land use; corporations, too, were understood as individuals. Whoever was seen as unworthy or did not use the land in the ways deemed productive lost their land. The gross domestic product was one evaluator of how our economy was geared. Toward profit at all costs. Methods of production led to cycles of overaccumulation and depletion. Everything became monetized, itemized, and surveilled. Dependability was touted as a feature, yet precarity ruled. Military installations dotted the globe accounting for more than half of all budget allocations. The wars we fought were both offensive and defensive. Warfare was an ever-present engagement. Domestically a punitive understanding of being in time and space created an ever-growing carceral state. Prisons were institutions where society confined those it did not want to deal with: the poor, abandoned, mentally ill, violent. A disproportionate percentage of people of color were made to serve time. Racialized violence and discrimination were systemic, ever-present. Hierarchies defined the society.

From kingdom, to nation-state, to corporate managed population, we transformed.

Carbon-based fossil fuel was our primary energy source, causing the climate to change at a rapid pace. Nuclear energy was also commonly used, which led to malfunction and failure. We ignored orders not to use sea water to cool overheating reactors. The radiation levels were so high that even robots could not enter some of the melted down facilities. Other energy sources were put into action, whose implementation required mineral extractions and fossil fuel to construct, transport, and maintain. Climate ameliorating strategies were profit oriented. Many modes of methane and carbon dioxide atmospheric extraction were proposed, some implemented, oftentimes causing deleterious interaction with atmospheric systems, exacerbating matters. Some methods gave us temporary hope. Some strategies worked in some measure.

The way we modified the landscape was extremely foul. We razed forests and planted monocrops to feed a burgeoning human population displacing native animals and plants. Humans, too, were displaced in this process. The Amazon rainforest had become a sandy dead zone. The polar ice caps had long since melted. Volatile weather offered little reprieve. Initially there was an infernolike atmosphere and many fires, coupled with tornados, hurricanes, floods, and drought. As the planet heated up, horses got tinier. We noticed some creatures making evolutionary adjustments. Others were not able to live in the changing world. Bees became extinct, most insects had declined. Still, for a time we were able to maintain coexistence with spiders, snakes, monkeys, fish, birds, and some other creatures. Then a little ice age came and went, a time in which we consumed cows, then dogs, and finally each other. After the ice age, the weather oscillated between extremes. Lately we've been experiencing unending solar flaring, high heat, and a lack of moisture.

Waves of violent outbreaks continued as most systems failed. Our social world became restrictive and localized. Yet the spirit of collective care was activated: neighbors offered their neighbors assistance, work-

ers helped fellow workers. Some of the animosity that troubled us began
to fade.

Mostly we worked in automated factories, modulating computer controls; there was very little physical involvement until everything returned again to analog and corporeal modes. We lived in corporate-
owned buildings that resembled individual homes. We leased the homes
with the money we earned laboring for the bosses and had to care for
their maintenance with the limited recreational time we were permitted.
We had no legal obligation to sacrifice ourselves; doing so was implicit.
The bosses told us what to think and obfuscated what they did not want
us to consider. They succeeded for a time suggesting that no one (least
not themselves) was responsible for social and ecological precarity. They
controlled us by granting and denying privilege, by organizing us in hegemonic scales of difference. The bosses: of industry, incarceration, and
war. This system imploded. *They toppled in beams of light, in a repertoire of forms.* We managed to replace this structure with a collaborative
plan of coexisting with mutual aid as our guiding principle.

The common environment was filled with metallic residue clinging to
the solar towers. The towers were an attempt to harness energy without
harmful effects that would cause additional feedback loops with the climate. There were employees who raked the metal debris off the bases of
the towers. Other such strategies to move away from fossil fuel were instituted and abandoned. They never met our energy needs.

Eventually everyone stopped owning most material possessions except the tools and equipment that were necessary to maintain the houses
and a limited supply of household items. Everything we required could be
rented or we could gain access with a subscription. As noted previously,
maintaining the functionality of the dwellings had become a central focus of life. The infrastructure was property of the corporations in whose
jurisdiction we served. The corporations owned everything. The air, water, food, all of Earth and other reachable planets.

For an indeterminate period, people kept up certain styles and man-
nerisms, then these tendencies faded. It is hard to say when the capitalist
time clock crumbled. The digits fell off the clocks, and the clocks rolled
into the great bonfires. No one took responsibility for the fires; they just
appeared everywhere. This was not something to celebrate. It was a different reality that we took satisfaction in, as our interpretation of the

world altered. It was not necessary to rehearse pleasures. Unfolding actuality was evocative.

The population had shrunk drastically. Having children was something we all dreamt about; pregnancies were quite rare and fraught, yet we bloomed, internally and externally. Babies were often born too unformed to survive. Pregnant mothers were placed in comas to maintain their vital signs before giving birth in order to increase the likelihood of a successful pregnancy. Newborns needing therapy received treatment at specialized facilities. They were hooked up to monitors, suspended in chemical baths, placed in specialized deprivation chambers, given transfusions with enhanced blood. DNA modification helped alleviate some emergent syndromes. Reproductive issues began gradually and imperceptibly at an unrecognized threshold overload. *My father said: Whose father are you rendering. My mother said: Whose mother are you rendering. My brother said: Whose brother is being referred to.*

The cumulative effect of generations of agricultural chemicals, ammunitions, pharmaceuticals, and other toxins of industry and war polluting the environment had a morphing effect on bodies. Sexual dimorphism disappeared. Everyone had varied genitalia. Most of the population was intersexual. We were for the most part delighted to no longer have to deal with the polarity of gender. The social conventions we held about our bodies were open and liberatory. We did not subscribe to the cruelty of body shaming and the ableisms of bygone eras. Ability had little significance to us, effort was where we placed emphasis. This was not wishful thinking; it was our agenda. Many had been transforming their genders for decades.

The near-total extinction of other animals and plants changed the planet and the way we lived. Some corporations had menageries of animals and plants that they maintained, privately, until the corporations also faltered. Zoos were a thing of the past. Zoomorphic diseases meant the interactions with other species were threatening to all concerned. With compromised immunity and the lack of effective interventions those that survived had to be cautious of emergent viruses and other diseases. Obviously, no one had pets any longer, either. It was difficult enough to maintain our well-being and provide sustenance for ourselves. Robot companions were a fad, they required expenditures for maintenance and energy, an expense prohibitive for most people.

Everyone seemed to have a manifesto memorized. This was a thing to do recreationally, to recite one's manifesto. There was great drama and longing in the recitations of utopian glamour. Almost everyone's manifesto contained the statement that they wished for the resurgence of forests and fields. Trudging through cesspools and garbage dumps of outmoded technological equipment, disintegrating military installments, and industrial waste had taken a toll.

There were those who recalled their ancestors speaking of the presence of whales in great oceans that wrapped around the globe. The globe had given off a bluish atmosphere when seen from outer space.

The decision to send excess spent nuclear waste into outer space had come to pass. This action caused the eventuality of nucleated material cascading to Earth. The teenaged workforce were the designated emergency crews; they were sent in when nucleated materials rained down, a frequent occurrence in the factory housing zones. They hosed down the zones with sand.

The oldest living member of the global society that anyone knew of was forty-five years of age and experienced neurodegeneration. Younger members of society experienced various forms of neurodegeneration and other physical and mental challenges. Our definition of health and wellbeing was continually changing.

Many members of society had given over to a collaborative way of group living. They seemed to live the most peaceably. *A life of spare parts, bucolic-mechanical, happy, happy, and most HAPPY, with flawless complexions.*

There were no hospitals, only mobile units sent out to assuage pain and suffering. Interventions were mostly palliative, hospice oriented.

Vehicles rode on conveyor belts, there were no roadways. Otherwise, self-ambulation was our only option when going anywhere. *We are the singing remnants.*

Joy had not been extinguished. Desire was perpetually revamped. People were energized by time and space and consciousness. Every day had some uniqueness regardless of the urgent requirements that demanded most of our energies. *Mother of all the mothers: Earth, mother's mother is the Cosmos.* This passage was stenciled all over the place, graffitied on the dwellings. It was a longstanding riddle and a vision to understand one's volatile positionality in a turbulent cosmic expanse.

There were still a few libraries that housed digital footage and for certain hours with a special pass we were permitted to watch YouTube and TikTok videos of all sorts of playful activity from the past. Watching any interaction with water was particularly compelling and great. People swimming in lakes, showering, fishing, floating on yachts, snorkeling, and watering their lawns were all popular themes.

The social fabric had certainly shrunk. It was a huge challenge to maintain the conditions for our survival. Since the population knew of no other reality, save for the historical vestiges in the library, they were not unduly depressed about the present or what was to transpire. *Give away and fall over feathers fabric memory journey flight unseen as horizons trying.*

The season of the sun was to be embraced, enjoyed. There was a popular festival held in the summer. Teen trapeze artists performed amazing stunts suspended over emptied rivers. Everyone who could come out and participate enjoyed their grace. Sunglasses reassured the delicate optics of spark. There were utopian clubs to chat about possible riveting scenarios . . . *Two forms of fabrication leaving down. Two downed legacies emptying form. Two shadows left fabricating horses. Two forms of legacy leaving down. Two fabricating shades of horsing left. Two empty horses of fabrication standing.*

Earth is a volatile environment of interactive elements and processes. We breathe in the atmosphere and release the atmosphere in a rhythmic tempo synchronizing ourselves with this world.

performance

The end of the world as we know it seems continually imminent. yet we live in the debris of many ended worlds, whose inhabitants continue to live on.

—Alexis Lothian

It is not that I have no future. rather it continually fragments on the insubstantial and indistinct ephemera of then.

—Samuel Delany

You begin to perceive that an animal or a plant and the lineage to which it belongs, and the planet itself, are like a flame; not so much a thing as a performance, always becoming something else; and that each of us and our species as a whole are part of the overall unfolding.

—Colin Tudge

communaLITy

The history of our dramatic past is convoluted and difficult to verify precisely. There is evidence of archived records; however, they were severely disrupted so that we can't apprehend for the most part how they were originally organized. Pieces of it are scattered around. Much of what still exists are tattered shreds, disjointed fragments. Occasionally we'll find a cache of books in fair condition. A loose-leaf binder with its contents intact. A buried subbasement of mostly disintegrated matter. Obsolete equipment, vehicles, weaponry, furniture, artwork, relics, bones. Most forays involve digging through layers of rubble. There are devotees who sort through the digital material on servers, hard drives, memory cards, DVDs, zip disks, and flash drives. Most of it is corrupted, scratched, broken. We've located flight recorders from downed airplanes, the backup data of a nuclear facility, several huge cloud computer data centers, forensic evidence, cemeteries. Our civic body for the most part has not been that curious about the accretions that reference a past that we have so little access to. We are linked to history by a continuum that is difficult to reconcile or understand. Recently our attitudes are changing. We dig around with greater enthusiasm. The past is never fully submerged.

It is the immediate present that engages and compels us, so it might sound contradictory that we refer to all moments in expectant terms as an ongoingness of an analogue future: instances of time that will become the present consistent with now (as now becomes the past) however many degrees tangential to it. Not all futures arrive at their destination. Some futures might falter. We contemplate the provisional and the possible within unforeseeable futures. The past is a building block of what substantiates the present. The future enters and returns to the present in ways both steadfast and emergent. It goes without saying that registers of time are manifold and elastic. The connectedness of all moments—past, present, and future—is a given. We are poised in a liminal state. We negotiate the present and the potential of other possible futures as we make incremental decisions that send us along divergent pathways, parallel tracks. We could as easily call our lives no-analogue because our present conditions are perhaps unique and unlike experience at other times—or so we imagine, supporting evidence is difficult to locate. The time theorists of our society make the claim that ours is a philosophy that treats the phenomenon of time divisibly flexible. We do not use incremental measurements to experience time or manage it; instead time is organized and relegated by body needs pretty much solely, and what is signified by the body is the communal body, the earth body, the cosmic body. Body need helps us register the constant present as a rhythm. The beat that the rhythm relates to is variable, diverse, and irregular, tugs us forward and backward throughout time. This registration does not have a name, falls outside of naming. Time drapes over us sometimes like a silken second skin, sometimes like irritable synthetic material. In somber moments history presents as a dead end, a forgone conclusiveness. History used time as its motivation and power, and we don't want to be manipulated like that.

There are no other animals on Earth besides us that we are aware of except for spiders, those creatures who defy taxonomic category, defy climatic conditions. The florae that persist are various molds, fungi, and algae that grow on rocks and on collapsed structures from wrecked civilizations, places where shade creates moisture. Microflora grows on our dwellings and in the air lung. There are also the hydroponic plants we nurture as well as the algae that we cultivate. Sometimes shadows form inexplicably in thin air, flickering about us, and we search for the forms that generated the shadows and their movements. There have been sightings of forms scurrying in the distance, or shadows moving with slow-motion pantomimed gestures. When we pursued the shapes and shadows in motion they dematerialized. We don't want to fully accept that we are alone. A thin thread of expectancy keeps our attentions geared to the horizon. Mirages are animate. Sometimes desire re-creates miraculous visions. Gardens and orchards. An image arises and there we are, harvesting fruit. Pale dewy light streams in on the grasses and the growing vegetables. Dragonflies hum by. Chickens peck between the rows of edible plants—corn, beans, squash. A furry dog jumps at our ankles. Massive trees sway in the wind. A snake slithers in a rain puddle.

Our collective encompasses everything we are. A civic togetherness based on mutual need and reciprocity. Our society is weary of categorization; any description is incomplete, partial. We just go on with the labyrinth of chores that demand our attention. We all pitch in in the ways that we can. The challenges we face are arduous, yet we find delight continually. A sense of camaraderie is readily expressed. It helps that we are not alienated from the work required. Just the opposite, work gives us connection to our goals and to each other as a society. Ours is less the top-down hierarchical approach of "management" that continually vouches for its rationale. Legalese does not play a part in our culture. Ownership is a thing of the past. Simple directions are welcome, as are straightforward summaries.

Our housing is constantly in need of repair. The siding must be reattached as it continually sags. Roofs blow off. Foundations have to be fortified. The blasting winds and penetrating solar rays make this a necessity.

Another major concern is the functioning of the air lung. This is crucial as it is our major source of oxygen. We repair and maintain its complicated concrete linings. The smallest of the teens head in together as a team with their tools. The spaces throughout the air lung are claustrophobic. The first team brings scrapers and chisels to smooth out the rough patches on the walls where residue builds up. The next group burnishes the surfaces to a sheen. Finally, a crew goes in with dusters and brooms to sweep up any scattered debris. The air lung is a complex hydroponic system that we have designed to grow single-celled organisms that photosynthesize and produce oxygen. Rotating trays are placed on racks that pass through on a conveyor belt below a sunroof. The lung must be kept continually moist. Condensation makes this possible. The air lung tunnels channel oxygen to our housing and our social spaces. The air outside our dwellings does contain oxygen, but the levels are not adequate. The air lung offers a supplementary source. Light-headedness occurs when we are outside for an extended period of time.

This task weighs heavily on us since the air lung is made up of lengthy tunnels that require unending maintenance. Entering the tunnels poses health risks and danger, so we use caution when working within the air lung system. We are susceptible to respiratory issues, and the air lung contains particulate matter. Sections of the tunnel periodically collapse. Having to do chores that are risky and dangerous is ordinary and unavoidable. No one is exempt. No one has special status. We are the commoners of the commons, as is our ethos. Here on Earth, here as Earth. We are an aspect of Earth's expression. We are a fragment of cosmic consequence.

Thankfully we've had moderate success with underground farming, so our food is almost adequate. Food preparation takes into consideration the fact that we do not have teeth with which to chew, only our gums. Tooth and hair loss were an outcome of exposure to toxins and radioactive waste. We often lack enough caloric intake and supplementary minerals, but our situation is vastly improved from a while ago when farming underground was makeshift and provisional. Before that period, people were nomadic. They scraped together an existence wherever they could find food, water, and shelter. Since we've settled and built our communal infrastructure there is a semblance of stability.

Same goes for medical care. There are technologies that were rescued during the collapses that destabilized global civilizations. Surgeries can be performed with nanotechnology, for instance. Palliative care is excellent.

Recreationally there are many spheres of enjoyment. Sensual diversions come in many forms. Some of us are partnered. On the whole we prefer to remain open to a togetherness as it arises with each other. We are committed to a practice of ensuring mutual good feeling, difficult as that can be. Though the environmental conditions are harsh and we cannot linger outside for too long without consequences to our health, the vast expanses beckon us. The subtle color shifts on the sands draw us out of our comfort zone. The lost buried cities are sites of interest. When making an expedition, we go in groups. Although mostly the expeditions are supply runs, they are a diversion from our routine. What we uncover is always surprising in its diversity of form and meaning.

Relations are polyvalent; our subjectivities are tightly interconnected. Some of us elect to have a surgical procedure that joins our brains and bodies. When the conjoined reach for consensus, they experience a surge of energy. This is one of the technologies that survived the meltdown of the previous societal order. Bodies are grafted using an organic glue that makes sutures unnecessary. A highly charged electrical pulsation device calibrates the conjoined body's nervous system. This procedure helps vulnerable people maintain a quality of life. The operation has a high success rate and is quite popular. We support one another this way.

Historians from another era might have been inclined to use the word *equality* as a marker of our social codes; we do not use this self-description. We all have varying, complementary abilities. Our adaptation is about discarding faulty linguistic constructions that baffle our fragile temporal personhood.

THE LEDGER

The ledger is available for everyone to transcribe experience. There are always writing implements on the podium where the ledger is placed. The ledger is always returned to the podium in the mess hall for easy accessibility. It is here in the mess hall where we pause to formulate our stories. It gets passed around while we eat or relax. Right now, you are reading the ledger that is, in effect, our group journal. Sometimes there are repetitions in the narrative, often similar scenarios occur, and we make note. If someone is inclined to document something, someone else might also feel it necessary to do so. In former societies taking historical account was paramount. Our notations are different. We don't record battles, property disputes, political machinations. Maybe calling it a ledger is a misnomer, we don't record financial transactions because we don't have currency. What shows up in the ledger are the ambient transmissions of the day-to-day. We have decided to make an improvisational record of our civic participation. Reliable witnesses of social transformation have been difficult to find. The ledger has become a means to explore our relation to space and time, or more aptly, spacetime. The propensity to use space and time interchangeably begs ontological unpacking. The convolutions of time make it possible, though challenging to sync up with simultaneities consciously. There are simultaneities of time, space, meaning, and presence.

We use carbon writing implements or dip pens into ink made from lampblack that consists of the soot from the cooling tower exhaust fans we scrap off and stir with gelatin and sweat as there is so little water. All condensation we collect is for drinking, bathing, cooking, and growing algae and other vegetables.

Mostly we do not have excess time in our day. We awake, eat, work, and forage for supplies in the massive waste fields where cities once stood. There are the remnants of the cities and, on the outskirts, the dumping grounds of those cities. From the numerous sites we recover materials from various epochs. Often what we discover on these outings is remarkable. Some of the material is collaged in the ledger.

This world is a commons: one immense undulating surface tension of uninterrupted space, and coexistence is our prime concern. The destruction that led to the current era dropped time out of circulation. Dropped history out of circulation. Time is still present; we do not doubt or dispute this. Still, time has been disrupted. It is impossible not to feel the impact of duration, pulse, beat, measure. Music immerses us in time, work immerses us in time, play immerses us in time, and we lose the sense of time in such instances. Time is philosophical, and its intrinsic qualities are multidirectional, expansive. The atmosphere it drags along is suggestive conceptual drapery that shades us from certain doubts and concerns. We keep the ledger for good measure. It is our only attempt at historicization. True, the air lung and our repurposed buildings constitute architecture and leave a mark of who we are. The ledger is significant because it is a textual polyphony. The exploration of language and thought in group form. Based on how a conceptual model bears down on us, we respond somatically to the symptoms of its meanings.

In the ledger we often attempt to explain our current situation, even though explanation as a mode is mostly anomalous for us. We are amused when we encounter in historical texts the phenomenon of lengthy synopsis, dissertation, and what is sometimes referred to as explication. We try not to dwell too long on negativity. Our sensual expressions don't merit description—they would take up all the precious paper as we engage with each other continually. Suffice it to say that our entire body is an erogenous zone of stimulation, and we pleasure in the discovery of touch, smell, taste, sight, sound, and intuition that heighten existence. We feel this way about the planet, an extension of our bodies, our home.

Some of us are in the mess hall to receive daily sustenance. Some of us scrawl in the ledger. Our sentience is a production. The mess hall consists of a hangerlike construction. Within the hanger are several dozen makeshift tables that we designed using material that can lay flat on two sawhorses. Some tables are glossy and gleam; others are rough and blend with the scuffed flooring. Few of the tables are in use. There are so few of us. Some of us prefer the floor. There is ample space designated for anyone who prefers to position themselves on the floor to eat, often a more comfortable option for those who are conjoined or have mutated anatomies that do not receive support from benches as they might have limited flexibility in their hips and knees.

The din in the mess hall is a whirring cacophony. Voices create a unified insectlike buzzing that becomes indistinguishable from the whooshing sounds emitted from the air lung. The mess hall is always open but there isn't always food available.

Pretty much everyone enjoys serving the sustenance. We decided long ago that the food servers should look elegant; they float around in silk sateen and gossamer cotton. Some have crocheted laces that drape over their torsos; others wear appendages of wool in coiled shapes. Capes are worn when the temperatures plummet. Accoutrements studded with opulent stones heighten body appearances. Usually, those dining are wearing our daily garb. We peruse the data, an irreconcilable history. We sample it, we wear it. Our clothing is made from recycled paper mulched together with reclaimed wool, cotton, and silk—remnants discovered as we unearth various patches of buried junk that hasn't disintegrated. Sometimes bits and pieces of historical remnants cohere to our skins; our smocks have a patchwork of fragments that make it through the mulching process. The team working today at the geothermal desalination center don smocks fabricated from a load of flower and vegetable seed catalogs that were ground down and refabricated into clothing material. We encircle each other, observing the numerous plants that once lived on planet Earth, our home.

The day began with the dull throbbing spotlight of the sun appearing to rise above the horizon like an inflated balloon drifting up in the sky. We've been experiencing a cycle of solar flares and coronal mass ejections that cast large amounts of radiation to Earth. Charged particles race to Earth at a speed of three million miles per hour, altering magnetic fields. The forcefields cause nerves to tense. The surface air temperatures rise dangerously during solar storms. The light becomes overwhelming. Particulate matter in the atmosphere intensifies the glare. Thankfully, the wind that had been raging has abated. The coursing sound of the sands shifting has paused. The atmosphere today is the tint and hue of the rocks that are scattered around the mess hall, calcite in shades of dull orange and light gray.

Presently a team is headed into the tunnels of the air lung. They convene in clusters around the door flaps that permit entrance and allow for the air to flow. There are forever-changing numbers of openings to the tunnels; these openings are where we make our observations. From these portals, we inspect what needs repairing. When an air tunnel breaks down, we hack open a new hole into the configuration and seal the former entrance for however long it takes to repair it. Making the concrete to rehabilitate a tunnel section means pulverizing concrete scraps we bring back from the waste fields and adding the necessary complimentary ingredients to create a catalytic reaction that bonds the materials. We warehouse ingredients for construction when we have enough time to collect and stockpile them.

The work detail did not go as anticipated. Four members of our society did not make it out of the air lung alive. The work on the central wall in the purple aster jurisdiction caused their demise. The bodies can't be retrieved; they are wedged in where the tunnel becomes cramped and narrowed. Our young ones who went in on the repair and maintenance mission were trapped in the inner casings. A team of older members were subsequently sent into the shaft to recover the bodies, but they realized quickly that attempting to haul them out would be too risky. They were redirected out of that part of the shaft before setting fire to the bodies. The best they could do was perform an onsite cremation. The ashes of those we lost will remain in the jammed catacomblike space until we release the pressure on the valves and expose the remains to the air current required to maintain oxygen levels. Later, we will redress the structural issue treating the problem from the exterior instead, a method that requires more resource, more effort. The young ones' ashes will mix with the concrete and silica, the fortifying elements used to restore segments of the tunnel's chambers.

The mess hall reverberates with pronounced choral overtones of low moans and high wails. Chord changes swell, ricocheting off the plastered walls. Bodies knock into each other in sorrowful connection. Everyone is teary-eyed, inconsolable. Those who can stand up in full spinal alignment gesticulate with their arms above their heads. People seated at tables express agitation. Rhythms tapped out by feet and hands on the rough surfaces of the tables and the floor create a deafening mass of sound. Sound can travel much farther than we are able to, sending grief in every direction. The loss of our four dears is difficult to accept.

a SHOW OF openness

Anomalies have been occurring. Now and again we notice forms appearing out of nowhere. Initially all we could make out were sheer blobs of light that moved in unusual ways. With each new encounter these manifestations materialized with greater clarity. After several sightings we were able to focus in, training ourselves to identify silhouettes that emerged in the atmosphere. The forms remained pellucid, but we ascertained that they were unquestionably beings.

Initially they were barely recognizable. Their appearance was blurred. We could spot one or two presences as indistinct outlines. Like low-slung clouds, their shapes hovered momentarily in our vicinity and then would soon disappear. After a while we recognized larger groupings. Now they are becoming more noticeable; we are becoming familiar with their features and begin to recognize them individually. Appearance is more detailed, more lifelike, though they are translucent. They are people. Humans. They are among us and we cannot ignore this fact.

When exactly they began infiltrating our social space is hazy. Our accounts don't match up. Pondering their arrival proves inconclusive. Some in our community immediately synchronized with them. They could perceive them before the rest of us could do so. All of us notice them now as they appear less peripherally along borderlines of the sensory.

During initial sightings we kept a cautious distance and tried to remain still, not calling attention to ourselves. We already blend with our environment. Our work clothing is the color of the sand and rock. Our skin tones the grayish color of the atmosphere. Now we are comfortable moving about engaged in our usual routines of the day. When they appear, our response has shifted from trepidation to curiosity.

At first it was unclear if they perceived us. The blobs of light did not rush at us. They were being cautious also, we intuited. As their features became clearer, we could read expressions. They seemed as startled, confused, and eventually curious as we were. For the time being we observe them with lingering hesitance.

A show of openness is important, we all agree.

To reach us they do not travel through the inhospitable terrain. They are cast through light and time. As if mirrors repositioned between time frames amplified and projected them, at least this is our hypothesis, as implausible as it sounds.

Why suddenly they've appeared we do not know. We wondered if atmospheric conditions had created unique phenomena. The sun has been flaring repeatedly. The intense light plays havoc on our retinas. A few of us have suggested they could be apparitions or figments of our imagination. Others of our community have posited that their appearance is a stress response causing hallucinations brought on by the demanding conditions in which we live. Speculation abounds. The other unusual development is that their appearance corresponds to a change in the algae gardens we maintain. Recently the algae have begun to grow profusely. The oxygen levels in the air lung have spiked. A lack of oxygen effects neurological conditions deleteriously: speech becomes slurred, vision blurred, thought processes altered, immune systems compromised. We feel the positive effects of the additional oxygen in our bloodstream. Breathing in a richly oxygenated atmosphere mellows us out. Cognition is improved. With the uptick in available oxygen because of the impressive outcome with the algae gardens our perception is enhanced. Or is this a case of wishful thinking?

We notice them particularly after we've spent time in the air lung maintaining the algae gardens. The algae seem to aid our perception of the others. Certainly, as mentioned, because of increased oxygen, but perhaps in other ways too. There seems to be a direct connection between the algae and light-filled people. The algae perhaps act as a beacon.

Our community has experienced constant loss. We are at a point where it is a strain to maintain the necessary systems that sustain us. The arrival of sentient beings fills us with expectancy. They are conduits to another reality.

CORPOREAL REALITIES

Our young ones are shrewd. They may be immature, yet they know about infrastructure and action. They have atrophied limbs, and with a deliberate gait they ease their heels when they move about. This is grace. They require sustenance, more than our society can provide. Malnutrition is an ongoing concern. We experience various stages of adaptation as a disintegration of human form takes place. We feel that these changes have positive attributes. The young ones champion any and all challenges set before them. Their tenacity is evident.

Young ones, little ones, the elderly members of our grouping. We use monikers as placeholders for states of being. Our conditions are relegated by epigenetic factors and Earth's and the cosmos's relationship with us.

For several eras, we supplanted our body parts with manufactured prostheses. There were technologies available to assist us in seemingly endless ways. Brain implants, dementia-delaying drugs, artificial limbs, synthetic skin and bones, organ transplants, vaccines, medicines, supplements of all sorts that enhanced the human condition. There was a push to eradicate disease. Longevity became possible for those with the means. Nation-states promoted advances in medical care to their populations; those populations experienced varying degrees of access.

Militaries were interested in having the upper hand. There were drug enhancements for soldiers. Feet were designed that, when surgically attached, gave humans the ability to catapult deep into the air, forward, backward, and upward, a mobility that allowed for bounding leaps and springing locomotion. Eye sockets were implanted with infrared capabilities, and the recipients could visualize in four dimensions. They were able to peer into walls and fortified architecture, seeing into the depth of the surroundings. Chips were implanted in the brain and heart to augment functions. Organs were grown in laboratories from fetal pig tissue, and other mammalian surrogates, then transplanted into humans. Artificial meat was produced for consumption. Soldiers and the rich were privileged with the healthiest diets and widest variety of foods and medicines. Humans were able to download aspects of themselves and upload their lives into the matrix of the Cloud. Cloud-based computing was a paradigm shift. An exponential amount of data could be accessed and stored, though it did come with the cost of prohibitive energy consumption and water use. Massive data fires occurred, exploding and razing facilities. Hackers caused the hardware to overheat and succumb to ignition. There finally wasn't a way to protect the data from overheating. Governments collapsed; infrastructure collapsed. The entire grid was connected and therefore vulnerable to these threats. Other calamities were caused by electromagnetic storms triggered by bursts of solar energy downing communication networks. Rogue organizations used human-built electromagnetic pulse weapons to disable national and international power grids also. Nuclear warheads and other lethal weaponry were deployed in massive conflagrations, never-ending wars for resources. The changing climate meant that reservoirs and rivers dried up, crops died out, famines were prevalent.

There is considerable archival footage of these scenarios. Technologies of this sort proliferated in the later eras when digital documentation was the norm. The enhancements can be studied even now; however, we are not able to recreate the technology due to infrastructural losses and resource challenges. Research and development can't be supported because we do not have an available test subject population or the capacity for errors.

At the time of these technological developments, punitive measures were instituted to hold citizens in check. Machines were programmed to manage the population with indirect threats and other means of social control. Surrogate technologies, such as artificial intelligence, replaced humans in most industries. One of the notable developments was a military technology, called BigDog. It was designed at a research institute in a major urban center. The dog machine consisted of a body made with finely tuned computers able to interact in real time with its environment. It could be programmed, but it also had autonomous thinking capacities. Hybridized machines with autonomous features changed the dynamics of social space thereafter in unforeseen ways.

BigDog was commissioned to attack insurgent strongholds in mountainous, jungle, or desert regions of foreign nation-states undergoing upheaval, countries that for several decades had continually experienced invasion. Resource acquisition was the main motivation for war. The technology was improved for urban deployment. The invaders, the same nation that originated BigDog, sent the canine machines into guerrilla combat against hostile enemy combatants, namely civilians, hunting them down in all-weather conditions, at all times of day or night.

Once successfully designed and fabricated, BigDog was inexpensive to operate. Its torso was encased in a bulletproof carapace that could take direct hits from land mines and rocket launchers. BigDogs were stealthy killing machines that knew no ethical limit and were inexhaustible. They did not suffer nervous breakdowns or syndromes commonly suffered by human soldiers and workers in those days. BigDog did not bleed and did not require state funerals with gun salutes and other formalities. No one mourned the loss of such an instrument of destruction. Essentially, they paid for themselves—if the land and resources could be seized from the native population, the thinking was that BigDog paid for itself. The first models were hulking and hideous. When their headless forms trashed a zone, they caused horrible outcries that spoke to the breach of the rules of warfare. The patent was trademarked so only the proprietary country could engage them. Other nation-states developed brutal weapons of their own.

International leaders willfully ignored pleas for sanity and reasonability. This technology was a way to reduce the human casualties of war, and ominously, the expense—the effect it had was the opposite.

Simultaneously to BigDog were developments that were smaller in scale, able to exist in the open; undetectable, unobtrusively stealthy. Such animalesque machines were called drones. Able to buzz about like a hummingbird or a bee, they were produced in multiple sizes. So miniscule and so effectively swarmed! An uncountable number were used as tools of surveillance flying forth through skies. Larger drones could deploy bombs effectively. Their applications grew as the technology became increasingly more capable of rendering destruction and death. Drones were called into previously unexplored theaters of war: civilian bedrooms, discreet antechambers, bustling pedestrian walkways—anywhere potential suspects were present. The president of a country, one day a week it was reported, generated a hit list; at the conclusion of the revolving day the drones were deployed to eliminate whoever was on the list. The assassinations were not made known to the public.

They were also quotidian as there were basic models available to the general public, cheaply and easily purchased. One boy filmed his parents having sex for one continuous year and frequently posted the footage on his video channel. One school child managed to get her principal sent to prison when she filmed him exchanging money for drugs outside the schoolyard. Someone obsessed over the migrating bird formations that flew through the town he lived in. He flew a drone with the migrating birds until the drone ran out of power and nosedived into the ocean.

Sometimes still, even now, we find drones in the trash heaps and archive reservoirs. They have been rendered obsolete by the lack of energy sources to power them. Occasionally we uncover a battery that has not totally corroded, and we inject it into a drone carcass. Rarely are we able to gain footage of our commons this way, but we have done so on a few remarkable occasions.

PERSONS OF UNKNOWN ORIGIN
IN REAL LIFE

Another obsolete technology we are aware of is virtual reality. Could virtual reality be what is causing the random appearances of others among us? Real people designated avatars to represent themselves and controlled the avatars using a joystick on a console—sending their avatars into other realities. We would know if our community had gained access to the equipment and an energy source necessary to reactivate virtual reality. There would be great excitement. No one could contain such developments as a secret. We are a closely knit society; our community is small. There's really no way to withhold much of anything. Furthermore, virtual reality was computer-generated simulation—it approximated a sense of three-dimensional form, so unless a singularity has occurred uniting the virtual with sentience, it can't be the case. We pinch ourselves constantly to verify reality.

At the onset we sensed the persons of unknown origin visually and intuitively. Later we could also hear and smell them. Touch has yet to occur. We continually muster the generosity to reach out to them, and in doing so we become hypersensitive of somatic registers.

They are here and then they board a bus and are driven away. A road appears out of nowhere and then dissolves into thin air. The vehicle they climb aboard is yellow. It has large rubber tires and can hold about fifty persons, but so far, the largest group we've spotted has been twenty or so. Others come in cars. They are different. Their purpose is different. They dress differently. They wear white encasing uniforms. The ones on the bus dress in various clothing, some tight-fitting, some loosely draped, some colorful and textural, some monochromatic. They are easier to perceive.

The fact that the two groups of people we are able to perceive are different from each other is an enigma. We hope to get some clarity as to why there are those who arrive on a school bus and those that are positioned throughout the area who wear the white uniforms and move in slow motion. The two groups don't interact. The groups from the school bus sometimes approach the ones wearing white but receive no response from them. To this point, we haven't noticed any communication between the groups.

The ones who disembark from the bus have a tour guide. This became apparent to us as we observed a man holding a megaphone, which he rarely used. He held it firmly by his thighs. His busily moving mouth projects the loudest speech of all. His voice is sonorous and echoes in and around the soundboards of the environment. He informs the visitors in his charge when to disembark the bus and when to board it when it is time to leave. He arrives and departs with each group.

Everyone from the bus seems confident in their body frame. They disembark from the bus with apparent ease. They all stand upright. They move with quick bursts of energy. They don't assist each other with their movements. In this way they are more autonomous than we are. It is unclear if they experience any pain or discomfort. Their spinal cords, straight ladders lead to their skulls. Their dispositions vary widely, as do their moods. All have a bushy amount of hair on their heads and their eyes are vivid, glassy, liquidous. Several wear sunglasses. Their skin, pliant, smooth. Skin tones vary. Umber, sand, olive, bronze. A beautiful array. It is tempting to guess how old they are. Our bodies usually expire before we reach forty revolutions around the sun. We do make note of the revolutions around the sun that Earth makes. However, we do not fastidiously keep a record of our ages in days, months, or years. Time dispossession is one way of handling our losses.

The tour guide scrambles up a rock outcropping and gives a demonstration while his fingers flutter about, then he races over to the storage bins and performs a monologue. From repeated exposure with various groups that visit, we are able to separate and filter voices and learn to distinguish the frequency of their vocalizations. The tour guide does most of the talking. The group converses quietly among themselves and occasionally someone poses a question to the tour guide.

We have an epiphany when we become attuned enough to recognize his name is Randy. Disaster tourism is a phrase he uses. He claims he has transported the passengers to a zone of least resistance, an unseeming nonsite is what he deems this place. He tells them they are on a humanly created island. Treasure Island.

An island? We are confused. We know of the endlessness of sand and the outcroppings of demolished cities that no longer have definition. The cities lie in rubble. Dead, inert. Never have we reached an intact ocean, or any body of water on our foraging expeditions or general wanderings.

He begins to narrate the history of the island beginning with its construction and then describes how it was unveiled as a staging ground for the Golden Gate International Exposition. The exposition featured flamboyant architecture and huge sculptures gleaming amid thousands of full-grown palm trees that were brought here. The theme of the exposition was the South Pacific; there was a Chinese village, Polynesian and Pacific Islander motifs were displayed throughout. Cultural artifacts from Japan, South Asia, and South America were featured in exhibition halls. European works were displayed. An exhibit by the University of California gave the public the opportunity to smash atoms on a small scale by using a cyclotron built for the exposition. Near the Temple of Religion was a garden that contained one hundred plants mentioned in the Bible. The Palace of Air Transportation touted airplanes and dirigibles. In another section of the exposition, a giant globe showed children of all nations holding hands. Concerts were conducted day and night. He tells of the galas and the throngs of visitors that included international celebrities and dignitaries. In two years, a total of over seventeen million people came to the island for the purposes of visiting the exposition. The exposition dramatized ebullient optimism, globalism, technological advances and pitched the United States of America in a heroic light, as a benevolent outward-looking superpower. Great swaths of illumination in red and orange, green and blue were cast on the Court of the Moon reflection pool with the Tower of the Sun behind it. From all areas of the island the National Cash Register was visible. It was a hulking building that read out the number of visitors on a screen that updated itself every half hour. President Franklin Delano Roosevelt waxed romantically from a piped-in radio broadcast during the opening ceremony: "San Francisco stands at the doorway to the sea that roars upon the shores of all these nations, and so to the Golden Gate International Exposition I gladly entrust a solemn duty. May this, America's World's Fair on the Pacific in 1939, truly serve all nations in symbolizing their destinies, one with every other, through the ages to come." The United States was lifting itself out of the Great Depression while another catastrophe was building. Germany had begun the annexation of neighboring countries and domestically began rounding up citizens considered undesirable by the regime because of their ethnicity, religion, political beliefs, disability, and sexual orientation. They were involuntarily hospitalized, forced into labor camps, or euthanized. World war was circulating in the atmosphere. It wasn't many years later that the United States rounded up its Japanese citizens and sent them to concentration camps in various desert locations in the west, treating them as enemies of the state.

It is difficult to hear all of what Randy says. The introduction to the tourists continues, detailing the many iterations the island has undergone. He gives an overview of the U.S. Naval involvement with the island: "Over there would have been the barracks and right there, adjacent, the training sites." The wind interrupts his speech. "Training for emergency and disaster response." Randy indicates as if talking to the sun, the beginning of the sentence cut off by interference. Sometimes their voices are clear and sometimes inaudible. He has more in store for them. "Some of the preparedness training included the detonation of simulated nuclear bombs." He points out that the group has gathered in the most concentrated area of one of the numerous toxic waste dumps. They are crowded around, standing, and talking on what is an abandoned landfill. There are significant radioactive remnants throughout the island. The other people, the ones wearing the white uniforms, are scattered throughout the parameter. He doesn't acknowledge them. The ones who disembarked from the bus give those in the white uniforms only furtive attention. Initially they focus on Randy. That's what we do as well. It is only later that we home in on the others.

We begin to piece together his narrative, and a comprehension of his rhetorical modality opens. When auditory and biometric frequencies overlap, a holism of resonance fades out the contours of our difference enough to understand these people.

Many congregated outside the mess hall before making their way over to the site of the fire, the location where the bodies of the young ones were cremated. The memorial ceremony commenced when a majority of us were present.

During the memorial, we see the visitors crowded around by their bus. They appear to be gazing into the distance as if contemplating something sublime. We cannot imagine what they see. We have been exiled from time as an oncoming phenomenon until these recent occurrences. Why suddenly our time dimension includes theirs is a thick question.

As the day wears on, little comes into focus except our bodies, the raging fire and grief. Stinging tears reabsorb into parched epidermal layers. We have added red and blue phosphorous dust to the fire and it bursts into a violet conflagration during the cremation. Violet-colored smoke is released from the air lung. Mourning rituals for the young are carried out with purple signification. While purple is a nonspectral color, violet however has the shortest wavelength on the light spectrum. Purple also designates danger to us. The Occupational Safety and Health Administration was a governmental agency that was instituted to ensure occupational health and safety guidelines. OSHA coding in purple designates hazardous nuclear material. The Environmental Protection Agency also issued symbols establishing hazard class categories. A starburst indicates explosives. A flaming ball alerts us to oxidizers. Skull and crossbones indicate poisons. If there is signage with a propellor it is important to be especially careful as this symbol represents radioactive substances. Canisters that are large and reinforced usually have toxic waste stored in them. Even in our current era we must keep in mind such coding when we forage through the trash fields, though often it is a moot effort. Substances have long ago seeped from storage vessels, leaked into the soil, spread around.

A duo emits plaintive phrasings on trumpets that gleam in the methane air. The instruments were crafted so that the player needs only two digits, and it is still a playable instrument if the musician has one functional limb. The trumpets are very light and easy to hold. The trumpets were forged from a cache of piping discovered in the junk outcropping behind the amphitheater. The drummer accompanies the horns with forceful heartbeat rhythms. None of us depart until the Earth has tilted toward night. Ultraviolet B light diminishes until the Earth again repositions itself with the sun for morning to occur.

ways we express togetherness

When a singular person makes a ledger entry it is customary to use the pronoun *we*, *us*, or *they* in all cases, at all times. This is because of the dependency we have on one another, how forever in conjunction with one another we are and with Earth, with the cosmos. We attend to a sociology of collective social cohesion; therefore, we avoid the third-person omniscient point of view.

We are splintered fragments of a larger whole that is undergoing a vast metamorphosis.

Our account fluctuates, the process is cumulative, additive. Autobiographical traces are veins in the rock structure of group solidarity. Autonomous, freestanding entities are incapable, cannot survive; a singular is lost without cooperation.

The singular who holds the stylus presently is a fourteen-year-old femme. This is to say we promote corporeal characteristics that we have agreed on are feminine, masculine, androgenous, et cetera. Naming such characteristics is mostly for personal growth and pleasure. Our anatomies are polygendered and diverse. Hardly anyone has the same organs in the same arrangement in the same location with the same functionality and with the attendant stimulated desires that go with the proliferation of beauty parts. Indeterminacy offers possibilities.

We gather in the bioenergy station, mix up vitamin drinks, and take them to the mess hall. She paws me for the stylus, and it is we who transcribe. My registration confirms I am an eighteen-year-old herm with wing sockets. We are desirous of we. Together we compile environmental findings.

Once we have initiated the recipes and while the chemicals mix in the bioenergy station, also called the kitchen, some retreat to the hammock room and succumb to the quietude while substances in the batch congeal. We enjoy the voluptuousness of relaxation in tandem. Others choose to be social; they take a break in the mess hall.

The societies that came before us were overwhelmed by forces set into motion that we are only vaguely aware of. Gathering sustenance from newly formed accounts of the present is pivotal. This is why the ledger is important to us. We dedicate ourselves to continual expressions of the present, our domain of active life. Communal notetaking is an aid to survival. As the stories accumulate, we are able to take stock of the dimension of time in which we live. The stories vouch for our existence. Group dynamic problem-solving and the social delight of writing make this a generative form of cultural expression.

The visitors, that's how we now think of them. They have crossed an invisible boundary into the world we live in and now we are aware that we've also permeated the environment where they exist. The island has come into focus. The shoreline is now noticeable. What appeared as blurriness is sometimes fog rising off the water. How startling to witness a seagull dive for a fish! An airplane flew overhead causing us all to panic. Astonishingly, a bright yellow flower seemed to emerge from the ground by the mess hall. On approaching the flower, it receded, fading into their world frame. It seems as if happenstance has created an overlap of our worlds. Simultaneous to their arrival a noticeable rebound of our algae gardens in the air lung had occurred. The microflora is showing signs of regeneration. The lichen growing on stones in the vicinity look brighter, glowing. A correlation with the florae in their world is purely speculative. Focusing on the florae does appear to stimulate the bond between dimensions to strengthen. Could it be that floral organisms are exploring a method of symbiosis that brings us together? The needs and intentions of plant life are of utmost importance. Without plants death is final, regeneration nil.

Today it just so happened that two from their party were wearing purple outfits, which fit in harmoniously with the funeral proceedings. Was this inadvertent? Perhaps they possess heightened perception and sensitivity and cared to be in synch with our ritual. We watched how they were watching, how they engaged with the porous realities of hyperspace.

THE HOLE

During an earlier era there was an event undetectable to the naked eye. We learned from documentation that in the year 2006 the Environmental Protection Agency, NASA, and the National Oceanic and Atmospheric Administration had announced the presence of the largest tear in the ozone layer to date.

Satellite and balloon stratospheric and temperature observations had yielded conclusive data that suggested an area of 10.6 million square miles was no longer protected from the sun's radiation. Suddenly there was a deficiency of 39.8 megatons of ozone mass in the lower heavens. The graphs depict a hole that resembles a sonogram image of a human fetus; the area that lacked ozone was shaped in a bulbous coiled formation languorously hovering over the Antarctic Circle.

Human-produced compounds released bromine and chlorine gases that penetrated the stratosphere, damaging the ozone layer. Atmospheric scientists speculated that it would take a decade for the hole above the polar region of the southern hemisphere to disappear, seal up, cease to exist as a reality.

Somehow the hole would seal itself. There was no information that we recovered on how it would happen, should happen—the healing. There was not much we found about the hole within the shards of history that appear as refuse in the junk piles, but it is something that fascinates us, so we continually search for more details. We live with the effects of an overheated, sun-stroked environment. The causes remain partially obscure.

Before the hole in the ozone layer appeared, the Earth had been swaddled in a layer of protective gases that comfortably diminished the impact of ultraviolet light. In fact, humans, other animals, and plants require absorption of substantial amounts of daily sunlight to produce necessary hormones and to promote body energy. An overabundance of exposure to the sun is detrimental. Once it became a concern that a hole in the ozone layer had developed, manufacturers began producing products that humans could apply to their skin (and to their pets) to effectively block the sun's rays. For most in the Western hemisphere it became daily protocol.

The lotions had unintended consequences. Cancer and other sicknesses were linked to certain active chemicals in the formulas for sunscreen. The ingredients were effective in killing off the coral reefs. The ultraviolet filters implicated in the sunscreen formulas had monster-long, complicated names that revealed their synthetic nature: butylparaben, ethylhexyl methoxycinnamate, benzophenone-3 and 4-methylbenzylidene camphor. The ingredients commonly found in most of the chemical sunscreens for sale around the globe recommended as protective agents caused complete coral bleaching at very low concentrations. Floral blooming habitats of majestic coral that had acted as great storied homes for fish and other diverse sea creatures soon rigidified into dead white skeletons. These chemicals were not the only factor in coral die-off. The oceans were heating. The seawater was acidifying. There were other sources of pollution that threated marine life. The oceans were transforming into mass graves.

The hole itself was a hole: something missing in action, recessed, evacuated, absent. It represented an inexplicable loss, a change in progression, an entryway for the sun. Coincidentally, the hole appeared in concurrence with an increase in solar activity. Within six years the sun went into a cycle of intensely turbulent coronal mass ejections. Geomagnetic storms hurled trillions of electrons and protons to Earth. In the northern night skies, there were brilliant auroras of purple, red, and green. Gaseous lights fanned across the night sky—rainbow spectrums on black velvet, foamy, radiant color fields. Solar winds brought aerosol flows of hot plasma to Earth.

The sky itself was a destination, an object of desire.
Ice hotels sprang up in regions of the Arctic where the show of lights in the night sky was prevalent—a unique, exclusive amusement for monied travelers. The wealthy few flew to a desolate outpost on a barren airstrip and for uniqueness were shuttled to the hotel grounds on a snowmobile that whirred at accelerated speed through snow mounds and drifts. The snowmobile provided transportation through an eerie environment

populated by wolves and white foxes. One such destination was Jukkas-järvi located in Sweden. Five hundred forty-eight inhabitants resided in the tiny snowdrift community. Many of the locals worked for the ice hotel, the largest ice hotel in the world. The ice corridors of the hotel were subtly illuminated with crystal and ice chandeliers glowing a frosty blue. Outside, the atmospheric temperatures hovered at forty below zero and the wind ferociously blinded. The hotel served vodka cocktails in designer snifters also made of ice, and artists from around the globe were commissioned to come to Jukkasjärvi to carve signature murals and install sculptures throughout the hotel. Ice sculpting was then recognized worldwide as a brilliant curiosity and sought after as money was no object. Corporate functions would often feature elaborate ice carvings as centerpieces.

When ice was not being carved it was being packed up and positioned on immense tankers and exported to oil-rich Arabian principalities, headed to countries like Qatar, where two overtaxed aquifers inadequately supplied its water needs. The water from the aquifers was too salty to use as drinking water, it could be used for industrial and agricultural purposes only. Whole nations had become dependent on the import of water as a major life element and commodity. Seawater could be desalinated but at a prohibitive cost. The price of water was roughly equivalent to that of a barrel of sweet crude oil. Along with the importation of ice, many of the same countries also imported prodigious amounts of sand even though deserts were the major land feature. Desert sand isn't suitable for construction because it is too smooth, too fine. Sand was the most abundantly used natural resource after water and oil. A global construction boom necessitated tremendous amounts of sand export. Sand was a commodity often trafficked by mafia groups. Beaches in the Caribbean and elsewhere were raided at night as armed gunmen supervised, bags were scooped up and illegally sold. Shorelines collapsed. Even so, glitzy condominiums sprang up in cities, along ocean fronts, in resort communities.

The jet-setting class careened around the globe, from Jukkasjärvi to Dubai, from Dubai to Jukkasjärvi. Hong Kong, Tokyo, New York, London, Paris, Rome, Mexico City, Delhi. In each location one could drink Absolut, a fancy Swedish vodka produced from glacier waters. Absolut was then no longer owned and operated by the Swedish people; the former state-operated company had been bought up by an opportunistic

French conglomerate, Pernod Ricard holdings, and each year the chemists at Pernod Ricard introduced a new tantalizing tropical-scented and flavored mix into the line.

The world was a global network with capital flowing through its circuitry. The hole made the circumstances of economies more visible. In stark magnitude, financialization drew everything into a debt-to-equity ratio focused on short-term profit for shareholders at the expense of social and environmental well-being. The conduits through which money flowed expanded exponentially facilitated by intermediaries in financial institutions who focused on how to dominate economic markets. To some, the hole was collateral damage. And life went on, as frenzied as ever. There were those with tremendous wealth and access to all that the Earth could bear. We began to piece together the totalization of the system and how it impacted every sector of life.

Super tankers carrying goods from one country to another mowed down giant whales on their migration routes, rainforests were razed to make way for monocrops such as soy and palm to feed a swiftly expanding human population. Products were at once underpriced—not reflective of the true cost of ecological damage inflicted by their production and simultaneously too expensive, drawing evermore of the population into poverty.

Humans had outnumbered every mammalian species on the globe. Every year the number of refugees and displaced persons vastly increased because the wars over land and resources created precarious circumstances for most living beings. Nation-states tightened their borders. Standing armies amassed, weapons were stockpiled or sold to the highest bidders.

The hole had personality, like a gaping mouth, an affective gesture of awe. The hole above the globe could not stop yawning and hyperventilating. The hole exuded the acrid fumes of vast forest fires, the pungent smell of trash becoming methane and the fragrance of melting ice. The hole enlarged to accommodate exiting pollutants, and it was broadened by solar radiation, searingly bright and intense. Humans with their numerous orifices intimately related to the hole. The hole was a perfect motif, a metaphor, a symbol intimately related to the body. We might be giving this hole undue significance. Our ignorance of the potentially more pressing realities that might have pushed the world's population into a terminal crisis remains a concern. As our ethos is that of connection,

we believe starting somewhere within a conundrum is a fair way of pro-
ceeding. Problems can develop subtly, remain undetectable until tipping
points occur. As we pick through the historical remains, we choose what
to give weight to. Every detail is of importance, but we can't study every
bit and piece. Most of what we find returns to the soil.

BOUNDARYLESS QUANDARIES

The forests, jungles, savannahs, and meadows have been razed and we know some of the reasons: the agro industry converted most of earth's arable land into factory fields that grow five main crops: soy, corn, sorghum, barley, and oats. The crops are for CAFOs: concentrated animal feeding operations. Seventy billion farm animals are raised for slaughter annually. They are fed a mash of chemicals and food substances that are not their natural diet. They have diseases and many cannot support their bodies. Unable to stand, they slump in the mud, in their feces and urine, or on hot baked soil. Thousands of skinned pink animal carcasses swivel past suspended on hooks. The pooling blood of the slaughterhouses overtakes the view of the tan tractor harvesting the fields that stretch for miles. The haze is caused by small filaments of stalk that have whirled out of the tractor blades and float in the hot air. To come anywhere near the fields is hazardous. The sharp particles cut like mini razors. Along the oceans of the world there are thick outlines of vivid green spongy sludge that bubbles and burps. These are algae outgrowths caused by toxic runoffs from the agro chemicals and waste used to fertilize the fields and raise the livestock. A woman in a blue suit points to a map that indicates the dead zones in the oceans. The topographical representation details the scant locations where wild fish remain. With red markings, the map shows the proliferation of industrial fish farms. Millions of fish swim in crowded nets. The fish are diseased, injured. A ballerina twirls by out of the corner of our vision. The musical score she dances to is incongruent to her movements. Explosions resound distantly. She pirouettes under the galactic refractions of a disco ball. The audience claps profusely. A steam locomotive rushes past. We see a horizon of exhaust pipes belching out thick fumes. Cut to a black swan gliding on a dark lake. Cut to a gray rhino on a savanna. All of a sudden, a mosque with a vaulted dome enters our field of vision. An imam intones the call to prayer over a powerful microphone. *Alhamdulillah.* A thousand worshipers bow in holy prostration on woolen rugs facing Mecca. A lightning bolt strikes the mosque with blue static light. What we experience next is a series of television commercials for all kinds of products: toothpaste that whitens teeth, adult diapers that are gentle on sensitive skin, a snack food that has the flavor of fire. Another jarring sequence of animations begins. A fight breaks out in a fast-food drive-through line. One person rips a bag of french fries from another person's hands. There is gunfire. Four people fall to the ground by their cars. We become disoriented again when the eyes of a calf are zoomed in on. The eyes are soft, expressive, and gentle. The feeling that the calf conveys changes the mood. The angle of focus shifts. The emphasis is on her torso and then her ankles, which are bloody, fungus covered. Thousands of cows come into view, crowding the horizon. The cows are confined in a restrictive pen. The cows walk on ramps toward a mammoth building. They are tased one after another after another in a relentless procession that leads straight to death. We've seen documentation of how cows are processed, turned into food, packaged, transported to supermarkets. There is a correlation opening up between need and death, death and need.

Death moves beyond filiation, or does it, as a process, as a state of mind, as a condition? In the rolling uncertainty of the questions that arise, the world offers us clues. That's when we see one of the performers. They lean over a cow and the cow transforms into sheer nothingness. Instead of the mono fields and the cows the other performers come into view. The early moon is a focal point in their setting, and it is also in ours. One particular performer walks steadily toward us. The performer is able to walk through us, as if we are immaterial, or they are. The performer circles around those of us who are standing in front of a garbage patch we were about to explore. Their breath forms condensation on our cheeks. The performer is taller than we are and looks slightly askance and peers into our faces, into our eyes. We notice this performer's eyes are not covered by a plastic shield that they usually wear over their faces, part of their uniform. The gestures they make begin to shed the skepticism that they telegraphed to us initially. Then they hold still, continue their gaze. The smell of plastic and crushed herbs rises to our nostrils. The performer holds a sprig of mugwort in their hand. Should we attempt to speak with them? They are mostly silent, unless quietly convening with each other after a performance. We don't want to disturb the peace.

We've been experiencing bouts of madness. Unhinged visions. Pockets of reality become heightened in dimension and take on various patterns. An instability of place and time. Displacements have become a frequent occurrence since the algae bursts and since the visitors and the performers exposed Treasure Island to us. Sometimes the barrage of sensory stimulations is horrifying; other sequences we feel ecstatic about. Affectively they encompass a spectrum of sensation and emotion as well as geographic location and historical time. The sensory stimulations are interoceptive and extrospective; that is, worlds unfurl in us as well as around us.

We are expecting a baby soon. The prospects for the birth are promising. The anticipation gives respite from other more disquieting outcomes. Our community continues to shrink. Still, we feel glee that a birth will occur. In the present, there is love, desire, enjoyment, and togetherness.

The performer holds a lake above their head cupping an unfathomable amount of water, or a giant crystal. When we look again it is a half-full water bottle that casts glistening flashes of light in all directions. The scale readjusts. A second performer joins their peer. One comforts the other. They embrace, eventually they both sink to the ground. They are distressed, we cannot figure out the reason. One is faintly sobbing. The other offers them the water bottle. They sip willingly, thankfully. With the lightest touch, we caress them, reassuringly. They seem to respond positively to our touch.

sustenance

Our farms are underground. We are able to grow genetically modified crops exclusively; all other genera were contaminated by the virulent DNA of laboratory-produced life-forms long ago.

Our staple is SVA, sustaining vitamin agglomerate, a combinatory food source made from the hybridization of DNA from bovines, corn, wheat, and squid. We call this food the sustenance. The plant-animal hybrid is a tough, fast-growing tuber that can withstand unfavorable growing conditions. It requires minimal hydration and ultraviolet light. The tuber grows in pellets of gravel and shredded paper that can be used as planting beds for several growth cycles. When old carpeting shows up in the waste fields, we can use it for our garden plots. The genetic material for bovines and squid was passed down. We continue the recipes we learned from our ancestors.

When the teams pulley up from tunnels in the ground with wheelbarrows loaded down in SVA, we hurl it at each other. The SVA is soft and rubbery, it bounces off our bodies in hilarious fashion. We never tire of this ritual.

We know from texts we uncovered about fields of interest like art history that a genre of expression called still life painting was held in high esteem. When we think of spending time rendering the SVA in colorful hues on subtle surfaces we laugh riotously. The SVA is the color of the stuff it grows in, a gray pulp. The tuber's shape is organlike and puffy. Of course, we do not disparage the SVA, we need the sustenance it provides; it is just that we would not endeavor to embellish its attributes in two-dimensional space using paints on canvas.

We understand every aspect of the SVA; it completely lacks mysteriousness. The SVA is rendered for sustenance and survival. We are allocated an amount of nutrition every feeding period, and the bulk of it comes directly from the SVA. Also, we use SVA as pillows and for sensual pleasure. When the tuber is rubbed against skin it becomes slippery. The flesh of the SVA is milky and has a sweet-sour interplay of flavors, even uncooked, which is how it is served to us at most feeding sessions. Ingestion of SVA gives us a sated feeling in our bodies. It is impossible to overeat SVA. Once the required amount of dietary nutritional elements is consumed, the body sends signals that it has reached saturation and we do not crave a single extra serving.

We do not know a wide range of culinary flavors. The synthetic sauces we ladle onto SVA stew are the extent to which our taste buds have experienced flavor.

We tolerate the consumption of flesh. It must be mentioned that when our bodies cease to function, they are brought to the molecular nutrition labs, where all the basic elements are extracted that are then made into supplements. These pills do not have much flavor. They have a slightly unpleasant aftertaste that is bony and gelatinous.

We wash down the SVA and the supplements with a liquid called wine. The liquid is squishy and malleable in our mouth orifice. Usually, it is red in appearance, although not always. Servers decide what to augment it with based on the inventory. We have a variety of food colorings that are added for nourishment and to excite us visually. Champagne glasses, beer mugs, coffee cups, snifters, and an array of vessels hold the libations to our lips. There are ceramic cups that have slogans like "Winner," "Only the Good Die Young," "Bitchin," and "Golf Champion 2000" and other mottos that read, "Everything's Coming Up Rainbows," "Florida Is for Lovers," and "Gator Country." The non sequiturs must have had great significance in another era. Some glasses allow for an impossibly small amount of liquid to be poured into them. In our collection are vessels that are large enough to store fluid we could not swallow in three sittings even if we had enough to go around. We have canvassed the zones and salvaged the wears. The vessels are cleansed with exceptionally fine sand when we are done sucking out the liquids at mealtimes. Sometimes there are kegs of fermented wine, and we all have a sensational time together. Usually, we cannot wait for the liquid to congeal and ferment, our thirst is too great and the supply too low.

As we sit in the mess hall passing around the ledger jotting down impromptu observations, an earth tremor sends us dashing for cover under tabletops and solid surfaces. The ledger falls to the floor with us and so do the dishes of SVA stew. Earth tremors are as common as solar flares and windstorms. We expect them almost daily.

The tensions of the earth's tectonic plates changed drastically once the polar ice caps melted. The mess hall is situated on the foundation where a renowned museum once stood eras ago. The concrete basement is evidence of a mighty structure thickly reinforced to hold substantial aboveground weight. We fabricated a roof of repurposed tin and somehow managed to paint it pink. The earth beneath us rumbles within the massive concrete walls, but they do not give in. Not even a fissure exists in this hulking architecture built to house art.

There must have been quite a lot of art to necessitate such a huge foundation is our thinking as we slurp the SVA stew with straws. What is art exactly—yes, we have read interpretations, definitions, summations, and manifestos from artists, curators, critics, patrons, collectors, gallery owners, and so on. We have perused many images of art: screenshots, paintings in gilded frames, sculptural artifacts, performative gestural happenings on video—the variety of it, the materiality of it (most of it), the diversity of it, the cultural applicability of it, the economic value factor of it, the discourses it inspires, the heightening of emotion that it carries with it, the pushing of ideologies. There is much to say about art, but it doesn't exist as a practice in our society because we don't categorize our gestures and efforts as such. Rather it is as if human impulses morphed into the total body, not something separate. Maybe this does not hold up as a statement—*morphed into the total body.* Here we also mean a social body that has become unhinged from history, from symptom, from form. Perhaps it is contradictory to be unhinged from chronology and engulfed or reabsorbed simultaneously as the total body.

We do not have uses for the art of memory or the art of beauty. We don't prize either. We do not fetishize our environment. We do not glorify death or life. We do not feel alienation or existential feelings as were described in the twenty-first century (the vein of the most prolific histories). The side effects are central; central are the side effects. All that we encounter. Interminglings of comminglings ad infinitum. We coexist in an intensely emotional, arduous situation. We are especially focused. Our gestures are not excessive; rather our gestures are integral. When we slide our limbs around torsos in an embrace, we mean to communicate compassion and reciprocity. We raise a heel to indicate pain. If we want to indicate fatigue, we gently wave our head from side to side. Ever so gently the motion creates the meaning, the meaning is inherent in the motion.

The quake tosses us around within the converted monolithic structure that we use as the mess hall. To maintain our balance, we strike poses that engage the palms of our hands and feet. This assists the bodies with more developed neurological conditions to coordinate their movements in preparation for the coming tremors—their speech capacity has given over to body motility, total body signage. Everyone has a mentor and if our mentor is by our side during such circumstances, they quickly assist in managing our balance, we help each other adjust to the motion. Our continuum does not rely on speech as a dominant form of communication—body gesture is where we place emphasis. Evocative affective twitching—the future multiplies thanks to you. Humming also is a form of communication. Thus, we have corporealized a spectrum of thickly visceral cues.

Earthquakes send vats of SVA stew tilting off tables and onto the floor. Our dinners are lost in the earth movement. Promptly the hair mops are brought out and we set to tidying up the huge gray concrete hall with its pink ceiling and pink roof above us. The mops are not constructed of actual hair. They are constructed of woven fibers from fabric we find. We admire hair so we consecrate our mops as such.

THe analOGue FuTuRe

Our condition is one of memory loss. We have difficulty storing long-term images in our bodies. If we try to stabilize the past it becomes inert, disconnected from the present predicament that demands most of our attention: survival. We have been relying on the ledger to give us a clearer sense of the comings and goings of reality. There was talk that the arrival of the visitors occurred once. Just on one occasion. That all other impressions were flashbacks or a symptom of faulty memory. The ledger verifies that they have made contact in our world multiple times. It also verifies we've been in their world multiple times. Whenever we meet the worlds meld. Time's center of focus shifts.

The bright yellow bus is here again, parked adjacent to our waste management machines. We saw as it made its way over a bridge to reach us. It paused, idling for a long time. The thick black diesel exhaust exiting the tailpipe of the bus choked us. No one has stepped off the bus. It seems they are having a meeting inside. The tour guide is giving instructions. Finally, the group unloads. It is a different group but about the same sized population. Roughly the same number of females and males and all seem around the same age with slight variation. The differentiations are interesting to us. We observe to see if there are differences in speech patterns and behavior. We notice skin tones ranging from dark brown to light pink. Our skin is mostly medium gray and spotty. The concept of race is described in many historical texts. We are the outcome of generations of genetic modification. Racial markers have no bearing in our society.

The other group, the ones wearing white uniforms, arrived a while before. They always come into focus first, perceptible before the bus arrives. They come individually, veering into our line of vision in cars. The exhaust alerts us, and the tires braking on asphalt stir our atten-

tion. There is a parking lot where they change into the white garb that is
so blinding. They disperse rapidly to the designated locations where they
position themselves each time. Before the bus arrives, they often sit on
the ground or lean against a building checking their phones. They must
receive a message that alerts them of the arrival of the bus, because by
the time the bus pulls in, they are already at their stations, already moving with slow articulated gestures.

We headed over to the liquefaction tanks for our shift. That's when
they came into focus. Our team was near the pipes that carry the liquid
that's generated. We greased the joints to maintain systemic flow. We
were wearing our flimsy paper uniforms.

Their modality of looking is often indiscreet, pointedly direct as to
be staring. We also take on staring as a response to alternative stimuli.
There might be a correspondence with their effects and how they influence us, but this is yet to be determined.

One of us attached the ledger to a makeshift lectern and placed it on
the platform by our work site. Usually, we require that the ledger remain
in the mess hall. Since the arrival of the visitors and performers we decide to take the ledger with us as we observe them.

We take turns jotting down transformations as they occur in the biome. Right now, we are writing about the experience of being watched—
rather viewed, regarded in a particular light. We are being viewed; we
are sure of it. We are being viewed as an eventful anachronistic occurrence. We are out of time but have somehow corresponded with their reality. They can see us. Their observational objective is to actually see us.
Are we blurry or in full focus we wonder. How do they perceive us?

The people wearing the white outfits, they must be performers. For
several iterations we thought they were working, but it never became
clear what their job might be. Now we understand they are performing *as
workers*. And performance is a form of work after all. Their suits are protective. From pieces of the conversations that have circulated between
the tour guide and the visitors, we ascertain that the performers act both
as forensic detectives searching for evidence that links the U.S. Navy's
culpability in the toxic dumping in and around this island and a specialized unit sent in to do remediation in a post-military industrial wasteland. We've tuned into one performer whispering to themself almost
inaudibly a running index of invisible contaminants on the island: arse-

nic, dichlorodiphenyltrichloroethane, dioxins, lubricants, mercury, metals, petroleum, polychlorinated biphenyls, radionuclides, volatile organic compounds. In hushed soundings they delivered an inventory of active substances. Their voicings sonically invoked each toxin.

After the visitors left, one of the performers came over to the podium and looked at the ledger. Cautiously they studied it. They turned a few pages in a careful manner. Perhaps to them the handwritten script is illegible. Their conversations are understandable to us, it would make sense that our conversations and thus, our written language are also comprehensible to them. They seemed mesmerized by the text. The whiteness of their uniform illuminated the pages of the ledger with reflective light. After a while they moved away.

Perhaps they never leave, and all time is simultaneous and instantaneous though a sensation of gathering, bunching, and fraying obscures the concurrences.

We store impressions of their hologramlike appearance in a psychosomatic archive of nerve endings and brainwaves. Our imagination pirates the impressions, manipulates them. Their visitations present the intersection of desire and the drama of extradiegetic overload. We have not been able to touch or feel their bodies; we do not know the attributes of their embodiment.

Correction. Some of us have endeavored to touch them. Gently, with care. The response was positive. We will field more information from the other team who engaged with them.

For now, sight, sound, intuition, and smell guide us. Several visitors exude a synthetic flowery scent that breaks down into components that cause dizziness, confusion, depression, nausea, respiratory distress, and neurological complications. Their clothing is coated in nanoparticles and their footwear is constructed of animal hides treated with chrome salts, ammonium salts, natrium, acids, and dyes. There is a low cloud of phthalates, linalool, camphor, benzoate, yellow 5 and blue 1, and other chemicals wafting over the group. Their flatulence gives us further readings. Traces of chemotherapy medications, antibiotics, painkillers, mood drugs, hormone replacements, and virility boosters leave a slight taste on the tongue. Wearing facemasks in their presence might be our best option. They generate many noises with flickering, handheld devices that ring, vibrate, and flash. One of the participants drops their device by a bush and we recover it later, recognizing minerals of rare earth involved with the technology. We know of the internecine battles fought over precious minerals in distant regions. The performers are covered in fabric that does not breathe; therefore, we know less about them.

When the school bus pulls up it is always unexpected, in broad daylight from a dimension other to us. Layers of time commune introducing an emergent sociality. Could we be remembering experiences from a previous existence, as in anamnesis? Astral projection is another example of the ability to travel within time displacements while leaving physical and etheric bodies at rest. Kings had at least two bodies: the body natural, and the body politic as it is written of. Enlightened beings were known to defy the logic of spacetime, appearing in multiple timeframes, reincarnating in new forms. Physical laws don't apply. Solid forms are not obstructions to a yogi who can move fluidly through spacetime, walk through walls, fly in the sky. Clairvoyance accompanies this magical ability. Different bodies in time can share an autobiography. There are stories about persons inhabiting other forms than their own in order to enter spaces. Persons becoming birds, becoming mountains, becoming rivers. Evolution itself is a form of time travel. Different forms of plants, animals, and minerals transform within time, over time. Molecular elements are recycled through time. We are, in effect, composite bodies, always returning as basic chemistry. What properties of electromagnetism do we not understand that would allow for the dispersal of presences in multiple zones? A multiverse coming apart at the seams is yet another possibility. There is a scenario in some footage we found called *Back to the Future* where a gendered boy, typical of the time, named Marty McFly arrives in "the future" on March 22, 2013, via a souped up energy-consuming vehicle that can travel the speed of sound. The machine he rides is called a DeLorean DMC-12 and requires plutonium to meet the requirements of 1.21 gigawatts necessary to transcend the present. His mentor acquires the materials, ostensibly from a group of terrorists. Some have speculated that what we are experiencing is the afterlife. We have merged with a divergent vitality postdeath. Others are sure that this is a dream. A dream of kinship across time. An act of transfer. Observing the arrivals and departures of animate beings begins as an extraordinary event. As more occurrences take place a sense of expectation grows.

An ontological breakthrough. What if the visitors and performers are not travelers, have not really journeyed anywhere? They haven't moved from their world; we haven't migrated out of ours. Perhaps what is taking place is a shift in the parameters of usual, assumed experience. A shift in what we consider to be normal life. They bump into us as if coincidently; it is a matter of translucency between membranes when receptivity is prime. Time by its very nature is shared. Time itself (the concept) is mutable. Everyone internalizes it slightly differently due to bodily registers processed by the brains of every living organism and geology itself, the basis of life.

In any event, the florae have been forecasting an ecological permutation. The outgrowth is indicative of a change.

Their quizzical expressions suggest that they are intrigued and unthreatened by our presence. We listen in on their conversations about ways of seeing that involve the anthropological gaze and an anthropomorphic tendency. They are critical of both. Filters can heighten perception or obscure how reality is parsed. The same goes for us. What are we not perceiving because we refuse to notice or haven't learned to understand? We linger on the significance of these encounters.

As we peer into difference, unusual vegetation comes into focus. There are plants that traverse the walls of a building. Great climbers! On their trellised stems are numerous giant blue orbs, blossoms the color of the sky. One plant's leaves resemble the teeth of a lion and is thus named dandelion. Everywhere we look we find nutsedge. Its leaves are shiny yellow-green, and its flowers are light brown spikelets in open inflorescences. There is even a rose bush. Roses are depicted ubiquitously throughout human history. We savor the sight of an actual rose, extravagant pink petals and spiky thorns! A smell so compelling and subtle wafts toward us causing us to become weak in the knees.

The ocean is a spacious presence and changeable. It has a magnificent personality as it surges and retreats. The day it rains in their world we stick out our tongues, wishful that the moisture will land in our mouths. After the rain, colors are enriched. The world we are being introduced to reveals more of itself on each foray.

An experiment conducted theoretically, actualized as a thought bubble. A simulation of an idealized present, a condition that hovers as possibility in quantum regions. A latent repertoire is regenerated.

For reasons unknown our thinking strayed away from the usefulness of theory, or theoretical thinking had been abandoned before we could grasp the precepts. The logic of abstract variables confounds us. We do not particularly ask "who am I?" such questions create vague and overwhelming uncertainties. Our philosophical outlook morphed toward tangible demands. Registered as a kind of background noise is an unsettling fantasy of the extra and the ultra—recontextualizations insofar as traces of embodiment are considered. Opacity. Observation. A theatrical stage almost totally bare. Suddenly a cast of characters take up their positions. The meanings of these phrases point to essence, what is essential in life. Performances.

The uncanny visitations have led us to pause in the fractalized liminal space of imagination to reach out and make ourselves available; we have yet to realize how to make this a practice.

We prioritize strategies that could aid in making them feel comfortable as they make contact with us. There is talk about forming a committee to think through these issues, a pressing concern as they are reappearing on a regular basis.

Meanwhile, an ongoing series of harrowingly close calls with extinction orients our daily life.

BIOMASS

It has been difficult lately to make notations in the ledger. A formidable issue arose. The challenge we encountered had once again to do with the complexities of biomass outgrowth, an accumulation of bacteria and viruses that cling to particles in water and rapidly proliferate, forming a thick jellylike substance. Pipes clog and water becomes tainted. The unrestrained growth of biomass threatens our existence. A fail-safe method of eradicating this menace has yet to be found.

We are forever worried about losing community to sepsis and other maladies that develop as a consequence of a bloom. As we were performing a mundane routine—the scheduled maintenance of some machinery—it became evident that biomass had grown out of control. The pipes leading away from the liquefaction tanks were totally choked with a noxious mass.

Biomass is nothing to take lightly; we cannot ignore it. Already it grew to such proportions that the system backed up and we had to shut off the mechanisms entirely. No liquefaction equals no potable water equals no hydroponic farming. There are many other ramifications to this that impact survival. The problem with biomass is that the slightest amount of it—a few cells—will infect the body and render it incapable of maintaining stasis. Once the cells get into the gut it is a death decree. We lament the challenges of biomass.

Biomass has positive attributes as well. Certain strains of algae-like microorganisms can be extracted from it. The nutritious strains we then transfer to the vats. The microorganisms grow abundantly, a food staple. Algae is our core vegetable component, in addition to SVA. We make shakes from juiced algae combined with potato tumors. Potatoes are hardy plants. This genus managed to weather the calamities. Even though genetic modification eradicated 99 percent of native species in the era before ours, the desert potato survived, and it thrives in the tundra wastelands that surround us in all directions. Potatoes tolerate the flaring sun, the windstorms, the parched conditions. Potatoes notwithstanding, we have the bone juice also, but there is nothing edible or redeemable to the bulk of biomass.

BM gets in, hazard. We are fairly sure it exacerbates our neurological conditions. Autonomic nervous system dysfunction is a common issue. Racing heartbeats, difficulty breathing, and digestive problems plague us. Micro particles cross the brain-blood barrier and multiply. BM is capable of fending off detection by the body's defenses. It coats cell linings. White blood cells, the body's defenders, do not attack BM because it mimics the body's cells. Increasingly the body is weakened and compromised. BM forms readily. For these reasons, we have to address each outgrowth in forceful ways. This requires exertion. Everyone chimes in with an inspirational tune. Choral singing around the pipes eases rattled nerves, the resonances of our voices ping off the rusted metal. *We are doing fine, we are fine, this is fine, sublime, in fact sublime. Blooming into an array, hey hey hey, we are doing fine, bring jugs of wine, hey hey hey, there's a fine line between feeling fine and towing the line, hey hey hey* and into the metal tainted sunset we sing.

PURPALIA

Our community is down to thirty-three members, and it has only been a short while since the BM flare up. Three darlings with end-stage dementia succumbed to infections caused by BM. Purpalia passed when they accidentally snuffed some of it. Their mask was defective; it had puncture holes. BM got into their lungs and then their gut. The BM flared and caused an inflammation that spread through their body like an inferno.

In a great gathering we unanimously commented as a group how mighty and resilient BM is and how we admire its vital qualities. We painted our faces camouflage green to signify our desire to subsist despite BM's hazards.

Four juvies perished not so long ago while conducting maintenance on the air lung. We miss them and we mourn them still.

The bodies of our loved ones who were overcome by BM were scrubbed with fine particle sand, swaddled in paper, and laid to rest for the ceremony. Later their bodies were delivered to the bone-juicing factory for processing. We have a limited means of procuring necessary calcium and protein; bones provide marrow rich in vitamins and minerals. Excavation teams also canvas for bones in the wasteland; the bones they uncover there tend to be bleached and of less nutritional value.

Our accounts of subsistence focus on necessity and ingenuity over personality and aura, but we drop these standards for Purpalia.

Purpalia's comportment said everything. They inspired everyone the way they engaged with work and their generosity toward the community was unfailing. They were a constellation of admirable qualities: expansive, tender, and witty, always preparing us for drama. Purpalia was a hall clerk who lived in the dormitory with the end-stagers helping to manage their needs when communication and movement was difficult.

Their partner is an end-stager who recently had a baby. The infant is maturing in the incubation ward off from the main facility, which is also dedicated to underground farming. In the incubation ward premature offspring are reared under the most promising conditions our community can provide. Only the workers are allowed in to maintain the integrity of the premises.

Purpalia was always responsive and deliberate; they understood intuitively when someone needed help with bathroom necessities or help with feeding. They could communicate nonverbally in meaningful ways. They provided the end-stagers with comfort.

We aren't supposed to single out individuals when we write in the ledger; this isn't our mode, and it really diminishes how the community is understood because interdependence is central to our lives. We are one working entity of flesh and concern. That said, I, yes, I feel compelled to single out Purpalia. They were my sibling; I grieve for them. Probably someone will come by, read this entry, and retract it by scratching it out. It does not even make sense. There is no holistic logic in speaking about them, or me. We all agree. There is durable consensus about how we represent ourselves. Our group solidarity is an ode, it creates harmony. Survival is a consideration at every turn. Our motif is the flower, how all the petals encircle the ovary of the flower, the reproductive site. We too surround a core logic, that of subsistence through group participation.

Purpalia is no longer with us. We all continue to benefit from their existence, how our joint existence bonds at the fleshy and psychic juncture of each of us. We don't think in terms of individuality; we are all coping with the exact same environment. We have tried to challenge this rationale, by pronouncing our bodies are different, capacities on a spectrum. Cohabitation and interrelation are crucial as a communal entity that is codependent for everything. We tend to each other. Consciousness is a network among presences. We cannot create individuals any more than we can create victims who shiver alone and suffer emotional pangs without support. We live and die as a hypersensitive communing organism ebbing and flowing diastolically recouping our social medium. Purpalia used to murmur, "Long live raw matter, long live the biome, our way station." They would say, "Walk with us," which of course we all do. To dwell on their life is to offer retroactive flow.

Unusual to have this taste in the mouth—the bitter taste of regurgitation. We had the bone drinking ceremony, they are inside us as sustenance, the heart of our marrow. Our united body causes me to write this eulogy for Purpalia as their substance enters our digestive system and rejuvenates us.

Two of the performers in the white uniforms pay particular attention to us as we conclude the bone drinking ceremony. They seem to experience our grief, or they grieve for their beloveds, too. One slumps over and lands on the dirt, another comes to their assistance, offers them water.

DRIFTERS, MOORED ARRAYS, AND SATELLITE DATA

A bold, greasy rain that coated and saturated surfaces preceded a fiery hot day. By morning the heat glistened, steam rose off the ground, the temperature a melting point of attention. The elegant concrete pond, covered thickly in algae growth, was a dense green carpeted hue. Resident swans didn't dare attempt swimming among the fast-growing organisms; the tangled vegetation kept them on the banks.

The organizers hectically wheeled around in overland vehicles surveying the site; they chattered rapid-fire on bright yellow walkie talkies. The entire obstacle course smelled of fuel exhaust, wood chips, perspiration, and sticky heat. The great GoogaMooga was being held in a park located on a human-made island off the bay of a densely populated western city. The park was a sprawling pedestrian course of concrete pathways through undulating lawns and trees orchestrated as a geography of leisure and lushness compared to the other areas of the island that were run-down, decrepit. The verdant blooms of late spring, a mere backdrop to the burgeoning event: a foodie extravaganza of pumped up, mammoth proportions. Eating with abandon was soon to occur. The goal was to maintain a continuously ravenous interest and selectively critical urges to go forth and explore food in a maximal way. The entrants were encouraged to gorge on hundreds of options and varieties of greasy, salty, and sweet combinations simmering within each tented pavilion marked by orienting signs that read Baconland, Rosemary's Baby Lobster, and Dinosaur Bar-B-Que.

The event was a budding example of foodie culture. Food moved beyond sustenance and a source of well-being to something approaching an obsessive and omnivorous hobby where passionate and studious approaches to food acquisition and consumption combined in a no-holds-barred attitude of total experience. Ardent foodies would report on their blogs about exorbitant cab rides to far-flung neighborhoods in search of the least normative eating experiences, foods that challenged the dulled taste buds of a population who ate mostly industrially produced starch, sugar, and wheat-based products, as well as factory-farmed animals. At last, GoogaMooga brought it all together, a surfeit of culinary opportunities. GoogaMooga, the foodie hoedown, slammed together the conceptual thrust of various snobberies and fetishizations in one gargantuan sprawl.

The huge public park was cordoned off blocking anyone who did not purchase an entrance ticket, and GoogaMooga organizers steadily worked to seal off all the entrances to the park, a unique challenge, like a nation's border, with forest underbrush acting as a natural gateway, a porous membrane. The organizers cruised in their overland vehicles, zigzagging through the park. They were the governing agents. Reams of plastic were unfolded and positioned into the shape of tents and pavilions. Stakes were rammed into the earth. The wildlife was already on edge; it was egg-laying season and the birds' biorhythms were disturbed by the hum and throbbing commotion that seemed to have no cut-off time. Raccoons took cover, as did mice, rats, chipmunks, feral cats, stray dogs, squirrels, and others.

People either adored or reviled GoogaMooga; no one was casual about their feelings regarding the event. The ones who felt chagrined concluded instantaneously that their beloved park was being trampled in the name of gluttony, that nothing but trash, trodden ground, and port-a-potty off-gas was yielded. The flow of humanity cruising for food was indeed a spectacle. Feelings of craving and satiation appear to be the ur-forms of contemporary life in that era. Food was commodity and erotic desire. The bodies of animals camouflaged as food items, steaming on grills then jammed between thinly rolled bread wraps. At the time, the animal-human divide was considerable. Human animals did not hesitate to envision the coordination between desire and death, the ambivalent reciprocity between killing and eating. But it was a one-way street. It was less likely to imagine the flesh of a human becoming the food for another living being, save in death, in decomposition. Life contained rich variation, although a major extinction of animals and plants both land and sea was in rapid progression.

The fact of GoogaMooga was one of the first access events we had besides the yellow school bus and attendant cars merging anachronistically
with our time zone. Randy and his group of onlookers and performers un-
knowingly alerted us to the possibility that we were not completely alone
in time and space. That somehow, under certain conditions, there was an
overlap of time or time was simultaneously realized in a mutually expansive dimension we could participate in.

Suddenly we found ourselves immersed in the precise setting of the
event, a circumscribed difference, entering the ostensible outside of the
present wherever it was to be located. We walked around the periphery
of the park, a space at once completely foreign to us and strangely familiar. We were drawn to the pond with swans on its banks, the trees,
and the hot, moist atmosphere, we were compelled by the crowds of people piling edibles on plastic plates, jamming the stalls to get more. We
watched the activity with awe. Immediately we were gripped by the concept of eating to one's "heart's content" and decided to schedule a communal meeting to decode the finer cultural significance of such rituals
once we returned our focus to our familiar ecosystem.

We had access to the park and the food fest. At the same time, there
was interference. This often occurs when we experience spacetime over-
laps. Dimensions shift suddenly. On this occasion the shift took place
most prominently within the sonic environment as an experience of
clairaudience. Auditory input recreated our sphere of attention. Boundaries were replaced, adjusted.

Sounds were coming in from multiple directions. The sounds of GoogaMooga were superimposed with a crackling dissonant noise, a staticky
feedback sound that amplifiers make. The effect was to shift our attention toward the ocean. The ambient noise of the food festival was completely overdubbed. Are those whipping winds we hear? Waves crashing? The sensation was of being in the path of a large storm, a cyclone or
hurricane, but then for a moment we were overcome by a swirl of fragmented kaleidoscopic colors as if a dance floor opened up before us, the
multiple LED panels strobing syncopated to the beat of the groove, colorized foggers enveloping the space with light and sound. Truss towers
positioned lamps from above and they flickered to the rhythmic patterns
of a kick drum. Bass notes throttled the air. Another superimposition, on
the dance floor we witnessed an expansive prairie in winter with camps
and fires burning. Drones flew overhead. People were chanting and sing-

ing. Many held signs. *"Mni Wiconi*—Water Is Life!" "No Dakota Access Pipeline." The Sacred Stone Camp on the Standing Rock Reservation came into focus. There were North Dakota law enforcement and private guards working for Energy Transfer Partners spraying the crowds with rubber bullets and tear gas. We could then make out the proposed path of the pipeline through the red smoking lights that illuminated the land, already bulldozed in places, and we listened to a powerful bass beat that carried the rhythm of the protests. The pipeline would channel upward of nineteen million gallons of fracked oil per day through Indigenous lands. A group of women elders stood around a fire in total silence, with their eyes closed rapt in concentration. Silence was a potent form of resistance. Multiple timelines intersected. The scene was ruptured again by a series of complex numbers and charts that appeared as a see-through overlay across the horizon. A hot pink line intersected a graph of undulating dark blue lines that looked like mountain peaks sloping upward. Readings from the TAO-TRITON Array were suddenly broadcasted. Climate research and forecasting information was being delivered in the form of crackling messages over our loudspeakers. The TAO array, a buoy was located somewhere in the Pacific Ocean. It took measurements of temperature gradients in the water. As if a film was cast on our world and the film was then being rewound, we could make out the buoy being deployed over the side of a boat, the crew lowering it with the help of a crane. Time zigzagged, speeding forward and then reversing. Confusion arose again when a distinct image floated above us and didn't move in the space of several breaths; we all inhaled in a state of complete horror. The image was of a man lying prone on the side of a highway with streetlights casting a glare on his body. He was pinned down by several police officers who then began kicking him brutally and assaulting him with large thick batons. A digital timestamp appeared that read 12:53 a.m., March 3, 1991. This act of police brutality was recognizable to us. Four officers were responsible for brutalizing Mr. King, while more than a dozen officers looked on. They did not intervene. Fire leapt into the foreground. Screams were the only sounds now. The screams become chants. This must now be the Ferguson uprising after Michael Brown was fatally shot by a white police officer. State troopers in riot gear send tear gas and rubber bullets into a crowd of protesters. Now the images scramble. What comes into focus in rapid-fire succession are giant open pit mines. The Mirny mine in Russia, the Kalgoorlie super pit gold mine in Australia, the Bingham Canyon mine in the United States. Massive visible scars cut into the earth. Deep recesses cut out by humans using monster equipment. We hear the grinding of rock and hear the trucks hauling the material away. The smell is dusty and metallic. The men driving the trucks look miniature because their equipment is gargantuan. The images disintegrate, fade. Some of us pass out there on the sand. A migratory swarm of monarch butterflies alights over our collapsed bodies.

The onslaught of imagery is a symptom of complex post-traumatic stress disorder. Traumatic events that are a fraction of cultural memory, archetypal vestiges impossible to shed, the horror embedded subconsciously. Though we have not personally experienced these events, they generate sorrow as harrowing as we know.

Language Movement, Vibration, Floral Transmissions

Fronds communicate. Language takes form in movement, as pollen dissemination, for instance. Living entities interact with blown-over seed crowns breezing via oceanic currents and temperature changes. Channels of motion: moist air descends, dry warmth rises, absorbed heat is distributed with subtropical high pressure, subtropic high points messaging atmosphere, the Coriolis effect; aerosols are tracers. Tropospheric wind patterns traverse, large-scale microbiological movements shift. Replenishing mineral nutrients are swept up in volcanic eruptions and cast as pulverized dust thousands of miles in the distance. The density of water and the particular density of air meet in levels of atmospheric condition.

Ask and Embla made their way along a cracked concrete path, foreboding in appearance. Signs warned not to trespass. Engulfed by heat and humidity, they slipped into a moody stupor that intensified the longer they merged with the park's biome. Their limp arms draped around one another; perspiration glued skin to skin. Glassy-eyed and dazed they ambled amid the overland vehicles steered by harried humans. They made their way through the foliage trying not to get run over. They intended to avoid GoogaMooga.

The couple rented an apartment on Treasure Island near the municipal park. Ask was immersed in a study of biofeedback of grassy environments. He hooked up sensors to parts of the brain in order to study how humans respond to stimuli from the sounds grasses emit. He angled a microphone to the grasses. His work demonstrated that grasses indeed give off low frequency hums and humans interact with these sounds in various distinct ways. Such capacities carry utopian potential. He had a wide range of collaborative interspecies projects underway.

Embla collected flowers and fruit that grew in fields and along roadways with which she assembled wreaths and garlands. She was an ex-
pert on plants of the Virgin as well as the vegetation relating to fair-
ies and naiads, the florae and fauna of the fairy steed, the fairy unguent,
the faes of the wells; those that plunged deeply in water sources, flowing channels. Sylvan knowledge passed down from laurel maidens and
wizened hags, sisters of flowers and the folk of sacred groves, spirits of
the dead that gathered below willow fronds, the hamadryads, the Elder
Mother and Feldgeister. A chapter of a book she was writing described
the sacred trees in Nandanavana, Indra's paradise, a grove filled with
trees like the Kalpavriksha, the wish-fulfilling tree of eternity that arose
in an ocean of milk, night flowering jasmine, gardenia, sandalwood, and
other blooming plants and trees.

As an ethnobotanist she studied forlorn histories teeming in soil. She
had written chapters on globe flowers and the deadly upas, the *Phallus
impudicus* and other ominous subjects that haunted woods and fields.
Devils perplexed fruit trees, lusting after succulent sweetness in the
form of fruiting orbs. Various herbs beckoned malevolent natures.

The Koran describes paradise in floral terms, generating an intense
focus on botany among Muslim scholars. She studied ancient Muslim
scholars of florae: Al-Dinawari, also Al-Kindi and Al-Tabari. Al-Tabari's
epic book titled *Firdous al-Hikmah (The Paradise of Wisdom)* especially
interested her, because he had compiled information not only on botany
but on climatology, philosophy, and astronomy as well. In the work of Ibn
al-'Awwam, hundreds of medicinal purposes of plants are outlined. Embla researched the very early Chinese writings on herbal medicines including the *I Ching* and works like *Esoteric Scripture of the Yellow Em-
peror.* She dipped into works by Egyptian writers. The Ebers Papyrus
described marijuana use for medicinal purposes and was important to
her. Her scholarship was transhistorical and also personal. Medicinal native plants and their usage among Indigenous healers were of great significance, a pharmacopeia of great diversity: cascara sagrada, eyebright
and horehound, sassafras, partridgeberry, tulip tree, slippery elm, and
white sage. Horsetail, lobelia, and goldenseal. The list was long, micro-
and macroregionally specific. Combined knowledge of herbs with ceremony made treatments potent, holistic. Yarrow, bearberry, coastal sage-
brush, mugwort, coastal buckwheat, and fremontia were all powerful

teachers. She researched the reciprocal and sustainable land management practices that Native people used.

Mugwort, or artemisia, held a particular sway over Embla. The plant had withstood the last glacial period, known as the Quaternary glaciation; and during the Oldest Dryas, Europe was almost bald, treeless. Artemisia was among the plants that thrived. It continued to proliferate during the warming up period of the Bølling–Allerød interstadial and did not die out when the ice came again, during the Younger Dryas.

Embla's considerations included so-called invasive plants that grew on lands of dispossession and disturbance. The plants that repopulated Teufelsberg, or Devil's Mountain in Berlin, a humanly created mountain made from the war rubble of bombed houses in that city yielded life-sustaining data. Areas of London that experienced air raids grew back with a surprising diversity of foliage. Chernobyl was another place she collected information on. And on the Sumatra-Andaman earthquake, which set off a tsunami causing major upheaval as it swept landward, flooding huge swaths of inhabited areas. Seeds returned via sky and sea, resettling, stabilizing, reworlding. Turtle Island (North America) fit the descriptor: dispossessed and disturbed. The adaptive farming techniques of Native farmers were not deleterious like the polluting agro business ventures where yield was profit and nothing was given back to the land, the soil. In places where there were cooperatives run by Native stewards of the land and others with similar working ethics, polycultures were nurtured using dry farming, prescribed burning, low-till techniques, and seed saving. It was possible to appreciate the holistic philosophies of reciprocity at play. Each plant carried conflicting histories with it. The edible and healing plant white man's footprint, the broadleaf plantain that Puritan settlers brought with them, made it easy to trace where they had been since the plant readily seeds itself, carried about most likely on the soiled hooves of their horses. Masanobu Fukuoka's *One Straw Revolution*, a tract on green gardening, motivated her work to be as sensitive to every aspect of how food could be grown, harvested, and distributed for sustenance.

In her satchel was a book explicating the herbs of Hecate, Circe, and Medea. She intended to sit on a bench and study the contents while Ask foraged for sounds among the thickets of purple top, little bluestem, and Indiangrass. Goldenrod vibrated in relation to prophetic oaks that whis-

pered remote secrets to receptive ears. There was an underground network of roots that allowed plants and other organisms to communicate, and it was possible to hear these resonances by means of intense
attunement.

Embla's sense of smell had developed so that she could tell what month
it was by the scents emitted in a specific environment, even down to the
week. Leaves gave off volatile chemicals that altered from day to day and
hour to hour. She sensed what flowering plants were in bloom. Seasonal
attunement drew her to the smell of decomposing humus to know what
stage of rot it was undergoing. She could smell sprouting roots below the
soil and the long tendrils of mycelium that sent channels of information
and nutrition from mushroom to tree roots and back again. Smell guided
her to the presence of worms and insects who did particular activities
during certain seasons. Microorganisms had certain distinct odors. She
could distinguish many molds, fungi, and viruses above and below the
dirt.

Oriented toward the tremors of leaves, stalks, bark, and roots, Embla proceeded through space and substance. Hercules amaryllis, Hercules phlox, heuchera Hercules, the *Aloidendron* Hercules flower, the latter
a member of the quiver tree family. Her stream of consciousness proceeded through floral identifications. Many flowers proliferate in *Alice
in Wonderland*: a tiger lily, a rose, lily of the valley, tulips, sweet peas,
blue bonnets, violets, sunflowers, thistle iris, and more. Alice encounters
flowers in a garden and they respond as if she too is a flower. A dramatic
moment when the flowers talk to Alice in a nonchalant manner. She is an
adolescent and is thus approachable as a flower, part of the biological expanse. The opportunity for exchange is extensive among living entities.
A rose for every lover, every grave, daisies to cheer, a larkspur may sym-
bolize an open heart. Stimulants, depressants, mood alterations in the
form of petals and stamens bending toward the sun and reaching out for
moisture. *The Wizard of Oz*, poppies. Fitful sleep. Chemical agents used
to incapacitate. An estimated seventy uniquely new synthetic chemicals
have been introduced, employed, and stockpiled as life destroyers during
the era of the Anthropocene. The numbers grow. Oz provided a space
of rehabilitation. A treatment center and a safety zone from the attacks
of the nemesis. Or Oz was the ultimate grandiose projection. A fantasy.
A coded depiction of Manifest Destiny. A garden of plenty exclusively
guarded, restrictions based on race and class.

By midday the stifling quality of the atmosphere was more oppressive than when they arrived. A weather announcer had warned that the ozone level was unsafe, the air quality had a high saturation of particulates. People should restrict their time outside, especially between the hours of 10:00 a.m. to 9:00 p.m. This was unfeasible. Their cubicle apartment was an airless chamber. No amount of air-conditioning lifted the lethargy. Ask and Embla intended to skirt much of the park because Googa-Mooga was in full swing. Or should they just stroll through to figure out what the hype was about? Neither wanted to pay the entrance fee. Both subsisted on various legumes, grains, and nuts, as well as vegetables lightly cooked. Ask was raised in a household of vegans, only his sister, two years older, deviated from the family norm. She solicited meat at her friends' houses or when the family ever occasionally frequented a restaurant. Embla was wispy but Ask was full-bodied, curvy, not lacking flesh, muscles, and fatty tissue. His body instructed every digestible cell of energy to be converted into the building blocks of corporality. He and Embla ate nearly the same portions from nearly the same menu, day after day. They were in sync on a primal level. This morning each had eaten a bowl of fruit and nuts. Embla wore sheaf dresses that had abstracted patterns, of leaves and flowers, similar to those found on vintage curtains. She favored fabric that was thick and rather rough; if it were possible, she'd wear bark, or cloth made from bark. Combining *codex*, the Latin word for "book," and an earlier word, *caudex*, or "tree trunk," she willingly wore pages from a book of trees printed on cloth. The tentlike structure of fabric much like vellum flapped against her body, catching slight breezes. Ask had a treelike body, and he tended to prefer clothing in rich brown and vibrant green hues.

Ask had decided not to bring his equipment; he didn't tell Embla that he brought just a notebook and drawing implements. Embla carried a straw basket under her arm, books, and a tablet. She often took video clips of the wind bending or agitating plants. They got as far as the perimeter of the park, and out of exhaustion and ennui, sat, inert for a time on a wooden bench. Several established New Zealand Christmas trees bloomed in profusion above them, the red bottlebrush flowers attracting insects. The buzzing sounds were hypnotic. The canopy was a soundscape that resonated to their bone marrow. Dialogue between them was at a minimum, though thoughts were being exchanged nonverbally. The heat parched language. They were as much in tune with the trees as with one another. The density of the heavy warm shade was a living presence. They both preferred a certain amount of discomfort when they worked. The body then was more responsive, primed to ecological cues. They used distractions to guide them into their analysis. Heat was particularly compelling. Heat slowed down thought processes, so each cognitive image appeared realized, full-blown, proximal.

Mood, barometric pressure, heat, the viscosity of the atmosphere, scents permeating the air; all contributed to cognitive engagement. They channeled environmental signals. The wood of the bench conducted the energy looping through their nervous systems. Embla inquired where Ask was with his data collection. He did not answer outright; he was absorbed in concentration. She noticed that instead of making vibrational recordings of the grasses in the vicinity he had his notebook out and had begun a drawing.

They sank further into semiprivate reveries. Ask began to make quick short strokes with a number two pencil in the notebook. He homed in on the trunk of the pohutukawa tree, the New Zealand Christmas tree as renamed by settlers who noticed the tree bloomed in concert with their Christmas celebration. He began to render the texture of the torso of the growing floral being. The demarcations were subtle. The tree was healthy, perhaps forty years old. He and the tree were the same age. The tree was actively swooning, thick in the time of pollination, producing crimson flowers that formed a crown of plumage. Nutrients pumped through the outer epidermal layer of the tree, sending replenishing minerals to the crown. A breeze blew and fiery blossoms drifted down to them. A human cannot presume to know what another human is thinking, nor can a human surmise what a tree is thinking. Yet there is a way in which it is possible to be in communication, and respond to indications of connection, whether human or tree—all sentient life exchanges information. Embla laughed as she looked in on the intimacy developing between Ask and the planted tree blazing red. An intensity of feeling flowed. They were all in a circuit. Ask's drawing was kinetic, alive. The pencil scratched at the surface of the paper with grasshopperlike movements the tree induced—a mental image transferred, made physical. The drawing didn't isolate the tree, rather it included where the tree made contact with the various forms of life that surrounded it. Pausing on the name of the tree yielded historical complications of place and time and contact. Settler colonists, in the process of territorialization, concluded on a name for the tree, ignoring and obfuscating a longer history of its roots in the ground, branches in the sky, and social exchanges with native Maori. There were multiple versions of a Maori legend where a youthful warrior named Tawhaki sought to avenge the death of his father by searching for heaven, climbing up higher and higher on vines before he crashed to earth. His blood spilled blood-colored flowers, the blossoms of the pohutukawa tree. Other versions tell that Tawhaki reached the tenth of the ten heavens, and he is thus associated with wind and lightning. Mental processes twist and turn like tree roots and find epiphanic heights, like branches reaching for the sun. Layers of reality shuffled and then agglomerated. This tree growing in California, far away from its place of origin, shared multiple axes.

He made another drawing automatically of a skyscape canceled out by the ash of an infernal fire. A fire that was yet to be but was coming. Not really prophetic—obvious, the personal recognition of a changing world. The watershed moment had passed and had been obscured. California and other western states will become engulfed by flames and burn for decades in which time plants and animals will be decimated and displaced. Major stands of ancient trees incinerated, multiple species eliminated. In the heat of the afternoon, in unseasonal temperatures, he intuited the future guided by the tree's insights. The drawing was dark as soot.

For Embla it was poignant to notice how the trunk plunged into the soil. Stuck in resolutely. Roots securely anchored the trunk that held up a colossal crown. Even coastal squalls did not disturb the tree. To be that committed to space, place. Socialization happens below ground with mycorrhizal connections: the relay of sugars and other nourishments. Interspecies symbiosis as fungal organisms share with the trees and the trees share with the fungi. There was no "hub tree" here, so how did the process happen without guidance and wisdom from a "mother tree"? So many of us are wayward, adrift, getting by without the benefit of secure networks. She noticed the odd drawing Ask had made.

"There will be fire," he offered when she looked over at him to consider his mark-making. The prescience of his remark rang an alarm.

"Did you feel something?"

"Yes. A world ablaze."

"Terrifying." She took her time to add, "induced perhaps by the thirsty red blossoms."

"The sun is blackened by the soot of the fire."

"What are you talking about?"

"Racing images overwhelmed me while I made the drawing. The entire Northwest was burning. That was the sense of the scale of disaster. At first there were patchwork fires. Then the fires connected. Moss-drenched forests become tinderboxes. Animals scrambled for safety but there was nowhere to run!" Tears rolled down his cheeks. He was spotty and swollen. His speech was lumpy. "Paradise. Every town and city was Paradise. Not the current fires, future fires." As it was, there were numerous fires burning unchecked in California, and neighboring states.

She handed him a clutch of fallen blossoms. "Let it all rush in." She did not mean this as an insipid command, rather as an ephemeral suggestion airborne as pollen. Power dynamics for Embla had to do with heartbeat, gravity, the hydraulics of plants absorbing moisture. Or power could be gossamer: the secretions of mushrooms, rain changing to steam, the hair of plants absorbing electricity.

They remained stuck, glued by sweat to the park bench. They readjusted their focus. Shadows ebbed and flowed, as if shadows were puppets lifted up and animated by outside forces ghosting and confronting them. An overland vehicle rushed past them laden with garbage. The stench wafted toward them. Rubber and perspiration blended. The fumes of rotting plastic, grease, and rat poison funneled up from trash cans. The tree's fragrance intermingled. A loamy reassuring smell drifted up from the ground. Ask began paying attention to the wispy Queen Anne's lace that grew around the tree's base. It bobbed while the trunk stood still. The white frothy petals noticed the slightest change in air circulation, the subtle flow that was always in action. Embla internalized the sensation of the flowers also. Light and shadow refocused the depth of field and lured vision into a floating world without perspective. The head of the flower pulsed. The stem bent into contortions. The shadows played against their ankles and shins. The light was so strong and canceling it could have been a snowbank she was looking at. She closed the book she had been reading and looked again at the activity of Ask's pencil. The drawing was animated by the floral tops of the flower that resembled spiderwebs. In fact, there was a spider. An orb weaver spider was perched on top of the frilly petals. Tiny. They could see its leg bristles that it uses to comb the silk. Why was the spider out and about? Usually orb weavers hide during daytime hours. A sparrow hopped around their feet and through the bottom leaves of the Queen Anne's lace and the grasses that grew at the base of the trees.

The shadow Ask rendered altered its contour. He erased the shape in the notebook and reworked the area. Attending closely to the negative spaces, he sensed movement emanating. The movement was independent of light and shadow. Every moment is a moment of creation and disappearance. There is evidence of everything recycling itself all around. Sweat beaded on his forehead then smeared across the page of the notebook making the paper translucent, the graphite crosshatching see through. Stippled lines appeared like code on the underside of the page of the notebook. He stopped for a moment, and they held hands. Then he resumed with shading and contrast using the eraser of the pencil. The composition kept changing. Intense focus culminated in diaphanous marks. Why was light emanating in the dark underbrush? The shadows stabilized. Pencil strokes delivered an accurate account of the spatial details. He worked in rippling lines rendering bright and dark. Then when he thought he'd worked out the dimensions and placements of figure and ground the ephemeral architecture of living presences shifted. What he had articulated was suddenly not representative. The shadows again rearranged parts of the design. He continually reworked the drawing, but nothing would sit still. Finally, he set down the pencil and approached closer to the plant, unhindered. A wider angle revealed perplexing anomalies of contrasts that did not correspond to the angle of the sun. There was a glare under the leaves in an area that should be shady.

They both shifted their postures having noticed the changes simultaneously, each independent of the other but in sync. Both were hesitant to formulate language, to speak of this with each other, breaking the spell. This was an occasion to be guided by ecological insight, not human constructs, though they seemed perpetually present, hardwired into the brain. Embla took a huge sip of air and it disappeared under her ribcage; he copied her somatic action. The intake of oxygen released the tension.

She entered into dialogue, but not with Ask. Her mind contacted the spider. Spiders have a mythic status inherent in cultural representation. She had to get past the symbolism to arrive at the present moment in time so the elements of cognitive semblances would balance out. She and the spider found a conduit for mutual language through the moisture in the leaves and the flower buds, the sea spray and the micro atmosphere created by breath and condensation. The spider immediately connected with her. They echoed what Embla had just intimated, but with different semantics. The spider projected a series of colorized templates. Green became brown, blue became black, yellow became red, clearness became opaque. Ice became vapor, wood became flame, dirt became dust. Her understanding was that spiders were almost completely blind. Spiders are able to tune the threads of their web like a musical instrument. She remembered what Beth Mortimer, a Royal Society University Research Fellow and leader of the Animal Vibration Lab in the Zoology Department at University of Oxford had said about spiders. "The spider can actually pluck or bounce the silk strings, and it can monitor the echoes that come back so it can locate objects." Mortimer's research was being used to design "soft robots" able to orient with the slightest cues of vibrational information thanks to a built-in multiscale sensory system. Could vibrations become colorized through synesthesia? Yes, that had to be what happened. Each of them used the information they shared differently. The spider catapulted off the flower on a silver thread extruded from its body and was then elsewhere, unseen.

Wiping her brow on the back of her hand, Embla began a sentence with actual vocal pitch and tone. She looked for the spider as she gestured with her fingers toward the leaves of the plant. "The spider's orientation consists of vibrations that I visualized as colors." She waited to let the words slip off her tongue. "That's how I interpreted what the spider communicated. Fire was communicated."

"I could listen in. I felt the spider's vibrations as a palpable language." Ask looked down to resume drawing. The pencil grazed paper but no marks could be seen.

With her moist hand Embla drew the flower toward her and as she did, she noticed the woman who often sat near them. The woman had a composure she admired. She sat absolutely still with her spine elongated yet did not appear stiff. They'd never struck up a conversation, but Embla was intrigued. There were signal lines between them. She could feel wave oscillations emanating from the woman. The woman had a floral nature. She doesn't have a place to stay, Embla intuited. She wore the same clothing every time Embla saw her. There was bag of belongings by her feet, books. Besides her dirt-stained hands she was manicured. They nodded to each other from separate benches.

Again, another overland vehicle traversed the path, this time empty of trash. A residue of stench followed behind the vehicle nonetheless.

"While you were receiving images from the spider a stream of sensations passed through me. Blurry at first, focus gradually adjusted. A meadow of mountain grasses tilting in the wind. Horses—no, they were ponies—they were petite and muscular, roaming freely. They had thick fur. There were patches of ice, a glacier. What looked like a woolly rhinoceros passed in the periphery. A spear flashed by. The rhino fell on the ice. A person wearing furs collected the carcass. He bundled it onto a sled with the help of others who came running toward the site of the kill as the animal fell. I caught a glimpse of the spear thrower. The woolly rhino hunter shared an uncanny resemblance with me, the difference being posture and the amount of facial and body hair!" Ask looked flummoxed, but not distressed. "Man on ice, hunting, augmented reality, the sun somehow blue, a giant ratlike creature scurried by, then the rhino. Primed to kill I felt the motion of the spear and also the woosh of air being stirred. The ice was real. It coated everything except a small patch of meadow blooming with flowers!" He swept his thinning hair back with a tossed gesture. "Being attuned to sound I was taken off guard to notice colors, never mind the whole prehistoric scene."

"That's incredible." She interjected, absorbing Ask's account of his daydream hallucination. "Synesthesia is a derangement of the senses that brings nonrational insight." She too brushed her hair with a sweeping gesture. "Sensations are doubled. Red is red, and, as I told you of the spider's account, red is also what once was yellow. A woman dropped her dripping umbrella on my foot the other day in a coffee shop and the sensation was of warm spilled milk. I can't account for the sensation except to imagine that it is part of a shifting dynamic where alternative cognitive pathways are excited by a disequilibrium. I think climate change is intensifying the rearrangement of the senses, altering cognitive awareness." Ask listened intently as Embla pursued her line of thought. "For one, added heat causes an organism to switch into a different regulatory mode, a phase change. Oceans are transforming into clouds. Forests into fire. Where before there were solid bodies, now there is vapor and ash— barely traceable, ephemeral. This hallucination goes outside the bounds of living memory. Your body is bringing stored temporal information up to the surface level of consciousness."

Moments passed. Ask's silence indicated to Embla that he wanted her to continue.

"History flashes up as images out of sequence as an organism in disequilibrium tries to make sense or stabilize reality." A flock of seagulls clattered overhead, blurring her phrasing. "Interpretation happens in fits and starts. One image bores into another and then is melted by emotion. Emotion is the psyche's atmosphere, or climate. How many generations back are you from your Neanderthal roots, I wonder? And am I too quick to assume you come from a lineage of Neanderthals because of your Scandinavian ethnicity—likely not. You might have diverged from somewhere else altogether. Humans migrate a lot in the course of one hundred thousand years, or don't."

Ask set down the drawing and shifted toward Embla so he could face her. She adjusted on the bench as well. They passed a water bottle between them. The spider instigated ancestral history to come to the surface. "A great-great-great-grandfather on my mother's side was from Yazılıkaya, in Eskişehir Province, what is now Turkey and once was Midas City, Anatolia, where the Phrygians lived. A few years ago, vandals dynamited some of the rock tombs, churches, and castles in the Phrygian Valley. The fairy chimneys are intact. I like to think that my interest in floral sonics comes from Anatolian descendants. There have been excavations in Anatolia with settlements dating back to nine thousand to seven thousand BCE."

"Yes, fairy chimneys," Embla echoed before he continued.

"The excavations at Çatalhöyük—a Neolithic settlement. Hunter-gatherers settled down to farm near the rich alluvial soils. Were the people Yamnayas who migrated there from present-day Russia and the Ukraine or older lineages of, say the Denisovans, or altogether other *Homo sapiens*, a different subgroup of *Homo erectus*? Mysteries prevail." There were excavations taking place all over the globe, revealing new settlements of people, unknown cultures, uses of tools, evidence of their relationship to the ecology.

Ask's digressions drifted until again the couple concentrated back on the florae around them. The heat held them in a torpor.

Embla got off the bench and crouched down so she could peer into the foliage. A constant return is necessary to see beyond paradigms and prejudices of sight—of all the senses. To remove the gridded lines of perspective and steer vision beyond sight so that senses merge. Seeing involves the interplay of coherence, consequence, and insistence. That's how Ask would start out in an explication, reverting to a syntax of Logos. He would start at a grounded point in an argument and then veer. He usually veered and it got interesting. Images are watery, color-saturated integrations of the imagination meeting a substantive material dimension. To generate an image requires an engagement with all of the body. She considered the integration of vast data streams of bloodline, all that is absorbed by the body: floral, faunal, mineral. Her eyesight felt compromised. Her vision went in and out of focus. The micro- and macrozooming gave her vertigo. Her instinct told her to give into the blur. It is within the blur that a new image could take shape. Reality that had been obfuscated, overlooked, came into focus. From the base of her spine running up to her cranium was an energy like cosmic breathing. Her central nervous system distributed electrical impulses through her body. The electricity of her body and the surrounding energy field had merged. The tree's energy torqued. The plants at the base of the tree throbbed. The shadowed spaces were no longer at the edge of consciousness. The darker spaces intensified, thus drawing her attention. She signaled to Ask hoping he would perceive what she was perceiving. A negative space forged independence from the tree and the underbrush momentarily. As the density of the recessed space was altered, the air coagulated. It remained translucent, yet there was a defined thickness. Ask noticed her probing intensity. He concentrated too. He tended to take cues from her when they were together outside, their fields of interest coalescing.

A thick humidity persisted but didn't land as rain. The Queen Anne's lace was magnified again by their attention. Native to Eurasia, the flower was yet another immigrant brought to North America through settler colonial channels. In 1604 King James commissioned a translation of the Bible into the English language for the Church of England; it was published in 1611. In the time that the Bible translation was underway, he sent three boats to North America—the Susan Constant, the Godspeed, and the Discovery—establishing the first permanent English settlement in North America: Jamestown, Virginia. King James had formed the Virginia Company of London; its goal was to expand colonization. In under a decade, the settler colonists were growing tobacco as a cash crop and had ushered in the plantation system, starting first with forced labor of indentured Europeans, soon expanding to enslaved Indigenous peoples and Africans. Tobacco had been grown in North America since at least six thousand BCE. The crop that Jamestown grew was of a South American variety that the Spanish cultivated on their plantations. Nicotiana tabacum. When did his wife, the young Danish queen, an avid lacemaker, prick her finger while making lace as lore has it? Queen Anne's lace often has a tiny dark purple floret at the center of the flower. The royal couple were unhappy in their marriage. James held court with a bevy of beautiful men, his homosexuality thinly disguised. Their troubles however, stemmed from other chasms, religion being one; he was an adamant Protestant, she a rebellious Catholic. He wore lace collars as flamboyant as the flower, as was the fashion for the ruling class. Did Anne make the laces for his blouses, Embla wondered. Anne's collars were more extravagant yet, extending to her ears in starched elegance.

The spider returned, descending on a long thin silken thread from a vault in the sky that had cracked open. There was a sticky monkey flower, a pink sea thrift, and also a wavy-leaf soap plant that became noticeable as the light shifted. She realized that she must have missed seeing the wavy-leaf soap plant earlier because the tepals (petals and sepals combined) open only at dusk and bloom until sunrise. She made note to come again to the plant in the hours when the blooms open up. It was also late in the plant's blooming cycle; the plant was nearly dormant. The soap plant looked spidery with its curled elongated petals. When a leaf is broken, green milk drips forth. Its tuber is edible (as are the leaves) and its sap creates a lather that can be used as soap. The flowers are bisexual. She knew this about the plant. Recently she came across a video channel of a man named Chad who posts survival-oriented footage. He uploaded an episode where he harvested the wavy-leaf soap plant's tubers and roasted them over a fire in a structure he built out of mud bricks in an undisclosed location in Mexico. The sticky monkey flower that grew here must have been recently propagated. It was just a small stalk, not yet in bush form, and buds of bright orange blossoms had yet to form. The pink sea thrift had numerous globes of medium pink flowers. The plant didn't mind the salty sea spray. All three plants are used medicinally by Ohlone, Miwok, and other Native people. For most other urban dwellers, local vegetation received barely a glance.

"Something that makes us eye-attentive to the eye." A Gerard Manley Hopkins line that she embellished through repetition when feeling a sensory overload from looking.

Ask knew to respond with, "that make my eyes sore and cross-colour things." The missing referents were more potent left dangling, out of bounds.

"You have to see it to really see it." Her mantra by which she didn't

mean an isolated sense at all, rather a magnification by all the senses together. And: "It is becoming impossible to detach."

"The plants have taken you in. As usual." He considered and added,
"us in."

They were both mindful of how space opened up vast inclusiveness.
The invitation was always there but not always recognizable. The possibility for contact and encounter was open-ended.

The Queen Anne's lace, sticky monkey flower, sea thrift, and the
wavy-leaf soap plant had parted their fronds. There was a form explicitly
alive scrooched down in front of them, nestled among the plants. It was
definitely a person. In a fetal position. The rhythm of their breathing agi-
tated the leaves.

Their intense focus augmented the space that the form took. Ask's
change of focus was intensified by hormonal shifts that sent a warning signal though his nervous system to prepare for unknown outcomes.
Fight, flight, play dead, or camouflage, the repertoire of mammalian responses. He added mimicry as an adaptive response, becoming like, taking on the qualities of the other, the environment. Emulating. He did not
mean appeasing a threat when he thought of emulation. That was another option, fawning. And if you are a tree, with great longevity, waiting
out a problem is the desired approach. Embla too internalized a plant's
ability to hold out in the face of danger. Plants cannot abandon their habitat in an instant, only through seed dispersal can a plant intentionally migrate. Or if the plant is rhizomatic, it can shift locally. Her study of florae
had given her insight into the radical complexity of diversity that lives
collectively in the understory and in the canopy. Trees and plants prefer
to live with their family around them, with a diversity of other trees and
plants closely interspersed. Sensitive sensors on the tips of leaves give
plants the ability to access information on changing situations around
them and in the vicinity of where they grow. Signals are passed between
trees, plant roots, and fungi. Warnings are signaled above and below
ground. The largest of floral entities are trees. When they are healthy,
they are resilient to the onslaught of most insect invasions, microbes,
and fire. A thick layer of bark protects the sensitive inner fibers of a tree
where nutrients surge upward to the crown.

Ask did not directly share ongoing observations with Embla; they
were both in a telepathic trance and sensed what the other was negotiating. They both continued to concentrate their full attention on the emer-

gent form in front of them. A calmness arose in breathing. The presence was also still as if frozen in the moment. Time had congealed around a nucleus of attention. This occurrence was like cell division, mitosis. And like fragmentation, a form of reproduction where part of an organism breaks off, drifts, becomes a distinct entity. Also, something mundane, the act of seeing something that may or may not be there all along and then the intensity of existence doubles. A memory resurfaces, a déjà vu. Body movements create a ripple effect in the forcefield, tension is released, molecules rub against each other and there is friction. A microcellular eroticism. Plants take in minerals, become mineral-infused, mineral beings, fauna internalize plants, become floralized. Minerals move in and out of various diverse states of personhood.

Any sense of autonomy dissolved the longer they both stayed where they were in transfixed attention. An ambulance blared its siren; the high-decibel pitch registered as an ambient layer of sensation. Embla's sandal crushed a bit of the lower foliage of the Queen Anne's lace and a rush of heavy essences opened gateways. A white serum oozed out of one of the broken stems. Insects were already ascending the plant, preparing to harvest the potent liquid. She considered if the hallucination of the form curled up in front of them was caused by the aromatics of a plant. Did one of these plants contain psychotropic qualities? Again, she forced herself to take a series of deep, mindful breaths, holding the air in her lungs for several seconds to bring her heartbeat back down to a resting level. The breathing ameliorated the agitation. The metallic taste on her tongue now seemed sweet. Again, the invocation of multisensory cues. What did the nerve endings of the body know of the situation that she didn't yet consciously perceive? She was able to pull herself outside of the immediate tugging sensation of shock and regroup to notice wonder and awe. "Fear demands feeling. . . . Courage implies a presence of danger." Plotinus from *The Enneads*, his commitments to the tutelary spirits and mystic passions connected with her understandings of soul work accomplished in collaboration with other-than-human presences, persons. As the fleeting terror diminished, she realized the void, or whatever it was, was passive, at least at present. There was a nonaggressive vibe. Another possibility was that the presence was waiting for her to react. Whereas Ask was drawn into a reverie of an archaic past, she felt the future unfolding. Flashbacks and mirrors onto a future.

The sun blazed as a fluorescent red orb surrounded by orange skies, the intense colors caused by the suspended ashes of forest fires burning up and down the western states. Both now sweated profusely but didn't relocate. More pedestrians walked by. Many headed to the food festival. The aroma was of seared meat and car exhaust. The garbage can near them filled up again with trash, little bags of dog poop and other sundry items.

"Have a sip of water." Ask handed Embla the thermos filled with chilled, filtered water from their apartment. The gesture helped him pull back from the excitement of the phenomenon of the form in the underbrush.

"Thanks," she whispered. Her cheeks were flushed. Suddenly to shape a single, simple word with her jaw and tongue took effort.

"All this has stripped the moisture out of me," he said, as she took several swigs. By "all this" he meant the intense attention he was committing to comprehend what was developing nearby. He dared himself not to look at the form for a minute. He then took a long sip when she handed back the bottle.

"I know what you mean. Something really shifted today. We always sit together studying microbiomes, but today I feel something, see something *beyond* or *into*. This might sound strange to say, but nebulous contrasts seem to have overlapped in formation, like a Venn diagram. That voided form we both spotted is where the circles of difference meet." The hot, aromatic wafts of Queen Anne's lace rose to their nostrils again. They both looked at the nested shape among the plants. Embla continued, "I'm feeling unsteady about perception in this heat and the crazed energy of GoogaMooga might be affecting my thinking, even at a distance." She paused and they both inhaled barbecue smoke mixed with a slight tinge of forest fire ash. "The plants might be playing tricks on us. There is a wavering of appearance as something struggles to find semblance. It's happening in front of us. Everything is normal. And there's a presence." She drew out the temporal longevity of each phrase. When she was done speaking, she looked over to see if the lone woman was still sitting on the other bench, but she was nowhere to be seen. She returned her gaze to the fetal form. It had shifted. It was sitting up.

Embla continued, "This is a manmade island. The geological record was disturbed when quarried rock, dredged bay sand, and topsoil were relocated here. In a true sense, the total shuffling of geologic time." She imbibed another sip of water and then paused to give Ask a chance to weigh in.

"What is forming before our eyes is so strange and yet seems totally normal. For the first half hour I sat here questioning my faculties, but now I've come to accept the possibility of an enigma." He adjusted his loose linen trousers. "You know this, when I record sound samples of plants it's not unusual to pick up irregular patterns, rhythms, and vibrations. I'm ready to be convinced of a visual equivalent. We are seeing sound. Or our listening and seeing have merged." They constantly updated on and put each other in touch with what they sensed. Even moments of silence were a kind of update. Both Ask and Embla had the qualities of epiphytes, plants that grow on the surface of other plants, that derive their nutrition from rain, air, and the detritus accumulating around them. They both reached out among themselves and each other to collect what they needed for subsistence, intellectually and emotionally.

"Let me look at your drawing again," she requested. He set it on his lap to face up at her. She traced the gap between the plants with her fingers. "There, a shape was there an hour ago when you worked on this. That's when I started to notice also."

"If only there were a stray cat in the bushes," he jested. "But that isn't it. It is an anomalous phenomenon." He was suddenly conscious of talking about the form in front of him.

The fact of the island being humanly constructed was always a topic of interest. They were drawn to Treasure Island because of its artifice, the fact that it was engineered out of material from elsewhere. It was built recently out of the social imagination and capital. Its radical newness did not mean it did not have an extended history: the stones were brought here from the construction of a reservoir on Yerba Buena, the island nearest Treasure Island; a bridge separated the two landmasses. The dredged sand too brought with it an archive as did all the various construction materials and imported vegetation. The biography of the minerals and plants had a legacy encoded in its geology and biology. It shared features of other massive earthworks: pyramids, mounds and pavilions that were made to inspire wonderment and admiration of their grandeur. In its case, a secular magnificence where capital moved rubble to form pleasure palaces and centers of military might. In its current iteration, and in this instant, food was being glorified: fatty, greasy animal products, sourced from industrial farms, many in the San Joaquin Valley, where much of the soil is so impacted it is almost as hard as stone (and sinking because agro companies have overdrawn water from aquifers, steadily depleting them). Driving along Interstate 5 near Route 198 she encountered California's largest beef producer, at the time, Harris Cattle Ranch (since sold to Central Valley Meat Company), where a staggering 250,000 cows stood or lay listlessly and exhaustedly on parched land under the blazing sun. A life-altering instance of witness, every sense assaulted by misery and an overload of rage. The factory megafarm was another such earthwork, created to impress a world of superabundance in the form of extracted life. Spectacles of artifice that influence how life is lived. Their shabby little apartment would no doubt soon be razed with all the development slated on the island. For the time being they had everything they needed. Shelter, a few windows, a door, a refrigerator, bookshelves, vases, a bathtub, dried flowers on the walls and ceilings. The structure would join a landfill somewhere becoming part of the mounds of refuse, perhaps humanity's most immense earthwork. For the moment, they were able to live sustainably with the energies and resources provided by their fieldwork.

They could now say with certainty that the person clinging to the foliage in front of them was human. The being was petite, maybe a child; but had muscle definition so maybe an adolescent, or young adult. They had speculated briefly that maybe what they saw was a baby deer, but there were no deer that lived on the island. The person's gender was indeterminate. Whoever it was could not be one of the performers they had seen of late in the area, moving in enigmatic formations. They were not here today, probably because of the food festival. The performers were easily noticeable because they were always dressed in personal protective clothing. They had misconstrued what they were doing when they first saw them. Maybe a chemical spill they thought? But why wasn't the public notified if that was the case? Had oil from a tanker somehow washed on shore and leached into the ground? They were aware of the island's toxic legacy.

Embla moved in first, got on her knees, adjusted the leaves aside as gently as she could without crushing the plants or threatening the presence. The person was breathing. She gently nudged the being's shoulder closest to her and noticed how they shifted, swiveled in slow motion into a seated position facing her and Ask. Embla seemed to see through them as if they were nonmaterial. Again, she felt a displacement in the chronological sequencing of time. Time was translucent. A new relation to time liberated an internal archive that was stored in her subconscious. Her throat tightened and a dizzy disorientation persisted as the scenery around her changed. A meadow bordering a lake came into focus. Suction pulled air out of her diaphragm and a light wind glided over the hair on her arms. An archetypal scene from her childhood overlaid the present.

An idyllic day, sunbathing in the vicinity of a mountain lake, the sparkling water bubbling up from a spring-fed aquifer. The lake, a dark evergreen mirror, and all around, verdant hilly contours caused by at least a mile thick sheet of ice that had slowly dragged over the surface during the Pleistocene Epoch that began 2.6 million years ago and ended about 11,700 years ago transforming the upper surface, revealing the basement foundation of igneous rock. The stream of images paused, and Embla could see the resemblance of herself in the form of the person lying on a towel surrounded by grass. It was her high school self, hair wet, posture stretched out. She would drive to the lake twice a day during her summer recess, once in the early dawn and again at dusk, and swim back and forth across the distance of the lake. It gave her a feeling of suspended animation to create a rhythm for her days that involved swimming when the light rose and when it set. Between those hours she worked for the parks department in the town in the valley below.

Her routine, or ritual, was to wake up as the sun rose above the velvet hills of hemlock, maple, and spruce, grab a towel, and jump in the shared family car. Her father, who left considerably earlier, had taken it on himself to bicycle to work most days, a twenty-five-mile journey. He was nearing retirement and biking to work centered embodiment before the impending workday, the drudgery of a sedentary office job. The lake was situated in the rural outskirts of a neighboring community. Much of the land was state forest. At most the resident population amounted to one thousand people living scattered on back roads, many unpaved dead ends; they lived in trailers, log houses, and ranch houses. Even in the summer, curls of thick blue smoke emanating from wood burning stoves exited out of skinny chimneys. The kids were bused to the school in the valley below, where she attended. The residents of the village were linked to the municipal sewer and power lines but there were many households that lived off the grid. Before cars were prevalent, people living there were landlocked on the mountain during the winter. Her great-grandmother's sister had lived in this community after immigrating from Sweden at the turn of the last century. At the time the village people farmed the rocky land that was difficult to plow, making it difficult to yield enough food to survive on. Most of the crops were grown as fodder for cows and goats. Kitchen gardens encircled the houses. Much of what was harvested from the kitchen gardens was canned. Berries were picked in the meadows. Root cellars were filled to capacity when harvests were plentiful. Privations forced people to work unrelentingly. The dead were buried on one's property. This chain of thought had her remember stories her grandmother would tell, of the bodies of the unrealized as she called them. "They were plentiful, the only thing that was plentiful." Her grandmother would express such details, sharing with her the memories that her mother recounted of her sister's life. What she meant were the miscarriages and infants that succumbed to illness. The women knew how to end unwanted pregnancies but often did not for fear of reprisal. An undertone of sorrow dominated the mountain.

The mountain lake was pristine (acid rain notwithstanding). The obsidian depths were of a molecular intensity that nourished bone marrow. Sorrow slowly underwent a process of clearing out, sinking deeper into the reserves of the earth, into the aquifers, into cracks in bedrock. Rain brought water from around the globe to the lake, affecting the electric charge of the water and the air. The accretions of history fused and blended. She swam through the sorrow, through the massiveness of emotional weight and physical pain. Her body stirred diffuse energies that clung to emotions.

The lake's energetic dimensions are conduits and also an integrated part of a terrestrial circulatory and nervous system. And too, all eleven systems of the human body are connected planetarily and not limited to Earth as they participate as expansively as energy is able to flux. The shock of the intense chill in contact with her skin stimulated her integumentary system. That sensation caused ripples of waves in the atomic structure. The water jarred her sense of what she was. Blood, tissue, bone. Her body consisted of approximately 60 percent water, the very substance she was floating and flapping within, yet she did not dissolve. Her brain and kidneys contained the highest percentage of water. Ninety-nine percent of her body was made of six elements: oxygen, hydrogen, nitrogen, carbon, calcium, and phosphorus. The other 1 percent was made up of five elements: sulfur, potassium, sodium, chlorine, and magnesium, and less than 1 percent of that of trace elements. Oxygen is the most common element in the body and its mass is present in the form of water. She was astounded to learn that her body mass was 2.5 percent metal.

The water that was the lake that she had swum in hovered above her as mist, as cloud formation, as fog. In the winter it was possible to see liquid, solid, and gaseous forms of the lake at once. Because the lake had partially taken the form of a cloud, it drifted. It would rain down on fields and valleys, in cities. Animals and plants sipped the lake, transporting it elsewhere. The lake within them subtly altered their DNA.

The trajectory from the parking lot to the lake was well defined. There were several pathways through a section of forest that led to a meadow and then the lake. The park service maintained the area, occasionally weed whacking the edges of the underbrush. Brambles grew up around the trails etched by human foot traffic. Root systems buckled underneath and above dirt. When walking to the lake she mentally prepped for the swim, her thoughts became focused once she parked her car. The hyperfocus was also a response to the threat of being a lone person, gendered female, and young, entering the remoteness of the lake at early or after hours to swim. Around the bend where the restrooms were located, she noticed an indented section of the underbrush. A human form was curled and twisted, the legs drawn apart and upper torso whiplashed sideways. It was dawn. There was no one else around. She mustered the ability to move her muscles and approach. The woman's eyes were closed shut. There was no expression on her face. The neutral look of the woman's features made it easier for Embla to move closer. The woman's body was strewn on top of mosses, fruiting bodies of pleated inkcap, viscid violet cort, and shaggy mane. Bruises were visible on her torso. Her skirt was hiked up her thighs. Crusted blood was caked to her feet. She squatted by the woman and reached for her wrist. The woman's arm swung to Embla's side. It was cold, damp, and heavy like rotting wood. She shifted her focus to the woman's face again to see if she could recognize her. She could not. A blackberry bramble was bent over her throat. Some of the bruising might actually have been blackberry stains. Embla lifted the thorny branch. The woman suddenly took a few shallow breaths, she was unconscious. She crouched closer to the woman, drew her hand over the woman's forehead, brought her hands to the woman's shoulders, and gently nudged her. The woman didn't respond. Embla assimilated the after-effects of the confusion she had about the woman's state. Her being alive was suddenly as shocking as thinking the woman was dead.

Later when the ambulance arrived, the paramedics informed her that the woman was in a coma induced by trauma. Embla followed the ambulance to the hospital in the valley. The woman had to be airlifted to a trauma unit at a regional hospital. Several days later the woman regained consciousness. When she learned the woman had awakened, Embla drove to the hospital to visit. Detectives had finished their interviews. She lay on a bed, enshrouded by stiff white sheets in the sterile room. Embla felt she had to see this woman again, alive, and responsive, in order to process the trauma of discovering her under a blackberry bush.

The woman seemed older than Embla—two years older, she found out later. Her complexion and facial structure were scraped into dimension by life's sharp edges. Her hair was chopped in an overgrown bob, a trim done at home with dull scissors. Bad teeth added to the stress of her look. Embla sat by the raised metal bed and introduced herself. The woman was named Rhonda. She had come to the village to help her aunt manage the tiny variety store near the lake. Her aunt had cancer as did her uncle. The store was on a country highway, a former Indian trail that intersected the local byway to the lake. Rhonda said she never swam there. The spartan store stocked the minimum variety of products: cigarettes, beer, milk, hotdogs, white bread, jam, candles, matches, dish detergent, ice, soda, toilet paper, ice cream, an assortment of candies, and aspirin. Mostly for the locals and the campers who stayed in the state forest, but out-of-towners also came to the store as they headed elsewhere over the mountain. The store had no security camera and resembled a cabin—poorly lit, small, dank, dark, with worn floorboards the color of soot. She was mostly alone in the store. The cash register never had more than two hundred dollars in it. She preferred to be alone even though male customers harangued her constantly with sexually aggressive taunts. She fended them off with nonreaction.

"A man came in, wandered around the store, picking things up, and then dropped all the items that he held in his arms on the counter." Her jaw stiffened when she talked. "The sound of all the items clanking on the counter was jarring after not having a customer for over two hours that day, before he decided to come in." She turned to the window half covered by a metal blind." He sweet-talked me," she said, "'come over here and get me a bag of ice,' and when I did, he grabbed me by the neck, yanked my hair, and hauled me to his car, shoved me in, and drove off." Her stricken look was righteous. "Then he impaled me with something, the claw side of a hammer, I think, though I'm not sure. I blacked out until we got to the lake. I struggled with him, and he bashed my head against a rock. That's all I remember; except I sensed the thorns of the blackberry bush on my neck. It felt protective in some way. I tasted blood and blackberry juice when I regained consciousness."

After the experience of finding the woman, the appearance of blackberry brambles caused Embla to expect a confrontation with dire condition, with presence congealing in the underbrush able to torque the day, the timeline. Her entire focus had been altered. She looked now intently for what might be concealed in the thickness of plant growth within mineral textures. Plants and the minerals they clung to and burrowed into camouflaged a secreted layer of reality, drove it into the earth. Attuning herself to plants gave her heightened perception. Plants were able to collapse time and space together into a breathable unit of intake. Vegetal life is a powerful converter of impulses, from the sun, of course, but also with breath, through absorption and decomposition. Plants share their energy and insight and insist on transformation. Florae is obsessive in its omnipresence, growing thickly over the surface of the earth. They, the plants, touch and feel interspecies encounters. The encounter with the woman garlanded with trailing blackberry cane fortified her for the situation that presently materialized before them.

DISASTER TOURISM, PSYCHOSOMATIC RECOGNITION, PHILOSOPHIES OF PLACE

Disembarking from the bus after the short circuitous ride from the academic conference felt spacious, just what I needed—a reprieve, a chance to experience alternative environments, partake in unknown qualities. We arrived at Treasure Island, completed in 1939 and opened as Magic Isle, a cluster of fairgrounds with a parking lot that could hold twelve thousand cars. The two vintage postcards from the exposition I brought with me gave me a clearer picture of where the pavilions had been: the Lagoon of Nations, the Court of the Moon, the Tower of the Sun, the various gardens, food stalls, and strange displays. One of the postcards shows two chinchillas in an airtight refrigeration unit, promoting the wonders of air-conditioning. Most everything from the exposition was razed when the navy came in, preparing for World War II. All that flamboyance lasted only two years. I had hoped my partner would be able to join me at this conference, but we couldn't coordinate our schedules and the international flights. She gave me the postcards as part of a going-away gift. The other half of the gift was my book on ecological philosophy that came out a few years back—a used copy she had found online, where on every page almost every other paragraph had been highlighted in either neon green or neon yellow marker, copious marginalia scrawled along the edges. She thought I'd be touched to see every page engaged with so fervently. I was.

We had met at a conference a few years back that focused on environment and the Anthropocene. Dior is an Earth scientist, an analytical chemist. I am a psychoanalyst and an academic philosopher fallen from grace, thankfully. I can say this now with no bitterness. Even philosophy can be a blood sport. The university, an arena of gladiators. If Dior had come along, she'd have met poets, performers, artists. I try to draw out her lyrical tendencies whenever possible. Not this time. She's neck deep in data that looks at climate change markers in the Eastern Gotland Basin in the Baltic Sea.

I would guess most of us had not ridden in a school bus for decades. This one was yellow, no less—quintessentially American. It excited my French curiosity for big, shiny American things. We piled on in a tumult, and then in a rush, disembarked into the sunshine to regroup in a motley semicircle to hear what our tour guide had to say. He had instructed the bus driver to pull up in front of a hurricane fence near an empty parking lot. It was a nondescript place. None of the glitz of Magic Isle remained. A postindustrial no-man's-land emptied of pedestrian life was what I thought based on its initial appearance. A terribly wrong assessment.

The various buildings and roadways came into focus as did the fenced in space. It was a space overlooked and anonymous but purposeful, there are layers of accretion: the access road, the hurricane fence, the outbuildings, and shrubbery. In this iteration there is little reason to come here, which is why we do, to peel away the layers of use and management and understand the history of the environment in order to comprehend what the present really is.

How might we penetrate normalized thinking and sensing, this was the goal of the outing according to our guide. bell hooks rang clear: "Attention is an important resource." Coupled with an admonishment vis-à-vis Giorgio Agamben that Claire Colebrook made when writing about a slip into the position of "frozen spectator"—a situation "in which images appear as ready-mades, that we can see both that there is no guarantee that we will be human and that it is human to forget oneself."

We are told to be aware of demarcation and boundary lines when and where one space merges with another. The fault line occurs when and where reality meets up with representation. The fenced off toxic waste is not obedient; it does not stay within the confines of the anodized metal enclosure. Not for long. We cannot see where it has dispersed; we can intuit that it has atomized and set aloft, making its way outside of the perimeter. Dust from Chernobyl settled here as it did on school playgrounds and on golf courses, on beaches and grassy lawns. Fukushima radiation washed in on ocean currents. Fine particles combine. Every crisis is an endless irritant, a compelling prompt.

We watched each other accessing the site. The sun held us in suspended animation. I pointed out a contrail developing a misty tail high above us as if to demonstrate chemical engulfment to the heavens. Our eyes shifted upward into the glare as molecules of unknown quantities dispersed into the arc of blue sky. Aerosol exhaust in the momentary shape of a headless serpent sent spent jet fuel to the breathable atmosphere.

Cloud formations took on unrecognizable forms. A San Francisco Bay meteorologist announced a long cloud formation in the sky called cloud iridescence, or rainbow clouds. All the colors that we as humans are able to perceive in our world appear in bent lighting. The configuration could easily be mistaken for a UFO.

I felt a momentary sensation of semiconscious itchy subtext as my thoughts darted to the reports of a strange outbreak of symptoms called Morgellons disease that occurred mainly in California affecting predominantly middle-aged white women, though there were exceptions. Or white women were the ones reported on; biases abound, especially when dealing with symptoms that could be misconstrued as "hysterical." As the disease becomes better known, a broader spectrum of people report symptoms. The initial findings describe fibrous strands coming out of skin—the body extruding what it rejects or cannot contain. The cause is unknown, but contrails have been implicated, and more recently, late Lyme disease has been attributed as an underlying factor. Those who suffer from this new and mysterious malady are often gaslit by medical experts. A sticky sensitivity prevails—a paranoia of intrusion by unknown pathogens. What is in the air, the soil, the food, the water that we ingest could be what is ailing us. I'm saved by a large rosemary plant that is there by my side when I glance down. As Juliette de Baïracli Levy, the great herbalist veterinarian once said, rosemary is the "dew of the sea." Instantly my worry was slackened by the potent sticky aroma moistened by sea breezes. Our cells shed themselves and regenerate. How much of the dust blowing about is cellular debris I wonder, the shedding of animal follicles, plant pollen, mineral dust? Fragments of bodies disperse. Are distributed widely.

Symptoms are the language of the present. Expressions in the body are expressions of the ecosystem communicating a legacy of experience, the climate is the sum total of inputs and interactions over time. The body (or climate) records its every move, all encounters are archived. Sensitive to the slightest offence, the body will make refusals in microgestures. Cumulative effect is a secret timeline shared between a body and its environment. The look of health can be a deceptive screen. I look about. My colleagues range in age between midthirties and perhaps fifty years of age when everyone tends to look their best, when maturity has seasoned exterior appearance and offered gravitas to spinal posture. I am slightly older, in my early sixties. Phase two of menopause is how I think of it. Menses is governed by the moon; menopause, however, is governed by the sun, a big difference. As estrogen is diminished, I notice a shift in how I understand the feminine in regard to sex and gender but also in relation to plants. Like the cucumber, I sprout blossoms both male and female, reliant on both to contribute to fruiting. The metaphor works when we overcome the aversion we have of being like plants.

Our tour guide reoriented our attention and set us again in motion. He began to walk forward along a neglected roadway with outlying buildings around, sun bleached and abandoned. Cans and bottles and blownaway refuse spotted the area with textures and reflective surfaces. He gave us a verbal set of instructions. We headed off in clumped formations, clustering by the facades, and quietly studied the surroundings. My frame of mind was tentative. Many took photos on their phones because this is the default response to new stimuli. I took out a black ink pen and wrote the tiniest graffiti onto a pale-yellow painted surface of what we are told was once a dormitory of a girl's school. The non sequiturs that flowed from my pen unleashed a rush of blocked awareness. The pen (and computer) in the act of transferring thought physically offloaded from body to paper to screen, or in this case, to the exterior of a building—is an outlet for the fugitive psyche's need for release. Phrases rushed out of my body all at once and I was not conscious of anything but the flow of urgent language as it took palpable form. The sun seared my back, a flooding of energy cast from millions of miles beyond, from another age of wide-ranging star clusters and galactic energy centers where light exploded into a presence and raced toward Earth and its surroundings in the Milky Way. Plants convert this energy into simple sugars and proteins, the biproduct enters our lungs as a primary substance of existence.

Two associates from our group lingered nearby and watched the scribble form. My spinal cord lengthened in their presence; my arms were taut. It was difficult to relax, I noticed I was self-conscious. They wandered off after a brief spell. Again, we were signaled by the tour guide. This time he whistled to us to come over to him. He then started to tell us a modified history of the site. Our busload consisted of thirteen of us—disaster tourists as he referred to us. I did a quick count and as is my compulsion I surveyed gender. The group presented mostly as female, femme: nine women, a trans male, and two dudes (plus Randy, a dude). This American colloquial is actually a term of endearment for me, preferable to *bro*, which I've found signifies patriarchal alliance and in its worst iterations manifests as fascistic identification in brotherhood, one such nefarious example being the Proud Boys. Several of the women were more likely nonbinary, nonconformist, with an emphasis on femme as far as I could detect. Emulating gendered mores of the past is fading. Gender is emergent. Randy's whistling was problematic. Deep breaths were necessary. On this excursion I vowed to let my guard down and give in to group communality if not conviviality. I wanted to see what he sees and take cues from the others. Randy, the tour guide—how he described himself—was intent on demonstrating a methodology of being in space, and I was willing to apply his ground rules.

We were guided to the edge of the island with a view of San Francisco across the bay. With his hands, Randy created a viewfinder that we were instructed to look through. He had effectively canceled out the ugly sidelines to reveal the picture-perfect ideal of composition. We were drawn into the staged persona of the city in the distance and all that it represented.

We were then let loose to wander and do so for about an hour, and in that time, I strayed off as others did too. Quickly there was no one around. It was as if I had been airlifted into the location because there was no trace of my arrival. How suddenly the atmosphere changed from one of an excited group dynamic to one of solitary contemplation. The sun beat down like an inquisition. I realized I was not alone in a cosmic sense. Fiery antigravitational force x-rayed my form. Perception occurred in black and white and there was a gauzy effect or a halo wherever my eyes settled on objects. I sat on the curb for a moment to collect myself and survey the area.

A settlement of makeshift low-income housing came into focus. Only a few of the units were occupied, the others had no curtains and there was a bit of garbage building up on the front stoops and in the spaces in front of the apartments where there were dead ornamental shrubs. The housing complex was neglected by management and the city. Were there pets inside some of the occupied units, bored and forlorn in the low light behind draped windows, waiting for an interspecies ally to bring them comfort? I had an urge to knock on a green metal door but immediately felt the prohibition of private property. Would I be trespassing? Wherever the stranger goes she brings the threat of intrusion, especially when whiteness is part of the equation. Instead of passing the invisible threshold at the apartment unit's entranceway, I sat on a nearby curb and paused to write some observations into a notebook and directed my attention to the celestial dome of light. The chemtrails had dispersed. The sky was opaquely thickened as if space could not possibly continue beyond the tonal expanse of medium blue atmosphere. There was a ghosted quality all around. As in dying, expiring, being put out, lacking regenerative energy—except for the ocean, the sky. Adjacent was a patch of overgrown grass and a chopped down tree, branches crudely hacked and scattered around. The stump was intact. Maybe there was a house or shed here at one time. It was now an odd patch of unused space. I moved to sit on the tree stump. Grass always mesmerizes me. It was illegal for several centuries to sit on grass in Parisian parks—until 1997, actually. The grass in parks was forbidden territory for people and their dogs. The massive green ruglike expanse of grass at Versailles was one of the first displays of the grassy lawn as emblem of ostentation, purely show. Although grassy lawns originated in Europe, as verdant spaces around castles for livestock to graze, I associate such greenery mostly with the American suburb, sports field, and cemetery. The endless mowing down. The endless chemical poisoning to achieve a momentary stalemate. The attempts at domination of the green life force, what sustains.

Opportunistic weeds grew prominently among the otherwise straggly mini front lawns of Kentucky grass. Weeds to dream with, hardscrabble plants with flamboyant leaves: mugwort; weeds to make a nutritious salad: purslane, dandelion, and lamb's quarters. We have got our identifications all wrong. The only sustenance here is mislabeled and then disparaged. The leaves' curvature begs attention. I projected onto their shapes a kind of symbolism or signal that calls out to other forms of sentience, suggests compatibility.

A stream of low frequency sounds was emitted from the plants, and my torso picked up the resonant vibrations. Impressed on my sensory apparatus was the chirography of their beckoning outreach. The syntax of foliated language danced in the microchanges of air flow, affected my thought patterns. Relationships that defy the barriers of consciousness.

Peripheral vision was different perched here on the stump as opposed to the cement curb. My knees were no longer crablike extensions protruding outside my arms as I squatted low. Another participant joined me in silence. She is a research movement practitioner. Her corporeal expression was fluid and full of energy with a tinge of depression. We made eye contact and then she slid her thighs over the stump and paused so our buttocks and legs were squished together. We both noticed a coreopsis plant springing out of the partially abandoned site with a profusion of yellow blossoms. It was a relief to gaze at a flowering life-form. The plant more than the shaggy grass suggested possibility. Favoritism. I spotted my bias and felt a pang of shame.

The demise of the tree was a mystery to us. We began a sporadic conversation that touched on everything from random acts of violence to psychic intuition concerning pain. She leads workshops in the Feldenkrais method. Her way of positioning herself on the stump was like putty, elastic and firm. Beneath an epidermal layer her bones were wet sculptures, she moved purposefully into a nested heap near me. Our energies flowed into another instantly. The tree stump we sat on conveyed both our heartbeats. The recharge was spontaneous. Moshe Feldenkrais, who formulated the practice, championed the directive, "If you know what you are doing, you can do what you want." This pliant woman goes around her neighborhood probing the environment for undetected new species. Not new to the ecosystem, new to her consciousness, possibly new to human consciousness. A method of encouraging transperspective. Her practice depends on treading lightly, all the while becoming more attuned to ways of sensing, ways of participating in relation to the ecology. The practice is a collaboration with others outside her taxonomic identification. I did not know much more about her practice; all I did know I learned from the few times we've had the opportunity to talk in fragmented Zoom windows. I asked her how she maintains a sense of continuity in the face of the myriad scenarios of doom. Doom is what I mean when suffering is normalized.

In *The Matrix* only a small portion of the population perceives reality, the others are held captive by a simulated illusionary present. And when history has been an ongoing act of obfuscation and ideological staging, how have perceptions been shaped, guided? She leaned over, blocking the sun that had propped itself on my forehead, and offered insight about human conceptions of earthliness. She told me the idea of the earth as a globe was first recorded in the *Rig Veda*, the oldest sacred Hindu text,

around 1500 BCE. We contemplated this solemnly. Worlds rotate away
and then toward each other. Sunlight hit the moon when we conversed
and the affinity we shared felt like it bubbled to the surface as carbon-
ation. While we were held together in a chain of significance, two of the
performers clad in white drew closer to us. Their presence was shadowy even as they inched toward the blaring sun. They care about the
well-being of the planet, that was the thought that came to me, watching them. Their identity was voided because of their outfits and because
of their gestures. They pantomimed the emptiness, the negative space.
As they performed I noted how careful they were about not stepping on
plants.

My early psychoanalytic focus delt with differentiation, difference,
and semblance on psychic objects of identity, using a feminist gravitational center. The key was to avoid binaries while dismantling the power
dynamics of gender that situated the male as patriarchal and phallocen-
tric. The feminine (and feminist) isn't the leftover baggage that resides
out of that construction, nor is the feminine "nature," yet nature plays a
part in the equation. Michèle Le Doeuff helped me to realize you could
be in something and out of it at the same time. When her work "Ants
and Women" was released, it set a mark of clarity to aspire to. She uncovered the splinters and things that trip up "the questions-which-have-
already-obviously-been-settled." I started to consider the relationships I
had whose meanings were subsumed in other dynamics that I remained
ignorant of. In full circle I eventually returned to florae, nature, the other-
than-human as a social framework that reorients meanings of essence
(which is not essentialism). Essentialism is a kind of quicksand deadlock
that I do not, did not endorse, though it is interesting as a construction,
nonetheless. The compelling task is how to move around and through es-
sentialist argument without losing cohesion while also anticipating expansive openness as to identity, a framework and ontological outlook I'd
rather call homeopathic metaphysics, as applicable to psycholinguistic
analysis. If Dior were here, she'd direct me to the periodic table for solid
bearing. Not to teeter between form and matter, rather, she would remind that the world is based on atomic relationships that deal with energy exchange on minimal and maximal scales. Form and matter are always in fluctuation. Waves and particles. Start there, she'd say to me.

I was antiautobiographical until a necessary reintegration with plants
and trees—for survival's sake I could no longer efface ecological reality,

how my body-mind participates in a fully saturated way that has everything to do with other-than-human sentience. Ecological connection put an end to the banishment that the dismissal from the academy forced on me. Two things happened: I reacquainted with my "self" while simultaneously releasing from whatever the self is.

My relationship to plants was influenced by the experience of having grown up in the intimate vicinity of a forest. The property line of our house was demarcated by a fierce outcropping of stinging nettles, beyond the nettles the trees gently darkened the forest floor and expanded in breadth. A psychic and somatic gift of alternative space and time composed of rooted living entities. Our property was a manicured, curated garden, even the pine needles were arranged for contemplative effect.

My mother placed curiously shaped rocks on pedestals and constructed walls and edgings for plantings. The garden was an exquisite living manifestation of her imaginative capacity to find interrelationships among animated forms of being. Plants and trees grew together as reciprocal infrastructure. My mother, as a stimulus to the garden, provoked its form and function. This labor required much of her discretionary time. The harmonic frequencies of living, growing, breathing plants were her meaning and her sanity, regenerative cellular structures able to call her into their demands of care and maintenance. Five hours of mowing, endless hours spent raking, collecting fallen twigs, pruning, weeding, planting, germinating, watering, thinning, mulching, composting.

Found in the pasture of a nearby farm were the odd metamorphic rocks that she stationed throughout the garden, punctuating its verdure. Their motley pockmarked forms expressed compression, erosion, cataclysm, and power. Lichen colonized the surface areas of the stones, slowly absorbing mineral content.

When glacial ice receded moraine deposits were formed, and rock debris was scattered. An erratic is a rock that differs from the types of rock native to the region. Erratic rocks wandered along on the path of the ice. The earth was scraped and buckled into new contours. Layers of rock that had been covered by sedimented rock and dirt were exposed. The weight and pressure of the ice exerted itself as an afterthought of the geologic trajectory of planetary matter.

The history of rocks is the archival memory of our planet's mantle, a solid crust encircling fire. Tossed and strewn inner earth settles on the surface tension of a spinning globe and a new layering event begins all over again. The stones in her garden had rested in an old growth forest for millennia that grew around them when the ice pulled away. Saber-toothed tigers and woolly mammoths were some of the creatures who might have scrambled over the rocks. Earlier, the rocks may have been exposed to great diverse oceanic epochs.

A mammal, a lineage of great ape in her sanctuary, she thrived when lugging a wheelbarrow loaded up with weighty found material ready to be repurposed into garden infrastructure. Sweat darkened the fabric of her threadbare T-shirt. Hours would transpire. My sister, an infant, fenced off in a playpen by the house, was held hostage by my mother's drive to commune with bioaffirmative space. I was, in effect, my sister's prison guard, and her only visitor because I was feral and out-of-bounds of the cage. I ricocheted between my mothers: my biological mother who was ensconced by my other biological mother, the garden, the forest, Earth. My sister, confined, solitary within the plastic fencing, underwent emotional and physical deprivation within concepts of domesticity and the family unit and, on hindsight, nature itself.

Told another way an autobiography becomes mythic, all-encompassing. It is impossible to consider the self without considering a network of relations. A different tense is necessary. The iterations become a volatile narrative. She is able to read minds. She unwinds a spool of language pertaining to her mother, an operative figure who conveyed her power through the manipulation of nature. Her life energy takes the form of hypervigilance, she anticipates the calibrated tensions underlying social configurations. They extend, reticulated throughout the family structure. When her aunt would visit, she noticed how her mother would enable her sister. Her aunt did not fight the ventriloquism of her mother's vengeance on sense-making. She witnessed these dynamics; they were building blocks of a puzzle indistinguishable from processes, meaning the puzzle had no contours. In the space of a breath's intake she observed how her mother manipulated the predicate of a sentence phrase. Her aunt picked up and extended the wrangled metaphor. The takeaway is that the organism is strengthened by fusion. Who begins a sentence and who continues it is not a rhetorical challenge from an ecological standpoint.

My aunt and mother's interlaced speech acts were chiaroscuroed sibling mirrorings, epigenetic projections, muscle memories of their mother, a Holocaust survivor from Poland who managed to hide in a barn when her family was rounded up and captured. Henceforth my grandmother spoke for her disappeared family unit in unison with the dead. A dead mother communicates through her child's nerve endings. The expression of her jawline revealed seismic information and where she was headed with it. Again, whose jawline, whose expression? The resounding symbolic figurehead of cultural delivery is the mother.

The reverie in broad daylight was interrupted by soft voices talking among themselves, yet I couldn't see anyone who might be whispering nearby. The voices continued: "We are unable to fully countenance the abandoned inventory of history that surfaces as burnt-out fragments and rotten slippages. We are entrained by consequences that percolate out of the present skewing and teetering in space. Our fixation on the now does not diminish how enthralled we are by the latent narratives that we forage for in the heaps." Then, like a flashlight in a cave haloed light settled near me, probed me. It wasn't intrusive. I listened intently. I no longer heard ambient dialogue. Instead, it was Randy who signaled to me to come back to the bus. The performers were gone. The other tourists were already crowded by the bus.

THE PERFORMERS
mia

The directive is to engage our bodies to call attention to the site in ways that might otherwise be avoided or ignored. Our bodies are pointers that indicate where there might be underlying tension or disturbance in the ecosystem.

There is a total of six of us, the performers. We disperse within a demarcated zone. Six plus Randy, who wears his normal clothing. We wear hazmat suits that are whiter than snow in the Arctic. The white of industrially produced synthetic fabric. Even though we shine brightly it is easy not to notice us. For one, our positioning is unexpected. Secondly, the way we move is measured, deliberately imperceptible. Thirdly, we were told to remain silent.

We come repeatedly to the island to perform. Treasure Island is made of dredged sand from the bay and quarried rock. One could say it was fabricated on a military industrial scale.

We perform corporeal messaging, layered meanings that become apparent if someone directs their attention toward us, shining out of range. The performances rely on the audience's senses and intuition. When we meet off-site, we discuss calibration and connectivity over distances. Because we don't perform on a stage, there is no protection, no boundary. The fourth wall is entirely missing. We are shielded by the thin membrane of white fabric that covers our bodies. The outfit is claustrophobic and also comforting. The suits make us nearly identical, indecipherable. A group mentality forms in our performance bodies. We constantly ask each other what each of us is holding, personally and for the group. Laura said to the group at our initial meeting, "Let's be vigilant about not taking our efforts and interactions for granted." Randy was not there to hear this, unfortunately. These meetings among ourselves are where we chart the dimensions of our working relationships and navigate the meanings of the performances. We work out techniques to help ground us.

In the distance, adjacent to me, Darius might be holding space by making slow deliberate movements that suggest caution. A rustle in the grasses might spur Laura on to engage a relationship with the plants that grow in the environment, for instance she might seek to establish a connection with the tall stems of wiry grass, parched and struggling to stay alive. Jay is fluid with their moves. They flutter with the fluctuating light, with the wind, blend in with the atmospheres of land, sky, and ocean. They are able to convert energies that circulate in space into their routine. When not performing they are meditative, nervous energy shows itself underneath the calm. Sae gets into the gritty details, and can see through walls, I swear. Her perceptive abilities are at the highest level. She also checks Randy whenever he is unreasonable. I haven't had a chance to get to know Shabnam yet.

If one of us is in another's vicinity we might look on for an instant at the other's body language, absorbing and incorporating it into our repertoire.

We make ourselves available to participate in these actions whenever Randy conducts a tour. He is a poet whose practice has branched out to include site-specific performance. The six of us who make up the troupe are also either poets, dancers, or musicians.

A colossal cumulus cloud dominates the vista of sky, and cool shadow prevails. I watch another performer lunge and twist their midriff. A limpid shape attracts my attention. A hallucination conjured by gentle pelvic motions starts to crystallize. The more attuned one becomes to submerged presences the more intimate time becomes. For a split second I look over to Darius and I record the alienation of the world. Western paradigms dissolve.

The barely felt presence that Darius has conjured is responsible for the breakthrough. Darius makes eye contact with me. I feel her pupils weighing on me. I can't be sure though; the gear obscures our features. When the cloud unmoors, I pivot around the dusty corner of a building and head out of focus from the others. The wind directs me easterly toward a fissure in the roadway, a minor tectonic fault line. Part of the road is sunken about an inch, the other side is raised; between the asphalt is a crack filled with sand, dirt, and rotting matter. From these nutrients a miniature forest has begun to flourish. In a scorpion position I'm able to examine the tiny trunks, the tiny canopy. Insects navigate the green swatch of the indented chasm. From an aerial perspective the forest twitches and sways with the coastal wind. The smallest mushrooms I've ever seen sprout from the rough aged copper-colored lichen that thrives under the seedlings. Hardly a car, truck or pedestrian travels this utility road. The micro forest is undisturbed for the time being. A cluster of microscopic red mites dart to a pebble. The moth that landed on my forearm a moment ago touches down on the top of the two-inch tree near the lip of the crack. In this position it is clear that the rumbling earth resonates and connects with all energies that are, at once, distinct and drawn into the entire unifying process of being.

Spending time as a giant on the edge of the forest reminds me that scale is contextual. My mind zooms in on a diagrammatic image of our galaxy. Earth is depicted as a pea-sized blue orb, a transiting pebble projected into deep space after an epic explosive scenario.

The last time we performed I got fixated on studying the surfaces we tread on because I want to know what the components of our planet are and to no longer remain ignorant of what dirt, concrete, asphalt, and gravel consist of materially. To know the origins of what I constantly step on and walk over gives me a sense of plantedness. Planet Earth is a rock, a rock in liquid, crystalline, and gaseous form, continually shifting between phases. A rock is a composition of minerals. Minerals are solid inorganic substances. The bulk of the material mass is electrified by the buzzing of electrons. Earth is in motion, part of an action-filled cosmic expanse.

The characteristics of planetary life become an obsession as I begin to comprehend the energy inherent in materiality. Treasure Island is a perfect case study because it was fabricated by humans, the accretions are recent and obvious. A microcosm within another microcosm: Earth.

The afternoon rests on our shoulders in a semioppressive way due to the heat and the lack of oxygen caused by being in a sealed suit. We've been waiting around and now the eco disaster tour bus has arrived. We station at our respective outposts.

Earth is a wet boulder hurling through a cluttered universe that may or may not form a boundary with nothingness. A herculean rock with many layers that intermix through cataclysmic and mundane processes. A rock is a composition of molecules that fuse together forming a gravitational center. Earth has a solid outer crust made of rock forming, silicate minerals, a highly viscous mantle, a liquid outer core that is much less viscous than the mantle and a solid inner core with a radius of approximately 760 miles. The inner solid core is made up of an exceptionally hot iron-nickel alloy.

Earth is a planet, not a star, the difference being that stars emit heat and light continuously because of nuclear reactions firing inside of pressurized cores of hot gas. Yet, Earth would appear a star, as electricity illuminates almost the whole of its surface area and human-created nuclear facilities with firing reactors working nonstop smashing atoms are everywhere.

The geologic record suggests that continent formation was episodic. Zircon crystal vestiges—the earliest of which have been dated are 4.5 Ga (4.5 billion years old)—were located in the Jack Hills area of Australia. They are the oldest Earth objects and were dated with a SHRIMP ion probe. Acasta gneisses formed between 3.92 and 4.02 Ga, straddling the Hadean-Archean division on the geologic time scale. Gneisses were exposed in and around the Great Bear Lake, the deepest lake in North America, located in the Northwest Territories of Canada. Geochronology is measured in Ga. One Ga is an abbreviation of gigaannum and represents one billion years. Ma, from megaannum, is the next unit of measurement and represents one million years, and the lesser Ka, or kiloannum, is a period of one thousand years. Maybe these facts are already obsolete, maybe older entities have been located.

I feel the rush of a continuum as viscoelasticity. A sensitivity of the torque necessary to rotate a spindle in fluid develops in my spinal cord. Like Earth, human anatomy contains an inner core of liquid and also solids: bone. When I move, I concentrate on the sharp right angles of joints connected to spongy flesh and the muscle mass that allows for contortion. I sit here perched on sharp gravel and sift the earth's chronology through my fingers. The amnesia of deep time vanishes when fondling rocks.

A wind gust lifts up fine particles of dust and momentarily I'm blinded by the irritation. My protective gear is missing its plastic face shield. Feet rise skyward, stomach muscles scoop into a concave shape, bucketlike, hips pivot slightly askew, and my chest forms a ledge. My body scrambles in participatory fusion. All the earth's water pours into the vessel of my body, and it's a paralyzing feeling because the weight is unfathomable.

The impossibility of water in a stone environment, yet Earth's composition is rheological. At this moment I contrast the planet's rockiness as I focus on the water that sits or hovers on top its outer layer and seeps into its fissures.

I rock back and forth syncopated with the ebb and flow of the tides that beat on the shore meeting up with this forsaken space. Darius suddenly towers over me; her legs straddle my shins. Her smoky quartz velvet shadow is plush, accommodates my fallenness. With soft shadow and shade overlaying my splayed form, I roll over and play dead. I assume a corpse pose and instantly feel a narrative of death invade my thought center. Absorbing the legacy of the naval station, one of the island's iterations, brings vomit to the back of my throat. Repetitive swallowing helps. Treasure Island was decommissioned in the 1990s along with the Presidio (a U.S. Army garrison) and Hunters Point Naval Shipyard—three major industrial-military waterfront installations, part of an embedded matrix of domestic and global American military installations presently totaling eight hundred, not counting U.S. military presence at embassies and missions. The military's presence is grafted onto the landscape in a forceful way.

These three sites represent the ongoing imperial aspiration and engagement on Native land, contrary in every possible way to Native intention, vision, and relation to Turtle Island. I don't think it is presumptuous to conclude this. Native struggles with settler colonial violence and theft, such as the recent land and water protests, speak to a different way of living on this land.

Once I agreed to perform in the troupe, I combed the internet and other sources for information about Treasure Island and the surrounding military sites. We all did. And we regularly meet to share our findings. Many of us visited the other decommissioned installations. These and other military installations are more toxic and lethal than I could have imagined. The Presidio was established as a fort by the Spanish empire in 1776. Mexico took it over in 1820, and then the United States in 1848. In the late nineteenth century, army forces gathered at the Presidio before invading the Philippines during the Spanish-American War. The 108 civilian exclusion orders and directives for the internment of Japanese Americans were signed at the Presidio by Lieutenant General John L. DeWitt under Executive Order 9066 that was then signed by President Franklin Delano Roosevelt on February 19, 1942. Ironically, the U.S. military had set up the Fourth Army Intelligence School, a language school to train Nisei Japanese Americans to learn the Japanese language and act as translators in World War II. It was disbanded after Pearl Harbor. The Presidio's final immersion in war was during the first Gulf War in 1991. The last remaining units were sent to Operation Desert Storm, a military operation ostensibly to get Iraqi troops out of Kuwait. In the 1950s to 1960s the U.S. military operated their most expansive applied nuclear research facility, the Naval Radiological Defense Laboratory at Hunters Point Naval Shipyard. There, ships from Operation Crossroads were sent to be decontaminated. For a time, it was called Treasure Island Naval Station Hunters Point Annex. The naval base on Treasure Island worked together with Hunters Point Annex on this objective. Operation Crossroads exploded two nuclear bombs, Able and Baker, at Bikini Atoll in 1946. The brutality stockpiles in my brain-body.

There's a dramatic photo of the dredging that the Army Corp of Engineers conducted in 1936 to amass the quantities of rock and sand necessary to construct Treasure Island. The island enjoyed a brief blip as a world's fair and then was quickly overwhelmed by the demand for a communication and command center for the Pacific theater as the United States entered World War II. Four and a half million military personnel were deployed overseas from Treasure Island. Thereafter, Treasure Island was used by the navy as a training center and testing ground for naval personnel to practice nuclear decommissioning. Decaying cesium 137 is part of the invisible archive of toxic substances the place tries to withstand. Randy listed a dozen toxins that are a feature of the environment of Treasure Island. Recently a local resident found a cache of gauges that were painted with toxic radioluminescent paint. The navy has made a half attempt to clean up Treasure Island. Articles online pop up all the time of radioactive junk piles still being discovered. One big one showed up under an elementary school.

There are plans in the works to reconstruct the island into an elaborate park and housing network in the near future. A slide show narrated by Fei Tsen, president of the Treasure Island Development Authority, a public agency tasked with overseeing the development of Treasure Island, gave an online presentation detailing the master plan for the island. It all looked so promising and thoughtful. The plan earnestly takes into consideration sea rise mitigation, issues of affordable housing, and access to parklands for residents and visitors, but I sincerely wonder if it isn't just another profit-motivated plan that will benefit developers and the rich who will inevitably occupy the glittering condos with the best views of the San Francisco Bay.

Darius wants to communicate something to me, so I focus on her with telepathic concentration. Images form. The participants in Randy's troupe are nonhierarchical, but Darius is our soul protector, a role that is generous and generative. She grew up here, she knows the stakes. Without Darius maintaining a sense of concord I think we would feel the weight of this place detrimentally, worse than we already do. We would perhaps be bullied into submission by the pressure to abide by Randy's objectives for the performance in ways that could cross the line. Giving up our agency. Relinquishing any sense of control or purpose. Not calling out the high-handed bullshit that he sometimes dishes out. If it weren't for Darius, we'd probably spend too much of the time figuring out how to deal with Randy, rather than focusing on how the performance is an important collective experience. Thanks to Darius our dignity and respect are guarded. Darius's unstated default is vigilance. Because she demands sensitivity we are always hydrated, we do not stay in the sun for long stretches. Regardless, we do absorb the ambient radiation from the toxicity of the site. The suits we wear look protective, but they are not designed for such exposure. Everyone had to purchase their own suit. Most of us opted for the same cheap brand that we found online. Randy had sent us a link to a hazmat suit that was prohibitively expensive. No one bought it.

The image in my mind's eye is a red target made by a split coherent beam of radiation. There is no context for the hologram. It floats in my imagination, and I break the corpse pose and roll onto my side once again gazing up at Darius's face covered by the shield of the white hazmat suit. Without knowing what the mental cue means I file it for future reference. We give each other clues all the time.

Randy is the explainer, we intuit. The red target has become a small globular shape and is translucent. It looks like a tunnel into space. I somehow trust that the crimson image is not a figment of my imagination, and trust in the situation gives relief. Still, it feels as if I had somehow breathed out a wormhole and what I visualize is an MRI of an internal manifestation. It hovers in front of me making it possible to peer into the contoured recesses. The raw shape comes in and out of focus. During the unfolding of this phenomenon, Darius swerves away and briefly follows the path her shadow makes. I gesture toward her.

At the side of a dumpster our paths diverge. Unspoken arrangements help us navigate together. The gangly tree by the dumpster nonverbally insists I assume the corpse pose again, this time with humor. Hyperawareness allows for communication with life-forms other-than-human. A nonscientific assertion, one that I have proven to myself. It takes a leap of faith to disregard ordinary filters that are part of human conditioning. I try to be with the tree, get a vibe from it, understand how it lives in the world. I try to take suggestions from the tree. A stench from the dumpster amplifies aliveness and deathliness in equal measure. I take advantage of the rotten smells. Nostrils focus immediately on disagreeable input. Within the dumpster unknown quantities of matter are merging. It is a chemical process that signals decay. I immediately realize that life thrives on decay. Holding still and deeply considering the odors intensifies a connection to the temporal location. The dead matter is shapeshifting. As I consider opening the dumpster lid to see what is inside, I notice there is suddenly a shadow draped over the sandy surface of the roadway and the microforest. The shape of the shadow is oblong, in motion. Randy's stipulation is that we not engage the visitors under any circumstances, not these specific visitors from the eco poetry conference or the public if we happen upon random bystanders. We must resist interaction even when we know each other.

THE PERFORMERS
sae

Figuring out alternative forms and expressions of collective action was what drew me to participate in the troupe. And, as participants, we were offered free passes to the conference, which had sold out, and even if it had not sold out, the tickets were exorbitant.

The sanctified, yet beleaguered status of "the individual" is perpetually subject to critique yet there never seems to be a breakthrough out of its framework. The anxiety I have around notions of selfhood and individuality is a pervasive conundrum that knows no bounds. I sort through philosophic options and don't ever arrive.

The historical moment beckons a reexamination of what is called "self." A society that prizes individualism diminishes life. A crucial paradox because it is necessary that rights and the general well-being of every single member of society is upheld. However, advantaging the one need not, should not, disadvantage the many. After all is said and done, "the individual" is an ableist construct that fails to reckon with capital's role in manufacturing personhood. I know, I know, all dialectical argument begins with Marxist analysis.

A collective system is in place to manage the juncture where individual responsibility tapers. This system could be enhanced, expanded. At the end of the day, someone is responsible for the heap of consumer waste that is generated: how the aftermath of rejected matter in bins and in plastic bags that is placed on the curb is dealt with. I want to get closer to that juncture where the individual and the collective meet. Closer to what is rendered invisible, obscured, falls out of "I" and "we" into a fissure, a blur, an abyss. The uncharacterizable holding pattern that wavers outside of opposites, oppositions. Getting into the minutiae of this takes me on a mad journey where seeing the forest for the trees is but a speedbump.

Jacques Derrida was weary of problematic dichotomies such as "good versus evil, being versus nothingness, presence versus absence, truth versus error, identity versus difference, mind versus matter, man versus woman, soul versus body, life versus death, nature versus culture, speech versus writing" and I would add, one versus many. Barbara Johnson, a theorist, in introducing Derrida's *Dissemination*, wrote the following: "In general, what these hierarchical oppositions do is privilege unity, identity, immediacy, and temporal and spatial *presentness* over distance, difference, dissimulation and deferment. In its search for the answer to the question of Being, Western Philosophy has indeed always determined Being as *presence*." Self-control, self-regulation, tastes, and preferences are all manipulated by market forces that place its focus on demographic groups. The individual is trapped in multiple nets. We handle our messy sighs.

Something diabolical happens when the individual is subsumed by the state: the institution and personhood becomes a biopolitical fungible "unit." Philosopher Kelly Oliver, whom I've been reading to prepare for the performances, writes of refugee camps and detention centers where refugees are nothing more than "collateral damage or units of exchange" and are thus "ultimately disposable." Unseen, as the humanitarian arm of society hides the evidence of systematic failures. Oliver turns to Derrida's "conception of unconditional hospitality" and his distinction between visitation and invitation to begin to rethink our obligations to asylum seekers beyond detention centers and refugee camps.

To situate myself I ask, what does any of this mean in this space?

I mostly don't know where I'm going with the rambling critiques my brain belches up. I just know that I don't want to sublimate the rage that throbs through my thinking. I perform and my mind continues to buzz. When Shabnam asks why I look distracted I don't say much, worried that if I spew this stuff out, she'll think it is ponderous, that I'm a mess. Sooner or later, I'll let on to my scrambled ideation. Everyone shares openly; it is inspiring.

The troupe hasn't established a shared identity politics, but we are able to engage embodied experience as it arises in time and use it over the course of each iteration of the performance. The affinity for one another that has developed is obvious. We've formed a meaningful bond among ourselves. The bond feels transgressive. The inner workings of our minds and bodies come together at this site. As we are not permitted to interact with the onlookers, we rely on each other and the environment for emotional feedback and support. Randy isn't a part of the intimacy we've developed. The leadership role he plays might be what forecloses the possibility of getting closer to him.

The air has a molecular value that registers disturbance. There are pockets of thickness where the air molecules gel. The focal point has shifted, from what to what I couldn't say. The shock of reorientation has a destabilizing effect. The gravel crunchiness, the wind, the metal clanking at a distant harbor, and the horns of boats on the water become paramount. My heartbeat is more pronounced, and I suddenly take louder inhalations of air. I sense the tightening of leather encasing my swollen feet.

During performances our attention is to be drawn downward, to the ground, to subterranean levels. We are to sort through the rubble, sift soil, move rocks, pass a Geiger counter over it all. Our gestures are to be done at the slowest possible speed. Randy suggests we come to a standstill every now and again and then slowly resume moving, almost imperceptibly. No sudden, jarring movements. Also, no individualized movements. Our gestures should be generic, whatever that means.

So, when there are two people suddenly standing in front of me looking intently at me, I disregard Randy's edict and return the gaze. They are not from the conference, seem lost. Without thinking I reach toward them, and this caused them to take careful steps backward. Again, I try an approach, permissive energy draws me to them. First impressions are loaded.

Easy, I tell myself, ease up. Savor the moment. This is a moment of contact. To be conscious of the point of contact is a microdramatical moment in time. You can feel the whirring, processing the who, what, when, where, why. Protection weighs in, as there is the necessity of establishing safety. I can't take meeting someone for the first time lightly or for granted, ever.

Their physical features are shrouded. It is an aura I notice. Their movements are gentle and careful. Not hesitant, deliberate. I choose to echo their gestures, demonstrating care as well. Their breath is more like wind, constant exhalations create a current of air. Their inhalations are magnetic when I do notice. My body moves automatically toward them. Their lips move in speech but there is no discernible volume. Something-nothing combine in form. I do not attempt to decode what they are saying because I'm too immersed in the all-encompassing experience of being in close proximity with entities, strangers of unknown origin. Then I see the person closest to me raise their arm and in their fist they have something. A permissiveness surges. In as much of an unhurried manner as I can muster, I reach toward their hand. They seem okay with this, perhaps it is their intention that I should meet them halfway in the gesture. A feeling of tenderness permeates the surround and is translated into touch. I endeavor to open each finger to expose their palm. Softness pervades.

In their palm is a piece of stone. The stone is not antithetical to softness, it has absorbed intention. They place it in my palm, and I bring it to up to my face to examine it. A jagged sparkling piece of anthracite. I look up at the person and their companion, then back down to the carbon nugget. As I look at the anthracite it turns to dust in my hand and I notice they are gone also, yet I feel their energy signaling something I can't quite hold on to or decipher. A lulling fugue state ensconces me after the mirage of presences dematerializes. Oblivion with a paranormal tinge. At the juncture where declaratory recognition forks off, an energized void appears, and then vanishes. There were two persons. Atomized oblivion without negative emotional valence. I have been characterized as tending to see the glass half-full. Now I see no glass, no water, only presence as an afterthought, and afterimage.

PHILOMELA

Songs of solidarity and songs of lament were sung by children and adults alike. Enduring a lifespan was a challenge; the stresses of unbridled political tensions, internecine strife, and other pressures social in nature whose effects were banal, commonplace occurred uninterruptedly. A song about a spider was a song of survival. *Down came the rain and washed the spider out. Out came the sun and dried up all the rain and the itsy-bitsy spider climbed up the spout again.* In another version of the song, most likely the original version, a more sinister tone is struck. The song goes: *Oh, the blooming, bloody spider went up the spider web, the blooming, bloody rain came down and washed the spider out, the blooming, bloody sun came out and dried up all the rain, and the blooming, bloody spider came up the web again.* In one minor episode in Greek mythology there was a boy named Itys. His name reminds us of the spider in the song. We know how life ended for Itys, the conclusive blunt edge. His story echoes that of the blooming, bloody spider.

We know that the Phrygians entered Anatolia from Europe by means of the straits, and according to the historian Herodotus, when they were in Europe, they were called Bryges of Birgs. The Phrygians died out or lost out to the Medes, and the Medes succumbed to the Persians, who called the region Beautiful Horse Country. Many invaders had raided and laid claim to the land: Alexander the Great, the Ottomans, the Persians, the Hittites, and the Romans. The fairy chimneys and other rock formations were used as safe houses, the rock churches were accessible through tunnels, and the underground cities were where scriptoriums existed, a place where printed matter and incunabula were stored. Within a trove of documentation, we found stories of Greek mythology. The stories are convoluted, as all that exists are fragmentary scraps. Recovered maps too are mostly damaged, and we collage them into new configurations.

Philomela was an Athenian princess. She wished to visit her sister, Procne, who lived in Thrace with her husband, a distance away. Tereus, Procne's husband, agreed to escort Philomela to their home in Thrace so the sisters could reunite. Enroute Tereus raped Philomela, then raped her a second time when she threatened to denounce him, so he cut out her tongue. Additionally cautious and cruel, he imprisoned her in a cabin in a forlorn and remote wooded area to prevent her from escaping. There, Philomela embroidered a scroll that depicted the crime and somehow managed to send it to her sister, who learning of her whereabouts was eventually able to rescue her. Procne, enraged by her husband, killed their son, Itys, and dismembered his body. She cooked the child's remains and served them to her husband. Philomela encouraged her sister to do so.

Philomela and Procne's sorrow and rage are a relation of feeling that collapsed in on itself, pulverized the form, smashed out the glass windows, and blasted the oak of the doors. The sisters fed the body of the young boy to the rapist. Why this made sense to them is a synonymous madness, the transference of violence from Philomela onto the son of the victimizer.

We have no more information on how the consequences unfolded in this iconoclastic period of conspicuous trauma and erosion.

Philomela, with her somber eyes, frontally superimposed on life in the thickness of space, could seem to disappear. From within the layers of her robe she held out a vessel filled with wine the color of blood made from grapes as she gave an account to the ministers and figures waiting by her. In this depiction her sister is not standing near her.

They had entered a labyrinth of trauma with many levels, where water seeped through, and the wind collided. We admire their struggles. By the time the sisters approached the deer watering at the stream, they had transformed, Philomela became a nightingale and Procne a sparrow. As a nightingale, still Philomela could not vocalize. Tereus too had been transformed, into a hawk. Memory pooled by the rocks. A cruel paradox began to take shape in the form of the psychic aftermath that trickled along history's path. Luckily, they could fly.

THE PERFORMERS
SHABNAM

The woman and man, presumably a couple, because of how close they sit near each other, occupy one of the benches on the fringe of the park almost daily. I become attentive to their observance of the foliage that grows near the benches. Sometimes the man crouches over, handles a plant. He uses electronic equipment to attach sensors to the leaves and then to his temporal lobes. The woman often sits on the ground, gently examining a plant or rubbing the trunk of a tree with her palms. There's something radical about their togetherness, which seems as much about a mutuality with the ecology as with each other. They don't communicate much, but there is a constant humming resonance between them. They seem two of one, or one of two, like-unlike, in symbiosis. A woman frequently sits near them. The woman has bags of books with her, nothing much else. She is always dressed in the same pair of jeans and a sweatshirt with the word *HERE* printed on it in sand-colored lettering. They all seem comfortable with one another. Do they know her? Once they shared their meal with her. This triad is a fixture of the park. Most times we are here, they are here.

A reappraisal of the environment occurs when we perceive there are others present besides us, besides Randy, besides the visiting academics and poets, besides the residents of Treasure Island. We notice anomalous presences. This happens collectively. I don't remember anyone announcing that they noticed something different. We all kind of came together one day and admitted to our perceptions. I feel a similar sensation when my ethnicity is noticed. When I'm in a crowd of Afghans and they realize I'm not Pashtun. I'm Hazaras. An invisibility becomes perceptible, changing the air, our bodies, our interaction. The aspirations of the nation-state are a fraught zone of contention. Nation-states subsume race and ethnicity under a banner of togetherness, unification, or see difference as an insurmountable, threatening problem. In the case of Afghanistan, the colonial architects were the British and Russians at the end of the nineteenth century. Their struggle to control the region was dubbed the Great Game. The Hazaras were once 67 percent of the population but now are somewhere around 9 percent. Hazaras were often sold into slavery until as recently as the late 1900s. There was an all-out killing spree waged against Hazaras in 1893 when Amir Abdul Rahman Khan, the Pashtun king, mandated the killing of all Shias in central Afghanistan. We are the result of waves of incursion and domination. It is said that the Hazaras are Mongols, remnants of Genghis Khan's vast army. Our history is a mood ring that changes colors. Sometimes I pass as white, sometimes East Asian, Native American. It takes a while for people to notice my Persian roots. Blue eyes throw everyone off. We came as refugees in the 1970s and my parents' outward objective was assimilation. This wasn't easy in a nonurban environment like the North Dakota town we lived in. We were sent there by a refugee resettlement program. In 2013 a white supremacist group began buying up property near the town, their plan was to establish an all-white neo-Nazi community with Nationalist Socialism as its political affiliation. By then my parents had moved to a suburb outside of New York City and I was an undergrad in the Philosophy Department at University of Michigan. Eventually they moved to San Francisco, where they live now.

Afghanistan is so thoroughly villainized by the West, politically, culturally. It is a convenient foil used to contrast a "modern, open democracy" against one of religious extremism, all the while in denial of its own rampant domestic religious extremism and racist ideologies.

Intergenerational trauma is smarting information I carry as an appendage. "Aren't we all traumatized?" is the rhetorical question my mother likes to ask when I crave details, dig at generalities. Past circumstances become intangible. The floor drops out, details falter. Or like a fog enveloping everything rendering everything indistinct. I think this is what my mother means to accomplish with deflection. When traumatic information does surface, it becomes a throbbing indicator into the future as much as the past. Momentary X-ray vision. The murky depth shows itself. "Mom, I need to know. I *really* need to know." I repeat. "I know you do, darling. Sometimes it is impossible to fulfil that need."

In 2005, we managed, as a family, to return to my father's hometown near the Ghorat-Hazarajat Alpine Meadow. We all broke down in tears when we arrived at the bluest lakes of Band-e Amir. As a child, he would bike to the lakes to watch bird migrations. "Shabnam," my father gestured sweepingly with dramatic motions like a conductor passionate about the symphony he was directing, "the lakes are imagination, the creative core." He instilled in us a precept, that ecology was at the basis of a person's perception. That ecology shapes expressiveness. "You may never see the snow leopard, their eyes the color of clouds, yet they guide visions." His comments bordered on prophecy—of the pronounced impact that nature exerted on beings. As a child I took these comments to be flights of fancy—nostalgia that had acquired too much patina, relied too heavily on emotive lyricism. These sentiments were carried over in the name my parents chose for me, which translates as "morning dew." When the sun set on the red cliffs of what is now Band-e Amir National Park, a Eurasian eagle-owl flew overhead in the bands of blood orange and pomegranate red streaks and then a Barbary falcon followed, I totally understood what my father was saying. A particular intelligence emanates from the land, the plants, the animals. The way the thornbush and grassland respond to the wind. The way the dry sponge of the sky thirstily sucks moisture from the lakes. The merged tonalities of wormwood, rue, and asafetida. The combined root systems of fenugreek, vetch, and astragalus. Scents of juniper and catnip heated by the late afternoon sun. We blended in with the ecosystem. Our coloration is the same, our texture resembles the textures of this region of the world. Travertine rock is a sense. We are also the colors and textures of elsewhere, a home long lost. The traces are barely perceptible. Like the Bamiyan Buddha, there for a long duration and then blasted out, pulverized, hollowed out, only an outline persists, a recessed shelf where the Buddha once existed. Could there be a more symbolic incidence of impermanence? The Bamiyan Buddha is crystal clear in my imagination, as if chiseled into the sandstone of my mind, and I also hold the emptiness that is the clearance of delusion. From dust, life will spring. A seed I brought back from a tamarind tree growing by my aunt's house in Kohe-Baba in the Fuladi Valley now grows in San Francisco, on the sunny side of my parents' house. Negative and positive space merge. I carry my father's optimism forward into a new generation.

Performing, for me, has been about exorcising overarching cultural themes that permeate a mentality of being in the world. I've been slipping out of a performance modality into a cultural forensic hypnosis, the spellbinding process of turning over each and every metaphoric stone to uncover a physical connection with lineage. This involves stripping away the veneer of cultural fantasy and examining what remains. I have flashbacks that make visible the collision of world views, of impressions that don't make sense because they are part of an imperialist derangement.

While performing today, I had cramps and would have rather flopped back in bed with a cup of tea, a book. Slowness was my medium. Darius was in a prone position wrestling with an anomalous energy she unearthed by the weathered, abandoned gas station. I thought of going over to her but remembered we weren't to engage in pairs.

Avoiding the troupe and steering clear of the visitors I made for the edge of the road leading to the bridge. Moving on asphalt felt worse yet than the gravel and the grass, but I put myself up for an endurance test in the face of exhaustion. The road caught fire and after the fire burned out, the ashes turned into poppies and a woman crawled out from beneath the shadow of another woman who was passed out near to where I was moving. I recognized neither of them. They wore stunning costumes: tight bodices of red silk and skirts of vegetable fibers dyed red that were ornamented with shells and flowers and they had elaborate headdresses decorated with feathers and flowers. They were Polynesian dancers. The scenario that unfolded was anachronistic Hollywood. It dawned on me that I could be visualizing the dancers who performed at the former fairgrounds on the island. The dancer who had collapsed near the road stood up and brushed herself off. Together they dashed across the road, barefoot dodging traffic. They looked stricken. What they were fleeing from I do not know. I ran toward them, and as I ran, I noticed my body moved through them. A sudden flash of verity in a challenging form, a movement to elemental meaning, or a phantasmagoria. The raging fire returned as an impression that burned at any semblance of empirical, verifiable phenomena. This wasn't the first anomaly I'd experienced, but it was by far the most intense.

THE PERFORMERS
Jay

The decision to join Randy's troupe was a quick one for me, though I had lingering apprehensions. Would we have any say on how we engaged our bodies at the site, or would the elements of the performance be dictated to us? Was there room for discussion in someone else's conceptual vision? What choices were up to us? Would we, in essence, be building materials or raw matter to be shaped and directed into form? These worries crept around my thinking. If these issues were not in the front of my thoughts, they tossed around in my subconscious. I am vigilant about such matters in whatever artistic or social engagement I enter into.

On certain days when we met to rehearse or give a performance, the instructions that were given shut me down. My muscles and joints would get rigid, and I would freeze in place becoming a blank slate, a defamiliarized entity, too vulnerable to the destabilizing forces of sex and gender. I came to see the performances as a gesture that allowed a release from reactionary personal form. A method that involved surrender. To let go of whatever built-up persona was being projected. I trusted many of the other participants. Joining in initiated solidarity. Our group, our motley crew, became if not family, then a queer assemblage, an emergent congregation.

The performances proved that concealment is possible in broad daylight. The hazmat suit confers anonymity. This feels soothing.

Consciousness is a steady interlocutor, with or without stark white costuming. The body pronounces itself alive, demands attention, needs food, caresses, a need of philosophy, a need of music, a need of ceremony, and don't let us forget sex. The body reaches out trying to decipher who will take care of them. The body wants to know who will avail themselves. The body may reciprocate kindness, may retaliate hate. The human body assesses signals: pheromones, scents, messages to decode and decipher.

There are times when walking home from the bus stop to my apartment I get entangled by sensation, overwhelmed to the point of acute anxiety caused by overstimulation. The bombardment of signals overloads nerve endings. I arrive home completely unraveled, pieces of me abandoned along the way. Panic elevates my blood pressure and I feel a burning nothingness. Hours pass and I still have not calmed down, the missing referents long gone, not that I try to remember the details of what overstimulated me.

Performing with the group might help soften the demarcations that I experience, with my body, self, and others—this is an aspiration I have.

A friend told me that a performance troupe was looking for volunteers. We would not receive payment. The artist who conceived of the performance did not receive any compensation for the project. He has a trust fund. This was a point of contention, his money, where it came from. The others knew him closely, as colleagues. I was thinly acquainted with him, had no personal baggage, felt no social identification. Sae, who tends to accentuate the positive, told me I could expect executive commands mixed with boyish good humor. I identify as boyish and lack the ability to give executive commands so the prospects of participating up close in person with such tendencies offered exposure to the qualities of a certain male repertoire, not that there isn't already a saturation.

There has been a radical shift in how personhood presents as gender identities proliferate. Suddenly, having a body does not have to be as claustrophobic. My pronouns are they/them and I prefer floral motifs. If twinkiness aids in the loosening of the patriarchal stranglehold, then I'll Peter Pan my way into the future for whatever it is worth. I'm a pinkish twink, a.k.a. white boi. Growing into my queerness in poverty with a single mother in a noncoastal state in a town far from a city created the conditions for amphibious mushrooming dayglow creatureliness. Guises are camouflage. My spots are changeable. Pink, but not a ham. I do not ham it up, I worship pigs. Newts, salamanders, lizards, and all changeling creatures amphibious demonstrate fluid participation in various ecological contexts. Many prefer moist forests—all require water nearby. My gender is amphibious. I require moistness, forests, water in my vicinity. Birds receive my adoration also. Twinkness resists ageism. Twinks are simultaneously old and young. Like Earth, the planet exudes youth and age simultaneously. Young life springs up on ancient bedrock, and the bedrock is young too, in relation to the cosmos's passionate origination: exploded potentiality within antimatter's forcefield. I wear my immaturity on my sleeve, fatigued of proving competence and expertise.

Darius got me tuned into trees, the healing aspects of the plant world. Growing sanctuaries. She said, "No self-flagellation in the presence of trees!" "If you are going to obsess, obsess about trees" was another bon-bon she delivered. Under a tree's canopy there is no threat of emotional bleeding, and tyrants of intent are held at bay. Why, because trees maintain a mood. Trees move slowly, generously, allowing for withdrawal. Trees are specialists at dissolving the toxic thoughts of humans. In a storm a tree will flail, do a mad dance with the wind, and then resume a calm stance. A mode to emulate. I study the trees because my life depends on it. I read a beautiful communique from an anonymous participant defending the Atlanta forest who states: "The slow time of the forest breaks through the fast time of crisis, and two different worlds slide past each other. In one, my fast-beating heart. In the other, the calm and patient vastness of a centuries-old water oak." Reports from the forest come from police abolitionists and environmental activists in a struggle to thwart a plan by the city of Atlanta, the Atlanta Police Foundation, and other entities to convert the forest into a herculean police training compound and a movie studio.

The sugary hormonal transmissions of trees are subtle compared with human communication. Human lingual output is a shifting field of calibrated messaging forever volatile and charged. Meanings burst their boundaries, a sentence springs ahead in space and time. A single sentence is cluttered with subjects, objects, actions, descriptors. Phrases seek out the magnetism of adjacent clauses. Thinking thoughts physically fills up space because words materialize properties of mind and body. Luce Irigaray writes, "A tree teaches us in silence." The act of reading a book is also the act of reading trees in that the text is absorbed by the tree's cellular fibers—something inaudible remains as a trace.

I arrived at Treasure Island early, the others aren't here yet, so I hang out by the administration building. The building is stark white, and I'm in a white hazmat suit. White on white is blinding. As my eyes are directed skyward to a shaft of topaz light, a flock of pigeons draws my attention to their roost on the ledge of a decorative facade that features stone owls staring out ahead, lions yawning or grimacing. Flowers and fruits drape over the edge of the limestone portico. The pigeons face the sun. They sit in a row absorbing the light. They rest against one another communally. Nature is cultural and emotional. A siren blasts, a baby in a stroller screams, car doors are slammed. An instant later, when my gaze returns toward the sun and to the portico, the pigeons no longer sit compatibly in single file. They have evaporated. I do note the giant pink moon in late afternoon. Have I ever noticed the moon so pink and enlarged? The visual tableau has shifted pronouncedly. Glitches in perception obsess me. Because of the slipstream appearances and vanishings, I pay close attention to the senses. Thus, the overload. The world does not know me in my rock phase channeling energetic blue ray vibrations. Amphibiousness relates to rocks. Rocks offer clairaudience. Stimulate the endocrine system. Cavansite on stilbite and heulandite. Three rock personalities coexisting together in gem formation. So marvelous! Pronouns shift accordingly, subject formations never end. Tangents are erotic.

Underlying eroticism is the feeling of something bursting, the violence of explosive tendency. I am like a fly landing ravenously on the very thing I have a strong aversion to, laying my eggs, sucking at the nectar that appears to everyone else as shit. Which is to say aversions transform content in ways hardly anticipated. Potent shit, probably something ruptured. A poet whose work I adore wrote, "your own madness is what you see as nature turning against you," and it rings true in my bones, so I swim there, or climb over the phrase as if it were a rocky ledge offering a vista. The personification of nature is a process and a practice. A related exercise: uncovering personhood encrusted by the civilizing notions of the human that clash with the ecological whole. This might include obfuscations of being-in-being with and as nature. Being bodily in the underbrush amid rocks and soil. Paying more attention to the burbling of blood in the veins.

For the performances we are required to wear a hazmat suit. A major toxic chemical producer also manufactures hazmat suits and sells them for a very low price. Randy wants us to be as identical as possible. We all splurge for the suit mass-produced by the corporation that has polluted much of the globe. Is the suit itself somehow poisonous? Unwrapping it from the packaging creates a threateningly acrid odor that will not dissipate. I shove it into a plastic bag and place it in my hallway for a while to allow it to gas off. Note to self: research the trademarked material to better understand what it is made of. A fabric impervious to toxic chemicals may prove to be chemically toxic in and of itself. Sigh.

The requirement to wear an outfit that renders us anonymous is interesting to me. Getting dressed and our clothing choices are perhaps the most individualizing human practices, or are they? A counter argument can be made that we dress according to group affiliations and maybe do not have that much leeway. Sae calls it appareling. A decision to dress in a certain way indicates how we center ourselves in group formation, as a symbolic community, sharing bonds nonverbally through style affiliation; our bodies, the flagpole on which we attach our flags. Unified dress codes signify either a consensual or forced acknowledgment of group identification. Prisoners, clergy, sports players, for example, all wear uniforms that simulate sameness. Fitting in is consequential. Ostracization happens subtly. We are metered and manipulated by a financialized system that seeks profit in every way possible, steering emotion, desire, outcome, and all the while we are basically composting and cannibalizing one another. At one level it is incomprehensible that alienation should arise out of absorptive tendencies.

After a week or two I pull out the suit and try it on. The plastic material is stiff and crinkled and continues to gas off. With a jerk of my legs, I manage to climb in, and it is as if I have entered the inner core of a strange plant or animal form. The crinkly layer of fabric is a shroud. Ambulation is slowed by the friction of the material between my thighs. It bunches at my ankles. When I peer down, I fantasize I see elephant feet, large pads of gristle under each appendage. I began to hear with my feet, picking up resonances; first from the immediate surroundings and then from much farther away. The suit compels me to walk nonstop. My feet amplify sonic tonality, and for the first time my body responds to noises from the plants and other voicings that were previously subaudible to me.

The first time I put the suit on with our group also getting into theirs, Shabnam came over and waved her hands in front of my face, "Jay," she said, "even though I no longer recognize you I'm here for you. Don't hesitate to call on me if the performance brings up heavy shit. Let our secret signal to each other be holding our arms out horizontally and flapping them as if we were moths or butterflies." We gave each other a hug and simultaneously pantomimed *I love you* as we moved closer to the others.

The reflective white surface glows in my dim apartment. The suit seems lit from within. Hazmat suits conjure scenes of disaster. Persons wearing hazmat suits do the dirty hazardous work. Wearing a hazmat suit is a badge of service, a sign of sacrifice. The performers in hazmat suits become the prosthetic outside. I want to explain the limits of this ad hoc thesis and determine how trust functions in the equation. If the group does not inherently trust their leader, what does this entail for the group, for society at large? The group puts its confidence in the leader and acts out the leader's commands. Someone has to take charge to speed up response time. I want to test the rationale behind the organizational strategy. Everything is pointing away from a top down, hierarchical model, a threat multiplier. Arriving at the scene of disaster within a historical formation where the historical formation, in and of itself, is the disaster.

Several years ago, a hazmat suit was offered to me. I put it on, a men's large stiff white oversuit. Together with an employee from the Department of Health I entered a building on the end of the block where I lived. I was the block representative; a community witness was needed. The neighbor whose residence it was did not answer his bell and had not been seen for days. The police, earlier in the day, used axes and sledgehammers to gain access through the front door on the upper landing. The entrance was blocked by a barricade of impacted materials. They could not penetrate the massive buildup and had to finally use a circular saw to cut through the metal gate on the first floor instead. There was concern whether the man was sick or dead in the house. The resident was actually in the hospital—he had been bitten by a rat and was gravely ill. He died several days later. For years he lived without a human partner with an evolving number of pit bull companions and their offspring in the three-story wooden structure. At first the man preferred cats and had more than a dozen cats living with him, but then, when his boyfriend left, he began living with pit bulls. No one seems to know what became of the cats. Wearing the hazmat suit upon entering his living quarters, I realized what a thin membrane shielded me from the teeming ecology of organic substances. The suit, made of thin flexible synthetic fabric, was insubstantial. Its boldest feature was its stark colorless glow, untouched by filth and disease—clinical, technical, not of the rotting, stinking realm of earth where decay is a cyclical process. Once the suit was on, I felt an immediate identification with the official from the Department of Health.

We entered through the first-floor landing. Holding on to his arm, we entered hell, a living, breathing hell accessible through the door of the domestic residence. Hell is not a dream, it is a set of conditions, and we hazarded them together, the two of us.

Gwen, the ex-cop, cheered us on before we entered. She lived across the street and had been abreast of the developments from day one. "Jay, make sure you come back out of there," she warned with her acrid humor. My comeback was a dry coughing sound. She said in a powerful voice: "I'll be right over here, awaiting your reemergence." I did not look over to her or I would have lost confidence.

The DOH official said generously to me, "Yes, do that," when I said to him, "I have to cling onto you." We immediately began slip-sliding in the accumulated muck by the doorway that led to an unlit vestibule. Substantiating hell appears to be much easier than claiming heaven.

We walked into heaps of rotting matter several inches thick, and it was difficult to get stable footing, I gripped on tighter to his arm. The outside world was shut out. The inside had suffocated. The DOH official had an LED Maglite that he used to illuminate a path through the pitch dark. Within an arm's length we began moving through woven cobwebs that entangled us and then saw that the windows were covered with thousands of dead flies, roaches, and other insects, several bodies thick. In the center of the room was an earthen mound of debris that consisted of broken rotted chairs, books, clothing, newspapers, and dirt all heaped into a circular hill formation. Everything was moist, perspiring. There was a tiny path around the mound. The two of us no longer communicated. We held our breath to seal off bodily contact with excreta.

As I clutched him, I tried to pay attention to the surroundings. Things came into focus at a delay. There were no right angles, no straight planes. There was no light except for the artificial blue ray cast by the flashlight that cut through the putrid atmosphere with laser precision, startling in its intensity. What was the genesis of the misery we were entering? Where was insight when all registers were on high alert? The thick grime had immense gravity. The pasty quaking substance was not quicksand, it was the outflow of the colonic circuitry of the underworld pulling us in. There was pressure in my knees and ankles to buckle, to give in. We exited the limbic system and proceeded on to the digestive system in a terrible labyrinth.

I tried to rebalance myself as we entered the cavernous adjoining space filled shin-deep with damp funk, a hummus consisting of feces and debris rotted into a mass. As the flashlight's beam darted around the sunken enclosure, we observed that everything in the room had decomposed. We began to make out the desiccated bones amid carcasses of dogs that were still intact. Men's clothing hung off moldy, splintered furniture. A few antique objects clung to the walls, covered in furry coats of mildew illuminated only by the light we carried in with us.

Together we made it as far as what appeared to be the kitchen, though there was little semblance of any function as a kitchen. Countertops were hilly brown surfaces. The walls were sticky with ooze. The flooring was also layered with waste and decay. There was a speckled amber light that glowed through the smeared window looking out to a garden as if into an unclean fish tank. All I could see were blurry shapes, but I knew the garden space was actually impacted dirt, more feces, bones, and pit bulls running free range. The dogs cannibalized their offspring and the weaker older dogs when there was no other food available. They were starving, covered in mange, and wounded. They suffered the effects of generations of inbreeding. We turned around and, in the hall, noticed an open door. We peered down into a cellar where there was an actual working light bulb glowing in a dungeon space. There was a soiled mattress soaked with sewage dripping onto it from the ceiling. This is where the man slept. Steven was his name.

As long as I knew him, he was always dressed in black trousers and a crisp white long-sleeved shirt, never a thread out of place. He worked as a waiter at a local restaurant. I would greet him whenever we happened to cross paths, but he would avert his gaze, never permit eye contact.

Toward spring one year I noticed he would constantly sit on his stoop, except for when he went to his job at the restaurant. Otherwise, no matter the hour, he was there, sitting on the stone steps with several dogs, all with the same color fur, a dusty pinkish off-white. A rat infestation had driven him from the interior of his home. He shared the house with twenty-three pit bulls vying for food and attention. The combination was lethal, and it was what led neighbors to call various city agencies to check up on the situation after attempting to talk directly with Steven. He refused any contact with neighbors.

After he died, his brother and sister arrived, and quickly a massive sixteen-foot dumpster appeared. They told me that they had no idea that Steven lived in this manner. They had not spoken to him in years. Before long the house was converted into two luxury units and sold off, pasts and futures imploding on another. A shifting baseline syndrome of forgetting, ruin piled upon ruin, history lost in dust and despair. The incommensurability of time's permeable membranes.

The hazmat suit gave me a momentary vantage point beyond my usual subject position. For the time I wore it I was both witness for the block and resident of the block. Inside and outside several worlds. I was covered in filth and also impervious to it. When I peeled off the layer of crunchy white material, stained and torn by the ankle, the situation became more real to me. This could also have been the shock wearing off. When I wore the hazmat suit, life took place in slow motion. There was no smell in that world. Without the suit I heard a ringing in my ears that extended down to my throat into my diaphragm. The taste of fecal matter surfaced in my mouth. We are not absolved of the interactions that led to this sadness. The history of suffering is a living history, it has energy and volition. We are culpable and liable, and for precisely this reason, a curse defined its powers as a territorial claim. A deafening roar of hereness. Heretofore and hereafter. Get off on, pass go. Get on a nucleated attention span. Double talk signifying an entitlement of nothing. Anything. For love, for peace of mind. Voids create vastness. The entryway, the hole.

I began to understand what I witnessed as a reverse Eden, where the disabuse of community results in an expulsion from home. Failing Steven was a failure of community. Pain and suffering got buried alive. Eden was about curious, all-inclusive interspecies sharing: tasting, smelling, touching, being touched. Only to be expelled by the godhead landlord. Reverse Eden happens in the wake when disconnection destroys persons and place. "When you hear the words 'reverse Eden,' what does it mean to you?" I queried my friend Laura out of the blue while on a FaceTime call. She looked up at the sky, a pixelated medium blue, changing to syrupy purple. A blooming tree with hot pink flowers encircled her skull like a fragrant helmet as she idled momentarily.

"Reverse Eden is when what once exuded nectar exudes toxic substances, but it tastes even better; we become addicted, we demand more." She paused briefly to collect her breath. "Factories produce it in large quantities. It is available in every form, in every flavor. It is lifestyle, commerce, and then it is our world!" she exclaimed as she pensively combed her fingers through her hair. "Our bodies become the substance, but there is finally a limit as to how much we can make, how much we can distribute, how much we can consume, and then bigger problems arise. A substitute formula is engineered. Our taste buds react positively to the new recipe, the chemicals are more powerful, more toxic."

Into the expanse of purple-blue voluminousness she went on, "It is like we've entered into a pact. We drink the Kool-Aid, if not willingly than reluctantly at first. There is a feeling of fleeting ecstasy, the feeling is shared experience individually purchased." She hesitated to inhale, "Collective dying. Think Jonestown without a messianic figure compelling us." Our connection faltered for a second and then she said prophetically, "We do not think of our predicament as dying, we think of it as living, and not everything has become poisonous."

Incessantly I think of Steven and the dogs and his house that rotted from the inside out whenever I am wearing the hazmat suit. The memory acts like a Geiger counter detecting sorrow and suffering. This place, too, is off the charts.

THe PerFORMerS
Laura

The relationships between object and sense. A merging of object and sense. A divergence of object and sense. Sense and object outside of epistemology.

The act of performing is propulsive. Adrenaline surges. Our bodies draw the spectator into a tableau that unites sky with land, thinking and feeling. Our performances are a form of chelation. Historical aftermaths, psychic aftermaths, and toxic aftermaths are drawn out. We huddle in an infinite present probing the occluded past. We probe a lost past; we hurl toward the future and land on our toes connected again to the infinite present. Time has a changeable quality. Time is a burning ember and a marching hymn. When the troupe performs, time burrows underground, resurfaces as cloud cover. Our rhythms absorb time as time absorbs our memories. Time and space become synonymous. Without time we could not return to that which we love and are attracted to. Time is graceful for having a past, a present, and a future. Some say futures, infinite futures, and infinite pasts and presents. Others speculate that the past and the future have merged since time began.

When we met in a coffee shop to briefly catch up before driving over to Treasure Island, Jay and I had a conversation about land acknowledgments and how this was a crucial piece missing from the performance. Jay said that they have never heard any artist or institution adequately acknowledge Indigenous struggles when making land acknowledgments. All seem to follow a nearly identical script. The artist or institution references the unceded territories they are on. This is an inadequate first step they say. They then proceed with the programing as usual. What did it even mean? Though sincere, the insubstantial gesture fails to address dispossession, the horrors of boarding schools and forced assimilation, land back advocacy, the return of sacred ceremonial items, ending containment, ending intrusions by law enforcement and incarceration, and respecting sovereignty in a broad, encompassing way. Jay pulled a book out of their knapsack and read from it. *Mohawk Interruptus: Political Life Across the Borders of Settler States*, by Audra Simpson, a professor of anthropology at Columbia University. I quickly jotted down what I could. "Iroquois peoples *remind* nation-states such as the United States (and Canada) that they possess this very history—a history of 'monocultural aspirations of nation-states . . . especially rooted in Indigenous dispossession'—and within that history and seized space, they possess a *precarious* assumption that their boundaries are permanent, uncontestable, and entrenched. They possess a precarious assumption about their own (just) origins. And by extension, they possess a precarious assumption about themselves." The quote by Audra Simpson changed me, it helped me understand something fundamental about power and perception. Nation-states are not invincible, no matter the military budget, no matter the punitive measures in place to maintain the system. I place my attention on the modalities of response that have been generated around the seizure of Indigenous land. I think of Diana Taylor's concept of "the ghost of oppositionality" as empowerment from her influential text *The Archive and the Repertoire: Performing Cultural Memory in the Americas*. Raven Chacon and Candice Hopkins developed a score called *Dispatch* that Laura Ortman and Marshall Trammel enacted with them recently, which I was fortunate to attend, where strategies of gathering and activating in solidarity with Indigenous struggle are creatively imagined. The score is based on the activism that took place at Standing Rock. The work focuses on roles of engagement, invoking direct action in communal form. They have thirteen categories of involvement, each with delineated protocols. Hosts are "people who live and have lived here for centuries," spiritual leaders are "Indigenous people from any tribe or nation, front line activists are 'native and non' ready and willing to engage directly with police, militia, or construction crews." Countersurveillers "surveille the police and encroachers." Temporary campers and sympathizers "bring attention to the cause, temporarily. Cannot or do not know how to belong to the camp." The performance of *Dispatch* brought to light the many intersections of the community, the state, and the land in gathering and witnessing in an effort to fend off and ameliorate the effects of colonization. Assigning roles for everyone to participate was genius. There is a role for everyone, even those adversarial to the cause. I shared these observations with Jay. Our conversation was brief because as usual we were running late.

The discussion that started in the coffeeshop continued on the ride over. Jay's notion of being in the world is a vantage point in motion. They are empathic. Every utterance is an exploration from a deeply considered ground even as it shifts: mercurial, quicksilver, philosophical, and experiential. I asked Jay if they are concerned with exemplary states of being, like enlightenment, or holiness, and they looked over while steering and smiled. Not a bit of irony or coyness. A grin and silence. "Okay, ethics then," I asked, realizing I would not get a reaction out of them if I paraded terms like *heaven* to them. Ethics are their bulwark. By offering up the whole gamut I hoped they would bite. Their smile rearranged my thoughts though. I felt differently suddenly. Less interested in discursive banter, taking in instead the resonances of nonverbal communication. I looked over at Jay again to see if their smile faded. No, radiant as ever. And not strange. Eagerness can be off-putting. Not with Jay. Jay's burn rate is steady.

I have noticed subtle changes with Jay. They are less talkative—yes, loquacious when they are engaged, but a prompt is necessary. They do not offer up conversation as they would in the past. They are not disinterested or reserved, just less verbal. Also, their body posture is different. They are more flexible. They sit differently. They look around more, past the humans, through the humans. Also, they learned a lot about local plants, and it is sometimes all they want to talk about except climate, weather. Yes, labor too is a frequent talking point. We rehash our disgruntledness with how we have to contract out our bodies as laboring units per hour, at the discretion of our employers. I receive two weeks off with which I have time to do as I please. Jay has four weeks accrued because they have worked at the same employment for over a decade. But, four weeks off out of a total of fifty-two weeks is a scandal. Lately we have limited the amount of time we use to vent our frustrations on this topic because it is moot to do so, as it does not improve our condition to expend energies grumbling. Jay is involved with union efforts and has motivated me to do the same.

Their significant others are goats. Tennessee fainting goats. They spend most of their free time communing with them. The goats adopted them, allowed them into their fold. The goats are part of a strategy by the city to manage municipal land with an attention to emissions reduction.

The goats were introduced into little fenced-off areas, to eat the grass on embankments and medians. Jay began to visit them on lunch breaks, after work, before work. The goats beckoned Jay. Jay explained that they crowded over to them, nudging and cajoling with body language. Jay began to occasionally bring their lunch and sit with the goats. Eventually they brought a sleeping bag and camped out with the goats when the weather permitted. When the goats are nervous, they instantly freeze, their muscles tense. Sometimes they fall over due to their anxious nature. Most humans ignored the goats after the novelty of their presence wore off. They are situated in difficult to reach areas, so contact with humans is unlikely. Leave it to Jay to establish a bond with the goats.

Is the intimacy I feel with Jay a holdover from our brief affair? Or did the closeness arrive once we disbanded with sex? Something to ponder indefinitely. Whatever is the case, I cannot lose them. They are my touchstone. I bounce everything off of them. Sex, no sex, an equivocal element. We might even touch more frequently now, postsex. We talk about sex, frequently, but not to titillate or make the other jealous. The way we talk about it is reportage. Factual. Who, what, when, where? The why ends up taking most of our time. The why is always a somewhat vexing point for me. Their relationship to their body, sex, and experiences with others is nonchalant. Their anxiety stems from ambient factors. When it comes to human interactions, they are breezy. They transitioned and they have more escapades now, more encounters. My relationship with my body is always a work in progress.

Jay recently asked me, "Shall we fuck? Should we resume where we left off?" I was momentarily taken aback, didn't anticipate a candid question like this. They asked me while we were driving somewhere—usually when we are in a car our conversations lead in this direction. They did not flinch. What I admire about them, they never flinch. I flinched, I said, "Sure," and then, "what do you mean?" a little too strictly and followed up with "did I hear you correctly?" We have not resumed anything in the way of sex, sex has become the elephant in the room. Always in the room, it defines the room, making presence almost autoerotic. Now I am feeling like we should "resume." Jay is great about impermanence, practices nonattachment flawlessly, demands nothing. They gleam atmospherically like an opal, their stone.

Prongs poke out everywhere with me. Sex and the experiences of having a body drive me into a tight circular pattern, where finally I regurgitate my own tail, so to speak. And maybe more problematic even is that I associate everything with childhood trauma. Jean-Jacques Rousseau's metaphor about the child being a young sapling, a plant or tree that can be pruned by a human hand but is nourished and guided by nature says it all. The pruning in my formative years was too harsh, and I continue to require constant exposure to nature. Trees are peers. To get me out of traumatic loops I rely on nature. The nonformal sensual interplay of pressures and atmospheres. I just haven't found my significant other, like in Jay's case, goats. Gathering with the other performers, masquerading as anonymous, unraced, and ungendered has a liberating effect.

The toxicity here, we know, is all around us, not just behind the fence with the placard that carries a warning. We carry toxicity in our bodies, drag it with us to this space. There is rocket fuel in breast milk, pesticides on the food we ingest. Most products we touch and live among are made of lethal materials with long-term effects not just for the purchaser of said product but for the entire ecosystem for generations to come. Nuclear facilities spill waste that spreads over the globe. Noxious gases are inhaled every time we ignite our stoves. Factory farms pollute. Rainwater is toxic because of concentrations of "forever chemicals": PFAS. The ubiquitous aspect of toxicity coupled with its invisibility gives it a terrible ghost presence. By agreeing to expose ourselves to the culprit we become stronger and weaker simultaneously. Our troupe was originally larger. Two performers dropped out because of worries about exposure. I am freaked out by the prospect of exposure. I toggle the risks in my mind. The giddiness of interactive pleasure alleviates fear. It helps me to deconstruct the anxiousness I hold in my abdomen. Let it go. Let it all go. We reassure each other. Some provide stats. The feel-good togetherness is worth so much. A sense of joy is rejuvenating.

Submitting to hazardous conditions knowingly is more honest than walking through life without admitting that the conditions of life under a neoliberal industrial-military complex are fraught with major danger. We are unsafe because the system does not care about well-being, only profit and control. I am rather of the mind that the bravado of going about spooning poison in one's mouth is ill-advised. But again, I totally get that our situation as humans provokes us to take on forms of self-medication and radical forms of homeopathy that involve ingesting what ails us as a healing strategy.

Randy constantly handles the soil, sifts it through his fingers, rubs it on his arms, throws it in the air—no explanation there, occasionally dabs a moistened pointer finger into a palmful and brings it to his lips, ingests it. "Acclimating," he explains, "when I sample the soil, I'm taking a somatic reading of the content." The exhibitionism and bravado cause disdain to rear up within me. Creating an atmosphere of discomfort or disturbance electrifies some people. Others vicariously feed off of the energy.

As we gathered before the performance started an unexpected rainstorm let loose, pelting us. We rushed to the school building and huddled as blurred sheets of precipitation fell. We hadn't suited up in our hazmat gear and were quickly soaked. Someone shouted, "Wet T-shirt contest." Will hardened nipples always induce a sense of shame and glory? Miniature mountainous peaks of flesh crested against fabric, nodes that signal temperature change, arousal. Some less pronounced and circled in bristly hair, others dotted pointedly on top a mound of raised mammary glands. Sex comes into focus and then recedes. There is not a heteronormative person among us, except, ironically perhaps, Randy. He is a he in a conventional sense, yet even conventions are changing. I will not foreclose the possibility that Randy too feels the oppression of gender, regardless of the benefits granted. We hyperattune to transformations, do not take anything for granted. There is a fair amount of inspection that is unwanted that we engage in, nonetheless.

The dry dusty road became soupy. Surfaces were slick with liquid. Individual raindrops are unique entities, and the waning light caught the circular water bodies in space causing glistening. Raindrops also arranged en masse; a molecular curtain created refractions of light. The spheres formed by the burst cloud were pulled down by gravity, the force that gives us our bearing. Droplets landed on our eyelashes; everyone blinked. The downpour lasted for a few minutes and then azure skies broke forth. The rain brought information from great distances. We tasted other oceans, other mountains, those that roamed around, those whose roots were firmly planted. Mineral residue glided over our tongues. Minerals entered our digestive system, our bloodstream. Some we will release through perspiration or urination, others become the fabric of self. Continuously feeling different is part and parcel of having a body because of ingestion, exhalation, and excretion. Materials with memories previously external become lodged within. Materials with memories previously held by our bodies are released.

We put our suits on and dispersed. I watched two participants whom I could not recognize wander over to the empty parking lot. They began to fidget. One of them began to convulse. Their body gestures were disturbing as if registering a surge of negative energy, picking up on imminent disaster. An electrocardiograph, a seismic reading. The ocean was a disk of light. The tide was way out, and I decided to center my attention on the horizon. Salt ions carry electricity through water, and the salt in blood channels electrical activity. Blood began to pound at my temples, at my jugular, at my diaphragm. The salted air gave off an aroma of iron, iodine, sulfur, and geosmin. I recently read about a chemical called lurlenol that is actually the sex pheromone of seaweed eggs that attract sperm. It turns out, the chemical pheromones of algae are quite diverse. The article also mentioned how marine worms and algae cause the release of bromophenols that produce a distinctive ocean smell.

A shaft of metallic light drew my attention. Where the light originated was obscured by clouds and an absurd double-arched rainbow so bright and multifaceted as to appear unreal. The edges were pink, fluorescent arcs that spelled out a hieroglyph of cosmic significance. The light did not quite touch down on the surface of the ground. When I concentrated on the light, I noticed my vision was slightly blurred. The light elbowed me on my left side. When I became self-conscious that I had not started to perform, I struck a pose. I adjusted my hips, knees, ankles, toes. In a rigid arrangement I bent over at the waist, touched the ground, crawled a few feet, and then moved to an upright position. As I returned to a mountain pose and then a tree pose, the light changed once again. Rain came crashing down. The upper regions of the atmosphere were now a green-purple, swirling and heavy. This time everyone had on waterproof suits, and no one left their zones. The rain hammered the ground and then in seconds let up. Exposed to the elements I got a sensation of being vegetative. How a tree's crown might feel showered in rain. What trees might experience when there is a slight change of temperature before and after it rains, how bark slackens and tightens. How glucose rushes to the upper boughs from a surge in electricity brought on by precipitation. The weight and velocity of rain as it pinged my leaves.

The column of light fluctuated slightly. It was still visible after the second cloudburst. I waved my hand through the light shaft to get better acquainted with it. Surprisingly, it was not a phenomenon caused by the sun. I could tell because blocking the sun with my shielded hands did not alter its intensity. The source was internal to itself, self-imposing. Another strange attribute of the light was that it resembled the watery translucency of rain. My hand went through the light and did not feel any resistance. When I tried this again, I realized that there was a sensation when touching the ray. I considered drawing over another participant to take a look but thought twice. An instinctive feeling dissuaded me. *Employ a process of deduction*, I instructed myself, while immediately moving toward inductive thinking. Then I was saturated by a mood of expectation. The specifics: synchronized electrical pulses from clusters of neurons communicated in a circuit awash in salt water, waves. Oscillations between alpha and beta brain waves, relaxed and alerted. All chambers of the brain fired. Then, blanked out as if entering fog. Thickness. Colorless, empty space. Space flattened out. As if one peered into space without eyes. This became more comfortable. Things eased. Brainwaves surely theta or delta. I experienced a free-flowing daydream.

I recalled that one of the other participants said something about feeling like a stone. That comment sounded strange. Easy to discount. To feel inert while participating in somatic terms, contradictory. Then I understood the nature of their comment. A feeling of the body that extended beyond the human. Mineral qualities dictated certain effects. We were being othered by the performance. We were undergoing structural change.

The light chamber was hollow and filled with energy. The glassy quality of light had a rigidity. The liquid nature of luminescence frozen in space. Glass sponges. Those creatures with the greatest longevity, tentatively estimated at fifteen thousand years. Graceful silicate spicules. A skeletal structure that resembled lace. The Venus flower basket, one type of glass sponge, grows its structure in a way that entraps a pair of glass sponge shrimp. The shrimp live out their lives in the sponge's bodily enclosure along with brittle stars. The baby shrimp offspring are small enough to leave the enclosure, find a glass sponge home of their own. I remember thinking, touch the light, touch toward it again, and the light was palpable.

Within the light column I detected sand. A space of exceeding dryness. A desert wasteland. Conditions were refracted through the light.

Entering the column of light with my hands drew heat to my nerve endings. The aroma of the ocean no longer existed. Palpable now was a chalky mixture of concrete dust and the searing sun overhead. Like an optogenetically engineered animal, I smelled the light.

There was an audible aspect of the light. The light communicated, giving off a reassuring frequency, but I did not hear sound, it was an internal sensation, in my cerebral cortex. My skull pounded, but I didn't have a headache. A low thrum drew me toward it. Ciphers.

I stepped fully into the shaft. I was ensconced by the light. My muscles felt like jelly. I glanced down at my feet to reestablish my bearings. What I saw resembled protoplasmic streaming—presences moving in a thickness, either liquid or air, also jellylike, slow moving. Amoeba and other microbial creatures that have bloblike bodies were undulating. Their bodies were see-through. One body contained multiples, like rainwater filled with bacteria and other tiny organisms. The microbial had come into relief, in high-definition focus as under a microscope. I was absorbed by organisms able to alter their shapes in varying forms. Then I noticed that I could see through my skin to bones, sinew, and muscle. It did not seem surprising. What was unusual was that a watery and dry quality had come together in this peculiar way. With utmost slowness and care to keep my attention focused, I spun around. I brushed up against something with soft hairs or whiskers—maybe it was fabric. My hips deflected something soft. Through a jellylike filter I could still see my surroundings. The trees, the school, the ocean.

Sae came over to check in on me, sensed something was unusual. "Laura." I vaguely heard her call out my name. I could not immediately reply. I was in the middle of a spinning motion that I could not voluntarily quit.

"Laura," this time more emphatically, but in a whispered tone, because we were not really supposed to talk with one another while in a practice or performance mode. Sae reached out to make contact with me and repeated my name in a plaintive tone.

"What's up! Laura, can you hear me?" Sae gestured and her directness snapped me out of an altered mind-body.

"Sae," I said, relieved as if we had not seen each other for a long while. I was grateful that she was there. "I'm fine," was all I could offer.

"What's going on with you, Laura?" Sae asked, but words were still not forming. I was caught in a freeze-frame between realms.

"I got so into the moves I kind of lost myself," I heard myself reply, acutely aware that Sae began observing me in a focused way.

"You were moving in a slow circular pattern," Sae probed. "I hate to say it—like a broken record. There was even a curious skip to your movements."

"Weirdly I felt out-of-body, or to be more specific, in a body with others." I paused. It sounded absurd. "This probably doesn't make any sense."

Sae was shaken, I could tell. Maybe details were best left unsaid or saved for another time when we could better go about coming to terms with the weird interferences.

"Come again?"

"Being in a unified membrane together with others."

"I don't understand."

"Neither do I!"

"Did you just experience an ecstatic state?" she offered.

"There's no way to categorize it, Sae," I said, noticing my breath slowing down. "I felt an unexpected togetherness—as if time melted and I was here, in a different time, and here, now . . . and there were others."

Some of the other performers looked over at us and noticed that we were out of formation. Randy gave that look that said, "Come on, what are you doing?"—mild chastisement, implying that he did not want us to waste time. His time. I realized I was parched and needed to sit down.

"Can we find something to drink, Sae?" I asked.

She was already escorting me, with her arms wrapped around my upper arm and elbow. Walking felt peculiar as we traversed to Sae's spot where she had dropped her knapsack. She offered me a swig from her water bottle.

Randy was still staring at us, if not glaring. Sae shot him a sharp look that said, *back off*. We walked through the gauntlet of his gaze. He did not impose a question to either of us. I was suddenly a bit dizzy and plopped down by the knapsack.

Sae is such a caregiver. Always knowing when to give and when to take a step back. I noted how much I appreciate her kind ways. Really the epitome of magnanimous. Only that word carries the feeling of sensitivity toward others. Her graciousness never feels like a compromise. She is the first to call out gendered and raced assumptions and will not suffer fools.

"Thanks for intercepting with your usual impeccable timing, Sae," I said as I closed my eyes, now reclining with my head against her knapsack. I felt wholly in this dimension body-wise, yet I continued to have auditory sensations that felt outside the usual context. Isn't much of the universe made up of a substance that is imperceptible? Dark matter—is not actually dark—it is translucent, light is able to travel through it without resistance, it is seemingly without physical qualities, intangible.

Might a gravitational change be the cause? Maybe the anomaly I experienced was not that strange in relation to cosmic architectures. Space contracts perpetually. Stars burn out. Black holes swallow massive areas of space. There could be micro versions of black holes perhaps, crevices in the surface of space. Voids that might actually contain life.

"What are you thinking about?" Sae softly murmured by my ear. She had also gotten into a reclining position with her head sharing a space on the knapsack.

"That we are biocosmological life-forms." Craning my neck, I was able to look into her brown eyes. Everything felt okay again. Sae and I are Asian. Sae is Japanese American. My mother is Chinese, from Shandong Province, her hometown is near the Yellow River Delta, and my dad is a white guy with Armenian roots. He passes as white. His ancestral home is near Carahunge, the Armenian Stonehenge. He took me there once when we visited his parents. The megalithic structure's name translates as "speaking stones" because the air flow between the rocks causes a whistling sound, and there are some rocks with perfect curricular holes drilled into them that also might be the cause of the sibilance. There are two other persons of color in the troupe, Darius, who goes by the pronoun she, and Shabnam, also she. My perceptions are often triggered by the foreground and background noise of racialized violence that can get so micro as to disassemble into pulverized dust and so macro as to rearrange all modes of living into blocking unbudging masses. The tension is an atmosphere within an atmosphere and negotiating it brings on hypervigilance. The stress adds a burden of proof, as if I needed to justify my perceptions. What is real? Can anyone say for sure? We all have secret lives. Aspects of our lives that light passes through. Existence is but one dimension of our cosmic experience.

"Have you been in touch with your uncle recently?" Sae queried. She changed the topic to help me get my bearings, I guess. My uncle works at one of the LIGO observatories. A Laser Interferometer Gravitational-Wave Observatory. He updates me on the status of gravitational waves in the universe. Even though they are pervasive in time and space, they are remarkably difficult to record and observe. It is true, I do riff off his metaphors. Gravity is one of my obsessions. If the oceans exhibit the intense effects of gravitational pull with the incoming and retreating tides, surely our bodies, filled with liquid, of weight and matter, are equally sensitive to the gravitational attraction of the sun and moon, of all masses in space. Dark matter passes through the body, through the Earth's core, through the cosmos.

We talked about my uncle briefly and then we grew quiet. The others eventually passed by us, waved, and indicated that they were leaving. We had been resting awhile. Time seemed to stand still. Sae agreed that our nap if it was a nap seemed to last a split second or an eon.

"Let's walk over to the place where the light was." I motioned to Sae. She looked hesitant but agreed to my suggestion. The atmosphere was overcast. Dampness hung heavy in the air. Someone's car radio played in the distance. The rhythms echoed the lapping waves. The tops of the trees were whooshing and bending. Many of the residents who live on this island were returning from work. We passed Sae's car in the parking lot and walked further, past the school and the fenced in space that Randy always focuses on to a patch of turf that once had grass growing on it but now was a burned-out median strip disconnected from the housing units and the park. It was a neglected patch in a crowded layout.

"I am willing to peel the blinders off, Laura." She spiraled; the ocean's reflection cast on her skin. "Let's do this." Now she was committed. "Submit to the light, submit to the darkness."

"Let's hope I wasn't hallucinating, or let's hope I was . . ." That foreboding feeling of insecurity. Not because of the feeling that the experience with the light gave me, rather, the feeling of questioning action. And that's usually when I take fatal action. Because there is nothing left to do.

"You were not hallucinating; I can tell definitively."

"How?"

"Because I could see you in the light, there was a numinous quality."

"You realize now you don't make sense." The streak of horizon glowed red in the distance, on the water. "That said, that's it, you totally nailed it." That red stripe. It commanded attention. "Like a womb space, being in the column of light was a kind of incubator of being." Sae was radiant, with the tint of red from the developing sunset cast on her. "Maybe there isn't enough light today."

"Wasn't it here where I interrupted you?" Sae stood at the exact spot where I was a while ago.

"That's it, that's the spot." We went with a heuristic approach to the unknown.

"Let's stand here together and see if we sense anything."

I joined Sae. Nothing happened to us. Initially, nothing changed. But one thing I could say is that sounds were intensified. The waves crashed in tonal multidimensions slamming the rock barrier reverberating the air, my body. As the water retracted against the sand the hushed lapping blended with other noises. A congregation of seals perched on a huge outcropping of rocks bellowed and yelped. Their fatty bodies plopped against each other in loud liquid slaps. They pressed into one another making purring sounds. The way their fur rubbed up against another, that friction, was palpable. The lyrics emanating from a car nearby were super clear. Frank Ocean was there, if in vibration only. His song unfolded in a synchronized choreography with the ether. Iterations of his song would travel through time, returning to the present on each replay. Each time it sounded it moved onward through spacetime. Sae's cardiac rhythms were syncopated, the sounds of her beating organ pronounced. I heard her shoes slide against the gravel. A fluttering rush of gulls flying off into the approaching night could be heard. A stirring wind.

"Anything?"

Should I reveal this new sensitivity to sound? I did not know. Was I placing too much on Sae's shoulders? She engaged a watchfulness for her friends, made sure they were okay.

"I got distracted by all the noises around here. You?"

"Laura, come closer." Sae motioned me toward her. "We need to be closer." She had a dazed look on her face. Wan. I shivered out of concern as I neared in.

"I'm here, next to you."

"Laura."

In the time that followed things became vertiginous. I felt loose in the knees. Sae went slack also. We no longer articulated in spoken phrases. We did not use our mouths. Yet we were communicating. Somehow capable of thinking within each other's thoughts. The air seemed hotter.

Dryer. I tried to indicate to Sae that I was here, with her. With a jolt I moved so that we were hip to hip. There were shadows everywhere and no shapes, or everything had become translucent. Static. I could look though Sae, within Sae. In doing so I also saw others. Presences.

"Sae!" I choked out a cry.

"Laura." I faintly heard her call my name, as if distantly, though I knew that Sae was standing next to me. We were still resting our hips against one another. A desert wasteland materialized. People grouped around us. Some were singing and waving their hands. I was delirious. "Who are you?" I ventured into the dry hot air. "How did we get here?"

INCHOATE REFERENCES

What cannot be said will be wept. Sappho, circa 1900, a book of translations, Sappho's voice transcribed into a different language, not the one she spoke or sang. Sappho, born in the sixth century BCE, on the island of Lesbos. What is not wept is gestured, pantomimed, danced. What is not danced is repressed, stored in the body's vault. Such regimes of containment are real, are solitary confinements. Grief and trauma are locked away in cellular tissue, near vital organs. The repressed data becomes a significant aspect of the body, its historiography. Cellular tissue carries carries critical data and instructions like a black box. The black box is a diagnostic kit. There are prohibitions against opening it up, a black box filled with grief and trauma. Information is often too hot, too triggering. The body that stores the information prefers not to revisit it. Some archives never get cracked open. Some go to the grave. Some get passed down to the next generation as DNA, muscle memory, epigenetic influences, culture.

The traumatic data will not rest. It will fester. Still the body attempts to hold the trauma in, has made a lifetime pact, a promise to carry it. The hurt tissue is cordoned off, its holding cell is restricted space. Just enough blood and oxygen are permitted through the barriers to sustain the traumatic information. The self, also known as the mind-body, performs intuitively, attempts to prevent the hurt from metastasizing, from gaining leverage, from taking total control. There is a sensation of violence when probing the vault, in unloosening the sutures, in returning to the site. Sharp pain results in a reckoning of release.

Time passes. Amnesia sets in. What was stored away is relabeled, recategorized. No longer recognizable. An estrangement occurs. A castigation. A refusal. Crises breach the databases, the athenaeums, the storage facilities. Soon enough there are fissures. There is reexposure, there is rupture. Eventually canisters leak. Files become corrupted.

There is said to be a way of organizing sentient time—history, but the information is inconclusive, bleached, scrambled, missing. The stockpile of remains are compressed into sedimentary, metamorphic, and igneous formations. The amount of content is viewed as geological stripes and layers. There are items of interest. There are things. Tools of use. Objects of adornment. Weapons of aggression. Functional domestic items. Buried in the dirt, heaped in dumps, consigned to storage units, placed in tombs. Some of the languages we have encountered remain indecipherable. We linger especially over evidence of the heart's information. Songs of love, lyrical effusions, the talismans of desire. Gifts exchanged, furtive notes slipped between parties, promises made in the form of whispered pacts. Seductive language. Language so tantalizing as to be liquid. Nonhuman love that circulates. Puffs of pollinated air, aquatic creatures enjoying their habitat, mountains loving trees. Plants luxuriating in the sun. Mostly ephemeral expressions that have long since dispersed.

What remains are trinkets constructed from precious metals, glass, and hard fired clay: votive figures, gold costume ornaments, a gold seal with a griffin, an ivory plaque, a death mask from the first grave circle, a vase with an octopus encircling it, a snake goddess from Knossos, and silver goblets displaced long ago from where they originated. *There is a Pylos before a Pylos, and there is another besides.* The classical proverb was written on a placard and was found among the artifacts. This caused us to consider the subtle differences of repetition, recurrence, and reproduction as it relates to people coming together to live, love, and work as a community.

The Linear B and Linear A tablets were originally found at Nestor's palace at Pylos. We found them in a cache with other artifacts from elsewhere. Pylos made us wonder if it was a place similar to what this place might have been like at one time. Pylos edged a shoreline, was prosperous, life sustaining. We can visualize a bay so blue and expansive. From the time that the Linear A tablets were discovered until now, when we have unburied them, no one has been able to decode their precise meanings. We take heart in this. The anomalous nature of the text inspires us. Our ledger too is possibly vague and obscure to others who do not live like we do, do not know us, have never heard of us.

The scrolls we found in the cache depict floating worlds. Visually we travel through misty peaks from one mountain range toward another, passing through gorges of needle-laden pines, occasionally encountering various people on foot, or riding horses, sometimes resting, or having a picnic under a tree. In several of the scrolls there is scant presence of people. Maybe a boat in the cloudy distance, a few shaded dwellings, rock outcroppings leading to steep peaks. A long, tall scroll focuses on a river, undulating from the top quadrant to the lower portion of the painting. The banks of the river are rounded and shrubs and trees cluster nearby. The feeling is calm, tranquil, remote. The river is the composition and the composer. The surface of the painted scroll has faded into mud colors and there is little contrast. We have to focus our gaze carefully in order to recognize the dimensions within the expanse. The rendering of ecological details is an alternative language of communication involving color, shape, tonality, and texture. If we had more materials available, we would opt to draw and paint. We make do with signage, marks, symbols, and letters. The sun and the moon, birds with remarkable plumage, fruits and flowers, other creatures with shiny fur, striped or dotted, and baring impressive teeth and claws show up, amaze. Lovers with robes undone rustle in silken sheets. Amorousness expressed in endless postures and positions. Deities sheathed in marvelous layers of fabric floating in swirls of color above verdant landscapes give a sense of a luminous psychic spiritual order, hinting that mundanity and the sacred are not mutually exclusive. Clouds are a spiritual valence. Other scrolls we dug up depict cacophonous events: battles, mayhem. Clashing spears and knives drawn, faces grimacing. Bloodshed. Conflagration. Black clouds of smoke. Violence for the imagination.

Another area we excavated contained many random objects that were easy to uncover. More talismans, votive figures, brooches, hairpins, masks. A crown that caught our attention had an intact placard. *Yorùbá. Beaded Crown (Ade) of Onijagbo Obasoro Alowolodu, Ògògà of Ikęrę.* It was made from intricately arranged glass beads of beautiful coloration, sewn into a conical basketry form that features a gleeful bird perched at the top. The crown has three tiers and on each tier on both sides (front and back) are representations of people. On the third tier are also representations of two equestrian figures. We imagine how the crown might be able to rewire psychic networks. The crown channels power from all spheres of life. There is a playful merging of forms. The beaded flaps that hang down on its sides would accentuate the face of the king who wore it as an emblem of healing and knowledge. We imagine how it felt to wear it in that time. We model it for one another. Dances are formed to honor the crown, the energy it exudes, the energy it inspires. We don the multistoried crown and celebrate kinship. Performer and audience are synonymous. Ramifications from the past come through us as synapse and pulse.

We found a ceremonial object that is made of leather. With it was a book that gave information about the artist who constructed it. The book describes the circumstances of the artist's life and the context that is important to know when considering both the artist and his creation. We held the leather shield gingerly. It depicts a bird with spread open wings receiving or generating rays of energy symbolizing the bird's heart-mind-soul-spirit. We intuit the deaths that were acknowledged in the care that went into its creation. Tentatively, carefully, sensitively, we tap our fingers against the taut hide. The shield resembles a drum. Buffalo stomping their hooves on the prairie grasses resound. Many large animals sprint into the distance; their breath forms clouds of moisture. Sumptuous brown fur curls in the wind. The buffalo are all around us now. Their radiant dark eyes gaze at us. We gaze back into their soft luminosity. There is sorrow and unrelenting fear, also knowledge—knowledge of the circle of life that inextricably links with death. Cycles of becoming placing everything in relation.

The energy from the shield gives us insight into the power of convergences. The buffalo are allies. We've never encountered a buffalo, yet we sense them. We will honor the buffalo. We honor He Nupa Wanica, Joseph No Two Horns, the Hunkpapa Lakota artist who constructed the shield at a time of settler colonial violence that came in many forms including land dispossession and attempts at cultural annihilation. We understand that the conditions in which we live are a culmination of this history. We study drawings made on paper torn from a ledger that are attributed to Joseph No Two Horns. His spirit is present. We do everything we can to aid the dead. Beating the rhythm of the spirit world has consequences. Worlds join and rejoin. The past summons us. The future summons us. We are between worlds, between timeframes. If history had a repetitious tendency, that repetition has now ceased. In its place are joints and joinings. The aftereffects are present, as reverberations through the seams of time. In our bones we feel the forty battles that He

Nupa Wanica fought in, from the time he was fourteen years old. The gunfire of the federal troops ring in our ears. Powerful resistance is palpable now, through the drum, the shield. The greenest grasses waving in the wind encompass our imagination. The solidarity of the warriors can be felt. Custer and his troops were crushed. The Battle of the Little Bighorn was a victory, and freedom songs rang out across the prairies.

The relentless motivations of settler colonial malice persisted, eventuating a name change for a place and for people who lived here for decemmillennium. That name, the name of the nation-state we refuse to utter. The land is returned as Turtle Island in our ledger.

Other numerous caches exist like this one. Places that housed treasures, riches, spoils of war, the wealth of the elite in the form of art, jewels, and currency. We smell the blood on the currency and on the gemstones, and it is mixed with the paint that was used to create sumptuous landscape paintings of a new paradise in garden form. The intricacies of construction enthrall us, and we study the techniques of labor. Monetary value has no effect or purpose in the way we live our lives.

Recently, what turned up really baffled us, but then we figured out its significance. A storage room of forensic evidence. Rape test kits, personal belongings, blood-drenched or soiled. Objects in plastic bags, labeled. One bag held the notebook of a young girl who had been abducted from her bedroom in the middle of the night. In it were drawings of unicorns, lollipops, and rainbows.

The chronological order of events is obsolete. Everything that turns up in our presence is the present. Some of the stuff we leave where we find it.

DReam OF

Breathe in the present, exhale history. Hysteresis creates traces, as lags are traces. The experience of more than one magnetic moment in any given magnetic field brings a different valence to the way history is experienced. We ourselves are confirmation of how history continues to depend on the present to carry it along and also how dependent we are on the residual infrastructure of history. After major disturbances, organic life continues to forge movement out of nonfunctioning relics. The scope of our struggles is partially inherited and also distinct to our era. Our cultural mentality changes at a pace as does our DNA, RNA, and the microfloral communities that live on and within us. We change with climatic conditions.

Dependency models are preferable. Competition only increases fallibility. It is blatantly obvious how interdependent we are, not only with one another in our community but with the world, all presences who world within the world. Worlding is active tense interaction. Two endstagers passed away and the infant that was being reared in the nursery died in close succession. The present tests our resolve. We feel a weakening hold on life. The algae in the air lung continues to grow strong, one ray of hope. More celebratory ceremonies to commemorate life are in order. We dance our hearts out on every occasion. Daydreams bring gauzy scintillations to the fore, or eldritch montages. Touching ameliorates stresses. We fondle in the day, and we fondle at night. Massage tight muscles, tickle the folds.

The continuation of lineages brought us to where we are at today. Sentient life in all forms rely on passed down retrievable knowledge stored in the body. An organism is actually a multiorganism. This means that. Other organisms in our bodies store and retrieve knowledge from within their bodies within our bodies within the world's ecosystem. Our plasticity is based on a host of factors, essentially the cooperation of others who help shape the flexing.

This is a time of extremely diminished diversity. Perhaps our era is similar in reverse to the stage when life initially took off on this planet, splitting and mutating, going down unique pathways. Single cells seeking multiplicity with each fork in the evolutionary road. Perhaps we are on course to return to the elemental beginning within a timeline.

Flailing arms and bulging eyes are ways to signal alarm or fright. We cannot scream. Our vocal cords cannot support high decibels. Vocal folds have atrophied. We are accustomed to close-distance vocalizations. There is little need to broadcast our voices over a long range as we live together in tight clusters. If there is something that triggers the need to communicate preparedness and gather attention, we tap a metal utensil against the metal necklaces we all wear. The sound travels quickly and is effective. The way one taps, and the duration of the tap, can indicate multiple messages. We have a way to signal that we must come together. We assemble and concur. There has not been a direct assault on us by other humans for generations. Our greatest challenge continues to be subsistence. This challenge is our meaning. Since we do not have much to sustain us on reserve, we must always work to generate what nurtures us. The social situation of subsistence is a collective effort.

They look lost, they can't dance, one holds a bone, the other a breastplate they pulled from underneath their shirt, an underwire contraption. "Do not worry!" we intone. Vocalization is more of a murmur. Effectively we use mirrors to redirect light. With angles the light bounces, lands on their white reflective suits. Springs back at us, illuminates us. Double shadows appear. There with there, overlaid. The light from the mirrors flashes against rocks and the windows of the homes in their world, this world. The ocean is glowing, is flashing. Eyes flash. Their teeth flash.

Our brief sojourns into other worlds of unintended exposure become regular. The performers are familiar. They dress in their suits, and we watch them move into position. Even though they are dressed identically we remember who goes where. We've grown accustomed to their names. The acoustics are less muffled coming through as surround sound. The fluttering wings of birds, the lapping waves on the shore, police sirens, the groove of a song being projected by a car radio. We hear with a greater fidelity.

The person's name is Darius, we hear her name called out by the other performers. She struggles with something near her left foot. Wrangling with negative space is a repetitive motif of the performance. She kicks into the air. Darius! Her name rolls off our tongue. Mirrored light gleams through a rainbow. Shabnam recognizes us. She was the first to establish a connection with us. Sae is nearby, she too senses us. Another presence named Laura is still as stone. Light from the mirror lands on her temple. She tries to brush the light away as if it were a physical object, a living thing. She scratches at it like it tickles her. Gently we encourage the light to stroke her. The illumination from the mirrors causes fluorescing. Tiny particles from the ocean cling to their suits and also our skin, picking up light waves. Everyone is prismatic, casts light. Laura is again inanimate. Laura! "Laura, embrace the light!" in a chorus we flicker. Jay spins toward us. Mia, where is Mia? we wonder. There, yes, there, collecting pebbles in the wave's froth. Mia seeks hard surfaces, compact rock.

Laura continues to hold a stationary pose as wind currents blow over her frame. The ocean entices the wind to gust. The tide is coming in. Our mirrors like the surface of the ocean are alive with reflections of liquid luminosity. The glassy expanse of water swallows the reflections. The sun beams onto the ocean, and the ocean beams the sun back to itself, simultaneously gulping it in. Sea plants absorb the sun's rays. Fish swim through the opal light, head deeper, their silvery, quinine crystal scales cause polarized light to ghost and glisten. Wavelengths shiver. Reflections caused by their birefringent outer layer give certain fish the ability to hide in plain sight. In great schools the mutating shapes of their swimming bodies refract and scatter radiance. A synchronicity multiplies intensity.

Familiarity brings affection. We are better at understanding the choreography of their gestures. Their features are less pixelated and hazy. Early on it was as if the magnification tripled and sometimes quadrupled them. Laura appeared in doubles and then doubles of a double. There is distortion, a sensation of looking through reflective surfaces, like layered glass coated with mercury. Sometimes they are hypermagnified, other times, they appear totally out of focus, vague. Synching our perceptions requires undivided concentration. Within the mirrors we catch sight of them with us together in a frame. A few days ago, a cat appeared suddenly like a mystical occurrence, strutting past the parked cars until the furry animal reached the tree stump. We hoped to encounter a cat. It climbed up onto the stump and slept there in a curled position until the sun set. The cat was utterly adorable, the epitome of cute. On another day Jay tried to pet it and the cat punched them with her paw.

Yesterday the performers were not here. The person who studies herbs and flowers, Embla, appeared together with her partner. Under one arm she carried a bag of books, under the other, a basket of fronds she must have picked around the perimeter of the park. She spoke quietly with her partner. They sat on a bench and studied the underbrush closely. She pulled out an enormous book from her bag, and when she opened it up, we saw an array of colorful, lifelike images of birds and plants on the pages. Elaborate colorized etchings of a hornbill with a rambutan in its mouth, an olive-backed sunbird collecting nectar from a Turk's turban flower, a spectacled spiderhunter with its beak in a scarlet passionflower. When talking to Ask she referred to some of the images of birds and plants as missing persons. Birds and flowers that had passed out of existence, gone extinct, in a short span, she said, in less than one hundred years. She burst into tears as she described to him how birds were killed for their plumage. The feathers were used to make elaborate women's hats in the Victorian age. The killing stopped fairly recently, but it was mostly too late for these creatures. They discussed habitat loss, acid rain, human encroachment. They were critical of certain forms of land management and cultivation processes. They used the word *war* to describe horticultural impositions by settler colonists who raided, razed, then established their settlements on stolen land. As we listened, we curled into a fetal position beneath the boughs of plants by their feet, quite like the pose of the cat we saw. Eventually Embla and Ask became aware of us. We remained as still as we could for as long as we could.

We paid close attention to their conversation. The tone shifted. The substance of the discussion shifted. Embla regained her composure. She went on to elaborate the development of nanobiotic plants that could emit light and could potentially replace electric lamps. There was a lab that was working on embedding nanoparticles into plants, inducing them to give off light. Luciferase, the enzyme that gives fireflies their glow, was successfully engineered into the plant's cells. The scientists involved were hopeful that eventually this biotechnology could be used to convert trees into self-powered streetlights, using the tree's metabolism. Other groups of scientists had already designed plants that could sense explosives, she said. Ask began to speculate how these changes might alter the sounds the plants make and what cascading effects might occur in an ecosystem when vibrational tonality was out of sync.

There was noise all about, but it was difficult to tell what was making the noise. Embla and Ask had hushed voices. Besides them all we could see were blurry shapes whizzing around us, distracting and unusual. We could smell rich, greasy odors. Smoke emanated from somewhere, indistinctly. There must have been several small fires burning to make this much thick gray exhaust. A sensation churned in our stomachs. We moved away when the smoke overcame us.

a VOID IS CaLLeD a VOID FOR LaCK OF INFORMaTION

Charlene fixated intently into the voided shadow that flexed in front of her. Contourless, liquidlike undulations defied explication. The shadowed area was both fuzzy and nondescript, contradictorily immense, a container of multiples, heavier in terms of gravity than the surrounding foliage, dense as to be swollen, enflamed, molten. Her eyes made scale adjustments, but still she couldn't understand what she was encountering. The intensity of the enigmatic occurrence caused her breath to constrict, and when she released the air from her lungs, she convulsed with the exhalation. Repeatedly she shuddered, sucking air into her body, tugging at the troposphere, enveloping cloud formations reaching her lungs. The release of the air in her lungs became vaporized, traveling within the nonspace that was a dimensionless physical constant of electromagnetic interaction between elementary charged particles.

The cirrus clouds previously floating above her head in ringlets relocated, taking the form of white petals in numerous flower clusters, creating a pattern of pinpointed light. A microuniverse momentarily replaced a macrocosm, the flowers were heaven, and if not necessarily brimming with holy detritus, certainly celestial, containing starlight and amplitude that radiated in all directions.

Voided shadow was how she instantly thought of the presence that seemed to want attention—it connected to her gaze. The flowers growing near her crested in a wave formation that swept them up, overturning their petaled crowns. This was doubled by what the clouds were doing above her. She became acutely aware of her surroundings. The identityless blob intensified how she perceived reality. A feeling concave, a smooth arc of sensation.

Emotions rushed along the curved slope of a clear bowl that was full of invisible substances. Her capacity to feel expanded. A capacity to give and receive responses was how the void related its importance to her. The greenery, the soil, the pebbles, the many organisms that shared an ecosystem were connected to her by a mutual life force. She wasn't sure if the voided shadow blob thingy was something to fear, to be repulsed by or savored.

White flowers nodded. Many growing entities enveloped her focus. All that was growing around the void became more detailed, more intricately relational. As if under a microscope, she could visualize with magnification every root, every stem, every petal.

A beetle bore into the tangle of grasses by her feet and disappeared into the underbrush. When the beetle appeared again it shone as a metallic object, iridescence gleaming under the sun's rays. It then melted into the green foliage, seeming to become leafy, stepping out of the order of Coleoptera. The beetle's circuitous path drew her in, the clouds drew her in. The main arteries in the dirt were lines of convergence. Roots coiled along the ground, dipped into the soil, signaling subterranean connection. How had the clouds been drawn toward her, and the beetle?

Occurrence developed around an energy field that looked to be a mirage yet could not be ignored. The displacement and rearrangement happened before her. Fata Morgana, distortions that involve images stacking, receding. But not on the horizon this time, for what she perceived was within an ecosystem of dense growing entities, not at a distance. Light from the sun or a reflection were not immediately responsible. Matter once too miniscule to perceive, in her case, due less to her physical makeup—hominid, mammalian, more about cultural perceptions—came into focus, the structural underpinning of terrestrial life suddenly made apparent. She now was aware that everything was in motion. Movement lubricated the world of objects in a bath of chemicalized locomotion. Her heartbeat's rhythm fit in with the ambient rhythms that gave the environment its pace.

Dirt was anything but still, rocks were not still, the sky was a panorama of shapeshifting dimension and amplitude. Time cannibalizes electromagnetic fields by counting and consuming digits that appear to disappear in a cycle of ingesting that does not leave anything out of its purview. Aggregated to appear as atmosphere, making appearances as light and shadow, electrons are both particle and wave. Other elementary particles have no mass, such as photons making up the quantum of the electromagnetic field. "*Et sic in infinitum*" (and so on to infinity). This phrase was written in cursive pencil marks on the borders of a drawing that the astrologer-physician Robert Fludd made in 1617, depicting "the nothingness that was prior to the universe," from his *Utriusque Cosmi*. The drawing is not a totally dense black square, not totally opaque. It is scratchy. A space for coming into being. *Aenigmate*—through a looking glass darkly. An enigma, or mundane reality in its fullness. She understood the drawing as a representation of an electromagnetic field of potential. Seeing nothing and then the realization that the nothingness is the about-to-burst potentiality of a universe coming into existence.

What she grasped as ecology in the fullest sense was a cosmic framework that included dark matter, contracting space, quantum dynamics, exploding stars, event horizons, as well as terrestrial environments and organisms. Nature had restorative powers. She conceptualized the ecology as a nurturing whole. Now she realized that the ecology—ecosystems of great diversity—were reality itself, in all of its largess and infinitesimal configuration, touching everything, a factor of every encounter. A dense core of a dying star that took eons to cool was but one element of the cosmic ecology known as the universe. Attraction and repulsion, constituting and destroying—limits were inconceivable.

In the time that she had forgotten the beetle, they—the beetle—had reappeared. A blue milkweed beetle. There are no "its." "It" is far too anonymous, generic, and detached as a marker for any living presence. The beetle was a person seeking to enrich their personhood. A whole, rich complicated life unfolded within a complex environment. The beetle had desires, intentions, methodologies, modes of perception. She read at whatsthatbug.com: "larvae are obligate root feeders, and adults eat the leaves of larval host plants: milkweed and oleander. Females are highly polyandrous, while males engage in extended periods of post-copulatory mate guarding." Would she venture a guess as to the beetle's sex? The sexuality of the milkweed and the dogbane corresponded to the life cycle of the blue milkweed beetle. The blue milkweed beetle required that their nursery consist of flowers. Emerging in early summer, beetles thrived while the plants bloomed.

The beetle was not a solitary automaton, acting robotically according to instinctual drives that could not be altered, though instinct played a role in navigating the tangle of vegetation. The beetle was in the world with her. She and the beetle mostly did not have to contend with one another, she thought, but then realized how humancentric the impression was. The beetle was subject to a humanly engineered domain, and humans were dependent on beetles for many of the roles they play in seed dispersal, bioturbation, pollination, and nutrient cycling. The beetle's social world involved encounters with other beetles, earthworms, other insects, birds, humans, other plants, and animals. *Hapless great apes, so full of themselves!* she thought to herself as she brought her face closer yet to the beetle. *My reality is with the beetle, of the beetle, as the beetle, not the beetle*, she mused, her breathing becoming gentle and regulated by her settled posture. She burst out laughing.

She was seated on the fringe of an outcropping of grass where it met a diversity of weeds that merged with thicker underbrush. Suddenly she shivered, the sun was lower on the horizon. The park had cleared out. She became self-conscious sitting there, alone. Alone with beetles. A particular beetle that becomes more active at night. The threat of random violence forced her out of her concentration on the beetle. She could easily be dragged into the bushes. By a human, or more than one human.

No, she was not going to be motivated negatively by fear. She stayed where she was as the skies swirled gassy magenta and fuchsia striations. The trees around her swayed slightly, and she took this as a benevolent sign to feel out her place on the periphery of a maintained area of the park. The smell of dirt and leaves grew thicker.

Focus for a sustained duration is what I need to do, she thought, exploring the feeling it gave her body. The tendency to scan over the surface level of the object-field was internalized by many factors. Looking too long and too hard had consequences. Studying conditions for transitional change was nuanced work. What had she projected onto the world? *Specifics*, she reminded her mind's eye. She was apprehensive of the gaze that focused like a spotlight on an object, diminishing the context. Part of the problem was the emphasis placed solely on seeing while ignoring or disregarding other sense perceptions. Sight was a convention of perception. Intellectually she realized senses do not stand alone. Sight is augmented by hearing, taste, touch, and something else unnamable. A billion synapses are responsible for each sensation as it registers between body and body. Touch travels through the body at a rate of nerve signals and hormonal release. Sensation does not typically happen in a vacuum.

What is the Rumsen word for an unnamable condition? She was not sure. Or the word for green? She recalled her father teaching her words for nature, *saka-ti* (grasses, weeds), and *moyoti* (a flying beetle). A smile crossed her lips as she mouthed the word *xoxoctic*, a blue-green color, it also signified "unripe." Her father's Nahuatl culture was passed down more tangibly than her mother's Ohlone language and cultural meanings. Fragments of lost memory reappeared amid the traumatic canceling. Grief pervaded everything. Sadness coiled in anger, and anger coiled in remorse. Sometimes she dissimilated in the face of her mom's reticence. "I am always looking for my mother. I will never know the depth or complexity of her stories. Many stories are so sacred, they cannot be repeated. They can be gestured to, but language wrenches their freedom. My mother's healing and my healing run parallel. I dream I will find myself in Indigenous plants, the soil, rocks, and the sky." Monologues loud and soft unspooled in her mind. She gently cycled through images of a decolonized future where trauma gets converted into joy.

While above her, sex. Stimulations and impulses. Much to do about nature paying attention. They desperately want to believe what they conjecture is true. These are characters of great pride. Only when they perceive others are in love with them do they burn. They overheard the warnings. Always swagger. What fire is in my hair? Why am I in ruins? Why are the trees filled with fruit? As if I was on stage for the first time, all alone. I caught the eyes of the flowers in my gaze. I do not know who reached out first. Something unlocked. The space opened. Sexual slander is catastrophic. They waste us. We are reduced to ashes. With ease. With total ease. Sharing women is more than sport.

Something her mother did relate about Charlene's grandmother clung. Her mother told her about how baffled Charlene's grandmother was by the transformation of Turtle Island by white settlers. "It is the same place, but it is not the same place," she would say, flabbergasted, and then would add, "how can this be the same place?" She would always end her probe with, "This four-billion-year-old home, we are here, the clutter can be cleared." Charlene's mom would always add with highest praise, "Such a lover." Sarcasm was not part of their rubric.

The violence that pulsates through white settler colonial patriarchal structures is negative capacity infiltrating blood, sweat, tears, land, and accumulative labor. A racist fraternal culture, a rape culture, a prison-industrial complex. The women he accused of recklessness. Names become slurs. Walk through, walk over, move through for a moment's titillation, a momentary swoon. An internal conflagration. The patriarchy that is also racialized touches all it wants, picks at will what it desires as a demonstration of dominance, dominion, holding the world, extracting from the world—life itself, held hostage. How could anyone not feel imposter syndrome when forced to fit into the formulation. And to be forced to pray to heaven on it. Shorn of hair, shorn of language. The construct, "woman" as a gender category is a cultural fabrication, the construct "animal" is also. Multiple channels scrambled. How then to tear it apart? Or stitch it back together in an altered semblance? The bigness of critique caused a burning smell of hyperbole to choke out thinking. Open awareness brings concerns with it.

She recoiled and then sprang back to her considerations. The skies were shifting. Thick, oily blue-scarlet clouds bunched by the horizon. Overhead a wind kicked up leaves and dust. The air circulating in her lungs pumped through blood vessels laced with sulfur, methane, the enzymes of rotting leaves, squirrel scat, and dog dander. A turbulent whooshing of atrial rushing pushed the pulse. "One woman plus one woman plus one woman will never add up to some generic entity: woman." The philosopher's words added a refrain to her thinking. She felt her place between forms, between formations, between theories and concepts, between intensities.

NIGHTTIDE, PLANT MOTIVATIONS, CHARLENE AND MILLY

There is a contemporary philosopher—she wrote a personal testimony of how she was banished from the academic post she had held for many years. Her banishment had social repercussions. She not only lost her job, her reputation, and her friends—she lost direction. All because the assertions made in her previous book too greatly deviated from prevailing conventions held about gender, sex, and power, presumably.

After the rift the philosopher pivoted toward ecology—florae specifically. Plants, especially forests, called her toward them, offered her a reprieve, sanctuaries she didn't know were available to her. Merging with verdancy helped recalibrate her sense of self. At a low point the only presences she felt embraced by were plants and trees. She told how they held her up, supported her physically, psychically, integrating her back into the web of life. In the thicket of dense foliage is where she noticed she had rejoined a forcefield of reciprocal energy. Within the communion of trees and plants she was able to learn again about togetherness and love. The trees aided her in reestablishing relations with humans, which had proven to be toxic, detrimental.

The philosopher, in her account of being rescued by green growth, had a realization as to how Western cultures had created an artificial division between what constituted nature and what constituted culture, that is, civilization. A profound alienation with nature (everything surrounding and including herself, actually) had been hard baked into her worldview. It took a major disruption to realize the rift. Once she did, she reassessed what she trusted, what she thought she understood; she questioned calcified habits of thought, received ideas hardwired to appear as self-induced, self-evident—natural! She interrogated the forms of conditioning that had created her identity.

In this division of life-forms, humans (white men) asserted themselves as superior makers of the world, assigning passivity to the earth, ecology, women, and others who were poor, or not racially white. Historically, as was Western rationale, the majority of the planet's population was considered passive, fundamentally incapable of rational thought. This was not remote history.

The philosopher, now in her sixties, realized latently the cumulative effects of this "great chain of being" formulation. She found herself castigated from the social circle she had depended on, paid allegiance to, participated in. Her network pushed her out, pushed her into social isolation. The philosopher was on to something, just like anyone who slips on the upward mobility ladder, the capitalist fever dream, the imperial wishful thinking machine that churns out proclamations of justice and virtue universalized to the point of oblivion. The rejection hurt, but it created a point of entry too. She began to understand how other forms of life extended themselves receptively. One of the first generosities she noticed was the plentitude of herbs growing in the cemetery where her father was buried. She harvested a sprig of purple thyme from her father's grave, tossed the crushed leaves into a salad, and felt the power of the plant's dimensional energy. The plant surely knew her father; it grew out of his remains.

One point the philosopher made that stuck with Charlene was her comment of how, when navigating implicit and explicit rules and mores of society she had been too mental. This at first seemed an overly simplistic point to make. And didn't the body—personhood—function on mental signals—the brain, an operating system? The brain as head of state made sense within an order where actions are dictated top-down by a figurehead, or a godhead of universal order. Mental activity is understood as powerful. More powerful, more important than physical activity. Society separates people into degrees of difference, often based on perceived mental capacity. There was the hierarchy again. This model gave little credence to all the participant members of an organism, an organization, a world. Anatomically a single organ does not function as all-powerful, with an unlimited jurisdiction of the body. It was prudent to critique one's becoming too anything, certainly too mental.

Charlene continued to sit under the vault of the cosmos thinking about the philosopher as her mind scampered over disjointed territories of consciousness. Her considerations arose and dissipated haphazardly. She had to engage contradictions in order to abandon them. She had to trip up on the cognitive interfacings between herself and the world. She gave space for the wild array of formulations that her imagination generated. Converting lifeways into commodifiable thingness perhaps is most antithetical to a holism with the environment, nature. Who maintains the reigns of production controls thingness. What does commodification demand? For example, whole forests of old stand trees sacrificed to make toilet paper. Mountain ranges of toilet paper. Trees cut, mulched, bleached, and processed into disposable items. Vast intergenerational networks of trees, shrubs, low-lying forest plants, and animals that lived within their canopies razed and displaced for disposable furniture, shredded into wood chips for lawn ornamentation. Unimaginable numbers of trees decimated to construct picket fences, to fabricate pencils, make telephone poles and railroad tracks. Pencils made in quantities as long as the distances of stars from this world. Houses made from wood, from trees. A necessity, dwellings. Wooden items in unending quantities, which initially did not appear troubling or threatening until one imagined wooden consumer goods piled up as high as skyscrapers, the skyscrapers crowded with wooden objects as weighty as all the birds on the planet currently alive and many who have perished before. Name any thing and then multiply it by millions, billions, trillions. Then retrace how it was made and from what living organism it was sourced. Thingification was also transmuted into digits, financialized units that streamed infinitesimally through electronic networks. She pursued the trajectory down a crazy rabbit hole. Not a rabbit hole, a humanly constructed chain of significance. No hyperbole was necessary when scrutinizing this model of world-making.

The philosopher now identified herself as a mutual citizen of Earth. She began to feel as a cell of nature, an integrated unit in a complex organism. The contours of her body did not end at the outer membrane of skin. She actively labored to produce intellectual capital. Her activities consisted of unaccountable gestures that produced effects both local and at times far-reaching, affecting the surface tension of reality. Her body transformed as it came in contact with other bodies. She was a white woman who lived in a nation that had actively colonized other cultures. She was a participant in global capital distribution as much as she was evidence of moist bodies: oceans, rivers, rivulets, streams, and lakes. The philosopher exposed the complexity of positionality; her life was an example of how and why someone could be a victim and an oppressor in a system of ecosocial trauma. The active shift in attention caused a ripple effect.

Testimonials can be resonant one moment and off-putting the next. A diagnostic probe is often messy, disruptive. Charlene felt compassion for the philosopher. She also felt frustrated and annoyed by her. The book the philosopher had written was a plea for a different order. It was a renouncement of the ways of living that had led to catastrophe upon catastrophe. Yet others had made these same arguments and they went unheeded, ignored, overlooked. Basically, the philosopher had given an animist understanding of the world her own twist. And with that impulse was a "born yesterday" quality to the philosopher's thoughts. The naivete of her privilege came across. Her epiphany followed the principles of a trope that was common in contemporary ideation. The philosopher was a privileged white woman, no doubt her learning curve was steeper, her insights less nuanced when it came to social divisions based on racism and inequity. "Who do you think you are?" she cried out, not referring to the philosopher per se, maybe to a cultural continuum that arrived in this here and now.

Then there was Charlene's response to the philosopher's emotional range in her writing. The philosopher had gained fluency with her emotions in a way Charlene felt she had not yet been able to. Charlene found herself drawn to the philosopher's intensified emotions, particularly her anger. Anger was a catalyst. It propelled. Anger was too much of a test for fear. Fear succumbed to anger. Sadness too could dampen fear. Maybe. What of the oxymoronic impulses of love! The philosopher's anger had an unusual taste in Charlene's mouth. A sound too. A throbbing tone that refused acquiescence, did not solicit acceptance. The philosopher (and, by extension, Charlene) had broken open, oozed out of herself. Anger had a fiery quality capable of igniting what it came in contact with. The philosopher's pitch was smooth and enveloping but anger was evident. Charlene did not detect vengefulness. What came across was refusal. It defined a limit, and that quality was powerful. The limit the philosopher set down in the sand opened up more pathways than it blocked.

This was the time of burning. Of social reckoning. Demanding change, making change. Of availing all mediums to amplify dissent at the corrosiveness of persisting hegemonic systems.

The philosopher's expertise was grounded in the cultural imaginary—

detecting what a culture knew and felt. The philosopher was a psychoanalyst and therefore understood the complex underpinnings of how spirit, mind, and body cohabitate, how social stressors and formative experiences influence selfhood. The book she wrote was an elegantly cogent message. A culture based on escapist consumerism would not necessarily endorse, let alone embrace her critique. The book contained a nest of inconvenient focal points that bore holes into the edifices of power. Again, it was true, the writing had its failings, the philosopher was fallible. Charlene appreciated that the philosopher didn't take an easy escape route. That she exposed her vulnerabilities. Charlene was convinced that plants would teach the philosopher to listen even deeper. All crises linked in fundamental ways. To address any one issue required addressing the web of interrelation.

The night sky squeezed Charlene's body into its expanse. She had been all in her head circuitously processing the philosopher's maxims. How airtight it felt, but also interesting and necessary to sort through the variables that the text availed. The sky presented a more expansive option. Particles of night encircled her and entered her orifices, her pores. She was porous. She became night at night. Within darkness she was indistinguishable. Possibly boundaryless. She could be sensed by others whose vision excelled at night because their retinas had more photoreceptors. She was perceived by smell and sound too. Touch. Night was a stimulant. The plants aided processing. The atmosphere was filled with reverberatory stimulations. She plugged into the animation of terrestrial expression. If there was a god, then she lived in god, as god, a microparticle of god—all connection, all material, all energy, all active and passive circulation.

No one was running from the scene where she sat, enveloped in night. The plant world is contemplative. Plant postures are meditative. Thinking involves a metaphysics of exchange in a quantum spacetime of flexing and expanding infinitude. Thinking is a complex multiorganism process. Cognition would not be possible if plants did not convert sunlight into sugars and breathable gases that the bloodstream delivered corporally. Even at night heliopotency is palpable. The warmth from the sun is absorbed in all bodies. She did not want to move from the warm grasses that she had been sitting on since late afternoon. Thinking with plants involved being with plants. Iron and oxygen, two of many chemical elements that coursed through her circulatory system, were as important to the plants around her. When dense little stars called white dwarfs explode, they send iron blasts through space. The main component of blood is the material of supernovas. The majority of oxygen is generated by marine plants: algal plankton, phytoplankton, and kelp. When considering personhood it is crucial to understand who and what we are in conjunction with.

In her mind's eye she visualized the philosopher superimposed by sea anemones bursting into cosmic rays. Oceanic breath twines with deep space explosiveness to form exquisite myriads. There was ocean inside her, and the air was oceanic. She could viscerally feel kelp swaying in the ocean's current modulated by the moon. "A swoon of particulates, petals, follicles." Had she thought this or heard this? The phrase had entered the horizon as extrasensory data. *Bending among.* The monologue in her mind was as sonorous as the ambient sounds around her.

The existential dread caused by environmental duress had a new name: solastalgia. It was palpable. Home and world were being destroyed, any sense of home and world. The confiscation and appropriation of everything that constituted life, with the explicit goal of ending others' worlds. The scale of the crisis had evolved to epic proportions with the prospect of the near-total extinguishment of life on the planet. Essentialism and polarization. Startling wealth and abject poverty. Lush abundance and total fallout. "I have watched as convenience, profit, and inertia excused greater and more dangerous environmental degradation. I have watched poverty, hunger, and disease become inevitable for more and more people." Prophetess Octavia Butler described rolling catastrophes in her fiction, and what she wrote was reality. An intermediary of a future who follows on the torn and mangled coattails of the past. The daily news broadcasted spectacular forms of suffering. She had to curb herself from itemizing the disasters. In the same newsfeeds a business-as-usual attitude attempted to occlude the facts of disparity and the suffering that arose.

Some institutions had thrived on disaster for more than five hundred years. Other forms were older yet and new forms emerged daily, stealthily, and also in plain sight. The algorithms moved quicker and what was extracted might be smaller increments. Because of speed and efficiency, more could be removed. There were regions on the planet that were completely razed of sentient life: dead zones. Surface mining including strip, open-pit, and mountaintop removal left gaping wounds in the earth. It was called overburden removal. Large corporations from the North appropriated rare minerals from precarious nation-states in the South. Near-total destruction of ecosystems resulted in the formation of inhospitable wastelands. Profits benefited few. Capital offshored. Sensoria eliminated. Sacredness dismissed. Lineages denied continuation.

Clouds moved in the company of stars. Fog drifted through the tall stands of trees. Formations arriving from other worlds traipsed through, signaled something distinct about atmospheric pressure. The clouds appeared momentarily ghostly, then again like puffy petals of a flower, then as huge boulders that melted into night, a sapphire immensity. Orion was no longer visible. His belt was shrouded by a thick haze that loomed overhead.

Charlene wrapped a woolen shawl around her shoulders as she reclined on her back, then she rolled like an egg so that her head was upright, able to see the migration of white forms frontally. Everything in her immediate vicinity was blanketed by night. The philosopher's psychological break coincided with Charlene's break, or so it appeared; chronological details were vague in the philosopher's account of her crisis. Both crashed while the world was crashing. Both were coming out of low points while upheaval prevailed.

She had recently started a relationship with a woman she met at the soup kitchen where she volunteered. A two-hour walk-in lunch period was offered daily in the hall of a local Unitarian church. The volunteers were instructed to refer to the recipients as clients. Milly, one of the clients, now lived with her. They'd become romantic partners. Milly was the one who introduced her to the philosopher. During their first direct conversation, Milly slid a book in her direction. The book had no cover, so Charlene did not know what to expect. It was grimy and barely held up as a book, and this intrigued her. It appeared to have emerged from the core of the earth, the dirt, the root level. The pages were curled inward as if they were a stack of leaves. Milly had slid the book in her direction like a calling card. Charlene accepted it. She then doled out peas and carrots with mashed potatoes and a sprinkle of parsley on a thick ceramic plate. Milly was unfazed by Charlene's lapse of composure. They did not communicate for several weeks. Charlene volunteered once a week on Thursdays. She was not sure if Milly had given up coming in. State and federally allocated resources were being retracted. Tent cities had sprung up in metropolises.

They found each other again at the fringes of the park in the same place that Charlene now sat. Milly was seated alone on a blanket gazing into the dense thicket of foliage. She seemed to be humming or purring. Charlene recognized Milly by the way she held herself. Her spine was upright, a straight trunk that extended to her crown. With feet underneath her sit bones and her sacrum exactly centered she appeared solemn and simultaneously kinetically charged. Charlene said something unintelligible under her breath, maybe just a sound to signal her approach. Milly slowly turned, glanced up, seemed pleased to see her. Milly's nails and fingers were covered in dirt, as if she had been digging in the soil and leaves.

Charlene joined her on the blanket without asking permission. Milly quickly glanced at her, but it was clear she was preoccupied by something. She continued to hum to herself. Charlene did not feel ignored, rather, there was a feeling of coming together. Everything looked greener somehow, motion filled. There was a breeze, so this was not unusual. She noticed that Milly had her shoes off, and her feet were as stained, grimy, and soiled as her fingers.

The humming in the air lulled Charlene. Her defenses dissipated. The solitary eye of the sun probed them. Both were bathed in lilac light tinged with an orange haze that made their skin tone shine. There was an exchange between them that happened outside the domain of human speech. Charlene began to be conscious of what she thought were Milly's thoughts, then realized she had become aware of the consciousness of other presences, not only Milly's. As Charlene looked closer at Milly's legs and hands, white veins became pronounced. The veins were thread-like, thin, and numerous. The veins were on the surface layer of her skin. The effect of the veins made Milly's skin glow multihued. The veins resembled mycelium, the underground network of fungi—its vegetative filaments are called hyphae. Fairy circles are made of hyphae. Trees communicate through these thin living threads. As she looked closely, Charlene noticed Milly's attention focused continually on the vegetation. While Milly was recognizable as human there was a plantlike quality that she exuded. She smelled of fresh earth, a mineral-rich rain-drenched smell. This impression would only grow stronger. Later, when they became intimate, sometimes Charlene could swear the woman's fingers were like thick rootlike extensions of the burdock plant, able to burrow deep in challenging, compacted soils.

Charlene sat on the blanket, inhaling the approaching night air. Milly did not move from her upright seated position next to her; she was silent except for the ambient humming that seemed to issue from her. Vegetative presences enlarged as darkness descended. Shadow and solid form combined. Milly blended in with the low-lying shrubbery. Foliage and the night sky fused together. The sounds of motor vehicles, breathing, heartbeats, dog howls, the wind, mechanized fans, and the humming became layered. When Charlene got up off the blanket Milly followed her home.

The morning after spending the night with Charlene at her apartment, Milly actually said, "I definitely needed repotting." They sat together drinking green tea. When Charlene returned from running errands Milly was still there, in a position similar to how Charlene found her on the blanket in the park: upright but not at all rigid. Milly sat near the window. The air in the room was tinted green. There was a faint aroma of chlorophyll.

Charlene would spend the night in the park like Milly had, for how many nights had Milly been out there she did not know. She had to do this to understand. Only by staying overnight, out of her comfort zone, would she be able to relate to Milly more fully. It was trauma work to remain calm and steady outdoors surrounded by night in a park in a section where the wooded outgrowth intensified darkness. The surprise was that she was not afraid. She was more relaxed than usual. She was cold but the chill was not unpleasant. She was back to thinking about the philosopher, wondering if the philosopher's forays into the forest occurred only in the day or had she ventured out at night alone also? Environments with a lot of plant and animal life felt more animated at night than during the day, though at the moment she did not see anything stir. Plant intelligence is about blending, merging with peer groups of plants. Charlene then heard the sound of rustling leaves and twigs breaking under the weight of a small mammal. She intuited shadows overlapping shadows.

Everything shifted suddenly when she became aware of a shape in front of her. The shape was human, crouched on all fours, straining. The gender unclear. With her arm extended, her hand open, Charlene rustled the fronds surrounding the shape. She continued to reach around the plant forms to try to see what lay there. She brushed against a tall stand of dark green plants. The ferns, sensitive, furled their megaphylls in response. The person responded.

For a moment in time, Charlene's senses wavered kinesthetically. Her senses were primed, overloaded. Bells sounded off in her skull. The spores of the ferns released in a microdust cloud. The sky made a whirring noise that was almost unbearable. The trees chattered among themselves and the ground cover snittered. The friction of the rocks was also noticeable. She felt transported back to the Cretaceous period some 145 million years ago when flowering plants first began to proliferate. Ferns could remediate contaminated soils, maybe that is why they grew in profusion here, at the edge of the park. She was in a grouping of sword ferns and the ferns hosted families of Reticulated Decantha Moths, *Thallophaga taylorata* moths, and *Diarsia esurialis* moths that circled around her head as if her head were a streetlamp giving off light. The buzzing from their wings was intense. Earth's gravity weighed down with an immensity she had not previously felt. Gravity, in this case, resembled attraction, drawing presences together.

Charlene observed the person's breath. The exhalations were visible in the darkness, and it did not seem peculiar to suddenly notice a person lying in the bushes.

INTO THE WORLD LIKE WATER IN WATER
CHARLENE

There is a time of night that feels infinite—as if time didn't exist and space itself has been absorbed into a totality of endlessness.

My thinking had loosened. I was out of thoughts. Stillness overcame me. My muscles relaxed despite the cold moist air that settled on me. I had a shawl and I wrapped it around my shoulders. The wool of an animal I didn't know warmed me.

My personhood seemed attached to the trees and plants around me. At a certain point, my body was almost unnoticeable to me. My mind seemed an extension of the sky. Pinpoints of awareness glittered. Consciousness shifted from internal animation to the external expansive world that rippled with subsonic sound and starlight.

Blood pumping to the heart coincided with the tree's uptake of water and nutrients. The sound of the tree's internal mechanism was pronounced. I was surrounded by vascular beings.

As I dragged my hand over some plants in the understory at the edge of the patch of maritime forest that existed in the park, I could feel energy accumulate as a forcefield. My hand gravitated to the plants. The hormone jasmonic acid is responsible for conveying touch signals within plants. I knew this intellectually having read a paper called "*Mimosa pudica*: Electrical and Mechanical Stimulation of Plant Movements." The information excited me so much that I contacted the lead author, A. G. Volkov, hoping for more information. Around me were a variety of fern—spiky yet tender. I sensed them out. I gently moved their foliage. I thought, *I am probably projecting anthropomorphically, because I sense the plants welcoming the gesture.*

As I touched the ferns, I noticed a person lying there. They lifted their head up toward me. The ferns continued moving in the breeze. I turned my attention toward the ferns and the moths that lived among the ferns—furry flying beings who were attracted to light. How did they perceive light? There were so many of them flying around me. Some landed on my hair. I did not dislodge them.

The form gently shifted from side to side, then gradually turned onto their backside. Their exhalations sounded like shishing. I registered the sound internally as a suggestion not to speak, which did not mean do not communicate.

Thought energies traversed between ferns, moths, night sky, my body, and the person peeking out from the vegetation. There was flickering energy of figure-ground, figure-ground. A breakdown in perception. Everything had shifted—how?

The figure moved again. Relocated. Then I saw only the ferns.

Moments went by. The ferns were brighter. Their fronds looked different from a minute ago. There was a luminescent highlight to the outer edge of the fronds. Perhaps it was their spores alighting on the night wind currents. Everything seemed distorted around the edges. Again, the sounds of crunching leaves and a scampering into the distance drew my attention toward the wooded area.

I got up, shook off a bit of leaf debris that had accumulated on my clothing, and swiveled my head around to see if any moths were still nestled in my hair. A few took flight and then insisted on landing again on my arms and forehead.

Something told me to get up and move about. I needed to increase the blood circulation in my lower limbs, which were nearly asleep. I decided to leave my blanket where I had been sitting for several hours and walk over to the ocean's edge. I had almost totally forgotten that I was near the ocean. There was a little path and I followed it. The tide was coming in. Salty water splashed against huge boulders along the edge of the shoreline. Swimming was not permitted here; the currents are too forceful. As I gazed at the ocean, I remembered the human form I left in the bushes. What was going on? Why didn't the encounter feel stranger than it did? Milly had prepped me for strangeness, and yet, meeting her wasn't strange.

Many marine mammals including sea lions, seals, porpoises, whales, and diamond dolphins live in the bay. The extensive gardens of flowering eel grass were a rich habitat for sea life. The lights of the metropolis lit up the skyscape, a numerosity of diamonds of light powered by natural gas-fired power plants and hydroelectric power.

Regardless of the prohibition against swimming, there was someone immersed in the water. They were using scalloped breaststrokes to reach the shore. Having attuned to the ferns and foliage, it took my vision a minute to adjust to the swimmer. I had hoped to shake off the unsettling feeling that I experienced among the ferns of someone nearby. Now to be approached by an anonymous swimmer in the middle of the night created an uptick in tension. Nonetheless I did not move from the shore. The waves were loud and high and curled into the sand. My feet got wet. My pants were now soaked.

I had a flashback from childhood while looking out at the water. When I was maybe five years old my parents took me to the ocean for the first time. I had only swum in manmade pools. We had a hotel room on the waterfront. Near nightfall, with the beach unpopulated, I insisted that I swim. I remember declaring to my parents that I intended to enter the water, but the story they tell is different from my account. They claim that I suddenly ran for the waves and plunged in without a moment's notice, without asking their permission. I seemed possessed. I disappeared among the crashing waves. They scanned the water and could not locate me. They said they screamed for me, but I did not reply. My memory is that adrenaline rushed through my body. I could swim but the waves were rough, and I lost my sense of equilibrium. The waves pulled me under and then above and I struggled to catch my breath, choking on water. When my parents eventually saw me, I was not alone. Four enormous sea lions had surrounded me and were pushing at me, helping me regain my breath. One clamped their teeth into my neck and gently dragged me toward the shore using their fore flipper to nudge me onto the sand. My parents grabbed me, and the saga ended without calamity. My parents were too stunned to lecture me. When I returned to the shore, the cohesion of my life returned. In the water, I was in another world. That other world accepted me. The terms of engagement were different and yet the same.

I came out of my reverie and noticed there was an additional person swimming in the night waters. They too were moving closer toward the shore. It had to be 3:00 a.m. by now. I had completely lost track of time studying the ferns while conjuring the philosopher's text.

The wave activity was hectic. White foam bubbled up and cascaded over the waves. The froth concealed the swimmers. One seemed frantic; both were having a difficult time making way to the coast. They were perhaps one hundred feet from one another. I didn't call out to them. The sounds of the waves were deafening at this point. My nostrils were filled with salt and sulfur.

Now up to my knees in the surf I felt the eel grass against my legs. Similar to the sensation of noticing a presence among the ferns, my instinct was to remain silent.

Motions slowed down, and there was a bright glare arising from the swimmer's bodies. At this point they converged on the shore. I stepped toward them. They both lay panting on the sand and waves washed over them.

As I approached them, they looked up at me. I felt a strange recognition, yet nothing was familiar about the situation. They both were men, both approximately twenty-five years of age, maybe slightly older. Both were wearing white pants. One was still wearing a white jacket. The other had on a white T-shirt. In their distress they had passed out. When one of the men regained consciousness, we together dragged the other swimmer further from the water's edge. As we knelt over him his eyes blinked, and he coughed. The other man carefully moved the hair out of his companion's face. To this point no one had uttered a word to another. I kneeled by the side of the man as he slowly regained composure. His companion did the same. It was clear they knew one another and had come from the same place. They were dressed in similar uniforms. They had identical cropped haircuts. They looked to be naval personnel.

As I knelt by the man's side along with his associate, I surveyed the water. On the tips of the waves, I thought I saw other figures. They bobbed in the froth. Their features were indistinct. I signaled to the men recuperating on the beach, pointed out to them the others in the water. The man who was in better condition looked over but said nothing. The other man was clearly in bad shape. He could not respond.

I walked away from the men on the sand to see if I could help the others who were still in the water. It was difficult to see them. They became obscured by the waves and then reemerged in the pale low light of the moon. A few of the men were actively swimming to shore, others were despondent, floated with their heads barely above the waves.

A commotion ensued. Pink and harsh blue flashing lights, sirens, tires breaking on loose gravel. Behind us three police cars arrived, officers ran forward with guns pointed at someone. The person's hands were raised as if crucified. Shots were fired. The man sank onto the pavement. The officers crowded the body. I could not see precise actions under the flickering lights. It all happened in an instant. Adrenaline coursed through my veins like molten metal. The sky was spotted with crass daggers of light, and I was worried I would have a seizure. Overcome by the cacophony of noise and light I stood, frozen in place, unable to dislodge myself from the scene.

Eventually I swiveled around after additional officers arrived. They began to cordon off the area. When I returned to where I had left the beached men, they were no longer there. The men swimming in the water were nowhere to be seen. At that point I slowly walked back to the wooded park to find my blanket.

navy personnel

Our cell was windowless and dank—there was one bulb buried into the thick plastered ceiling, that was all. Not seeing trees or plants affected me greatly.

I had a cellmate. We washed ashore together. We had been held in that building, in that prison hospital for months.

Previously we lived in the barracks and worked in another building and also on a drydocked naval ship that was used as an instructional demonstration site. We spent most of our working days on the contaminated vessel. We were members of the crew that had brought the ship back from the Marshall Islands. It (and we) had been irradiated by a thermonuclear blast. The toxicity levels were not disclosed to us in detail. Few asked pointed questions. We understood that probing would not be tolerated.

The contamination was not visible. We were told there was a thin film of radioactive material that needed to be removed from the ship as well as thousands of drums filled with liquid, presumably also radioactive material that had to be disposed of. Various government agencies were involved, but the navy directed the operation. It was classified work.

After we completed the assigned cleanup, we were placed in the prison hospital. It was actually a psychiatric prison. We were to remain there until we were discharged. The reason we were incarcerated in the prison hospital was because of our homosexuality. My cellmate and I managed to escape. My cellmate was my lover. His name was Edward.

I joined the navy to be in the vicinity of marine life, especially marine florae—for instance, eel grass, Neptune grass, and turtle grass, the billowy underwater gardens of grasses—and to be in the company of men. The primacy of sky and ocean appealed to me. Being for long stretches away from land, riding the high seas with a small community of tightknit personnel simplified life. Navy life was uncomplicated in many ways. When we were on the seas for weeks on end I could breathe deeply. The ocean does not give up secrets easily.

We were involved in theaters of international conflict yet there were occasions for relaxation and play. Sometimes we would anchor at a certain latitude and longitude in the middle of the ocean. A few of us would dive from the deck into the waves. One of the men would arrange to fetch us in a dingy. Afterward, after showering, we all were again dressed in nearly identical uniforms. Our tasks were the perfection of redundancy, and to do a good job was to be punctilious and neat. We were navy personnel first and foremost, sailors secondarily. This distinction was lodged subconsciously.

The Marshall Islands became what was termed the Pacific Proving Grounds for the U.S. Naval nuclear bomb testing program. Detonations began in 1946 with a series of bombs called Crossroads. These were the first postwar nuclear test detonations. The first of the Crossroads bomb series was dropped on Bikini Atoll on July 1, 1946. It was named Able, and the second, named Baker, suspended ninety feet underwater, exploded on July 25, 1946. The objective had been to test the impact of nuclear bombs on warships. A joint task force of the army and navy arranged a target of ninety seafaring vessels throughout the lagoon. Some of the ships were loaded with live animals specifically for the purpose of testing nuclear bomb effects on living beings. Pigs were included because their hair is similar to that of humans. Goats, rats, and other animals were also positioned onboard the boats for the bombing. Those bombs were both Fat Man plutonium implosion-type nuclear devices. After that the navy went ahead with additional series of atomic bombs: Operation Sandstone in 1948, Operation Greenhouse in 1951, and Operation Ivy in 1952. We arrived with our ship to Bikini Atoll in February 1954.

The navy forcibly removed the inhabitants of several islands prior to testing a series of bombs called Operation Castle. They were relocated to a neighboring island that could barely sustain life. It had no fresh water, little food, and very little habitable land. They were told that once the tests were over, they could return home. That was never a realistic possibility. Most Marshall Islanders were severely impacted. They were and are continually exposed to life-threatening levels of radiation.

We were brought to Bikini Atoll to assist with the detonation of the navy's biggest thermonuclear bomb test, euphemistically called Castle

Bravo, one of seven such tests that were part of the Operation Castle series. Echo, one of the tests, was canceled; the others went ahead. After the Operation Castle tests there were other series of test explosions to come. In total the United States dropped sixty-seven nuclear bombs on or in the vicinity of the Marshall Islands between 1946 and 1958. Several islands were totally obliterated by the explosions.

When Castle Bravo was detonated, we were on our ship, part of an enormous naval task force. Our ship was miles from the area of incidence, yet we were engulfed in a cloud that soon spread out seven thousand square miles, raining down pulverized radioactive coral that resembled snow. The fireball itself reached four miles in diameter. The impact of the Castle Bravo explosion was larger than imagined and the fallout considerably more significant. Personnel and natives on other islands also had to be evacuated after the detonation. The inhabitants of Rongelap and Utirik atolls were not evacuated before the blast and consequently suffered acute radiation poisoning. Gamma and neutron emissions made their way around the globe. We were not informed of this, though diagnostic tests were conducted.

Already the bomb test had been delayed by ten days due to adverse wind conditions as air currents swung from side to side. On the tenth day the command signaled with the go-ahead though the conditions were borderline. We were all up and prepared by 3:00 a.m. Tensions were high but sheer bravado ruled. I did not sleep for several nights leading up to the detonation, I don't think any of us did.

We were constantly told how important these tests were for national security and for civilization in general—that was the language used—these bombs were a *great step forward in progress*. There was a last-minute flurry to check emergency protocols, make sure communications were functioning. In the brief break I had, I went aboard the deck and felt the ocean's power holding us up. The moon was a waxing gibbous. The night was incredibly clear. The Milky Way draped over us like a gauzy jeweled scarf. I could make out Alpha and Beta Centauri and the Coalsack Nebula. The constellations Sagittarius and Scorpio were visible. I contemplated the sun's orbital rotation around the Milky Way, a route that takes somewhere around 250 million years to complete. I exchanged furtive kisses with my lover, who was also my commanding officer. That night offered no opportunity to find a safe space to be together. We briefly merged and retreated.

As morning dawned energies were high. At 5:00 a.m. an alarm sounded. We were to secure positions at our stations. The ocean had a film of starlight covering the surface making the salty liquid appear molten. A sick feeling ran through my veins, into the pumping chambers of my heart, and back out again through the pulmonary artery to the lungs. An intense discomfort settled in my abdomen. I could anticipate the blood surging and retreating into zones of my body. I wanted desperately to go on deck and simply breathe near the ocean, but I had to stay at the controls. The commanding officer was noticeably shaking but then adjusted his posture.

Before the detonation, we strapped into seat belts to protect ourselves from possible upsetting seismic activity or wave disruption that could cause injury if we were not secured. We were instructed to remain at our work positions; under no circumstances should we venture on deck. Curious questions formed in my mind: *Is it possible to see the surface of an object without seeing the object itself?* then, *Is the surface always part of the object?* My brain tried to countervail the impending event with thought puzzles. I began to question aspects of perception. How sensing was partial, contextual. The body is wired to respond to conditions favorable or adverse. Most stimuli are ignored. Intrusive thoughts fluctuated at a staccato pace. Another nagging, jagged question. *How to imagine the dispersal of a megaobject?* I was up against the limits of my imagination. In a haze of speculation, my sense of sound and sight halted momentarily. I felt a sixth sense, not fully formed, and my sense of smell was heightened. Everyone had a cup of coffee by their monitors. In that momentary blur, all I could sense was the stringent, acrid smell of the hot beverages combining with the distinctive chemical smell that wafted off the treated fabric of the control room chairs. The ocean too gave off a powerful scent. Saline reached my nostrils and coated hairs and skin with a slightly abrasive residue. Our bleached uniforms, the metallic smell of the boat, and the drifting seaweed in the water added to the aromatic mix. The heavy air in the control room contained the collective sweat pheromones of everyone positioned there, intensifying the nervous excitement and anxiety that was building up. I made eye contact with the commanding officer. He offered me our furtive sign: we would tap our left shoulder with our right hand to indicate connection, to let the other know they were seen.

Our ship shivered in anticipation of the blast. A convulsion ran from the ocean through the hull, vibrating the metal and our bodies. The primed energy had enormous pressure as it surged through everything. Days before I had been able to get a quick look at the explosive device that was to be detonated. It weighed close to twenty thousand pounds and was encased in aluminum. It represented a sum of intelligences centered on destruction. At the time I would not have consciously articulated it as such. The violence registered subconsciously. After seeing the weapon, I had plaguing nightmares that left me staggering through the morning and afternoon hours, unsure about what to do with my thoughts. Almost a decade previously, two megaton radioactive loads were delivered onto civilian populations in a war zone by the U.S. military. Hiroshima and Nagasaki. They were the first ever nuclear detonations used as warfare. The consequences were horrendous—the acts, heinous, a turning point, and a point of no return.

There was a beehive of commotion that engulfed us. Everyone seemed to be moving a dial, rustling paper, calling out a message, tapping out code, gulping their coffee. The ship rumbled heavily. Its engine generated bassy vibrations. Someone's medallion of Saint Francis with its slippery gold chain fell to the floor and coiled into the shape of a snake. I picked it up after scanning the room to see if anyone was missing it. I put it into the depths of my trousers. It falling to the floor as it did seemed to signify something, but it was impossible to decipher whether it was positive or ominous. In the last few days there were many occurrences that seemed like signs giving boding messages. Again, I shifted my focus to meet the commanding officer's gaze—much to my relief he had sought me out as well and for a split second we gave each other a look of profound significance.

Then everything became calm. During the minutes approaching the detonation the atmosphere became silent and tranquil, caught in amber. The ocean was still. The crew was on autopilot now. We breathed in tempo to our mission, protocol directed our every move. Our vessel, a destroyer, was more than thirty miles from the projected blast site to avoid directly experiencing the thermal effects caused by the explosion. Every ship had a trained staff of medical officers who were prepared to administer first aid. For more dire consequences, it was difficult to imagine what measures had been planned. That information was beyond my jurisdiction.

The bomb was detonated from a cab shot on a manmade launching site near Namu Island, part of Bikini Atoll. Zero hour was 6:45 a.m. on the first day of March 1954.

I was a witness and a participant of a demonstration of energy at a zenith level, a fifteen-megaton blast. I noticed the pupils of the commanding officer reflected the tangerine orange burst of light, they resembled tiger eyes or the eyes of an owl. As if he were seeing with night vision. Others resembled tree frogs with bulging orange-red eyes, the cone cells of their retinas filled up with blast light as they stared ahead. We were no longer the persons we were a split second ago. We had morphed into insects able to perceive ultraviolet light or had transformed into snakes able to recognize infrared light. The strongest technologically induced force had infiltrated us. The blast light penetrated through metal. Later, sailors mentioned how even with their eyelids closed or with no proximity to a portal to witness the explosion directly they nonetheless saw orange-yellow radiation. The radiated light had X-ray capacity. We were translucent jelly. We were skeletal remains. Any notion of civilization was obliterated.

Our physical survival coincided with the dying of some ineffable quality of being. The ecological importance of this event was pronounced by a burgeoning mushroom cloud that formed that looked like cotton candy. We learned later that it climbed to a height of sixty miles in ten minutes.

Our ship had slipped into an alternate universe. In that immediate period a harsh vacuum sucked the breath out of our lungs, out of our blood. Flesh and bones felt flattened. The bomb exerted massive pressure on the surface tension of the ocean. A shock wave generated from inside the fireball traveled through water and air. It was soundless because low-frequency sound waves are imperceptible to humans. The equilibrium temperature was molten. A double flash occurred. We were far enough away not to experience direct burns. We had been informed at a debriefing that the temperature of the nuclear explosion could reach the temperature of the interior of the sun: one hundred million degrees Celsius.

I did not personally see the mushroom cloud until much later. The portal I was able to look out of faced the opposite cardinal direction. We were shown photographs and a movie of the moment-to-moment unfurling of the plume days later.

Once we were permitted to move from our stations we did so in slow motion. Ambling about seemed difficult for everyone. Many chose to stay sequestered there. Several men bumped into another, blandly excusing themselves. A voice came on the intercom giving us instructions. We were to stay by our workstations until nightfall. Meals would be distributed in brown bags. We were not to go anywhere until further instruction. A portable latrine had been positioned behind a subdividing panel at our station. After a while, a classical radio channel played Bach's Mass in B minor. How uncanny.

The navy deemed the mission a success. This was the new arena of atomic, biological, and chemical defense methods. Collateral damages included the place called home for numerous families. The coral reef surrounding the island had vanished. The palm trees were gone. All that formerly existed there showered down in the form of irradiated calcium debris and ash that appeared like fresh snow falling.

In a few days our ship turned direction. As we changed course, I pronounced under my breath the names of the three islands that no longer existed: Bokonijien, Aerokojlol, and Nam.

We were headed to a humanly fabricated island off the San Francisco Bay: Treasure Island.

It was late at night; a commotion of lights and sirens caused us to awaken. Several of us scrambled to dress when we noticed that again we had merged with the other reality. The ocean pounded against the shoreline. As our eyes adjusted to the low light, we could see that two bodies were lying on the sand near the water's edge. In the distance there were lights flashing in all directions that were very disorienting. We had heard sirens before but never quite so blaring and immediate. We avoided the altercation with the police and instead moved along a stone embankment toward the ocean. We moved slowly and cautiously toward the men collapsed on the sand. We kept our heads down, almost crawling along.

One of them sat up and assisted the other. They were wet; they had come out of the ocean. They wore white clothing, uniforms. Both had bruises and looked exhausted. There were circular indentations on their skin. In places there were needle wounds. The hair on their heads was close shaven. They did not initially notice us. We swayed with the breezes wondering what to do next.

Because there have been increasing encounters with other persons, we have taken to wearing face coverings—masks with slits for eyes, nose, and mouth. The masks are circular. We collectively chose floral designs, based on the seed catalogs we recovered that depict remarkable plants that lived in other times. Plants with flowers that grew in inflorescence are our favorite. Clusters of flowers spring from our peduncles. A cardinal flower with numerous tubular blooms. A hydrangea, puffy, or a lilac, tiny stars in tight arrangements. Bleeding hearts. Many wear marigolds—*cempasúchil*, a flower with which to remember the deceased. If only hummingbirds would seek nectar secreted from our nectaries. Hummingbirds no longer exist where (and when) we live. And the cherry, a flower that reminds of the pathos of fleeting beauty. The blooming plants of the seas, oceans, rivers, and lakes also beguile us. Our day smocks resemble kelp.

Something terrible had happened to them. They were in horrible condition. We contemplated how we might help them.

We balanced beside them. Our flowers bobbed. We saw them clearly through the handmade petals of our masks. The pair was positioned on the sand; one man was stretched out flat against the sand, barely breathing, the other man knelt by his side. Once they became aware of us, they were confused but too tired to react.

There had been another person near them. She departed abruptly when the flashing lights and sirens began to blare. We saw her for but a brief moment. We think she is the person who we saw earlier, sitting by herself in the park. She headed in the direction of the forested area of the park we have become familiar with.

One of the men remained unconscious. They both looked miserable. We could do little to comfort them except to rock gently holding hands, interlocking our energies and sending it forth. We formed a circle around them hoping that our presence would bring solace. We hummed quietly, steadily. We hummed in harmony with the wind.

There was a distortion of focus as sound, smell, and sight merged and retreated. The pulsating police lights put us on high alert. Other shapes and shadows darted around the periphery. When we first arrived, we heard several gunshots. We were not close enough to see the action. Then we noticed there was a body on the ground, shot dead, splayed by the car. The police rushed to the body with their guns pointed. It is unclear if they were responsible for shooting the person.

Eventually one of the men stood up for a moment and looked around before dropping to his knees again. He was profoundly disturbed. Tears ran down his cheeks. We continued to encircle him. We did not want to push too hard with our energy. With our feet in the sand we stood together and held a vigil for them.

Again, distortion. An overload of sensory information. Sounds were amplified. We could hear their hearts pounding. This tends to happen when we stand together in group formation. Our senses get magnified.

In the night sky a sextile between the moon and Neptune would bring comfort; we expected the mood to change.

We knelt to be closer to the men. We formed a simple nucleus. By all appearances they are young. One man's complexion was warm brown, the other man's complexion was bone white with pronouncedly bluish veins. Around his eyes were dark gray sunken circles. They appeared to care for one another deeply. One man continued to cry softly over the other man.

Both the men required medical attention. Their injuries covered a large portion of their bodies. On closer examination, their skulls looked bruised and dented. The contusions did not appear to be caused by anything that might have occurred in the water. They sustained the injuries prior to their swim. Some of the bruises looked to be older than others.

A thin film of algae and other microflora covered their epidermis. Perhaps that is why we could perceive them clearly. They also would have digested a large quantity of microorganisms on their swim with the intake of ocean water. Their bodies radiated a faint glow. Microorganisms, especially those with luminescence, aid our ability to perceive that which is outside our usual timeframe. We are still unclear how time and space converge and synchronize. We have somehow become able to see through time. Our situatedness is slipstream. We are illusory. We see in double vision.

We entered more energetically into the space. We intuited that they noticed us for a moment and then the moment passed as flickering light. Morning approached. The sun began beating harder on us. We had to retreat. We wanted to offer more of ourselves. We wanted to console them.

Our community would be anxious if we delayed our return. We promised to check back on the injured men if we could. Before departing several of us knelt down beside them. The man who was conscious looked at us and smiled for the first time. We had the ledger with us. We had been carrying it with us to take note of the hybrid timestreams. We reached over to him and carefully placed the ledger in his hands. He said thank you. "By the way, my name is Darnell," the man said to us. We said, "We want you to have this book." Then, spontaneously we left. Their pain was familiar to us. We empathized deeply. Handing our ledger to Darnell was the only offering we could give.

Our ship, a destroyer, led a defunct warship that had been directly hit by the atomic bomb blast back to the United States—to the naval yard on Treasure Island in San Francisco Bay. The navy wanted to study the impact of the bomb on the physical shell of the ship and also understand the level of radiation that it had absorbed. We underwent decontamination training. A mock ship had also been constructed for instructional purposes. It sat on a dry dock at Treasure Island. That ship too was covered in radioactive material.

Returning to the United States promised us some downtime and a chance to try out our land legs again. It had been almost half a year that we had been on board the destroyer. In the area around Treasure Island, gardens of eel grass grew. I was excited to dive around the perimeter of the island amid the grasses.

By this point, Ed and I were very tight. We hoped that time off the ship would afford us more opportunity to be together. There was the bustling metropolis of San Francisco nearby.

It was spring when we arrived at our destination. We were given accommodations in barracks near the facilities. The island swarmed with activity. Because the island was a communications hub and a repair station for naval vessels, thousands of naval personnel came and went.

The decontamination site was up and running shortly after we landed. Every day there were two shifts of fifty navy personnel who were involved in the cleanup. We were assigned brooms and mops and also wire scrubbers to work at the invisible substances. This duty did not feel entirely disagreeable. When we were on deck, we were treated to the blissful coastal atmosphere: bright sunshine and ocean breezes. The work was tiring but by no means drudgery. We filled buckets with seawater and splashed it over the surface areas of the ship while we scoured away.

We were given the bare minimum of instructions. Where to report, who to check in with, who we would be working with. We were divided into crews of four individuals. Together we helped one another to carry supplies and equipment and generally we encouraged each other. The camaraderie was wonderful. The work clothing that the navy assigned to us were jumpsuits of thick canvas material. When a shift concluded we were scanned with a Geiger counter and our clothing was collected and washed in chemically treated detergent under high temperatures. Both ships were also scanned daily in order to take successive readings of the radioactive levels. We were monitored and screened for any unusual health issues. We were instructed to immediately inform the medics of any developing condition we might experience. There was a routine form we had to fill out describing our overall health. Was the tongue swollen? Stiffness in the joints? Trouble urinating? Blood in the urine? Trouble with ejaculation? Sore lips? Skin lesions? Hair loss. Upset stomach? The most common complaints were contact dermatitis—an insidious rash that spread from the area of contact and crept along the body, along with headaches, diarrhea. Some had trouble breathing. Some suffered hair loss. The personnel who expressed symptoms immediately were mostly those who were assigned to paint parts of the ship with a glow-in-the-dark paint made from radium.

On the first day of work I experienced no symptoms. The second day I came down with a nonstop headache. The third day I had constipation, then diarrhea, then I was fine for weeks on end, scrubbing at the ship. My crew was assigned to the upper deck—we were outside most of the time, in the direct path of the sun, ocean air circulating. We took relief in the fact that the navy monitored and screened everyone continually.

I was not overly anxious to be working with cesium 137 and whatever other radioactive substances the ships were doused with or what radioactivity remained from the blast. We were ignorant to the fact that cesium 137 moves easily through the air as a crystalline powder and readily dissolves in water, as its chemical compounds are salt molecules. When swimming in the waters around the naval facility I did not give the presence of cesium 137 much thought. I was unaware that cesium 137 gets absorbed into concrete and soil and was, therefore, all around us. As we scrubbed and splashed our mops and scrubbers around, we inadvertently transferred the radiation from one area to another. The ground, the ocean, other plants, and animals inhaled and ingested these substances.

We got in the rhythm of cleaning the ships. Our crew was close and enjoyed each other's company. Ed worked in another division, though he was always around, often onsite. My off hours were spent almost exclusively with him. We'd stroll around the island and also go for a night out to San Francisco. There were plenty of men who had boyfriends. We kept our relationship discreet.

San Francisco's nightlife was welcoming compared to any place I had ever been. Nights flew by at the Black Cat or at Finocchio's Club. But there were raids by the police. Tommy's Place was raided, and the episode really tamped down the mood for a long while. We went to the Paper Doll, and it became our mainstay. Access to these venues didn't come too soon for me. Once there I understood belonging. Ed was no longer my direct superior once we returned to the States and that was a relief. Our power dynamics changed; polarities shifted. "Darnell," Ed would say to me with a twinkle in his eye, joshing, "top or bottom?" Our sex was anything but vanilla.

When a national syndication ran a feature on San Francisco gay life, Ed appeared as a barely visible bystander in a photo taken at a gay bar on Polk Street. All hell ensued. The navy suspected our entanglements. We were interrogated and subpoenaed. I was guilty by association. Over were the nights, shirts off, sipping cordials, dancing to Faye Adams, Ruth Brown, and Big Joe Turner. Or how we'd nurse the night to the point when dawn's first filaments of light teased us, barely awake, still in need of each other, we'd listen to *Study in Brown* by Clifford Brown and Max Roach. We'd shed languid tears over Dinah Washington's songs when the fog and drizzle increased the melancholy. Or get rambunctious with Ben Webster blowing away on his saxophone after smoke and fire in some bar. We planned to move into a flat together after our service with the navy was over. There were plenty of available rooms in the Castro and other places.

After we were interrogated by the navy, Ed and I could not see each other. We were placed in separate solitary confinement cells within a naval detention center. Soon we were moved to the naval hospital—a psychiatric facility on the island. It was a gargantuan ugly white edifice that gave me shivers even before I was forcefully admitted.

Things got way worse. Our heads were shaved bald. We were forced to wear a pajamalike outfit that was demeaning. I was always chilled to the bone. None of the heaters seemed to function. Next came the battery of tests. I was never not taking a test. Aptitude, mood, on and on. They experimented with drugs. All of them, horrible. Nothing recreationally pleasant or able to offer a distraction from the situation. I felt either an intensified anxiety or an indescribable dullness. Next came electric shock. And procedures I never learned the names of. Injections and X-rays. Constant grilling in an interrogation-style method. Threats and shaming, it never let up. In their classification homosexuality was a sickness. Thousands of gay soldiers went through the battery of tests and demoralization. The navy discharged gay soldiers in San Francisco. My experience was worse than the firsthand accounts I heard. Racism and sadism go hand in hand. There was one day when the torture was too much to bear, and I vowed to get the hell out of the hospital. I would find Ed and we would leave. Our escape did not go smoothly.

THE PERFORMERS
DARIUS

Having spent my childhood growing up on Treasure Island it has taken
me a moment to come to terms with the stuff that arises when we perform here. The experience is peculiar. I scan the island, and I'm in two
places and times at once. The little bungalow where we lived is still here.
Same color. Beige. The same battleship-gray door where we entered and
exited our comfort zone each day to join or retreat from the world. Same
bushes, untrimmed. Same bay, same ocean. I feel attraction and revul-
sion for this island.

Others in my extended family pursued careers in the military, but not
my mom and dad. They arrived here as a second massive wave of people
leaving—fleeing the Jim Crow South. They chanced on Treasure Island
because rent was affordable. Maybe the city relocated folks here, I'm not
sure. Now my parents live in San Francisco. When we lived on Treasure
Island there were predominantly postmilitary families that had stayed
on.

I go to graduate school at University of California, Berkeley, the university hosting the conference. Sae and I are in the same department, in
the school of forestry and agriculture. We bonded in a reading group that
focused on the work of Booker T. Whatley, George Washington Carver,
Rudolf Steiner, and Jerome Irving Rodale. The focus of my research is
Indigenous land stewardship, precontact and postcontact. I've been engaged with traditional no-till farming techniques and irrigation methods,
diversified plantings, selective harvesting, seed collection, and other
land management practices that are low impact. Traditional Native agricultural systems of managed wild gardening use no toxic additives and
do not rely on mechanized equipment. Seed banks that collect wild, local
seeds are a subject of interest. I visit the Akwesasne Freedom School in
Hogansburg, New York, for research. The year-round curriculum gives

local children the opportunity to plant and maintain community gardens. Another part of my research includes the Oneida Community Integrated Food System, an eighty-three-acre farm in Oneida, Wisconsin. Besides these organizations and a few other out-of-state farms and gardens, I focus most of my energies on in-state horticultural developments. In a working group we strategize food sovereignty and biodiversity and look to working models that organize around such tendencies. The link between food and medicine is emphasized. The connection between giving back to the land and reaping harvests is at the core of our practices.

Sae and I are also poets. Our poetry tends to be ecologically focused. How obsessed can one be! She lured me into joining the performance troupe. A good opportunity to deal with traumatic residue, I thought, a good chance to think into versions of the narrative I have concerning this place. It is emotional to be here. Divination and crying—they are linked. I can prove it. The thought passed my mind and I had to smile. Tears clear vision for clairvoyance. Otherwise, I had nearly no expectations for any outcome. To date I haven't written any poetry centered on the experience of performing here or about collisions with childhood memory.

The day I agreed to join I had an encounter with another person in the department. They were pontificating about something and as they got all pink-faced and heated, I watched the galleon etched into their upper arm start to wobble on waves delineated in navy blue ink and felt nauseated. Who gets a tattoo of a galleon and then espouses leftist politics! They were going on and on about some departmental dispute—their points well taken—yet as I became hypnotized by the galleon tattooed on their skin, I became incensed. It triggered me to think about how it functioned as a symbol of transatlantic slave trafficking, how galleons carried people and goods across the Atlantic. A running list of the extractavist goods that traveled on those ships ran through my head. Abducted people, tobacco, cotton, hides, flour, rice, gold, pearls, indigo, sugar, cacao, textiles, wheat, maize, pork, manatee lard, wine, brandy, rum, ammunitions, and so on. The great forests of Europe were razed to make the ships, displacing vast populations of humans and other-than-human persons, decimating plant life, bringing on poverty and precarity and an endless cycle of violence. Wherever fleets of galleons landed, misery followed, bodies and resources plundered. After the microaggression of the galleon sighting, I wondered if I made the right decision to join the troupe, though the two situations were unrelated. Sae had looped back to the department lounge, where the fracas was taking place. She caught my attention and then thankfully broke up the conversation. We departed together. I breathed a sigh of frustration and relief.

The galleon, though, put me on a long daydream that intersected with the ongoing nightmare of white supremacy, settler colonial domination, the police, imperial hegemonies, and the nefariousness of large seagoing vessels. Last week a tanker carrying commodity goods into the port of Oakland ran into a family of whales, killing several, including young whales that were still nursing.

My mother's mother's mother's mother (my great-great-grandmother) and her relations held the distinction of creating for themselves the means of escape. They commandeered a small boat to get some distance from maniacal torture and endless drudgery. The family legacy has been passed down like a weathered nautical buoy withstanding harsh waters. We never lose sight of that marker; it always bobs to the top of our familial memories. Braving the waters, ad infinitum.

After surviving the voyage in the hold of a filthy, disease-ridden, overloaded galleon and having been abducted, stripped, shackled, and eventually sold to a planter in Alabama, my great-relations waited to get the lay of the land and a working knowledge of the clockwork of plantation management. It was a smaller homesteader farm in a disputed, sparsely settled area, not prosperous. Isolated, near waterways, the ocean.

The story goes that the enslaved people on the farm quickly collectivized. They worked against privileges and status that created the divisions necessary to maintain hierarchy—divide and rule. The farm had less of the two-tier structure of in-house and field enslaved, which might have had an impact on the solidarity that formed. Years passed, season after season of sowing, tending, and harvesting. The farm had a diabolical rhythm. Everyone was in the groove. This story is probably much longer and more complicated than it has been told from generation to generation. The seed of the story survives and is about survival. The details are mixed with the land, the plants, and the ocean.

Every move the planters and the overseers made was observed and studied tactically. They knew that the overseer would run to a burning crop. They knew that the planter would wake out of bed at an alarm and run out his front door toward his horse and head to the conflagration.

Despite all the violence done to them they rejected the genocidal tendencies of the planters and had no interest in emulating the settler colonial paradigm of the Europeans. They knew of an herb that grew by a stream that could put someone into a stupor. After hours they made a big vat of the unctuous concoction and stored it in carved out melons. By creating the necessary distractions, under the cover of night they were able to dig out several strategically placed shallow pits, covering them in thin branches and dirt to look untouched. One was situated by the front door of the planter's house. The others were enroute to the fields. The pits were lined so the herbal bath would not be absorbed by the soil.

At the appointed hour at daybreak other distractions were set into motion. Fires set. As projected, the planter and the overseer and other plantation management stumbled into pits where they were overcome by the herb. They were quickly bound and secured so they could not make a pursuit once they awoke. The pits were covered over to conceal where the men were tied up and confined, affording more time for the getaway.

Those fleeing made their way to the coast, and whoever had agreed to go got into the small boats that were stashed in the reeds. They arrived at a string of small islands inhabited by an Indigenous community who had been displaced from the mainland. New forms of solidarity formed. The islands were marshland, thick with foliage, abundant with food, and shoals of fish swam in the waters.

Stories of rebellion usually only make appearances in history as cautionary tales of how hatched plots go wrong. Vulgar details overstate how hazardous and impossible it is to attempt to break out of a system. Or they are portrayed as romantic notions of wish-fulfillment. When really, every effort of collective pushback is a sea change. It is as much a simplification to make the claim that plantation management was always successful at creating divisiveness among its intended victims. Solidarities are obfuscated in the historical record. Furtive power clamors for truths disguised as hyperbole.

The part of the story that is emphasized by my family is the potent herb. How the mind-altering quality of a flowering plant that grew in such abundance in that region offered the power to transform lives. An interspecies realignment. One "species" coming to the aid of another, an instance where the taxonomy falters.

The settler colonial objective was to tame the wilderness. Terraforming the continent involved the replacement of diversity with monocultures of tobacco and cotton, later wheat, corn, and soy. Was the herb my ancestors asked assistance of an African plant? Were its seeds stored in a bottleneck gourd, transported as food or medicine? Nightshade is of African origin. So is jute mallow, sorrel, pangola grass, castor bean, tamarind, kenaf, and cotton. There are dozens of plants indigenous to the African continent that were brought to slaving centers. An ethnobotanical lineage has been maintained. An estimated thirty thousand slaving voyages were made. Surely many of these trips involved the transportation of seeds and plants for future gardens. There is an account of an enslaved woman bringing grains of rice woven into her hair.

The plantation ecosystem was an extraction ecosystem, and many of the aspects of that system are still in place. The environment was subject to the exploitative practices of settler colonial planters who reengineered the world for production and profit, not sustenance, or subsistence. Native plants were eradicated to make way for vast monocrops tended by people in bondage. Within that horror I'm able to find one encouraging fact: plants nurtured people and plants were nurtured by people. A point I dwell on, and a fact overlooked. Sugarcane was raised by humans; tobacco, watered and tended by humans, relating an intricate embodiment of interspecies relations. Most of the planters did not know much, if anything, about farming or gardening; they were merchants. Native and African expertise made survival possible. Tending to gardens directs energies toward sustenance, mutual care.

Aiding growing life *is resistance*. Labor that involves sustenance for collective benefit is social. Fannie Lou Hamer demonstrated this on the Freedom Farm Cooperative she set up in the 1960s in Sunflower County, Mississippi. White landowners evicted black sharecroppers and tenant farmers for demanding more pay and attempting to vote. In 1960s Mississippi only 5 percent of black residents were registered to vote. Those who tried to register had their lives threatened. White supremacists tried to repress and intimidate Hamer in every way possible including shooting at the house she was staying in, but she was undeterred, famously saying, "The only thing they could do was to kill me." Hamer went ahead with her vision to establish a collective farm to help with community food security, making land available for the community to farm, and provide affordable housing. She understood collective farming as economic and social autonomy. Sylvia Wynter has been an influential figure for me as well. She makes a fecund point that although the plantation was a "superstructure," this definition hides the "secretive histories" of enslaved people activating plots of generativity. Her writings underscore the "plantings of people" in new ecosystems, "not in order to form societies." Yet the formation of new alliances happened. Planting took place in many diversified plots, many gardens were formed on the interstitial land between monocrop and forest, monocrop and field. The plot is what is imagined. The plot gets a makeover, a reexamination, an alternative conceptualization. Plants have ways of plotting their futures. One seed is a multigenerational world about to unfold.

"The plot?"

"You dig it!"

"Dang, plots!"

"Shit's real"

Such is the running repartee between me and Sae concerning plot, plots. There are several iterations. What is growing in the plot, has died in the plot, is composted in the plot, hence our joined focus. The plot is always-already crowded with life and death, with intention, with archive. Scratch the soil. Disturbing the plot has consequences. Better to work gingerly with the organicism of the plot up against regimes of power. The plantation structure and its system of commodification and violence overwhelmed the plot, but look now, shifts in consciousness are occurring. The plot was never lost. "Peasant farmers, agroproletarian workers." The seeds of the autochthonous are vibrant. Dormant matter is significant too.

Wynter writes that victory against such systems is pyrrhic. So real. The sheer taxing effects of these challenges are absorbed into the all-encompassing effort of living. The cost is always life.

The department gave Sae and me some funding to conduct experiments with urban gardening techniques. We tinkered with plot dimensions, the scale of the walkways between plots, where to plant varying heights of plants. We also positioned plants that need more moisture or more shade with those that require full-on sunshine for the majority of the day. Placing plants that are hardier next to sensitive plants brought great results. Certain plants fend off insects and other organisms that damage specific vegetation. We paid attention to leaf shapes and the negative spaces between leaves. We noted how we flexed for the plants and they in turn flexed for each other. We got to know them individually and as groups. We were amazed by the robust outcome in such small plots. As we review our findings, we are reevaluating concepts like "yield," which is tied to market dynamics. Survive and Thrive is our motto and growing ethos.

What is it that we do not notice that notices us?

What plants get selected by humans as worthy of attention (and reproduction) out of the numerosity of living presences? Desired characteristics are bred, engineered. Settlers didn't realize that the plants that were growing on Turtle Island at the time of contact and conquest were intentional in the landscape, were being looked after, encouraged to grow. What they encountered was by no means an "undiscovered" Garden of Eden.

Plots inform us about breathing in air, noticing breath, noticing entanglements and alliances that are often hard to detect or understand.

Extend.

Extension has become my go-to gesture. In an age of boundaries and declarations of personal space and violations of space I become curious about extension. How to extend. Plots often look like they have rigid boundaries, but they do not. Plots need not be containers. They are porous, extend skyward, encourage burrowing soilward, generate contact with organisms and the atmosphere. The cultivation of many natures possible and necessary. Boundary rules often sanitize, neutralize, create hegemony and same-same identities that then create antagonisms with the outside, the others.

Plants grow to extend themselves. They anchor one part of their body and then extend in all directions as a motivational claim. Extensions call for a quantum dynamic that gives space and time an opening and a method for how relationships can flourish. Time needs to flow; space needs to expand. The generative sources of space are only realized through extension.

The plot never stays put. We bring manure from cows to the plot, we compost tea leaves from misty tea farms in Taiwan, India, and China, avocado rinds from Mexico, banana peels from Honduras, lichi pits from Indonesia, apples cores from Seattle. We harvest and consume the fruits and vegetables we grow out of these scraps and animal dung. The minerals and vitamins constitute our bodies. We shed, the plot sheds, and organisms extrude into the soil. Skies dump water from giant moving oceans in the atmosphere into the plot. Water that once was circulated in the body of fish, or in reedy marshes, or on a mountaintop as snow cover. A bobcat traipses over the snow, and his residue clings. The snow melts with a bit of bobcat in it. The plot is infiltrated by plastic particles because plastic has infiltrated the entire ecosystem. Pharmaceuticals become trapped in the soil or dragged to the ocean. Chemicals from agribusiness find every nook and cranny to settle into. Everywhere are organic compounds that have never before existed in the course of human civilization. My imagination runs wild combinatory mixtures: opalescent eyeshadows worn on fashion runways melt with a glacier, interacting with the rocks underneath; bat sweat slides down a dank cave wall and is saturated with the components of a slippery lubricant used in the nuclear industry; pearls of moisture that pool in the crowns of palm trees on a Pacific island contain microamounts of underarm deodorant from sports players thousands of miles away; and snail mucus from gastropods living in dense jungle foliage contains ingredients found in hand sanitizers. All the tears shed have been reconstituted over and over again, somewhere, and then, somewhere else as something else, as someone else.

Steady state energy or equilibrium do not exist in the plot.

Extend into the nasty factuals.

Shaped by notions of private property, finance, law, industry, and nationhood, contemporary formulations of space involve movement and exchange in global markets through financial networks and algorithmic computation, in courts, in schools, in prisons. The plot is a space for a microrebellion borne of a diversity that arises despite these systems. I look for unruliness in the plot.

Extendedness has provoked disorientation. Something uncanny has taken place. For several performances I have felt spasmodic irregularities. There are blurry incidences. Wondering if the blurriness is neurological, I take it easy. Dwell longer at a time. The blurriness feels like shifts between microclimates. When I come upon sudden changes in the texture of air or intensity of light I slowly immerse myself in them. I try not to withdraw suddenly. With as much calm as I can muster, I hold space in a different spectrum of time. How or why this is happening, I am not sure. In and out of these pockets of otherness, I fall in and out of my childhood. My body feels empty, I come across other people who appear empty. Almost formless, or is it a play of light? The place that was once the backdrop of my childhood imagination has been absorbed by a history and a mythos that I attach to it. Histories populate spaces.

Angel Island radiates a green energy and rock solidity across the San Francisco Bay. From where I'm positioned, supine by the huge granite boulders that shore up the embankment, I look out, feel its presence. The island is verdant because of recent rains; the ocean surrounding it also glistens emerald green. In high school, I found out that immigrants, mostly Asians, were processed on Angel Island. Because of racist policies, namely the Chinese Exclusion Act, thousands of Chinese immigrants were detained there. Asians were also screened and quarantined at Angel Island because of the fears of bubonic plague exacerbated by the xenophobia and the white supremacy of the late nineteenth century. A fort was established on the island to service the U.S. military in World War I and World War II. The fort became a detention camp that held Japanese Americans and German Americans and also Japanese and German prisoners of war.

If I gaze westerly, I can see Alcatraz Island, another island set up as a defense installation and later used for incarceration. This island served as a military prison, and then a maximum-security federal prison. This "evolutionary" sequence is the underlying motif. The fort, a modifiable structure, can be "upgraded" to adjust for ever more intensive campaigns of domination and appropriation.

My parents participated in the protests in solidarity with Native activists who staged a lengthy occupation on Alcatraz, taking up quarters in the abandoned prison. The Northern California Pit River Indians call the island Allisti Ti-Tanin-Wiji (Rock Rainbow or Diamond Island). Alcatraz is graywacke sandstone formed by submarine landslides that contain mollusk fossils 130 to 140 million years old. Meanings of the palimpsest glisten within layers of a chronology as atavistic recognition. The stone holds solidarity. The protest chants are recorded in organic and inorganic substances, in solid crystals. The stone and the plants steady the vibrations in their molecular structure.

I walk by our family's former bungalow whenever I come out to Treasure Island. It has a draw that pulls at the marrow of my bones. What is most discernible are emotional sensations that the memories conjure. How it felt to leave the house to walk to catch the bus for school. Coming of age in racialized America, noticing it as skin, as gesture, as glance and banal interaction. All the ways that assertion announces itself. All the ways in which cancellation plays out. Something other than defense and offense. A monster equation of becoming through discontinuation.

Also, how strength and courage grow like vines gaining momentum. Now the house looks weatherworn and desolate as most of the houses do on the island. Plans for gentrification are on the drawing board. Most of the current housing and surrounding structures will be taken down— tabula rasa, erase it clean. Nothing here is quaint or redeemable to the planners. The asbestos siding will be demolished and carted off to a landfill. The trees too will probably be removed. Sleek glassy structures will rise up to replace these houses. The new edifices will contend with impending ocean rise and other climatic challenges. Once again, massive earth moving efforts. Making the glass sheets for condo constructions has a huge carbon footprint.

Microfocal intensities. PTSD clashes with present offenses. I chew some roadside chamomile. A calmness ensues. A little rosemary and sage to rub against, the aromatics waft. We grew the herbs in front of our bungalow. The bungalows were formerly homes for military personnel. That legacy is quite tired and ragged by now. Slumping inward. Ingesting itself.

As I check my focus, I make a hand gesture to Jay. I notice they are fumbling with something. They try to grab something that I cannot see. It appears that they cannot see what they are reaching at either. They aren't quite swatting. Rather testing the shape of a contour that is imminent, coming into being. I have an out-of-body experience. I imagine I am a *Wiwaxia*, a subgroup of mollusks, a soft-bodied animal that resembles a crown of pointy feathers. My impressions of the *Wiwaxia* are entirely generated by a fossil I once was introduced to by a colleague in the Paleobiology Department. They were creatures that had scales covering their bodies somewhat similar to the contemporary pangolin. In addition to the flat rows of scales, the *Wiwaxia* had spiky extensions, or dorsal spines, that radiated out of their back like long plumage. Their habitat was nowhere near here. I extend toward them in time and extend like them in gesture.

Jay is still fumbling. What is up? It is worrisome to see them bumbling about. These are not the moves they usually make. They tend to work in a vocabulary of angular pivots. Slow and deliberate. Right now, they are thrashing in the air.

The last time we all came together to practice I sensed something was different about Jay's interactions with the environment. I tried to broach the situation with them but got nowhere. Something is different. I keep sensing it too. Focus is either stronger or shifts to an indefinite quality. The fluctuating sensations arrive and retreat. Shabnam said hallucinations are sometimes advanced warnings or signs of things to come. I didn't have a chance to follow up with her on what she meant, but the gist of it made total sense to me.

This is a site for experimentation. We make body gestures that evoke the hidden recesses of our subconscious. I respect Jay's determination to push the boundaries. It might be rude to come across too inquisitively when Jay is in the process of transforming their repertoire of moves. But maybe they will want to talk with me about it. I want to compare notes.

I notice Jay talking, but no one is around. Are they saying something to me? Unlikely. I am too far afield. The ocean is murmuring, there's noise from cars, birds are making a ruckus. Planes streak the sky. There is also an extremely loud helicopter overhead. It strikes me how much ambient noise there is when I stop to listen. I wave to Jay. They do not notice my hand signals. I decide to leave it alone and approach them afterward. Since we are not to engage the bused in onlookers, I don't think about them much. They take a position in the background. They usually take some photos, take some notes, huddle in little groups together, conversing. Or Randy keeps them spellbound with his talking points.

Now is the time for me to get deep into my purpose for being here. Try out divergent forms. Get into history as a study of body politics moving in action with ecological reality. Absorb the linguistics of other-than-human participants. Learn to communicate in those languages. Breathe it all in. *Hrim*: the seed mantra. Adding a *la* sound to the mantra can paralyze speech. To get to a stance where all is one, speech needs to be subdued. Hearing supplants listening. Hearing for flows of energy, flows of consciousness. A seed mantra to access invisible sound, infinity, divine energies. The ego hides, takes a pause. Plots and extension. Hiding and then again being overt, acting unruly in a destructive way. Two types of views: vertical and oblique. Layers of military history. Layers of advance and withdrawal. A sequence of events too complicated to be mapped. Only partial excavations. Aerial photography reveals burial grounds, areas more and less effectively policed by the standards of the state, caches of warheads hidden in bunkers underground. I am tripping. I am processing psychic overloads at warp speed.

The helicopter looks as if it might land on the parking lot, but then, in the last instant buzzes away. It tears at the sonic fabric that embedded everything just a moment ago. *Min-min*: sound of air screaming. The helicopter's whirring decibels will travel to the outer cosmos. It will only take 12.6 minutes for a radio signal to reach Mars from Earth. To Jupitar, 43.2, to Saturn, 79.3. The sand beneath my feet responds to the helicopter's frantic beating. Gravel and dust agitate. A gritty friction blocks other dimensions of sound. Blades against wind and sand particles rub against each other. The ground is particularized. A fraction of space buckles between forms. We really only ever touch each other's auras. Unless there is penetration, consumption, dissolvement.

The hazmat suit seems whiter than ever, and reflective. I see duplicates of myself dotted across the ocean. Dressed for inspection duty. Dressed as a joke on incorruption.

I am never bored by the minutiae of the unearthing process. *Are you bored?* I question the miniature critic who resides in my psyche. *Actually not*, replies that voice, my identical twin.

In the midst of temporal attenuation, I swear I see two sailors sprawled on the beach. Then I scan for Jay. Jay continues to paw at the space around themself while walking toward me. The hologram of the sailors fades. My palate registers spirulina, with an aftertaste of chamomile.

The gross body, the subtle body, the causal body. Physicality and etherealization. Anything but body coherence. The versions are prying themselves apart and also melting together. An orgasm mutually achieved earlier in the day with, should I reveal their identity, maybe not. Little gushing rivulets pushing out suddenly from a mound of dirt. Definitely tremors, quaking. Release from the groin and up the chakras. Body remoistened. Seeds can take hold.

I sit down as an automatic reaction to astonishment. *Are you sitting down?* I hear my psyche mutter questioningly.

Once I am seated, I am indeed calmer, and the cascade of images dissipates. I focus. The blurred vision I experienced earlier has begun to yield shapes. To my absolute amazement the forms have appendages—legs and arms, in fact, there are heads, and torsos, one head per person. My bewilderment suspends me in ether, a nebulous condition of awakening to unknown phenomena. I respond by reaching out. My reach is directed to an arm, whose hand is swaying like a sea anemone in an oceanic current.

An electrical charge bolts through my neuromuscular system. Autonomic nerves respond in a way I have never experienced. My total body recenters. My hand meets up with a form entirely composed of light in the process of becoming moist, supple. The form crouches down, and I am suddenly at eye level with a sentient being, a human in fact, different, yes, though certainly human. There are other people, but I focus on the person near me.

Their expression is so different, their posture also. With this encounter I give in to the longest, penetrating direct stare, but it does not feel invasive or inappropriate. The being responds in kind. There is no malice.

My overloaded curiosity becomes empathic trust. This makes me think the person is a child, who else would extend total trust?

The person is taller and also more bulbous than a child.

My smiling lips betray wonder. The awe I feel has spirited into exquisite allure as a sense of personhood expands before me—as allocentric connectivity. The methods of the gaze have to be refreshed from my brain center to my central nervous system, the systems that categorize and access human-to-human activity—a multifaceted physiological process.

There is a sparkling quality as if every sand particle is a crystal glinting in sunlight. As I look around, I look through the person in front of me. They are barely materialized. They flicker in front of me. They reach out.

The taste of saltwater, kelp, and herbs permeate my mouth. My saliva is suddenly gritty. No smell can be detected. An incredible thirst arrives. Breathing feels heavy, like dragging the world into the recesses of the body. A sip of water becomes crucial. My water bottle is by my feet, and I grab for it. The turquoise enamel gleams brilliantly. What a giddy feeling to have transported water in my very own turquoise carrying container!

Everything wobbles in a jellylike tub of light. It takes a second to refocus. To see the person again. And the others gathered around them. If I readjust my center of attention, I feel vertigo. I'm thankful that I'm in a seated position. The hazmat suit is bunched around my legs and torso so there is little recognition of my own body. I glance at my legs like they are foreign matter. The suit is so bright! Like space junk faded by solar rays.

They and everything in a matrix of their social space appears sand colored. There are tonalites of taupe, sandstone, burnt sienna, and a more granite-toned gray. As yet, I can only see an oval portal in space through which to access them. Around the edges is clearly the usual world in which I exist.

My attention shifts momentarily to the performance, the fact that we are gathered here as artists. Art might be good at generating incipient recognition. If so, something is happening, like catalytic generativity.

I feel anticipatory of the present as it continually reasserts itself to appear seamless.

Performing with the *Wiwaxia* in mind is not a passing fancy. Animals that resemble plants greatly interest me. The *Wiwaxia* has these qualities. They look like sea grasses sprouting from the ocean's floor. This ancient animal comes to my mind as I grasp again for the hand that reaches toward me. How am I perceived?

The person I notice appears camouflaged within a landscape of sand and dry, powdery dirt. Their skin tone is mottled somewhat, with tones of brown, red, tan, and light gray. Their eyes are also distinct. One eye is bluish, the other violet. I cannot place this person into a racial category, and when I think of doing so, I shudder.

Uneasiness enters. I have to look away, as I am caught in two frameworks, involved in an enigma or an optical illusion but everything tells me it's not a trick of light or a mishap in seeing. My rational mind has not overridden the situation. I blink in a present tense—the past and future are its suspending agents.

The *Wiwaxia* has characteristics of a thistle. *Cirsium andrewsii*, endemic to California. Thorny and delicate. I equate this plant with resistance. Thistle (as did the *Wiwaxia*) have awesome things that they can do, that they do, how they impact their environment. A copious feeding source for pollinators, the thistle. Why the spikes? To avoid being eaten. It is a defense mechanism I can relate to. Red brushlike flowers grow on bristled stems in habitats of disturbed soil. Other thistles are listed as invasive. Maps indicate where the spread has overwhelmed indigenous plants. The *Wiwaxia*, did they come to land? Are they relatives of *Cirsium andrewsii*, possibly connected far into the lineage?

My colleague brought dirt samples from our various plots to a lab for testing. The findings were remarkable. There were particles from the benthic domains of the ocean, there was sediment of rock formations from as far away as the Indian subcontinent, also microevidence of material from all seven layers of the earth. The findings revealed nanoscopic and larger pieces of tourmaline, garnet, kunzite, rhodonite, mariposite, obsidian, opal, benitoite, and other gems. Petrified wood was abundant. Clay and absorptive materials were found intermixed in the granules. There were also traces of DDT, cesium, rocket fuel, atrazine, and many other hazardous substances. Plastic was also present. A colloidal mixture that is plastic and viscous because water is a bipolar medium. Within the sediment were teeming life-forms. The report came back with listings of bacteria, viruses, fungi, algae, protozoa, mycorrhizae, and actinomycetes—that, when I inquired, is one of the living elements that lends soil its smell. There were nematodes, earthworms, millipedes, and insects. Included were various pathogens. The chemical and biological fertility of the soil relies on an incredibly intricate and complex interactive microbiological community living within diverse materials and weather conditions conducive to their thriving. The soil is electrically charged. Matter millions of years old and organisms born moments ago coexisting. That poem in the volume *If They Come in the Morning . . . Voices of Resistance*, edited by Angela Davis. Ericka Huggins. She got it.

> The oldness of new things
> Fascinate me like a new
> Feeling about love about people.

The person attracting my attention is wearing a headdress, some plumage on their head. Feathers? Floral sprigs?

earth science

THE TALL TEXTURE OF CATASTROPHE IS ERODED, IN SOME DEGREE,
IS MINIATURIZED, IN SOME DEGREE, TO MAKE A RE-CREATIVE
VISION POSSIBLE, BEARABLE, EVEN AT THE END OF TIME (OR WHAT
PASSES FOR THE END OF TIME).

—WILSON HARRIS

GIANT MOUNTAINS, CZECH REPUBLIC BORDER WITH POLAND, EARTH INDICES, GOLDEN SPIKES, RESONANCES

An international scientific body called the Anthropocene Working Group (AWG) established in 2009 has been tasked with endeavoring to pinpoint when, precisely, humans began impacting the earth in an all-encompassing way as to necessitate the establishment of a moniker for a new geologic time period. This new present-day epoch has been named the Anthropocene. The AWG has organized thirty-five scientists into teams to work at eleven locations around the world. Other auxiliary sites might be explored in the future. Their work is collaborative and also competitive. Each team hopes to locate the most convincing marker, called a Global Boundary Stratotype Section and Point (GSSP), also known as a "golden spike," that indicates an irreversible crossing of a geological threshold. Each site offers crucial clues in the form of radio-isotopes, remnant plastics, and other toxins that reside indelibly in the core of the earth, in ice, in stalactites and stalagmites, and at the bottom of undisturbed lakes. Their findings will be presented for final assessment to the International Commission on Stratigraphy (ICS). The results will then be ratified by the executive committee of the International Union of Geological Sciences (IUGS). A final summary will be compiled and presented. The data needs to prove a globally synchronous moment in time that can be correlated with evidence from all of the sites around the world. There is general consensus among scientists that the climate cycle known as the Holocene, a homeostatic period that began at the end of the glacial period nearly twelve thousand years ago, has ended. The higher divisions have not changed. The Quaternary Period, which began 2.6 million years ago, continues—*Homo erectus* appeared in Africa in the beginning of this period. *Homo erectus* has been altering the earth for a very long time but it is contemporary, industrialized humanity that accelerated planet-wide change.

The AWG has summarized a compendium of anthropogenic effects as follows:

> Phenomena associated with the Anthropocene include: an order-of-magnitude increase in erosion and sediment transport associated with urbanization and agriculture; marked and abrupt anthropogenic perturbations of the cycles of elements such as carbon, nitrogen, phosphorus and various metals together with new chemical compounds; environmental changes generated by these perturbations, including global warming, sea-level rise, ocean acidification and spreading oceanic "dead zones"; rapid changes in the biosphere both on land and in the sea, as a result of habitat loss, predation, explosion of domestic animal populations and species invasions; and the proliferation and global dispersion of many new "minerals" and "rocks" including concrete, fly ash and plastics, and the myriad "technofossils" produced from these and other materials.

Many of the effects will persist for millions of years. Each category of disruption represents a magnitude of disaster not experienced before by *Homo sapiens*.

Core samples are taken and examined. Toxic accumulation and cycles of depletion in stratified layers are compared for their distribution and intensity. At one site, while a team was in action, everyone paused for a moment to process the news that for the first time in human history, carbon dioxide emissions had gone beyond 420 parts per million. They learned about the record high accumulation of carbon dioxide in the atmosphere from a local radio broadcast that one of the scientists played loudly on their cellphone. The occurrence was indecipherable to their senses. The day had been unremarkable, not particularly hot, or cold, quite comfortable. What the numbers predicted remained in the domain of their imagination. They quickly returned to what they had previously been focused on.

A subalpine plateau in the Krkonoše (Giant) Mountains on the border between the Czech Republic and Poland. A four-foot core is extracted from the peatland in the Giant Mountain range.

My name is Petra. I'm a researcher who specializes in paleoecology and biogeography at Adam Mickiewicz University in Poland. I'm in charge of the excavation at Giant Mountains. Several assistants have traveled here with me. Together we pulled out a tube of sediment: brown, viscous, greasy, and hairy looking—the decaying arm of a Neanderthal. The area is peatland, waterlogged; organic matter doesn't fully decompose. For a moment we are all amused. Later, in the lab we'll make jokes again because the stump really does resemble a hominoid arm. Science takes a back seat to the spectacle of withdrawing something from inner earth that has distinct anthropomorphic features. But it is not the limb of an early human, or any mammal; what we've excavated is the residual material of 149 years of built-up accumulation from many sources, quite possibly containing traces of mammalian tissue, certainly macrofossils will show up, as well as pollen and traces of other unique signatures. We will closely examine the material record to determine what elements are present in the composition and determine when the extant humanly produced elements accumulated. The sample is an expressive biopsy of the layers of the planet. The giddy moment passes. With utmost care and precision, we lay the core down on a preprepped tarp, it is still tightly bound by the plastic canister used to lift it out of the ground. We then meticulously roll the tarp up around it for additional protection. It will be stored in a tub of dry ice until it reaches the lab.

One of my assistants, Liz, says that taking a core is invasive. There are organisms living in the sample that will die. Liz stands at the sidelines, assisting me in a subdued mood. She is the mood ring. We can detect atmospheric conditions by her expressions. She feeds measurements into a graph on a tablet. Liz has voiced her issues but participates fully. Her work is always meticulous. I briefly wonder how anyone so sensitive can exist in this world. I consider myself to be sensitive as to how findings are collected, sensitive to the inquiry itself, what it means to probe a living planet for signs of distress, a living planet, home to numerosity. I guess I share her misgivings. I'm more aligned with her ethics than I first allow myself to consider. My livelihood depends on not straying too far from a set protocol of scientific mandates, yet I often do so anyway. While I have been contracted to make a finding of the material properties of the core sample, I am also conducting research that deviates significantly from everything I have learned, yet I am convinced my meanderings run parallel in unforeseen ways. I make a note to self to encourage Liz's instincts.

I have, over the last year, used simple instrumentation to detect vibratory registers of materials I collect. Basically, I use a tuning fork to home in on the resonances an object gives off, including the core sample and other materials I find myself compelled by in the environment. I borrow this practice from Maayan Tsadka, a composer and sound artist

I happened upon on the internet, whose recent composition, *Sonic Botany: RA'ASH ADAMA (earthnoise)* drew my attention. Her performance was filmed outdoors in various locations. Tsadka defines her work as an interest in "the memory of matter; an amorphous memory of space that registers, remembers and repeats the acoustic occurrences in different time-scales." In one sequence she is seated in a cave, using her lips to hold a leaf in her mouth as she regulates exhalation to create tonalities. The compositions Tsadka makes require a level of engagement different from field recording, though the recording of the ambient sounds in the environment are important. She plays florae, it is her instrumentation. The sounds she generates are signatures of time fluctuating in response to animacy. The metal of the tuning fork has a role, as does her corporality and the materials she invites into the composition. The pressure and temperature of air affects sound. An acoustical wave will ride a gas, liquid, or solid. There's also ultrasound and infrasound to consider. I recently learned about the time crystal, a quantum object that repeats in time rather than space and never loses energy, never halts its motion, and is almost frozen in time. That's the arena of aural presence interesting to me. Noticing the intensity of focus with which she holds a tuning fork to a dried seed pod encouraged me to emulate her approach. Engaging similar practices created a rapport with ecology and geology in ways I hadn't anticipated.

Making sonic field recordings is similar to collecting material samples in the field. The properties of the environment express tonality, texture, density, and weight. Sounds affect living organisms. Sounds imperceptible to the human ear affect ecological conditions. A sound becomes elusive as it recedes, subsiding to the point of being submerged under the cacophony of the surround (and internal registers of vibration). How do different forms of sentience experience the dissipation of sound, I wonder.

Tsadka's conceptualization seems important for attuning to the consideration of climate disruption and the all-encompassing impact it is having. Some changes are subtle, at a subatomic level regarding properties of being that involve how everything resonates. I attempt to attune myself to the disturbances. The goal is to prime all senses simultaneously to be able to perceive disturbances, avoiding a fixed center of attention. Physical changes involve mental and spiritual changes. As a scientist I am not opposed to such lines of thinking. I've been encouraging it. Preparation is a process that involves shedding thinking that won't be helpful or useful when variables change. The impulse is preternatural. Coming this far in my research only to be attracted to an additional set of questions that stimulate engagement with ecological histories from a different angle is perhaps a breakthrough. What is now compelling me, I start to understand, is actually more of an extension of my work rather than a detour. The bicameral nature of my pursuits has, perhaps, put my career in jeopardy because of the dispersed focus, though science as a constellatory discipline is morphing. If the environment is constantly shifting and changing so too are the principles of objectivity. A speculative edge has always provoked scientific inquiry. Now is the time to go a step further in stretching the capacity of hypothesis. I relinquished a sense of control; the modicum of control I thought I had in whatever domain I focus on. This, too, has been a gradual process of release. More and more, I sense how other forces steer the direction, that my ego has little, if any, command over most decisions. I was convinced I was studying one aspect of ecological reality when I was being subtly directed toward something else tangentially.

The brochure on a rack in the entrance of the bed-and-breakfast states: "Geologically, the Giant Mountains formed in the period of the Proterozoic and Early Paleozoic eras, with orogeny processes producing the first appearance of the massif called the Krkonoše-Jizera crystalline complex. Mesozoic weathering, Tertiary alpine orogeny, subsequent water erosion and recurrent Quaternary glaciation gradually transformed the natural appearance of the Giant into its current form. However, it is human activity that has altered localized areas of landscape over the past millennium." The brochure articulates how vast eras of time can be compressed into language. The Paleoproterozoic era is when oxygen first appeared in the atmosphere beyond a trace level. A staggering thought. Tectonic plates shifted drastically, the cores of continents collided and rifted. Plants had not yet appeared on land. The Great Oxygenation Event occurred during this time; prokaryotic photosynthesizers, including the newly evolved cyanobacteria and eukaryotic algae, emitted oxygen that drastically altered the atmosphere. Initially solubilized iron in the oceans absorbed the oxygen. When the iron could not absorb any additional oxygen, it became airborne. The Proterozoic geological period extended from the end of the Archaean eon, 2,500 million years ago, or 2,500 Ma, to the start of the Phanerozoic Eon, 545 Ma. It was a period of orange methane skies and green iron-laden oceans. A vast fantastical spacetime. Descriptors burn into the brain cavity.

The region holds promise as a golden spike site because it has a history of high-density coal processing, and the peatbogs accumulate matter for clear analysis. Modes of extraction and labor are absorbed by this place. During my childhood in Poland, coal-firing plants sent fly ash into the atmosphere; it was strewn everywhere. My family lived near one of the biggest mines in the country: Maja coal mine, located in Wodzisław Śląski. Many in the region had asthma and other respiratory illnesses; now they have cancers. Presently, 55 percent of Poland's energy consumption is from coal, and 75 percent of its electricity derives from coal. Coal firing is now regulated and is considered by many to be "clean"; the byproduct coal ash is used to make concrete and mixed into asphalt for road resurfacing. Coal burning is most likely surpassed by nuclear explosions when it relates to chronostratigraphic considerations and the golden spike. We look for lead, cesium, plutonium, and other trace element concentrations.

In the Giant Mountain region, chronology is congealed, hardened into stone, or mushy, thanks to the peat; deep time is extant as distinct layers and loosened, mixed through disturbances. The dirt, ground down evidence of intergenerational activity. Mosses, grasses, and cloudberries growing on the Krkonoše-Jizera crystalline complex draw water through pores in their leaves and through their roots, liquid crosses several cell layers to reach central channel tubes in their xylem. Plants do not have a metabolically active pump like a heart so the mechanism of powering the circulation of liquid happens with negative pressure caused by evaporation pushing flow through vascular tubes. Today a cloud that burst yesterday is making its way inside the nodes and internodes of plants as they recycle forms and functions. The mosses growing over the rocks appear as fur.

Mosses draw me to their soft, pillowy world. As I hike around the crystalline complex I become lethargic and find mosses coaxing me to lie down. I submit to the unspoken suggestion. Do the mosses emit a sleep-inducing chemical? I wonder. Or do they produce a subtle resonant tone that draws me to them? Cyanobacteria associated with mosses fixate nitrogen from the air. What else are they performing? For miles the zone is soft reddish hazy overgrowth with featherlike extensions of lime green.

The mosses are tough and soft. As I lean into the softness, I experience a tingling sensation often described as an autonomous sensory meridian response, an auditory-tactile synesthesia that travels from my head to my toes and to my fingertips. Time spools in a suspension between senses. Time is expressed in the phenology of leaves and petals. I meditate on the seasonal cycles of plants as I drift off into subconsciousness. Listening is absorptive. I listen as time absorbs time with zero contradiction. Listening encourages nonattachment. Sound negotiates the environment with a broadcasted range of tonalities. I'm convinced time and sound have the same objective, that they travel together, always on the move: they are involved in cocreation. Acoustic spatiality is time itself, which is involved with everything, life and death intertwined as a continuum of resonances. In the immediate environment, I became aware of how everything is being affected by resonances, as well as circulating sound, each offering a unique dynamic. But it is the combinatory layered involvements created in sound that strike me. The ambience of attack and decay mixing and flowing in a matrix. The core was safely contained in the large plastic carrying container; I could relax. I could extrapolate infinitely. I could become other.

I fall into a light, translucent sleep as if levitating atop the mosses. My subconsciousness transplants me to the floating world, a fourth dimension now available experientially. The meadow of mat-grass, knee timber, and mosses cause a harmonization of the rate of respiration of the mitochondria in my body with the respiration of the green growth around me. Chemical reactions become pronounced. Protoplasm and protoplasts. The sugars in my body and the sugars in the plants correspond.

Zofia, my other research assistant, awakens me. She needs the key to the bed-and-breakfast. She lost her key somewhere in the mosses and no amount of groping for it leads to recovery. She stands a few feet from where I recline hoping I'll wake up—she waits like a statue, not uttering a word. The shadow that her body casts causes the air to become damper, chilly. The slight change in temperature and light reactivates waking consciousness. When I open my eyes, I immediately give her my key before she has the chance to ask. With an astonished look on her face she whispers, "You are green!" I don't know how to pursue her outlandish comment. She turns and runs toward the bed-and-breakfast. Within a minute she is a speck in the distance. All that can be seen of her is her dark gray windbreaker. With my cellphone I take a selfie to see what Zofia means. I have a green aura. My skin tone has a greenish glow. The tuning fork is in my bag at the bed-and-breakfast or I would take some readings of the vibrations around me. The selfie image suggests that I am trembling because it was out of focus. There is much more work to do to understand the resonances and frequencies of these mossy, windswept lands.

SAN FRANCISCO BAY, CALIFORNIA, UNITED STATES, SKEPTICISM

The effort we make to log periodicities to determine when humans entered a new geological era is not without controversy. The term *Anthropocene* has been batted around since the 1980s and only gained traction in 2000 when biologist Eugene Stoermer and atmospheric chemist Paul J. Crutzen popularized it. Crutzen passed away in January 2021, coinciding with when our team had gathered in the lab to study the cores. I became aware of the term in 1990, when I was in the process of finishing up my PhD. At a conference a fellow panelist used the term. The term added to the jargon of our field, but I quickly understood this was broader than the domain of science. The term would affect how humans thought about terrestrial existence. Some feel the term leaves out the critical effects of capitalism and have given the epoch the name the "Capitalocene." I tend to agree with theorist Donna Haraway that more than one name is warranted. She and her colleagues came up with the name "Plantationocene" to "account for the devastating transformation of diverse kinds of human-tended farms, pastures, and forests into extractive and enclosed plantations, relying on slave labor and other forms of exploited, alienated, and usually spatially transported labor" and also to acknowledge the ways in which plants make sentient life possible. Haraway also proposed "Chthulucene" as a working term to signify kinship relations across the spectrum of species. The time to decenter the "human" is upon us.

There are eleven teams in total, representing the Anthropocene Working Group. We have concentrated on the specific timeframe of the 1950s to 1960s to find the golden spike. Other theorists, and as I continue to research, I add myself here, want to push the date back to the time of European contact with the Americas. Fifty million (probably a low estimate) Indigenous people died as a result of European colonization in the Americas. Ecosystems were greatly impacted. Some suggest going

207

back in time further to the Agricultural Revolution, the dawn of farming, sometime between 12,000 and 15,000 years ago. Our final summaries will be submitted to the Subcommission on Quaternary Stratigraphy.
There will be a global meeting held in Europe where our findings will be
presented. One spike will be determined emblematic for its concise rendering of a boundary line, an emergent era.

Wrestling with myself I grapple with thoughts about climate, planetary life. I often wonder if it is a feedback loop of compromised thinking
to place all the agency on humans when the planet itself contributes to
the dialogue. Earth's responsiveness to all extant terrestrial (and cosmic)
conditions is actually what guides this suspended circular island that or-
bits the sun—a momentary island in a blip of time. Other weighted bodies and nonweighted bodies in the cosmos exact influence, greater than
can be presently calculated. Tipping points are occurring faster than humans can wrap their heads around the problem, let alone develop solutions. At a global temperature rise of 1.1 degrees Celsius, where it is presently, it may be that five tipping points have already occurred. Global
systems move far quicker than climate analysis. It is impossible to be
stand-alone, so to speak; and to place humans in an exclusive, exclu-
sionary category is facile. That interdependences have been unacknowl-
edged provokes havoc. Climate change is the ultimate wake-up call to
interrelatedness.

Humans—disproportionately wealthy, white, Western industrial leaders making decisions about energy, transportation, infrastructure, and
living in all its intricacies—are historically and immediately responsible for the unfolding catastrophe that affects everyone, though not uni-
formly. Race, class, and gender determine the severity of effects experienced whether they be related to health, income, housing, access to food,
safety, and a feeling of belonging. It is ugly to have to draw attention to
power and where it is seated. Will the solutions follow historical prece-
dent? Zombie arguments amplify the confusion on how to grapple with
existential questions.

Now the intended goal is to spare humans a fate of die out, extinction.
Other animals and plants appear to be an afterthought in this calcula-
tion. Due to narcissism and bias, it is convenient to think of humans first,
at the exclusion of the interwoven processes that sustain a delicate equilibrium for a time, allowing for humans and other sentience to flourish.

Humans are just one variation of how materials organize, how life expresses itself.

Clarification: I am not trying to discount the human baggage surrounding responsibility and action. I have no illusions how the planet has become toxic, how extinction of the diversification of the planet's plants and animals is taking place or how carbon dioxide and other greenhouse gases have accumulated in the atmosphere. It is easy to make a running list of the culprits. Methane: biomass burning, livestock agriculture, fossil fuel production, rice cultivation. Carbon dioxide—everyone is aware of the reasons for its accumulation. The use of fossil fuels engineered the architectures of Western modernity. Better to lay it all out in the main corridors of our critical attention and get to work on some strategies for living differently. I do not think there are solutions, per se, but there are strategies that humans can take that will aid survivability as an interspecies goal. Because what is the point of human longevity if all else fails? I do worry that we'll get it wrong. Again, we'll get it wrong.

As a scientist, a microbial geneticist, it is clear to me that it is crucial to describe the problem in open, fluid, and inclusive terms. Again, I engage Haraway as a jumping off point when she writes, "The sciences of the Anthropocene are too much contained within restrictive systems theories and within evolutionary theories called the Modern Synthesis, which for all their extraordinary importance have proven unable to think well about sympoiesis, symbiosis, symbiogenesis, development, webbed ecologies, and microbes. That's a lot of trouble for adequate evolutionary theory." So, what do I mean by more open, fluid, and inclusive terms? Sometimes I am not sure. Emergent planning will arise, human actions and actions outside of the purview of humans—as is usual of earthliness—will coalesce. There is a microlevel that is just now being taken into serious consideration. Major terraforming is accomplished by miniscule organisms. Codes are circulated, translated, enacted, mutated. Codes are communicative commands. DNA and RNA are two such examples. There are others. Nano, quantum. Codes that are made by presences that are difficult to determine if alive or not. Diasporas of cosmic code make their way to terrestrial environments and vice versa. Senders are receivers, receivers, senders. My scientific niche is proof that there is vast diversity within these quandaries. I tend to be skeptical of anything larger than ten microns.

Though I am a scientist I question self-determination. I question objectivity. I question evidence. Facts are always dissolving and shifting and altering. Facts have finite terms of validity. There are too many factual details to account for. Subjectivity and objectivity always work in tandem no matter how clean the lab. So, I focus on inflections.

Rav is one of my colleagues on this project. He's figured me out and gives me wide latitude when I get into a jag about predicaments that have no definitive answers, when I have the need to rehearse my hesitations and, frankly, just vent my frustrations. I'm forever appreciative of his generosity, I hope I'm not taking advantage of his stamina to hear me out. His patience is exemplary. With the others I remain professional, stay within the boundaries of our association.

There is so much going on right now. Distractions that beg attention. As we work, whales circle our crew. They appear in distress. Jerry, another colleague, does some research. The Northern Pacific gray whale has decreased in population by almost 24 percent in half a decade. Evidently the whales are starved; they can't build up their blubber. Their food sources in the Arctic have disappeared. They are washing up on the shores of California, dead. The largest living forms of sentience, dying around us. Four Pacific gray whales in the span of a week alone were found in the San Francisco Bay. How can we not partake in their struggle, their misery? We circle a dead whale on the beach, and even in its bloated condition notice how emaciated it is. Part of me wants to drop everything and somehow come to the assistance of the whales, but how? For the entire time we've been working on this project, the whales have been dying around us. We internalize the distress the whales are experiencing. There is also a terrible irony in the situation. Dying is individualized in the United States. It seems impossible to witness or connect with collective dying, collective death. This has become obvious in the time of the pandemic and the time of mass extinction. There's a major disconnect. The bandwidth necessary to receive the information hasn't been inculcated. My mother is in hospice in her home and as she tunes into the nightly news, she wonders out loud why everything is dying, having lost the filters necessary to sublimate the onslaught of death. When I visit her, I unplug the television and stream music in, or better still, welcome engulfment by the hum of the refrigerator, the song of birds and traffic outside her apartment window. "Shayla, thank you," she says in the softest voice.

On my mind for a while too is something nebulous. The displacements of terminology. The loosening taxonomies, the breakdown of signs. My colleagues who grok the data amaze me with their confidence in the results. I worry how our data, incomplete as it is, might easily be deployed by big corporations, intergovernmental agencies, and nation-states in times of crisis. Science is hauled out as the standard-bearer of integrity and ethics, yet we know this isn't always so and has not always been the case historically. Scientists can be overridden by profit-driven motivations, directed by industry. Biases affect science. An ethics isn't necessarily built into process or application. Studying the cores intensified this realization for me. And the reverse gives me worry too—that critical science is being discounted. That alarm bells are blaring but being ignored. Rav, noticing I am slipping again says to me, "All we can do is focus and follow our questions. I'm just quoting you back to yourself, Shayla." Regardless of the possibility that our questions take us off the grid, into unresolvable territories, out of professionalized jurisdiction, out of our psychic and philosophic comfort zone, we must pursue the questions that arise. I did say that, and I do stand by it. The cores are fascinating. Everything is in there: organic and inorganic matter, plant, animal, and mineral remnants layered and compressed. Maybe some answers too, and more questions. The core is our litmus test.

SIHAILONGWAN LAKE, JILIN PROVINCE, CHINA, A LAKE LIKE AN EYEBALL CONTAINS A GOLDEN SPIKE

Goal: examination of the sedimented layers (varves) from core samples extracted from the maar lake. We are here to take accurate paleoenvironmental records. Sihailongwan Lake is nearly a perfect circle with water a bright blue the shade of turquoise in certain atmospheric conditions. The lake gives the sensation of being an optical illusion. It looks like a cut-out, as if the sky had filled in negative space in the middle of a forest. The lake is part of the Longgang volcanic field.

Volcanic activity is responsible for the creation of maars, eruptions create the craters. Steam blasts through ground material leaving behind shallow formations that fill with water. The banks of the lake are made of tephra, glassy particles that built up after a volcanic eruption. They resemble a skateboard rink that grew trees, that's how pitched they are. There are nine maar lakes in the region. Magmatic history and parental melt last in the basement layers of rock. The coring sites are in the middle of the lake, like the center of an eyeball, open, gazing upward. In the warmer months our neon bubble markers float on the water's surface.

We took the samples in winter when the lake was frozen at a thickness of half a meter. We skidded on the ice in our high-tech boots, trying to gain traction on the shiny frozen surface. Several snowmobiles accompanied us, loaded with our gear. Our basecamp was at a village several miles away.

Before joining the team, my work consisted of petrographic and geochemical research. I focused primarily on magma flows to better understand crystal populations. Magma undergoes several processes when it travels within the earth's crust. Magmatic processes generate crystals of varying scale. I became interested in the large antecrysts, crystals from progenitor magma that form when not in equilibrium with host magma but get reincorporated before eruption takes place. Because of the paleovolcanic activity of the Longgang volcanic field, I was assigned to work closely with a paleogeologist who specializes in collection and analysis of core samples that reveal sedimented dust and detritus. There's one other team member, a geomicrobiologist. For this study we are taking cores that give representation to the last one hundred years with the 1950s through the 1960s being the decades of interest as we deliberate when to mark the beginning of the Anthropocene. We'll prepare samples for thin-section microscopy of pollen, dust, and the microgametophytes of plant seeds that produce male sperm cells. We also came looking for spores, microscopic plankton, and the diversity of other palynomorphs in living and fossilized form. Forensic botany, plant genetics, plant physiology, and plant evolution come together to reveal changes in growing patterns among plants and animals through time. The diminutive world of microfossils gives us the historical information about climate change that we need to determine emerging patterns that help us better understand catastrophic climate destabilization, to begin to know what to anticipate in the future.

I may be the odd person out, because I'm a gem person, less so a fossil person, and I don't focus on biogenetic substances. But it is amply clear that our team values the diversity and range of our combined knowledge base. There are processes that transform fossils into gems. Living organisms become carbon, become stone, become diamonds, for instance.

The other members of the team have studied fossils and the residue of organisms that have existed as long ago as the Cambrian period, when the first terrestrial land plants were found in the record, a lengthy green lineage. The arrival of plants is constantly shifting, being pushed to an earlier date. Molecular and genetic studies often focus on the liverwort family as being one of the earliest forms of land plant. Mosses are directly related to liverwort plants. Early plant life was cryptogamic ground cover, no seeds were involved. These plants carpeted the land while floral marine organisms proliferated in the oceans. The search for the cysts of marine phytoplankton gives clues about the carbon cycling of the oceans, among other things. When dealing with eons of time it is impossible to stay within a conscribed, well, *box*.

Our work brings together the considerations of abiotic and biological drivers. As a mineralogist I relish coming in contact with biota, especially the microorganisms that lived millions of years ago that we can locate in the sediment layers. Sometimes the same organisms still flourish

213

in the environment. Jiaqi, the paleogeologist, jokes with me, "Feng, we need your quartz rigor to accurately ascribe the correct time to fossilized life!" "Yeah, I know, who is going to offer crystal precision if I'm not around." I may be the least precision-minded of the group. I work with rough estimates and often speculative numerics. When I visited the Giant Crystal Cave in Chihuahua, Mexico, my first impression was that I was inside an imploded clock. The crystals look like fallen clock hands; a chamber filled with immense fallen clock hands. A mining company had pumped the water out of the cave, making it accessible. We were allowed to clamber over the enormous gleaming white crystals of selenite. Never have I felt such wonder. There is evidently another cave above the Giant Crystal Cave called the Cave of Swords, smaller in size, with sleek stabbing crystals. I was not able to enter. Since that time, the caves have reflooded.

The geomicrobiologist in our team bridges whatever gaps exist in the modes of our collective scientific study. Her name is Xue, she also goes by the name Barbara, but prefers Xue. Her expertise is extremophile organisms. We often refer to her as the extremophile, a nickname that immediately stuck—how could it not. "The extremophile is rolling in late today," we called out when she arrived at the lake an hour after us because her snowmobile had issues. Xue gets into the minutiae of extreme environments to understand how plants and animals cope in those places. Carbon-based life has its sweet spots. There is a plethora of organisms who thrive in zones where carbon-based life is threatened: in high salt concentrations, in radiation, in toxic environments, in the extreme cold, in the extreme heat, in the dark, in the deep. Some organisms live within rocks. Everyone seems enamored with tardigrades, also known as moss piglets or water bears. They can squeeze the water out of their bodies and roll into a ball, almost like a microscopic pebble, maintaining homeostasis for decades. These microscopic creatures are able to withstand the conditions inside of a volcano, as well as the deep freeze of Antarctica; even outer space is no match for their capacity to endure. Extreme pressure doesn't faze them, nor does radiation. Xue is quick to point out that what feels good for one species is not at all what another prefers. We know this intellectually, but ramifications can be overlooked.

Catastrophes are catastrophes for some and not for others. Xue's favorite example is the purple ocean theory. "Mauve waves crashed," we listened as she recounted an era of early Earth when purple tides ebbed and flowed, swirled, and crashed against much different shorelines. Her account took us back some 4.5 to 2.3 billion years ago when the oceans might have been partly anoxic and sulphidic, containing low levels of oxygen. This period was a time when organisms used anoxygenic photosynthesis. Instead of having chlorophyll to help absorb sunlight, organisms relied on retinol to absorb light, specifically, the green portion of the sun's rays, reflecting back purple coloration. "There are niches where you can see this today," she elaborated. "We live in a time of reflected green light." She demonstrated to us with a sweeping hand gesture that moved our gaze to the thick forests encircling Sihailongwan Lake. "The Great Oxygenation Event decimated the purple-reflecting life-forms, blue-green algae began colonizing the oceans." Two contemporaneous places to witness this purple phenomenon, she told us, are the Grand Prismatic Spring in Yellowstone Park and the Trapani Salt Pans in Sicily. "Never rule out a return to a purple world," the extremophile said dramatically. "We are getting there with the frequency of red tides." Jiaqi added. Color is often a clue. And the core itself is multicolored, revealing differences in banded layers, known as varve chronology. The macroscopic photographs of pale diatom laminae and dark organic detritus and other sedimentation are always stunningly beautiful to me. The Sihailongwan Lake cores are striations of white, dark brown, yellow, and lighter gray muds. Lacustrine deposit samples, meaning those that are extracted from lakes, are important to compare with cores extracted from other ecological sites. I think of us as the eyeball lake team.

My trip was nearly halted by an unsettling series of events. I was invited to Chicago by a colleague whom I had not seen in a while. I accepted. We would spend a long weekend catching up, that was the plan. Nadeem is a veterinarian for aquatic animals. While I was at his place, he got a call that an elderly fish was in distress. He had been monitoring the situation for weeks and it was determined through a conference call with other veterinarians and aquarium staff that the fish would have to be euthanized. The fish was experiencing organ failure. The creature, a lungfish, was more than ninety years old. He was brought to the aquarium in 1933 from an aquarium in Australia. His name was Granddad, and for the last few days he had not touched his food.

I was quite interested to meet this Australian Lungfish, Granddad. To catch a glimpse of him before he passed. He is of a lineage that has existed for at least 380 million years, and for the last 100 million years the species has changed only slightly. Granddad had both lungs and gills as is distinctive of lungfish. Australian lungfish are from a region in Queensland. They live in two rivers: the Moocooboola River (renamed the Mary River by settler colonists who moved into Taribelang land) and the Burnett River—I was astounded to find out how hard it was to learn of this river's Aboriginal name. A search came up dry. It was obfuscated by the legacy of white, male, colonial "discovery"—Burnett refers to the name of surveyor James Charles Burnett, who came to the region in 1847 on an exploratory mission. The *Journal of the Royal Geographical Society of Australia* published a dictionary in 1943 of the vocabularies of four representative tribes of southeastern Queensland, but it does not include the name of the river (nor does it include the generic name for river). In total the dictionary is nine pages long. The closest word to *river* I could find in that dictionary was the word *creek: kir ar.* The nearest semblance to *water* I could find in that dictionary was the word *rain.* In Wakka Wakka language, *rain* is *kuwong; kuang.* I consulted most of the institutions in the region, including the language centers. Most of the Aboriginal speakers who were fluent in the local languages of the region have passed on. It is important to learn the true name of the river, the name the inhabitants of the land gave it. It is crucial that the name of the river is not erased or absorbed. The Aboriginal Gubbi Gubbi name for the fish is the *dala,* a sacred, totemic fish. An ancestor of humans. Gubbi Gubbi land includes the Mary River Basin and its catchments and the Glass House Mountains. Eating the dala or climbing the mountains is prohibited and will bring bad luck. There are several other lungfish species that live elsewhere throughout the world, but the Australian lungfish is the most ancient.

Consciousness of expansive durational time is in this fish's DNA. I hoped to look deeply into his eyes to gain an understanding of an evolutionary continuum.

When we arrived at the aquarium there were many people gathered in front of the large glass tank. It had been determined how and when Granddad's life would be terminated. We had about two hours of time together. The mood was expectant and somber, but also electrifying. Humans dictating the life and time of death for a member of another species certainly felt strange. I was nervous and a bit upset about the conditions of his impending death.

Granddad appeared ancient and tired, but I was told that this is nearly how he looked and moved most of his life: slowly and purposefully, his scales and skin a grayish green. His scales reminded me of the scales of a pangolin and also scaled armor worn by soldiers of the Roman Empire. His doleful eyes were clouded, and his skin and scales mottled, indicating his seniority. He was brought to the tank with his mate, now long dead. I was told how they both would submerge to the bottom of the tank and rest indefinitely, eventually come up for food and air now and again. I wondered about Granddad's early memories prior to captivity. I wondered about the carceral nature of aquariums and zoos.

Granddad was moved to an auxiliary tank, much smaller and with an open vault so that he could be accessed easily. After a moment of silence, my friend and another member of the staff secured him, and an injection went in subcutaneously. This happened rather smoothly but Granddad did thrash around for a second. As he thrashed, water from the tank splashed me and I felt a jellylike substance in my eyes when I rubbed. It must have been biofilm living on the body of Granddad. I did not think much of it until sometime later, as we left the aquarium, after my friend had filled out paperwork and debriefed with his colleagues. When we sat in the car, heading out to grab lunch, I could tell that my eyes were reacting. My vision was blurred, and my eyes were bloodshot. "Would you take a look at my eyes," I asked Nadeem. "Your eyes?" He expressed concern. "Yes, I got water from the tank on them, they feel inflamed." "Oh, this isn't good—your eyes are bleeding!" he exclaimed, and I could tell he was moving the car into another lane. "I'm taking you to the hospital, immediately!" he said with punctuated alarm. "Feng!" Nadeem said my name with increasing alarm, but I could not respond. I blacked out before we reached the emergency room. Thus began the odyssey of identifying an organism that seemingly had never been observed in Chicago, or in Illinois for that matter. The organism was anomalous. The hospital sent a sample to the CDC, and they advised a treatment protocol.

When I regained consciousness, Nadeem was still with me. "How do you feel?" he asked, looking down at me encased by stiff white cotton sheets in the hospital bed. The question felt immense, too gigantic to respond to. All I could say that made sense was that I felt I was in a rubbery cocoon and that the world had become a parched, brutal environment, without water, without flow. Scratchy. The air was causing friction. The taste in my mouth was foul, regurgitated plant matter decomposing on my tongue. "Granddad squirted something noxious into the tank and at me before his departure from this world!" I said as emphatically as I could, as saliva coagulated in the cavities of my mouth. And it turned out this was valid. A virus had entered my bloodstream and was feeding my immune system a series of codes that it could not recognize. It was as if my voice emanated from an underground chamber. The weight of wet soil dampened the vocal range. My eyes expressed symptoms most dramatically. The whites of my eyes were erased by a thin film of green-gray, and when I looked around, I saw everything as if through the perspective of a swamp or muddy water hole, yet I felt parched.

My amphibious transformation did not persist. Within three days of a heavy deployment of antivirals I was seeing clear-eyed. The doctors gave me permission to leave the hospital. Within a week I boarded a plane for China to drill and examine cores from Sihailongwan Lake for black carbon, char, and soot, among other particulates. Mercury dispersed by coal plants and chlorine from nuclear bombs were on our list of chemicals to check for.

Something was altered though.

Water is a medium. Liquid is a transitional form. Air contains water, as vapor. I noticed this now, intensely. And ice, that state of liquid frozen hard, I could feel it as if ice were a form of bone. The harmonics of water drew me into black-blue sound. To say I could see water molecules was an understatement, my senses had undergone an adaptation.

Nadeem texted me, "What's up Granddaddy?" along with a photo of the elderly fish. "Did you cut a hole in the lake and swim away?" Emoji of a wave. "Can you even read this text or are you too busy swimming around in the chilled waters? How's your sight?"

What kind of response could I give Nadeem when the rate of respiration of the mitochondria in my cell tissue was different? That water felt like blood and blood, water.

I texted him back, "Nadeem, <<<333, you get it, you get me!" and I added, "I owe you big time."

"For what?" Nadeem texted back.

"Because my consciousness has been altered. You introduced me to Granddad. Plus, you bloody saved me."

Dailiness had taken on a dreamtime quality where every instance of water rushed back to me as impressions of deep tissue feeling, experiences I remembered I had had with water and those that I intuited, part of a secret chronology, not lived, imaginary. Granddad and his habitat range was one moiety, the other was expansive liquid consciousness. He was a part of me, we were divided, I was navigating toward him in uncharted waters of my imagination. Somewhere between the realms I was floating, while walking and being a person in real time, going about my business as usual, splintering, and absorbing dreams as a scintillation that unfolded as reality. Then a tight hardening membrane began to encase me. I was immobile, estivating underground. The land had become exceedingly parched. All was dark and silent. Coiled in a stick shape my mind was filled with sensations of many environments. In the Congo, or maybe Rwanda. My pectoral and pelvic fins changed shape and dimension while retaining my ancestral structure. Years elapsed. Internecine battles went on above ground. There was much bloodshed, fighting with AK-47s and other weaponry provided by proxy countries. The wars were not only there, in that region; they were global. International weapons manufacturers from the Global North spurned on local tensions, exacerbated antagonisms, goading conflicts from behind the scenes. Soldier armies were mainly comprised of young boys. Recruitment happened with incentives offered, or the boys were summarily kidnapped. The wars created more orphans than there already were. Blood seeped into the ground. Corpses were buried nearby. Weeping and moaning could be heard under the ground. The grief and suffering were magnified by an ongoing drought. I dreamt horrible nightmares. Eventually the strife ended in a stalemate. There was calm for a period. A purple storm cloud developed for days. The dry spell was finally over. Rain fell heavily and the soil became moist again. With squirming motions and my teeth, I was able to break out of the membrane and swim into the currents. A new era had begun.

CRAWFORD Lake, MILTON, ONTARIO, canaDa, accReTION IS an expRessION OF Time

Winter. Hard, frozen ground. The lake ice has a chimeric quality. The solar glare at noon polarizes the aura of a full moon that still hangs in the sky. They come to collect hard evidence that is often soft, mushy, viscous. The evidence: long, compressed tubes of sedimented organic and inorganic matter; accumulation built up over decades, centuries, millennia. Presently, the goal is not to go back to the start of the record, rather to focus primarily on the 1950s to 1960s, the era of peak nuclear detonation and prevalent coal burning. Following World War II, humans entered the Great Acceleration, a time of greater industrial expansion than even the Industrial Revolution. Data of the last centuries, with a specific interest in recent history, from the start of European settler-colonial intrusion in the Americas and the arrival of capitalism and its global spread is being considered as part of this critical timeline. Human activity bears on ecological reality in a myriad of ways as to affect Earth system levels. This month it became even clearer how real this is. The early warning signs of the collapse of the Gulf Stream were reported again, with the implications of the severity stressed. The proposed new era implicates humans, particularly those in the Global North and its overarching forms of extraction, accumulation, financialization, and militarization. The golden spike is an indictment.

The core falls apart if not handled properly. A tube filled with accretions must be extracted with the greatest attention to detail. If it is not kept at a frozen temperature, it will ooze or break in pieces. The sediment will run together making it impossible to distinguish one time frame from another. Such extractions either involve the injection of liquid nitrogen into the sample to keep it frozen or use a gravitational method of extraction. Here at Crawford, they've designed a unique mechanism to pull the sediments up to the surface: squarish metal tubes that are filled with dry ice and alcohol, freezing the sample on contact.

Crawford Lake is contained within a sinkhole formed by eroded limestone. This fact was realized by a scientist in the 1970s. Such a phenomenon is called a karstic basin. The same process formed caves and crevices in the area. The lake is deep and small. A water body surrounded by dolomite, a sedimentary rock made by lime mud and magnesium-rich water postdepositionally altered. Limestone and dolomite indicate an environment of shallow, marine ecologies where calcium carbonate mud accumulates in the form of shell debris, fecal material, coral fragments, and carbonate precipitates. Crawford Lake is notable because of its undisturbed sediments; it is a meromictic lake; layers of water do not mix. The agricultural history of the indigenous Iroquois is preserved in the sequentially deposited seasonal sediment laminations. At its greatest depth the water is dark, dense, and static. The lake bottom is anoxic, which means there is no oxygen, and the water is saltier. Only extremophiles can withstand such conditions. The walls of the lake are thick, so wind doesn't stir the water. This layer does not mix with the intermediate and surface levels of the lake. Whatever lands on the bottom settles undisturbed. The lakebed is a vault of the past.

Time series analysis confirms that microscopic fossils are excellent historical representatives. Pollen is one of the most durable materials. The team is also looking specifically for industrial spherules blasted out of smokestacks and radioisotopes from nuclear fallout that get absorbed into the atmosphere, into rocks and trees that accumulate in the lake. There is, of course, redundancy. The independent AWG scientific teams are essentially probing for similar findings. Ultimately, all teams have to find evidence of the same man-made particulates at the same time register in all of the core samples collected globally.

Before working on the Crawford Lake site, Jacqueline and Amir, palynologists, worked to collect core samples at a karstic body of water known as Lake Aguelmame Sidi Ali in Morocco, shimmering as blue-green sateen in intensified heat near the Atlas Mountains. Temperatures were over 110 degrees most of the days they were there. A notable facet of the lake is that it holds its water in, there is no runoff within the collapsed cave formation that makes up its containing walls. Others of their Moroccan team had focused on Tiguelmamine Lake in the region. Climactic drought is sinking the water level of Lake Aguelmame Sidi Ali, and the plants able to grow around its edges are rapidly changing. Once their work in Morocco concluded, they joined two paleoecologists in Ontario. The experience at Lake Aguelmame Sidi Ali gave them insight in using the surrounding plants, animals, and minerals as reference points. Understanding what forms of life are presently living around the lake is to enter the lake's ongoing ecosystem and glimpse how it participates in larger Earth systems that are shifting and changing. All lakes are caches of vivid data. They met scientists who were documenting the changes from beech-maple forests to oak-pine forests sometime between 13,000 and 15,000 CE. Significant amounts of *Zea mays* (maize) show up in the sediment around this time. Maize is one of the most diverse species and provides numerous uses: food for humans, feed for livestock, and present-day industrial applications such as in the production of biodegradable foams and plastic adhesives. Purslane, Indian chickweed pollen, sunflower, fern spores, and bracken were present in their data. Purslane and Indian chickweed are Iroquois pot herbs, so it is certain that the Iroquois were living here at the time. Earlier in the record, at the time of the Pleistocene-Holocene transition, artemisia and Poaceae were abundant—it was a meadow environment then. Gradually woodland developed with the introduction of evergreen *Quercus*. *Quercus* gave way to *Cedrus*. In recent times, the environment has experienced degradation due to logging and grazing, as well as climate stresses. What persists now are plants that can contend with a parched environment: Spanish juniper with its fragrant, resinous berries and foliage that donkeys and goats munch on and other scraggy, low-lying plants with thorns. The lake environment is changing now, too. Lake Aguelmame Sidi Ali has a changeable personality; it could be said that the lake is, in fact, a person, and in community with other persons. Through Jacqueline and Amir's encounters and their colleague's stories, Lake Aguelmame Sidi Ali, Tiguelmamine Lake, and now Crawford Lake became intimate presences they drew close to, getting acquainted by spending time and dedicated attention.

Jacqueline was entranced by lakes. Bodies of water were composed of tears and the perspiration of sweaty encounters, of off-flow of mountain snow mass and the residue of coursing rivers, of dew on the densest jungle vegetation and the thickest forests, of calving icebergs in the frigid Antarctic, of the glistening condensation on mushrooms and mosses, the moisture on the membranes of flowers and leaves, wetness from the tongues and epidermal layer of mammals and amphibian slickness beading off. Moisture becoming air-bound and then resettling into crevices in the earth as liquid or snow held suspended in stone vessels of collapsed caves or carved out containers from meteorite impact, glacial indentations, depressions caused by flooding, and debris damming water into basins. Tectonic, volcanic, landslide, glacial, solution, fluvial, aeolian, shoreline, organic, anthropogenic, meteorite. She'd describe her personality as lakelike, the people she formed intimate relationships with, rivers: ephemeral, episodic, exotic, intermittent, mature, old, periodic, permanent. An oxbow lake: a meander in the river becomes disconnected and forms a lake. Maybe that was the most accurate way to understand her mentality. Amir was the ideal working partner because he was unlike either lake or river—maybe oceanic, yet she could not specify the qualities of what she meant by this except to think: more expansive, more modular in his fluidity among bodies, more inclusive of water, fresh and salty. She and Amir felt great fondness for each other. They shared the same devotion to their work. Working to uncover properties stored in deep time conferred information about perplexing questions of how life was possible through time. They referred to each other as each other's spouse, in jest and also seriously. You are my science husband; you are my science wife. They were bonded, not wedded. Planetary life offered erotic entanglements as a form of being. Possession of one body didn't satisfy her. She kept her intimacies with other humans in the periphery; her focus was centered on the primal energies of lakes. Lakes were long-term relationships between rock or dirt basins and water. Amir was in a long-term relationship with lakes, yes, and also with Mia, his partner, whom he referred to as spacious. Jacqueline trusted Amir's intense connection to Mia—in fact she felt a sense of gratitude that Amir's romantic attachment meant he held a different position in her life and didn't feel threatened by the dynamics of their own brand of intimacy. The crucial aspect of Mia was that she too was oceanic. Amir had just returned from San Francisco, where Mia was participating in an ongoing, site-specific performance. Conversations about Mia triangulated their conversations. Mia was a poet and performer. They both found stimulation and relief in bringing Mia into their exchanges. She was somehow always in the room with them when they were in a room and outside when they were outside together, or simply in the world together, at the same time, sharing space.

The cores were extracted in the winter and taken back to their lab in Ontario. By summer they had made several analyses and were preparing the data to present at a conference in Dublin the following summer. The conference would bring together everyone researching the golden spike sites that the AWG had organized. Their samples made a convincing case that the golden spike was geolocatable in the data that they had collected.

An epoch of time is difficult to pin down exactly. Pinning down events in time, they realized, was a human obsession, a game, and often a distraction. Time was coincident and inclusive, also slippery and eruptive. Time could be an infinitesimal split and a *longue durée*. Time involved compression and layering. Time was a conceptual problem; they were scientists and their study focused on registers of time in a sedimented presentation. For Jacqueline, the golden spike might prove ultimately that radionuclides are most comprehensive as a marker, yet, in terms of world-changing patterns, she held that the combination of imperialism and colonialism brought with it an entitled, self-serving "destiny" and was a significant contributor of catastrophe-making through time. She and Amir had countless Zoom conversations with Shayla, the scientist working at the San Francisco location, about this. He had introduced her to Shayla. They'd become friends, though they had yet to meet in person. Amir hung out with Shayla occasionally on his travels to San Francisco to visit Mia. He had encouraged Shayla to check out the performance work that Mia was involved with on Treasure Island, and Shayla had taken him up on it.

Jacqueline and Amir were well aware that their work participated in a Western scientific framework that was both academically and industrially inflected. Their papers would end up in chasms as deep as the lakes they studied, read by a few insiders, as "obscure" as ancient diatoms in an anoxic environment. The information they gleaned would appear in a white paper, and then, perhaps, as a footnote within the white paper of another white paper read by a specific niche of palynologists in their broader field, adding to a sedimented layer of ideation that was quickly buried by accretion. Industry would benefit most, having the data well in advance of arguments made about the havoc wrought on ecosystems.

They prepared their data on many late nights at the lab. Conversations erupted in the middle of their elaborations of graphs and charts.

They worked in tandem, each looking at the same charts and data on different computers.

They had been discussing the dumping of radioactive waste along the California coast, especially off the coast of San Francisco. Much of it has settled in the Gulf of the Farallones National Marine Sanctuary. The dumping which went on from 1946 to 1970 is the largest dump of nuclear waste in the United States. The U.S. Navy was responsible. "The ocean is a repository of dubious secrets." Jacqueline looked up from the glowing computer screen to Amir, who was bobbing in an ergonomic task chair, the mesh sufficiently supporting his body, he had a pen in his mouth that he took out and twirled with his fingers after each utterance. She knew where he was going with this. He continued, "Nuclear residue notwithstanding, I keep having this internal response that we've pushed the timeframe up too much." The date he thought they should be looking at would consider settler-colonial impacts at an earlier juncture. The committee had made a preliminary decision to concentrate efforts on the nuclear bomb era as the main focus, even before actual voting had taken place. Nuclear bomb deployment of radionuclides in the strata were more succinctly expressed. He continued, "The results have to show indisputable proof rather than emergence." Jacqueline listened soberly but didn't respond. On this they both concurred. They'd had similar conversations about the issue of the timeframe. It was a loop in their conversation. They were both silent for a bit.

Jacqueline broke the silence to redirect the conversation they were having. She asked, "What was it like to see Mia perform?" They both were at the hot water dispenser now, pouring it into mugs to make tea.

"Unlike anything I've experienced, frankly. The performers wore protective gear. Hazmat grade. They reminded me of forensic scientists, which was the point, I guess. They moved slowly. The performers were dispersed widely on a section of the island. None spoke. There was an eerie energy about it. I didn't drift too far from the bus that brought us there. Mia didn't want to tell me too much before I took it in. She said it was better to fully immerse in the actions without preconceptions. I abided; I didn't probe her with questions."

"The images you texted me look like workers sent into the damaged Fukushima Daiichi nuclear plant. Intense!"

"The performance was jarring actually. I felt unsettled. There was a feeling of loneliness and crowdedness that came together. Treasure Island is a dismal place."

"Could you recognize Mia?"

"I couldn't. I didn't try to. Her body gestures were obscured by the suit. I accepted the collective anonymity of the performers. My curiosity was directed elsewhere. Something about contact felt extremely important. The acknowledgment that's made of another life, another presence. What happens at the moment of reception, and then has to happen again and again; these repetitions, the basis of social relations. In the case of the performance, contact was restricted—forbidden, though this was unspoken. The prohibition against making contact signaled a break in the social contract—at least that's what came up for me. I navigated the environment itself, instead of focusing on the performers. I felt myself extending toward the sky, the ocean, the ground, the air. Some force was percolating." Again, they both were silent for a moment, allowing Amir's comments to sink in.

Jacqueline lowered her mug to the counter. "I can't help but think about how we are making renewed contact with fossilized organisms and materials sometimes eons old, tracing a trajectory, understanding ancient life-forms in a new light." Her words seemed vague compared to the sensation her thinking was creating. The screens on the computers flickered on their faces, rendering them pixilated and shadowy. A whale screensaver projected onto Jacqueline's face. Amir, too, had a blue glow.

The cores they withdrew contained trace materials that were older and younger than the sedimented layers in which they appeared. They found matter from exploded stars billions of years old mixed with seeds grown within days of falling into the lake. Time in material form was a collective arrangement of anachronistic properties.

"Everything leaves a trace." He was thinking about the cores and what Jacqueline had said and also his thoughts returned to the performance. He had had an inkling of simultaneity during the performance. As if there were more performers than he could account for. Mia had told him there were six performers in the troupe yet he could swear he had seen more. Each performer had a shadow and the shadows had shadows, and in this case the shadows embodied light-energy. The shadows moved independently and in tandem with the performers. His memory had stored images that contradicted rational thought. Always reverting back to a rational marker, he tried to decipher why he apprehended more bodies than conceivably there were. No explanation came forward.

His thoughts veered wildly. He was struggling to make sense of the barrage of images that suddenly flooded his attention. His mind was generating fuzzy archetypes. Images of people—mere outlines with little demarcating detail of facial features, indication of sex, ethnicity, or age—appeared in his mind's eye and dissipated. The figures appeared as if along the evolutionary pathways that early humans might have taken. He cycled through questions that barely made sense. The more he probed, the blurrier his line of thinking became—ludicrous even. Anatomically "modern" humans appeared one hundred thousand years ago, at the time there were deviations, different strands of the human family. Fifty thousand years later, humans again changed significantly. Behavior took on different forms of expression. He imagined a group of shaven men encountered by unshaven men who had never before considered the removal of bodily hair. How strange it would appear not to have facial hair. The shadows he saw on Treasure Island were time-deviant, either from a past or a future, he could not tell. Or had the past and future collapsed into the present?

The night before the performance, he had slept poorly. Dreams interrupted calm, restorative rest. On the bus enroute to the performance, he wondered if what he had dreamt was something he had read somewhere or was the narration of a film he had seen but forgotten. The off-kilter aspect was that the people in his dream were early humans—maybe Neanderthals. They certainly weren't contemporary. The dream felt lifelike, as if it were a memory, though isn't that what dreams can do—release the uncanny from its otherness? The dream was a bit cheesy. Really cheesy, actually. Maybe because imagining early humans conjures melodramatic imagery. Men and women in fur loincloths eating from giant bones, sleeping in caves, hunting with daggers. Echoing through his skull was a phrase completely foreign to him, that didn't sound like any contemporary language he could think of. *You'll weid, you'll woid.*

When he arrived with the other spectators at Treasure Island, his dream was sublimated by the stimuli of the performance. The sea breeze interrupted compulsive thinking. The sun offered itself as a focal point. Shadows begged attention.

He intimated that he could perceive them. What would draw their attention to him, he wondered. Fluttering his fingers, he conjured body movement that he hoped would indicate he sensed their presence. The shadows moved at a different pace than the performers, yet they were in relation with them. The shadows crowded the performers. Not every performer had multiple shadows; however, most did.

He was careful not to be rude or invade the space of the performers. Engaging vocalization felt wrong, like a threat. He sensed he had to rely on alternative forms of communication to make a connection. He formed an image in his mind of association. Reaching toward another, shaking hands. He felt a pull from the shadows. At one point he noticed they were crowding around him; they had moved away from the performers toward him. He welcomed what was happening.

BØLLING-ALLERØD INTERSTADIAL, SEEDING EDENS, AMIR'S DREAM

Before Jericho was Jericho we lived here. No one remembers the former names of this place.

We settled in the Hebron hills. The ice was retreating all around. The sea released warmth creating a blissful change in temperatures. We remained hunter-gatherers but decided to dwell here, in one place.

Some years were spent living in caves and temporary shelters made of stone, grass, and wood until we could build ourselves more lasting forms of housing. The cave we first lived in was later called Shuqba cave, located on the northern bank of Wadi en-Natuf, in Palestine. Later, Levantines and Chalcolithic Anatolians came to the region. Migration was a constant. Someone always occupied the cave, whether big cats or *Homo sapiens*. Other groups of hunter-gatherers moved around in the north, or east, some westward. Presumably there were those who returned to the south from where they originated.

Our relations are called the Natufians—again, not our name for ourselves. A name alone would not suffice to mark how we understood ourselves. More than ten thousand years after the fact a British paleoarcheologist named Dorothy Garrod had rummaged around the site, collecting evidence of our existence, and gave us this name retroactively. She found a carved amulet one of us had made representing a bull-calf, a symbol of energy and regeneration. At the time she found our sacred object, it was considered the oldest evidence of prehistoric art.

We lived here in the time of the Bølling–Allerød interstadial, a period of glacial retreat. The climate presented periods of searing heat and debilitating cold. The swings could last for decades or centuries. When we decided to settle in this region the weather had become milder, moist. We'd climb up the butte and face the sea. The air was delicious. Sea spray misted us, a pleasant combinatory feeling of hot sun and cool water droplets landing on skin. In the immediate environs there was an abundance of trees: willow, poplar, fig, pistachio, hawthorn, and oak, along with fragrant juniper shrubs. Eagles, hawks, and falcons soared overhead. Goats ambled about the hillsides. Our memories of ice were long and involved hardship, a way of living that was charged with consequence. Now we no longer had to seek out refugia—areas of abundance surrounded by ice—in order to survive. The environment once again supported a great variety of plants and animals.

Up on the butte we'd relax at night, gaze at the starry cosmos, notice the occasional flying object. We made fires to roast meat and boil grains. We ate emmer wheat and barley as our main staple, supplemented with fruits and other vegetative growth that was nutritious and easily foraged. Small mammals came around smelling offal. When they came close, we snared them, or used our slingshots, adding to our food supply. From the ocean, not far away, we pulled many edibles, some with hard shells we smashed against the rocks and others that swam we caught with nets and roasted in our fires. Ocean vegetables were a staple. Many varieties of kelp grew prolifically.

Everyone was continually on the move, but we chose to eventually settle. Reaching the decision to stay put in one place came about through consensus, we discussed it day after day whenever we were all seated together. This was a place that could sustain us. With our extended families we had traveled as far as the Taurus Mountains, in the Levant, staying briefly in places we'd been before and those we hadn't, then when the weather changed or the food ran low, we'd pack our cooking utensils and hunting gear and set off again. We had many harrowing and also pleasant experiences along the way. Whenever we returned to Jericho, we felt the most contented.

Others followed the ice as it retreated north. Up north the land was still bald, trees had not yet grown back everywhere. The ice crushed and froze expanses of forest. The ice dragged rocks and debris and the weight of the ice and stones created gutted areas that filled with water. Where the ice had melted there was a dense groundcover of wormwood, chenopods, mosses, cotton grass, and purple saxifrage—a tenacious plant able to break rocks, that's why it got the name "rock breaker." There were steppes growing thick with Labrador tea, with its hairy legs or stems, bearberry too, which attracts owls and other birds, and the pink tufted plant with star-shaped flowers known as moss campion. Expansive areas had been overtaken by cushion plants and other vegetation that could withstand strong winds, cold temperatures, and the huge animals that trampled through: reindeer, horses, saiga, antelope, bison, woolly rhinoceros, red deer, and jerboa, a hopping rodent. There were bones and horns scattered everywhere. We got reports that there was so much hunting going on that quickly the large animals were pushed into extinction. The retreating ice also threatened them. Very grim scenarios. The woolly mammoth and the *Smilodon* succumbed around this time. There were many animals that caused everyone to practice extreme caution when foraging. Lions, hyenas, bears, and other sharp-toothed creatures roamed about.

The long periods of the ice had left a mark on people. There was a thirst for the kill. Anyone that did not show themselves instantly to be someone we recognized or who posed a threat, we killed. We also brought strangers into our group, as lovers or as prisoners. Previously, during the time of the ice, there was openness about others we met randomly along the way. During that long period, working together with strangers was necessary. Sometimes to get food we had to chisel out a carcass from the ice, a laborious task that required collective effort. When the ice began to melt, aggression became prevalent. Everyone began fighting for the best place to live, hunt, and forage. Our strategies of ambush become more lethal. Our offspring knew nothing of the ice times. It is incumbent on us to convey what it was like to live with ice of such magnitude, so they can carry these stories into the future. We tell our children stories of the ice at night, before they drift off into sleep, their dreams a practice ground for living in conditions they have never experienced.

Our group remained small and tightknit when we were moving frequently. Once we settled down our community grew. We have the opportunity for more sleep, relaxation prevails. Our feet don't always hurt. Our backs can rest. We don't have to carry everything under our arms or on our backs. Unknowns abound, but not behind every tree and bush. We have an expanded familiarity with the environment. The time we have to relax has created constellations of familial groups. Children run around in great numbers! They are well protected in our group. When there is a threat, they retreat to their homes. As our population expands, we all assist with the construction of the houses. Many of the houses now are made of neatly piled rocks with a wooden roof. Or we use mud bricks.

Both create a sound, dry environment. We add sediments from rivers and lakes to the slurry that we use to coat the dirt and stones with. It contains silica and the fossilized remains of tiny, aquatic organisms named diatoms. Adding the slurry to the surface keeps unwanted insects out of our dwellings. Silica is white; we also coat the insides of our structures with the paint, the prepared walls give us more illumination when we light animal fat lamps at night. We have also noticed a glow that the diatoms give off. The diatoms are millions of years old. Their frustules are still intact. The crystal form of their bodies is like ice, water held in suspension.

Recently a group we weren't familiar with arrived here from the east and gave us a bag of seeds. Their generosity gave us pause. We set aside our suspicions and welcomed them. We weren't sure what to do with the seeds—we'd always just spit them out. "Yes, but haven't you noticed what happens when you spit them out at the right time?" they asked us.

They told us they had come across an amazing garden that seemed endless, with numerous edible varieties of fruit and vegetable. They told us the large expanse was maintained by a group of people living amid the plants. The plants grew in multiples and were arranged conscientiously. The trees were trimmed, and the garden was weeded. Every fall the community collected seeds for next year's growing season.

"Look at the seeds," the visitors suggested. When we opened the bag there were many of various sizes, shapes, colors, and textures. "In exchange for the seeds, let us stay with you for a season and we will teach you how to grow the vegetables that are grown in that fabulous garden that we encountered on our travels." They repeated the word Eden several times, but we were clueless as to what it signified. We decided to let them stay with us and share our dwellings and our foods. They used words like $g^h reh$ and $\acute{g}r\,h_2$-nó- and when their utterances made no sense to us, they looked at each other in dismay and said she_1 and also $yéwos$ and then translated their phrases differently as $situn$ and then again looked at their friends, laughed and said $simen\ sermn$. They pointed at the seeds and repeated the words. They said, "You'll $weid$, you'll $woid$," with conviction. We strained to catch their intentions. Eventually what sounded garbled became meaningful.

Talking now augmented gestural signs and expressions. Words rely on tone, pitch, volume, inflection, rhythm, and rate. Some cultures communicated with clicks or whistling, others used symbols, glyphs. We shared a motley plethora of sounds. The aural world was expanding. Soundings are not exclusive to *Homo sapiens*. Trees interact sonically with wind. The oceans create a cacophony of tones. Plants give off particular frequencies related to the uniqueness of who the plant is and where they grow and how they relate to the atmosphere. Other animals chirp, whine, chatter, cry, and sob. To us, as hunters, sound is of paramount importance. Other animals communicate among themselves. Listening is strategic attunement. Our babies are the noisiest of all. Jackals, wolves, antelope, foxes, and squirrels know how many babies there are in our group and if they are hungry or upset. We don't have especially sharp teeth so we must carry sharp spears because our babies draw dangerous attention to us. When all seems quiet, the cosmic expanse itself is not silent—galaxies hiss, stars, nebulae, and other celestial bodies emit radio waves; an unexplained roar sounds out in space.

These visitors—they knew much that we didn't. They were going to teach us to grow plants. "$D^h\acute{e}g^h\bar{o}m$ teaches," they murmured with awe in their voices. They were trying to convey to us the genius of the Earth. Then there was a storm and they said, "We told you so." Their assessment of weather patterns was impressive; they made forecasts based on environmental cues, something we do also, but not with as much success. They poured some seeds into our palms, and we handled the dry hard carapaces. Right off we were tempted to roll them on our tongue and then eat them. To crack them between our teeth, splitting open the kernel. Many seeds in the region are edible and life sustaining. "We'll show you how to prepare a plot by readying the soil and digging holes to submerge the seeds." "It all sounds slightly sexual," we offered shyly. "Yes, it is sexual." "Plant reproduction is sexual." That night we sat on the butte in deep thought. We had to form new questions.

The next day they said they would give us an in-depth demonstration. They would begin by showing us a flowering plant and indicating where on the flower the female parts and the male parts were noticeable. All of this time we had been walking in spring and summer through cloud puffs of pollen, unaware of the sexual implications. Pollen is the sexual phase of plant life. "Great," we said. We looked forward to the lecture on permaculture. Tomorrow, too, we would properly celebrate their arrival with dances and nutritious foods.

The late spring air was mild, so we ended up gathering together on the butte until late in the night, passing around a fermented beverage we make out of lavender and grape mash. There was enough of the libation

and wooden cups so everyone could have ample amounts and feel sati-
ated. A fish dinner was served up, followed by a fern salad and plenty of
tubers salted and flavored with herbs. Everyone comfortably reclined on
their backs, with eyes to the night sky, as stories circulated. Talli and
Emisum had supplied us all with fluffy pillows to rest our heads on. They
had sewed them over the winter and were thrilled that they could be put
in use for this special gathering. Eager to get to know the group better we
listened intently and probed gently with questions.

One of the seed carriers, Rainy, wore a thick rope around his jugular
with a tooth of a wolf dangling onto his chest. Rainy had a huge dog with
him, a Saluki. He told us the dog helped him hunt. The wolf was also his
ally. One day while hunting for boar with the Saluki (he called the dog
Gray Cloud because of his blue-gray velvety coat), they found a disturbed
wolf den and in it remained a lone infant cub. Rainy stashed the pup in
his satchel. When he brought the baby wolf home everyone told him to
get rid of it. It would bring back luck. Rainy ignored them. With all his
focus he nursed the pup. Finding a steady milk source wasn't that difficult after he had also rescued an errant goat on the hills near the Zagros
Mountains one summer. The group he was with made large circles on
their hunting journeys. Previously he had only killed goats, never studied
their behavior up close. They were quirky creatures. Humorous. The goat
looked at him with her funny eyes, rotated horizontally to stay aligned
with the earth. Goat pupils are horizontal and rectangular so that they
can see panoramically to avoid predators like wolves. Maeaza was the
name he gave her, a word from a language from the Fertile Crescent.
From his makeshift hut he'd call her, and she would answer him with her
strange screams, as would the wolf cub, in his own language. The wolf
became Maeaza's protector and best friend. Gray Cloud took to the wolf
too. The wolf became known as Vruk, a Sanskrit word Rainy had learned
on his travels from a group he met in the Damascus basin. With a stylus he crafted from a piece of wood, he taught himself to write the sen-
suous cursive word वृक. Rainy collected languages as he collected seeds.
"Rainy", we queried, "you don't have many weapons with you, why is
that?" "Vruk and Gray Cloud give us plenty of warning of incoming danger. They can read the intentions of others. With a wolf and a dog giving
us environmental feedback, we do not fear traveling in unknown lands."
The information about their dog and wolf companions was interesting to
us. We hadn't previously encountered such relations. We are closely at-

tuned to foxes. We believe they have paranormal abilities—they can see through matter, they can shapeshift into different forms, they understand emotions keenly.

Rainy's group spent many years in Hittite regions, along the Kızılır-mak River, which they called the Marassantiya. There, many *Homo erectus* and *Homo sapien* groups intersected. Some were ice people. They had lived through millennia of glaciation. Names like Neanderthal and Denisovan were tossed around, but in truth, there was no strict division. Everyone was a composite of many forces, many experiences, many people. People were constantly intermingling, forming many new cultures in regions from which they came and went, depending on where the ice was, depending on where the animals and plants were living. Some sought division, others embraced difference. Some communities were landlocked and thus insular, never exposed to others.

Comparing information was critical to our understanding of the world. On the tundra, according to the visitors, it was mostly possible to trap ground squirrels, rabbits, marmots, and foxes when larger animals weren't present. For several years there was such an abundant population of ground squirrels that they could be seen out of the corner of one's eyes at all times. If you napped in the meadow, squirrels would scamper over you in a matter of time, tickling your beard, getting into your food pouch. They made a stew with squirrel, fennel, and the bulbs of parsnip and cranesbill, sprinkled with oregano.

They told us detailed stories that added to our understanding of how, when the ice retreated, the land was strewn with rocks and rotten matter. They gave firsthand accounts of whole forests preserved under the ice in a flattened, sometimes macerated state. In many places it was difficult or impossible to walk. Sometimes the air was gassy and pungent because of the decay. In these places extra caution was necessary. The oozing matter could suck a body up in minutes, leaving no trace. They witnessed a group of aurochs become frightened by a lion and dash into the sticky, viscous pool never to be seen again. Children who like to play in the mud and are always seeking adventure often disappear by the suction of muddy lagoons. Rainy lost a child this way. His dog companion would not venture into the lagoon, aware of the danger. The dog howled at the fringes of the wet murk, indicating to Rainy that that was the place where his child had entered.

The passing ice had left huge scars on the land. Most of us had seen such things with our own eyes or we heard stories passed down by our elders about hills that were bashed into by masses of relocated dirt and rock. Rocks were fractured and dragged on the paths of the ice. Lakes were formed. Sometimes veins of gleaming gems appeared in newly exposed crevices. Visitors who came through the region sometimes brought with them jewels that glowed in spectrum colorations. Our settlement had a number of special stones, including sapphire, amethyst, aragonite, and malachite. We treasure these stones. They give us power. It is difficult to quantify or qualify, but the auric energy is palpable.

The people who visited with their seed bags had designed sturdier shoes than we wore. Our footwear was essentially sandals made of tough seagrass that we beat against rocks to soften and make pliable. Their footwear was heavy, made of leather, and reinforced to keep out the frost. They decorated their boots with elaborate stitching in rich colors. Some had matching tunics, also stitched with colorful threads made from hides or from dyed flax. Even Gray Cloud wore adornment in the form of a collar with gems sewn into the leather; when there was cold weather, they bundled Gray Cloud into a leather vest—the cold did not agree with the dog. Gray Cloud was like a son to Rainy. He told us he acquired the dog from a group of Iranians in Mesopotamia who knew how to breed dogs. We had previously never heard of such a practice. Apparently, it was becoming common. Indeed, Gray Cloud was like no being we encountered in nature. In the sand, Zidanta, one of Rainy's traveling party, drew an image of a small cat that we were also unfamiliar with. Zidanta told us that cats make wonderful companions and they rid the area of rodents. Nirved, Zidanta's brother, added that cats get comfortable and quickly take over one's sleeping area. If there are cats, they will most likely be sleeping in your sack with you. They get to know you as well as your lovers do and use similar tactics to get attention. The study of interspecies mental processes was part of their skill set. They all laughed and then Pamba, another hunter of their group, mentioned how when Rainy acquired Gray Cloud his mood was so uplifted that when they camped in Golpayegan, Rainy spent the next two days etching into a rock face a self-portrait: a hunter on horseback with a falcon and a dog by his side. He said he was able to achieve a likeness of Gray Cloud. After the story was recounted to us, we asked why Rainy left out flowers in his mural. Golpayegan is known as the Fortress of Flowers or the Land of Tulips, we were told, so why didn't he make sure to add them. "The tulips are sacred," he said, it is improper to depict them. We became quiet, absorbing this.

Rainy and his entourage felt fatigued and indicated they would like to sleep. We offered them several houses to rest in. Mostly their group traveled with horses or mules, but because of the terrain, they had come this way by foot, trading their horses and mules with another group heading elsewhere. It had been an arduous journey. They had blisters, calluses, and bunions. Several had splints on their legs from falls they took at various parts of the hike. They told of a spot in the mountains where faces of rock crumbled off with little pressure, leaving dust and debris around, a treacherous area. We had exhausted them with conversation; it was time for rest.

In the morning, before the visitors awoke, we organized a performance. It is customary to welcome guests with dance. Foods were prepared. Finally, when the sun rose and streaks of gold and pale pink lifted up off the horizon as if crushed flowers were smeared across the sky, we made sure each house had a jug of water and milk. When they arose, we served them hot biscuits made from pounded chickpeas and fava beans sprinkled with pepper and everyone passed around the bowl of honey. Abisare served tea to stimulate us. Because they were going to deliver information on seed growing, we decided to do our flower dance for them. Basically, it is a dance to honor the plants that grow around us.

After breakfast was consumed, we gathered around the open pit of sand where performances are held. Six performers joined in a circle formation. Their arms were the boughs of trees or the fronds of plants and their torsos represented trunks or stems. Toes performed the roots. The dance transformed them into trees and flowering plants, the wind and sun stimulating the movements of the dancers. The performers appeared as fluorescing presences as our senses tuned into the wavelengths of ultraviolet and black light that in normal circumstances we do not perceive. Every other dancer was a floral entity, either a daisy or sunflower. Every other dancer was a tree, a mimosa or black locust. When they are mimosa, medium green streaks appeared to glow. As black locusts, they emitted an intense yellow-green aura. In the center of the circle the gemstones were placed on a tiny platform. The gems fluoresced also. The performers mesmerized everyone. The performance relaxed the boundaries of the known and unknown, of the animate and inanimate. Dreaming in a waking state was possible with the aid of the flower-tree-gem dance. We turned our attention to the seed demonstration after the dance was over.

Decisively growing seeds caused us to worry. This activity could be detrimental to the earth, could it not? The visitors showed how growing a plot involved removing what was growing in that space. They suggested hacking and chopping everything out. "Expose the topsoil" they commanded. "Trowel the dirt with a forked tool." They had a tool such as they described with jagged fangs that could vigorously scrape through the soil. It is not that we forage for food without modifying the ecology. We thin certain plants in spring to allow the plants we depend on to grow stronger, to receive optimum sunlight. Selectively removing the plants that don't provide us sustenance makes it easier to find the ones that do. We make pathways in the meadows so we can easily find our favorite plants. In the forests we've established where to walk, so we can locate mushrooms, bark, herbs, and roots. What they suggested to us is to make gardens separated from the surrounding land. With the tools they brought they opened up the earth and made a rectangular plot that they edged with stones. They lifted the dirt up and inserted seeds that they spaced about a fist apart in neat rows.

ernesto cave, trentino, northern italy, half lives

The inner architecture of a cave is anything but static. Slowly formed structures build up from the cave floor and suspend from the ceiling in these damp subterranean spaces. Soda straw stalactites, also known as dripstones, can look like infected tonsils coated with milky liquids. Stalagmites emerge from the floor of caves in undulating spires. Speleothem sheets occur when moisture settles on walls and floor surfaces, slowly accumulating, creating what can look like a sticky ooze of coagulated liquid. They are fed by a combination of seepage and fracture water.

Water flows from the ground at surface level into the cave ceiling and continues down projections of calcified minerals and walls onto the cave floor until it leaches even deeper. The chemistry of water that percolates through the cave reveals the aboveground world of industrial and agricultural off-gassing and leakage, fossil fuel emissions, nuclear fallout, and other manmade substances.

Fluids evaporate and the residual materials harden. The golden spike will appear in the lateral banding on a dripstone, accumulations that form as dripping substances harden. The anthropogenic sediment forms a very thin layer—sometimes only a millimeter or two of residue and is thus easily disturbed.

The United States and other countries began atmospheric nuclear weapons testing in the 1940s. The firing of the weapons created discharge of carbon 14 (C-14) into the atmosphere, among other particulates. The Treaty Banning Nuclear Weapon Tests in the Atmosphere, in Outer Space, and Under Water went into effect in October 1963. The greatest density of C-14 occurred right before the ban was enacted. Radioactive isotopes have an unstable nucleus that decays, emitting alpha, beta, or gamma rays, until stability is reached. Plutonium is very rare in the natural environment—when it appears it usually indicates nuclear detonation. Burning fossil fuel leaves a different signature. Fossil fuels are millions of years old, the remains of the lineages of animals and plants that have transformed into chemical compounds that readily combust. Anything over fifty thousand years old is "radiocarbon dead." The age of fossil fuels far exceeds the half-life of c14. Comparisons between stable isotopes such as carbon 12 and carbon 13 that appear in the mineral deposits called speleothem can be made with the presence of carbon 14. Annual laminations of carbon isotope values reveal information about the changes in enrichment that pinpoint anthropogenic impact.

Radioactive isotopes, such as radium, thorium, and uranium, also occur naturally in the environment, in rocks and soil. Uranium and thorium can be found as trace amounts in water. Radon is present in the air. Carbon 14 is also a naturally occurring isotope that exists in trace amounts. I and the other scientists focused on time signatures at Ernesto Cave are interested in the production of c14 through neutron reactions. As carbon 14 indicates nuclear explosions, a spike in carbon 14 is what we look for. This gives us the ability to precisely gauge materials with bomb-pulse dating, observing how parent isotopes transform through radioactive decay into daughter isotopes. The daughter isotope is the product of what remains of the original isotope. The radio daughter—another name for the daughter isotope—acts like a clock, giving evidence to the passage of time. The more radio daughters, the older the sample is. This is a process of a neutron changing its species by emitting particles and radiation, seeking to become stable. After seven half-lives there will be less than 1 percent of the original amount of radiation.

Carbon 14 and other nuclear fallout has managed to find its way into the carcasses of animals in the Mariana Trench—perhaps the most inaccessible place on Earth. The way elements travel excites, and also alarms, my sense of being in place. Noticing and studying chemical shifts is about tracking tiny indicators as they enter ecosystems, and thus, food systems, bloodstreams. The bodies of humans, animals, and plants absorb radioactive material and other toxins. Fragments do not respect boundaries, being somewhere is always multiple because of the way elements move, resituate. The relocation of substances can be a profoundly slow process or involve rapid change.

The geologic architecture of caves conjures the alimentary canal funneling nutrients from mouth to anus. Caves provide a slow-drip passage through time. Decay schemes are accessible. This cave has all the properties we are looking for in our efforts to indicate a golden spike.

Ernesto Cave is damp and fragrant. Petrichor wafts with the cool smell of salt. There is strong air flow through the chambers of the cave because of the karst system that allows for drainage and air penetration. There are minute traces of hydrogen sulfide; the rotten egg odor of the gas is barely noticeable. A fetid smell is also caused by rubbing against limestone or quartz with our boots.

There are numerous caves in the region. This particular cave was happened upon in 1983 when a forest road was constructed between Enego and the Marcesina Plateau. Within the cave, artifacts of prehistoric hunters were found. There were animal bones, tools, and hunting weapons scattered about, relatively intact. There were also rusted beer cans and cigarette butts strewn over the artifacts—probably a couple of teenagers ventured in. They didn't disturb the relics of the prehistoric hunters.

Caves are part of the ancient underworld where the present rushes in in the form of wind, or trickles in as water, fluorescent humic and fulvic acids derived from aboveground soils. Ernesto Cave is part of the Calcari Grigi di Noriglio formation of limestone formed in the Early Jurassic period. Dinosaur marks are imprinted all over the place. On a morning I have free I head out to hike Monte Zugna and I am thrilled by the perfect impressions in the stone. Obsessed, I then travel by bus another day to Altopiano della Gardetta in the province of Cuneo to take a look at the fossilized tracks found there of a crocodilelike reptile who left ten footprints that look as fresh as if they were made that day. The dinosaur survived the mass Permian-Triassic extinction event 252 million years ago, and this means an ecological niche was left intact. The tetrapod, *Isochirotherium gardettensis* as it is called, was somehow able to withstand extremely heated temperatures and acid rain on the Pangaea mainland after the volcanic eruptions that caused global climate change. The creature looked on the ocean that encircled the land, Panthalassa. When I visit, white flowers dot the meadows, and the jagged peaks rise up into cerulean blue skies. The color is oceanic. It isn't difficult to imagine an epic water mass covering most of the land.

The dinosaur resurfaces from a distant past as an indentation in the rockface that recorded its scrambling motion along a muddy seabed. What was once at sea level is now a towering mountain range. Its claw marks are legible, as if it had been climbing only hours before. I was deep in thought, ambling along the trail with a dispersed group of hikers—we had loosely formed a pack. One of the hikers I briefly climbed with commented that what the reptile saw on a daily basis while sauntering along the shore of the primeval coral seabed is still here, with us, only it had rearranged into alternative patterns and forms of life. It was a simple and profound thought. "Thank you!" I called to them. They had already dashed off ahead into the blazing horizon of light, casting dust and pebbles in their wake, gaining distance. They revealed ephemeral and durational qualities in one instant. The perpetual metamorphosis of life is something I remind myself of. Time is the agent that brings this phenomenon into focus.

The world has a way of evoking jarring strangeness while also enabling a familiarity that induces oblivion. The footprints are odd as to be otherworldly and place everything around in relief. Later in the day I am struck by how I walked amid trees and rocks with the sun beating down and didn't bat an eye as to how terrific and strange it was that an exploding solar body steadily heats our globe from a great distance, or how usual but also peculiar was the fact that we live among countless leafy presences oxygenating the planet and among other living beings whose differences in survival strategies are bewildering and utterly necessary for a functional ecosystem. Compacted soil supports the weight of living bodies; there is food to nourish life, and all the while persons dream dreams within the scope of their sensory system's expanse. Caves have become familiar environments for me after several years of crawling around in dark wet cavities. When I describe that my day job involves spelunking to recover data in the form of built-up secretions from eons ago the reaction is awe.

"Lily," my mother chirps on the phone when I call her from the mouth of the cave before going in with our small team, "make sure to sing to the cave." She insists on acknowledging everyone with song, and she includes nonhuman presences in her acknowledgments. "I will, Mama, I fully intend to—the notes that feel right are coming to me." "Don't worry about what you sing, rocks will harmonize with you." "Okay, Mama, do I ever say no to you?" She began humming "La Vita" by Beverly Glenn-Copeland. I overlaid the words on top of her pitch-perfect vocalizations. "And the body says 'remember you gotta breathe,' the body says 'take the time to grieve,' the mind says 'let the silence flow.'" When the refrain arrives, we enter into a duet, "My mother says to me 'enjoy your life.'" I sing "La Vita" to the cave after I make my way in, in reverence of the internality that permits our entry. Janice, who is responsible for the analysis of the biogeochemical cycling of sulfur in speleothem archives, heard the tune. "You're affecting the data!" she jested. And no doubt, on a subatomic level it is true. Her attunement to the nuances of ecosystem dynamics is incredibly sensitive.

We'll soon be heading back to our labs at the University of Newcastle in Australia and the University of Birmingham in the United Kingdom to play out the fluorescence imaging and synchrotron X-ray fluorescence mapping of strontium and transition metals for the last three centuries. There were many tests prior that gave us data on atmospheric pollution that can be verified as well by tree ring analysis from trees growing near the cave. We will compare with core samples that represent earlier eras.

On our last day collecting samples we come across soft, viscous moonmilk and do a very unscientific thing; we, the paleoclimatologist team of three smear our fingers in it and paint our initials on a wall of the cave, much like prehistoric artists would, a practice called finger fluting. Then we plaster the fluid all over each other. Janice has short, cropped hair that is crystal white like the moonmilk; she becomes a fluorescing entity from deep earth when we were done with her. Forehead, arms, neck. I am with Janice, the more the merrier. Dean only permits moonmilk on his lips and eyebrows. We glow. We finish taking a few more samples and then head out, wearing the cave slurry aboveground. Into the tiny bar in town we go, slathered in cave minerals. It comes down to what you chose to circulate. We circulate moonmilk, sulfur, carbon, and calcite, plus our blood, sweat, and tears.

LITTLE cayman Island, central caribbean, forests above and below sea level

Our AWG-affiliated team was scheduled to travel to the Cayman Islands to collect cores from coral colonies, but due to the pandemic, international travelers were not allowed entrance. Thus, our trip was put on hold, subject to a phased reopening. Instead, I found myself in a different context, on the Gulf Coast collecting samples from a source I never imagined would be revealed. A fully intact cypress forest some 50,000 to 60,000 years old was discovered submerged along the Alabama coast. The preserved ice age forest is situated sixty feet underwater near Dauphin Island, Alabama. The cypress grove had been buried by sand and settled sediment thousands of years prior by rapidly rising sea levels. Almost a decade ago, Hurricane Ivan, a category five storm, disrupted the seabed, exposing the forest. A fisherman became curious about the area of the ocean as fish were being caught at a disproportionately high rate. The seafloor along the coast is mostly sand, not conducive to large fish populations. His first thought was that someone had discarded objects into the ocean to attract fish. People dump all kinds of trash and heavy objects in the water to lure fish. He got some local divers to take a look. I got a call from a local environmental reporter soon after. Would I like to take a dive, collect samples, survey the forest? I recruited a few colleagues I knew would be interested and a small crew was assembled. Each person I texted, texted me back the exact same message: "Cindy, count me in!" The outing came together in a heartbeat. It was an opportunity not to be passed up.

I gathered my gear at my lab at Louisiana State University and made the three-and-a-half-hour drive from Baton Rouge to a dock on Dauphin Island. The ride is a familiar one. I've come to walk among the shell middens piled up in the forest of huge moss-draped oak trees on the tiny barrier island. The middens or mounds were formed by Native people who gathered to fish and steam oysters on the island. The discarded shells along with charcoal, potsherds, and fishbones built up into mounds. The Alabama Indigenous Mound Trail Organization lists the earthworks made by Native people in the area. They state that in 1975, archaeologists from the University of Alabama conducted excavations at this site and identified evidence of a long sequence of prehistoric settlements that range from the Bayou La Batre-Tchefuncte culture of the Gulf Formational Stage approximately 4,500 to 3,200 years ago to the Fort Walton and Pensacola phase of the Mississippian Stage around 900 to 500 years ago to the Mobile tribe that occupied the area at the time of European contact. According to Alabama Audubon, the island contains a wide variety of vegetation quite distinct from other Gulf barrier islands. There are a number of species growing on the island that are representatives of plant families found as far inland as the Appalachian Mountains and from as far south as the state of Yucatán in Mexico. The plants were brought here for medicinal, ceremonial, and culinary purposes. Making good time I crossed the three-mile-long raised Dauphin Island bridge well before 8:00 a.m. and arrived at the dock on the island shortly after. When crossing that bridge it is sublime to hover over the surface of the glinting waters as if soaring, gravity held at bay. The shimmering light set the tone for the day.

Everyone was on time, eager to head out, fueled by adrenaline and coffee. The boat departed as planned, 8:00 a.m. sharp. We powered our boat quickly to the coordinates as there was a flurry of anticipation at what we'd find.

By 10:00 a.m. we were diving around in the waters of the Gulf of Mexico. "Let's see if I can bring up a stump." I called out, and off the side of the boat I plunged into the swirling saline waters. I wore black, suctioning skin-tight scuba gear and held the anchor line from the boat so I could later find my way back up through the silty waters. Emulating a manatee, a turtle, a sea snake, I felt the water was familiar, ancestral. I was raised in a coastal town in Maine, so I am accustomed to frigid temperatures. Swimming to feel hypothermia was what I considered thrilling as a teenager. The balminess of the Gulf enveloped my senses with awe. Its warmth swaddled my body. Euphoria has an elusive, ambiguous nature, but right there at that moment, I could pinpoint elation.

Ron, a paleontologist who was first to go in the water, encountered several curious sharks that swam around him and nudged his camera but otherwise didn't bother him. He discussed the encounter right before I jackknifed into the water. "They were juvenile sandbar sharks, a species of requiem shark—thick skinned, not particularly dangerous, they approached me nose to nose." He was beaming from the interspecies encounter.

Carlos, a microbiologist, and I—also a microbiologist—are unfazed by any danger the young sharks pose. We relish the chance to swim among sharks, turtles, fish, and other oceanic life. The ancient forest emboldens us. This area is anything but a dead zone. The trees act much like a coral reef does, drawing life to the intricate labyrinth of trunks and branches. A region of flourishing in an otherwise threatened ecosystem.

The knees, trunks, and roots of the trees rise out of the murky depths. Flashes of fish ricochet sunlight, illuminating the water in tones of aquamarine, celadon, teal, and dark azure striations. An octopus with its three hearts, nine brains, and blue blood transforms its epidermal layer from spotty orange to mottled blue-purple before it flies past suddenly, blending in with the surroundings so completely, I can't see it any longer. There are two stingrays and a sea turtle that glide by. No sharks while I look around gently kicking the water. Oceanic life-forms swim within a submerged coastal forest, the air displaced by water. After a while of swimming through the forest with the fish it isn't difficult to imagine the same fish swimming in the skies, among the clouds.

Sixty thousand years is a blip. Yet much can occur in brief time spans. Epic events take place in short sequences. In past eras, global warming approached speedily. Samples from the pristine forest speak to a time of enveloping heat and rising waters. As promptly as scientists want to get in the water to observe the forest, so too do entrepreneurs who plan to harvest the wood to make high-end furniture and other marketable items. I imagine how interior decorators and furniture makers might salivate over this find, eager to transform the wood into sleek tables and chairs. The location of the forest has been kept a secret because of the differing objectives. Now, as the trees are again exposed to oxygen and other elements, they will soon decompose, changing form again. Water is a protective agent. It can suspend forms in time. Change is a form of continuity.

On the boat, Carlos, Ron, and I are joined by a marine biologist, a dendrochronologist, and an environmentalist. We will sample the trees, insects, and plants in the area and study rainfall patterns. When I'm back up with a basket of wood samples, Carlos says to all who can hear, "Nothing is arbitrary within ecological reality." His statement might sound like a non sequitur to anyone who hasn't heard us in dialogue. We have a running joke about the meaning of arbitrary and the meaning of random. We are here to remind each other that connections are often opaque, difficult to sense. Though we repeat the mantra endlessly it still is helpful to me, it realigns my relation to the environment, a reset. We are microbiologists, maybe this affects our sense of humor. The likelihood of two microbiologists, childhood friends, in a boat, off the coast of Alabama studying ancient, submerged forests is for sure remote. Our backstory is that we happened to grow up in the same northern city in Maine, and both of us went on a similar path of study. Portland is mostly white, but there was a significant influx of refugees in the 1980s when we were growing up. Refugees from Vietnam, Cambodia, Afghanistan, Iran, and Eastern Europe resettled there. Carlos's family was one of the few Mexican families living in Portland and my family one of the few Native families. We lived in the same neighborhood, went to the same schools, helped each other survive. He leans over to give me a hand; I climb the ladder and then shimmy onto the boat. Carlos's disposition is serious and calm, but oh so hilarious when he wants to be. He asks if I sensed if the forest has given consent to the probe. I tell him I consulted the forest, asked for a signal. I say I can't be sure if I understood the permission clearly. In my eagerness, I can't say if I've projected my desires.

We look for causal relations, it is what we are trained to do as scientists. There is a basis for seemingly arbitrary events, the human lens is often not fine-tuned enough to comprehend the labyrinth of interconnection. Randomness is confused as arbitrary. A certain randomness is a function of the way the system operates. It is a bit of a rabbit hole at the extreme macro- and microlevels of perception. The terminology itself buckles. Carlos takes out a handsaw and cuts a slice of a tree limb. "Cindy, here, look at this." He hands me the slice to inspect. Tight and narrow rings indicate stressed trees. Soon we learn that the forest's organic matter is too ancient to radiocarbon date.

Out of my wet suit, into dry clothing, still on the boat, I hear my phone. It is Leanne, my daughter. "Don't worry, Mom," she texts. I run my fingers through my hair nervously. She repeats, "I really don't want you to worry. I did get doused with pepper spray at close range though, and then pushed to the ground." I hold my breath as her message discloses the details. My daughter is on Vancouver Island, on the traditional territories of the Pacheedaht, Ditidaht, and Huu-ay-aht First Nations in the Fairy Creek Forest and Central Walbran. Primary, temperate rainforests. Some of the last significant stands of old growth. She continues, "I'm fine, I am. Sarah and Jason drove me to a hospital. The spray got into my eyes and throat, I'm okay, my eyes are fine. The Royal Canadian Mounted Police sprayed at a group of us who were crowded together. They'd begun arresting others in our group. I fell on the pavement. I'm getting patched up where I hit my head and then I'm going right back in. It is terrible, Mom. I wish you were here." I've kept up with the excessive use of force employed by the Royal Canadian Mounted Police at these protests. Leanne continues, "If they could they'd tear our faces off. They were there in throngs pushing at us." The RCMP is one arm of the state that persistently aggresses First Nations people. The RCMP is the very definition of a settler colonial power illegitimately controlling destiny—*destiny*, a word I detest, because it holds within it a concept of society that thinks of the future as a trajectory along extractionist lines that leave a sickened vacancy, a recipe of destruction.

"You are going back??" I react, keying a phrase messily, my sympathetic nervous system is triggered, but I am not surprised. Emotions exhibit in the form of sweat beads on my skin. My blood is a hot snake that feels like taut jelly under the skin. The submerged primeval forest is momentarily not my focus. Carlos quickly glances over with an empathetic expression, sensing my concern. I silently mouth my daughter's name to him. My colleagues give me space to process Leanne's message. They are busy tagging large tree samples. I think again about randomness and arbitrariness in relation to the forest struggle and again, the systemic rears its head. She's sent images of decimation. The ground parched, no trees or underbrush remaining, post-clear-cut environments. She posted photos of old-growth trunks stacked in hulking pyramid formation, to be hauled away to sawmills. Another image Leanne attached showed a new road cut into an old-growth forest. It struck me because the contrast was blatant. Massive tree trunks knocked down and in piles at the sides of road. The soil along the road was torn into—still alive. The road would lead to more extraction, plain and simple.

The protests are the largest acts of disobedience in Canadian history. Leanne has sent me running lists of the plants and animals that call the forest home. To ground myself I reread the list, picturing lineages of their terrestrial presence. Frilly horsetail, deer fern, moonwort fern, skunk cabbage, orchids called white adder's mouth, four hundred species of moss, lichen; an oceanic species of lichen called old-growth speckle-belly lichen that has migrated astonishingly far from its place of origin. Many lichens who live in the forest have yet to be named. There are families of black bears that wade in the rivers, who feast on salmon, grizzlies who roll in the meadows among wildflowers such as buttercup, bird vetch, and foam flower, Canadian lynx whose acute hearing gives them the ability to locate a mouse 250 feet in the distance. They all coexist in the area. They make dens under fallen trees, sheltered by the densities of the forest. Goshawks soar above the tree line. Fishers and wolverines live in the underbrush with red-legged frogs. Elks occupy the terrain as do marbled murrelets, who nest in the high treetops of the forest when they are not at sea. Most of the plants and animals live in peril, as clear-cutting makes existence increasingly impossible. The marbled murrelets are debilitated by oil spills on the ocean and the clear-cutting that goes on in the forest, a double whammy.

The trees on Vancouver Island are some of the oldest living organisms on the planet. Some stands have persisted since after the last ice age. One of the biggest stakeholders, Teal Jones Group, owns the tree farm license, granting them 9,459 acres of old-growth forest comprised of yellow cedar, red cedar, old fir, and hemlock. The Ditidaht, Huu-ay-aht, and Pacheedaht nations petitioned the government to stall old-growth logging for a period of two years to initiate stewardship plans. It is a highly contested situation. Many of the Native people in the area have had issues with the protestors and have asked them to leave. Simultaneous to the protests, news broke about the discovery of a mass grave of 215 Indigenous children buried on the grounds of a residential school, also in British Columbia. Again, the RCMP are implicated as they were often responsible for the removal of Indigenous children from their families and transporting them to the boarding schools.

I text Leanne and see if I can lure her to Alabama, but I already know she won't travel simply to comfort me. "I have to be here, Mom—you understand!"

The samples from the submerged primordial forest ask me to refocus. Will there be evidence of heavy metals that seeped into the wood? A shift in carbon isotopes that are a result of carbon emissions from fossil fuel combustion? What about 4C, 239PU, 241AM, and 137CS—nuclear testing products? My instinct is yes. If they didn't show up it would be even stranger. Has agricultural runoff from the coast reached this part of the Gulf? Pharmaceuticals? Testing can be endless because of the diversity of compounds. Spent rocket fuel—somehow the stand-in for human-made toxic chemicals—will it show up too? And there's the plastic that is tangled in the branches of the sunken trees. Other garbage is down there. I collected the eyeless head of a Cabbage Patch Kids doll hung up by a branch, an action figure soldier covered in algae, and a pink plastic tampon applicator on the ocean floor. Everyone came up with an assortment of trash. It isn't part of our study but has a depressing impact on our reception of this incredible discovery. The forest's existence is coming into full view after over sixty thousand years of being submerged. It will be scrutinized with the most high-tech equipment in the world, looked at under powerful microscopes, measured and documented.

Leanne receives my text along with the image I sent of the underwater forest that I took with a waterproof camera and responds with an emoji I don't immediately recognize. "What is it?" I ask. "A water flea. It is the smallest oceanic critter I could find in emoji form! I think of it as a water flea. It could be a land flea or even a fly." It completely makes sense. Our terms of endearment are water flea and forest flea respectively. Fleas show up in the field. Fleas show up in the cores. Fleas show up in conversations about zoonotic agents. Fleas show up in my domestic arrangements. I live with three cats, two dogs, and a foster goat. "Mom, a goat?" "Yes, a goat, consider yourself duly informed." She was flabbergasted that I decided to foster a goat. I send one more emoji to her, a fox, and spell out *tsítsho*, in her great grandmother's language, Mohawk. We are a family of foxes that don't mind the occasional flea. May the fox and the flea give her strength and fortitude. Long live the forests!

eastern GOTLanD Basin, BaLTIC sea, RaGInG secrets are aLSO ROCKS

The core we are working with was retrieved in 2018, at a depth of 241 meters from a central area of the Baltic Sea, a rather shallow and brackish sea that is notable for its sparse water exchange with the North Sea. Like the other golden spike scientists, our team too is testing for radionuclides and other markers of human activity that present noticeable configurations. The core bears out human impact in many ways. At a specific length of the core, the lithology is noticeably different because of the high increase of organic carbon. You can see this with the naked eye, unaided by microscopes. We are zeroing in on this section and dating it as well as scanning it to measure the elements within the sediments.

In whatever spare time I have while hanging around in a hotel room truly fatigued by data—data collection or data analysis—or in airports and after-hours at the lab, I pull out books to distract—or inform, I'm no longer sure which—as my impression toggles on any particular day. The books I'm immersed in now are *The Adventures of Simplicius Simplicissimus*, written by Hans Jakob Christoffel von Grimmelshausen, and *Don Quixote*, penned by Miguel de Cervantes. The two are perfectly paired. They both offer commentary on indomitable aspects of the human spirit. Both are timely even though *Simplicius Simplicissimus* was published in 1668 and *Don Quixote*, published in two parts, the first part in 1605, the second in 1615. They are another form of "core sample." A sample of European culture in a self-contained vessel, the printed page, the book. Storage containers of sensemaking and absurdity. It becomes my hobby to decode both. To see how the past bears on the present. Not that my reading list is a prognostication tool or anything more than subjective interest.

Nothing prepared me for *The Adventures of Simplicius Simplicissimus* except life itself, at its banal, quotidian level. Ribald humor and atroc-

ity. Farce and fable stand next to science in describing this era. I have
to balance the science I practice of demonstrative outcomes and verifiable proof with a descriptiveness that circumvents rational thinking.
That doesn't attempt to thwart the fantastically absurd aspects of reality. Chapter 4: When he is ten years old, Simplicius's home is seized,
plundered. Thuggish cuirassiers abuse his father, killing him and everyone in sight. Simplicius takes to the road, he's now a displaced person,
he hides in the forest until a hermit helps him. He sets out again, traveling through the carnage and wreckage, stepping over corpses, narrating
as he goes. The Thirty Years' War, which began as a local religious conflict—a civil war in Bohemia—ended up ravaging most of Europe—the
dynasties of the House of Hapsburg and the House of Bourbon contend-
ing for the control of Europe. Simplicius's story is about surviving in the
midst of that war.

The story that Simplicius tells is reminiscent of the Kosovo Albanian
experience in the late 1990s. Ethnic, religious, and regional tensions at
that time were exacerbated to the point of genocidal terror. In 1999 I was
sixteen years old. My father died in the conflict and my mother was raped
and beaten but survived. Between February 1998 and June 1999, life for
Albanians involved death marches, mutilations, rape, mass murder, and
expulsion. We fled to Athens and eventually became refugees in Berlin.

Our life in Berlin reoriented us, at least superficially. By my senior
year in high school my mother had tried her best to put the war behind
us. Her survival methods involved disassociation and repression. Time
consisted of yesterday and the distant past, but the genocide was not on
the timeline, it stuck as a nightmare in her dreams. She thrashed in her
bed at night or paced the dingy narrow hallway between the bathroom
and kitchen. We didn't ever talk about it. No one dared broach that quag-
mire. All the emphasis was placed on my education and finding a positive
outlet for my older brother, who seethed with submerged frustration and
anger.

My interest in large water bodies led to an eventual degree in analytical chemistry. I wrote a dissertation on the Holocene history of the Baltic
Sea. I furthered my skills with mass spectrometry imaging to be able to
construct visual diagrams of molecular configurations. Tiny biomarkers,
tiny objective indicators of what goes on in an environment. Water has
a forgiving quality, materials break down, dissolve, are eaten, disperse.
Hypoxic seas are different. Whatever sinks to the bottom resists decay

because there is no oxygen to break down matter. There are few if any living entities in hypoxic bodies of water. I became interested in these special water vaults. I made an analogy between hypoxic bodies of water and the deep-seated trauma of postwar life.

When I began graduate school, I took to wearing a wide-brimmed hat made of canvas in a dark wine color and upped an outrageousness in all social matters though I was studious and always got the work done. My mentor, Teodora, who was also my thesis advisor, was the person I spent the most time with. She was a decade older than me. She was responsible for guiding me through my research and was the one who suggested I pay attention to biomarkers and their molecular mass as they relate to particularities of chemical changes in the waters of the Baltic Sea. With funds she scrounged up from outside institutions and donors, the department was able to purchase a high-powered MALDI-MS—short for a matrix-assisted laser desorption ionization mass spectrometer. The technology was new and coveted and now we had one in our university laboratory. The MALDI-MS was a prosthesis for me. An extrasensory organ. Firing at the matrix crystals with the laser brought me satisfaction bordering on joy.

We frequently did field work together collecting microfossil assemblages from the Bornholm Basin in the southwestern part of the Baltic Sea. I made it a priority to crack jokes and perform pranks. Teodora was always sober, tipped toward somber. "Dior, I'm laughing, I just don't express mirth with body gestures and sound." One day I peed over the edge of the jetty and the wind blew urine back at my ankles and shins. Some spritzed up at my face. I used the tissue meant to protect the sample vials to clean myself up. Then my hat flew off my head and into the sea. I dove into the frigid water. That day I was wearing thick cotton velvet from head to toe and my outfit became heavy, drenched in seawater. Teodora extended her hand and tried her best to haul me in.

We spent summers researching in Sweden and Denmark and also Estonia and Lithuania, in different areas of the Baltic. One summer I was reading the *Inferno*, obsessed with the lion, the leopard, and the wolf that Dante encounters. Influenced by a fear of interspecies relations, Dante chooses to walk a circuitous route through several hellscapes instead of coming to terms with the animals he encounters whom he profiles as savage beasts. Would it have been so difficult for him to extend a morsel of food to the wolf, one wonders? The wolf is dispossessed, in need of sub-

sistence: "a starved horror ravening and wasted beyond all belief." My
ethics radar runs rampant. People are able to absorb levels of suffering
and misery and remain cold, detached. *Don Quixote* is a paranoid book
in places. Don Quixote confuses a field of windmills for giants. Simplicius Simplicissimus, famished and delirious from exertion, finds himself
with his head on the lap of a hermit who strokes him gently. Simplicius
accuses the hermit of being a wolf whom he thinks is planning to eat him
alive. The hermit assures him he will do nothing of the sort. He wants to
soothe Simplicius, not devour him. He offers Simplicius some water and
greens and a chance to rest in his shabby hut; it is all he has to give. In
the end, Simplicius becomes a hermit. In hell or the afterlife, as in this
world, trauma smelts down or combusts a person into smaller particles
that drift or settle, rearranging into new forms. Some new forms don't de-
viate much from their predecessors.

Our lab received the core sample for the AWG research last year from
a consortium of Baltic-based paleoceanographers. The core was pulled
from a sediment layer that dates back to the Little Ice Age. It was extracted from the Bornholm Basin, part of the geological era of the Littorina Sea, named after a prevalent species of mollusk that lived there
at that time. The Littorina Sea was the penultimate stage in development before becoming the modern Baltic Sea. Teodora proposed a trip
to collect water samples from the Bornholm Basin. I readily agreed to
accompany her. By this time, our relationship was no longer just professional—had it ever been? She was a surrogate mother to me, then
a sister, eventually my lover. The carnal pitch of our bond caused me
moments of consternation because I couldn't tell if we were reaching a
violence of assimilation.

Last summer we flew to Bornholm Island, part of Denmark. We stayed
at the Green Solution House, innovated to be totally environmentally sensitive, trademarking a concept called Cradle 2 Cradle, where the building materials are either fully recycled or biodegradable. The hotel and
conference center exuded privilege and self-congratulatory pride; it unsettled me. Most of our time was spent outside, away from its purity. We
hired a boat and collected water samples several miles from the shore.

The day before we were scheduled to return to Berlin, we set out for
Gudhjem to visit the rock formations of Helligdomsklipperne—angular
granite and volcanic stone rising above the shore. At the base of the cliffs
is a spring with holy water. During the Middle Ages, we had read, parish-

ioners would bring water from the spring to the chapel nearby as an offering, hoping their illnesses would be cured. We sipped it and I flicked chilly droplets onto Teodora's face, she dabbed her finger in the frigid spring and rubbed holy water on my lips. "Is it rude to guzzle holy water?" I asked. "Let's fill up our water bottles," she suggested. I watched her imbibe a modest sip.

Further along there were designated walkways weaving among the rock outcroppings. We left the path and clamored high onto one formation called Lyseklippen, Candle Rock. Rowan trees were in full display with berries so orangey-red as to be miniexplosions. Ocean spray pelted us. Much of the island has been intermittently submerged under water since the last ice age, causing erosion to the rocks. I felt a tremor as if the sea had sent a shockwave in our direction. Water hydrology is a form of divination. Water is telepathic. It knows in advance what will happen. Maybe because electricity travels so freely in water. A gust of wind made me teeter. My absurd hat managed to remain glued to my skull. Teodora stepped closer to me, and the sun pierced my retinas in such a way that I felt vertigo as the sea continued to exert pressure. "Dior, watch out!" Teodora cried. My feet firmly gripped the rocky ledge, but I was mentally off-kilter. She extended her arm and I grabbed her and yanked her. I could feel her spine twist and her feet lift off the surface. For an instant I couldn't see her—again the sun momentarily affected my vision. Then I heard her skull hit the rocks twenty meters below. I tasted blood in my mouth and felt blood in my throat. What had happened splintered into a refraction of light. The protruding rocks over 1.8 million years old, the surface tension of the water, the rowan berries—all contributed to the surge of energy that ran through the meridians in my body. There was the faintest differentiation of energies that were exchanged, yet I was sure I had pushed her. Still, something impugned my capacity to judge what had happened. Numbness set in. Over and over, I replayed the accident in my mind. Finally, someone saw Teodora's body and then came to collect me off the ledge. Police interrogated me for less than half an hour. The next day I left for Berlin. An investigation was deemed unnecessary. I went back to "my life," absorbing the loss as a symptom of war.

This summer took me back to the Gotland Basin. I spent several weeks in Riga, Latvia, to run toxicity texts and exposure status evaluations. Lavern joined me. The Gotland Basin is a major dump site. The basin contains a vast quantity of chemical warfare agents (CWAs), such as sulfur mustard, cyanide, and tear gas. There are incendiary bombs made of benzene, phosphorus, and cellulose that can ignite on contact with air. Most of the corroded munitions have sunk to the basin's floor. The release of the payload depends on the state of the casings. The munitions are washing ashore in several European countries.

Lavern and I met at a conference on the environment and the Anthropocene. We've both heard, read, and used this word so much the color has drained out of it, yet we know it is valuable as a base word for the dissemination of information concerning a shift in geologic timeframes. She presented a paper on the therapeutic effects of ecological immersion from a philosophical perspective. The paper delved into cultural understandings of human relationships and healing in regard to plants and forests. It was personal as well as psychoanalytic. I listened to her presentation and we talked afterward. Something clicked. We came to share our traumas in little vignettes.

Teodora's death came up in conversation as Lavern and I were nestled under a down coverlet in an inn in Riga, nearly asleep. We'd both had a couple of glasses of wine with dinner. From all the hiking my muscles were of a jellyfish consistency. And after a bath I was numbly relaxed. In a semiconscious state, it nearly slipped off my tongue, the detail I never share. It could be considered a secret. Teodora's uncle, a Serbian, was my mother's rapist. He lived in the neighborhood, three houses down from us. I don't think Teodora was aware of the connection. Maybe she was. She was living with her family in Montenegro during the war. One time she mentioned her uncle and I froze in place. Teodora, I think, knew I was obfuscating something and realized that to probe further would have been crossing a boundary. A part of me murdered her that day on that craggy outcropping on Bornholm. And then there was Lavern getting close to the matter. She has a talent for prying me open regarding sublimated material. Still the door was shut, I parried. What came out of my wine-stained mouth was opaque, suggestive: "nosce te ipsum," from a passage in *The Adventures of Simplicius Simplicissimus*. "Each of you, know your own mind." Delphic oracles repeated this maxim to Roman envoys according to the account of Simplicius Simplicissimus. It is inscribed in the forecourt of the Temple of Apollo. It can be translated more simply as "know thyself."

The San Francisquito Creek emptied into the San Francisco Bay until the dam was constructed and the water collected into the Searsville Reservoir. Dam construction was completed in 1892. The project included flooding over the nearly defunct town of Searsville. Some say it is an underwater ghost town that continues to haunt. It was active as a pioneer mill town supplying lumber for the building of missions and gold rush towns that irreparably disturbed Native tribes. The town failed when the forests were used up and the hillsides leveled. The tribe that calls Searsville home were and are the Muwekma Ohlone Tribe, and they are still in a fight with the federal government for the restoration of tribal recognition. In 1975 Stanford University closed the reservoir and surrounding land to the public and established the Jasper Ridge Biological Preserve, a biological field station. The reservoir is being allowed to slowly fill up with sediment and transition to a meadow habitat. Currently it is 95 percent filled. The cores extracted in 2018 give us a high-resolution archival record of the last 126 years of geochemical activity. In little over a century, the reservoir has been polluted with numerous toxic agents. Like our colleagues at the other AWG sites, we are looking for evidence of fallout from nuclear tests in the form of various radioactive isotopes as well as lead, mercury, pollen, and other indicators of anthropogenic impact, such as the burning of fossil fuels, roadbuilding, and the ever-increasing use of plastics. Specifically, at Searsville, we are interested in how logging, livestock, and agriculture affect the record. Substances become concentrated wherever they land. The sedimentary layers reflect social history in chemical form. The stratigraphic sequence of the core is disrupted in places, indicating earthquakes.

The dam was originally conceived of by Leland Stanford, an industrialist and politician who came to the area during the gold rush, amassing wealth and power. He needed a source of water for his immense estate. He obtained the rights from the Manzanita Water Company and made an agreement with the Spring Valley Water Company, who would operate the reservoir to supply Stanford's land with water. Stanford and his wife, Jane, founded Stanford University as a memorial to their only son, who died shortly before his sixteenth birthday from typhoid while on a grand tour of Europe. By 1919 Stanford University had secured the possession of the water rights and the title to the dam. The university continued to purchase more land in the area.

Stanford served as senator and governor of California. He was a racist and a xenophobe. He passed discriminatory legislation and recruited volunteers for U.S. Army battalions that hunted and killed hundreds of Native people. In his inaugural address on January 10, 1892, he proclaimed with brutal, hyperbolic vitriol, "To my mind it is clear, that the settlement among us of an inferior race is to be discouraged, by every legitimate means. Asia, with her numberless millions, sends to our shores the dregs of her population. Large numbers of this class are already here; and, unless we do something early to check their immigration, the question, which of the two tides of immigration, meeting upon the shores of the Pacific, shall be turned back, will be forced upon our consideration, when far more difficult than now of disposal." Stanford University was modeled after a Spanish mission, a colonial system of forced labor and forced conversion to Catholicism. The university used a caricature profile of a Native person wearing feathered regalia as its mascot until 1972, when a petition by Native students and staff was circulated and the mascot was changed to an image of a tree. It took the university until 1989 to repatriate 550 Ohlone skeletal remains, but they still maintain other Native artifacts in their possession.

It is a mixed blessing to work where I do, doing what I do. For now, this postdoctoral fellowship at Stanford is where I need to be, focusing on long-term diversity dynamics that are responsible for ecological fluctuation. It feels pertinent to be working with our local AWG-affiliated team of scientists, though I question their occasional pop science performances when giving talks with titles like "Humans Are Powerful: We Can Kill or Save a Species, the Future Is Ours to Choose" or "Rescuing Species," where emphasis is placed on one of the threatened trophy status animals everyone is rooting for: tigers, polar bears, for example, and choice is made to seem almost casual, clearcut. I groan when another such PowerPoint video lecture is uploaded onto the internet featuring students glued in their seats absorbing the watered-down content.

Spending time at the Searsville site, at Stanford, and commuting back and forth to Oakland has drawn me into a triangle of considerations. Artifacts are rearing up all over the place. My attentions have had to shift to varied focal points, each calling on a particular sort of attention. One afternoon, back at my apartment, I received a FedEx package. Inside, carefully wrapped in tissue paper, was a well-worn journal, thick with handwritten entries and collaged details, and another book, also a journal, though its origins were harder to detect. There was a note attached. "Aiysha, your uncle wanted you to have his journal, and this other book too, love Dad." I set my uncle's journal on the desk by my computer. The other journal I stored on my bookshelf for later consideration. I made a cup of tea and came back, picked up my uncle's journal carefully, opened the cover, the spine cracking when I did so. Throughout it there were images glued or taped to the pages. Cards from clubs and cutouts from porn magazines, yellowed and brittle with age. My dad found the journal in my grandmother's possessions when she died recently. It was wrapped together with the other book, with a note to give it to me. Her son, my uncle Darnell, died of complications from AIDS in 1987, in San Francisco. I sipped a breath of atmosphere from my living room and the air felt saturated with salt crystals, the smell of yellowed paper and acrid smoke from the fires raging throughout California. Firefighters have been wrapping the giant Sequoias in resistant blankets to protect them from the Paradise and Colony Fires that are 0 percent contained at present. Last year was also a brutal unprecedented year of devastation. The western United States was consumed by flames. Fires raged in several countries. In Australia, bushfire killed or displaced more than three billion animals. Fire is the basis of my thoughts these days. I have to think with and through fire to exist. Fire was Darnell's sign, and it is also mine.

My uncle Darnell's handwriting is cursive in delicate filigree, yet easy to read, though the ink is nearly purple due to fading. I had the distinct pleasure of spending time in his company in the early 1980s, when I was a kid. We'd hang out, listening to his extensive record collection. Most notably of which he was proud were albums he somehow procured from Egypt, Algeria, and Morocco—North African pressings. I adored hearing roving tales of his time in the navy. He'd open his thickly painted green front door and stand there welcoming me. He was tall and dapper, smelled of bergamot and lemon zest. Sometimes his hair was straightened, sometimes he wore it in a low taper fade.

Our family had moved to Bernal Heights, San Francisco, not too far from where he lived in a compact flat painted bright green on the edge of the Mission at Potrero Avenue and Alameda. Scraggly eucalyptus shedding over the house and ground gave the appearance that the house itself grew fronds. A menthol scent and the odor of concrete pervaded. The apartment hummed with the traffic of Highway 101 and the Central Freeway rushing by.

Before his death he had become reclusive. We didn't know he had AIDS—at least my parents never let on if they in fact knew. He was ill, that was disclosed to me, but I didn't know his life was threatened. There wasn't much explanation offered as to why I could no longer visit Uncle Darnell. Just vague obfuscations, "Your uncle is not feeling well. He doesn't want visitors." Uncle Darnell never came to our home, no reason was offered. He had a long bout with a rare form of bladder cancer years back but seemed to come out of it. We were not sure if he really fully recovered or if AIDS complicated his recovery.

The funeral was closed casket, unheard of in our family and community. The iconic photo of him in his starched white navy uniform, a seductive glimmer in his eyes, was propped on an easel next to the casket. My father said he honored Darnell's wishes to be buried in a lime green woolen Willi Smith jacket. My dad said he found Darnell's favorite article of clothing neatly pressed hanging in his closet, his glad rags ready for the occasion, as if death were a dance party on *Soul Train*. Lime green was his go-to color. His bedroom was also painted in a vivid version of the hue. When the sun set, the room became the shade of dark mosses and forest understory. Bouquets of flowers came from his friends with cards attached, always signed with first names, mostly male.

Darnell's journal on closer inspection seemed composed of several journals rearranged into one chunky book. The dates were wide-ranging. The first entry was from 1954, and the last was dated 1986. The book wasn't organized chronologically. On many pages there was a date and instead of a handwritten journal entry a collage of images or a doodle stood out. Some pages were crossed out.

The entries concerning his cancer gave me renewed commitment to the study of sedimented cores and the evidence they hold of detonated nuclear devices. Declassified information continually points to covert involvement by the U.S. government of the testing of nuclear weapons. The dumping of spent nuclear materials no doubt continues, in "sacrifice zones," unsurprisingly located where white folks don't live, at least not well-heeled ones.

The other book was peculiar. It took me several months to return to it. I don't know why I hesitated to examine it. There was an otherworldly quality to its construction and the vibe it gave off; it contained a strange energy. Not negative, quite the contrary. It exuded a soft and gentle quality. I enjoyed how it beckoned me from the bookshelf. It was thick and large and seemed weather-beaten. As if it withstood a great duration of time. It was made of a type of a handmade paper I'd never encountered. Handwoven rope encircled it. The rope itself was strange too, made of human hair intertwined with what appeared to be a hemp material or paper. I came back to it after fully weaving my way through Uncle Darnell's journal. I slid the rope off without damaging it. The rope curled into the position of a resting snake. Before opening the book, the first question I had was why Uncle Darnell had meant that I receive it. Posthumously. I had no idea what the book held in store for me. I had no reason to believe it would shatter every preconception of time and space I had been confident of, saturated in. Here was evidence of how worlds arise and remarkably transform.

DARNELL'S JOURNAL, VISITATIONS, TREASURE ISLAND AFTERMATHS

My lungs filled with seawater. I saw Ed bobbing in the waves, he looked weak, stricken. Dark tendrils of bull kelp entwined his skull. The tide pushed me away from him. No matter how I tried I could not navigate toward him. Eventually I managed to crawl to shore. With the last energy I had, I dragged Ed onto the sand as far from the onrushing waves as I could. Delirious, I collapsed next to him. A woman emerged out of the forested park, came over, and tried to revive us. Her demeanor was quiet, meditative. She sat in a vigil with us. In my delirious state I remember I was grateful she didn't alert the police. She made me feel less vulnerable as she sat with us protectively. Then I must have blacked out. When I came to there was a group of people encircling me. The woman was gone. These entities cast a glow, not a shadow. There was a luminescence that arose in our midst. My skin had a pearlescent sheen. The people crowded around sparkled also. I wasn't sure if they were singing softly, humming, or mumbling. A resonant frequency spread from the ocean through the atmosphere, through our bodies. Ed was unconscious. The group huddled around us; they were concerned for our well-being. Because of debilitation, there was sensory confusion. They appeared as flowers! As if a ring-shaped garden had grown up around us. The air was sweetly tinged. The pain I felt morphed into a dull throb that was endurable. I was listless, in a liminal state, but alert. I questioned if they were human but was unconcerned. I drifted into a dream state. Apparitions of benevolent flowers peopling the coastline brought relief. My thoughts had become wistful. Their presence ameliorated the stressfulness of the situation. Ed looked peaceful though overcome by his condition. I leaned against him. I tried to keep his body warm. It put me at ease when I noticed he was breathing steadily. One of the flowery presences encircling us offered a gauzy scarf. I draped it over Ed. Another bent down and reached over giving me a book. At the time, I didn't know what it was. It was wrapped in fibrous rope. It was large, an unusual shape. They placed it under my arm. I think I eventually rested my head on it. I didn't have the wherewithal to process the gesture.

At that moment the scenario changed. Everything took on stark contrast. The shimmery quality of the light disappeared. In the distance on the water was an ominous monochromatic shape. The dark form congealed into a ship. None that I'd ever seen ocean bound, but I recognized it was a galleon. A Spanish flag flapped from its masthead. A dinghy came to shore. Gradations of form and color reappeared. Looking on from my vantage point I could see several men in woolen knickers and top jackets the color of the sky on the brightest day, accented in blood red with flashy gold buttons running down the front. Though they were dressed in spectacular fashion, I could smell their stench from where I was positioned. Their skin was oily leather that hadn't been washed for months. They approached the group of people that had gathered on the beach, all of whom were stunned by the approach of the galleon that was now anchored a distance away. Everyone then turned their attention to the boat that had landed on the shore bringing forth so much commotion. I assumed the crowd on the beach were Indigenous Indians.

The dinghy went back and forth to the galleon picking up and unloading people and eventually livestock onto the shore. Other small boats joined in, ferrying humans, animals, and supplies to land. There were cows, sheep, goats, pigs, and chickens. Most were hogtied. Other animals were in crates. The cacophony of noises was overwhelming. Smaller creatures—unintentional cargo—scurried to shore. Rats, mice, and lice, most notably. They were thrilled for a chance to set foot on land.

The scene in front of me flickered. The atmosphere blurred. Cloud cover floated just above the cresting waves. Had it rained momentarily? I recall thunder, or was the noise the waves crashing against rocks? Temporality presented as jarring segments ricocheting along multiple axes. I did my best to seek grounding in the tumult of the emergent strata of time.

My attention refocused again, to the confluence of people assembled on the beachfront. The population density was larger. It must have been later on the same day, or the following day. Now there were clergymen milling around, as well as the soldiers I had seen earlier. All, I presumed were Spanish, based on the flag that flew on the ship's mast. Their crew brought ashore paraphernalia for their missions, presidios, and pueblos. They yelled at the Natives not to drop the wooden boxes they so prized. One Spaniard of the militia dropped his breeches and defecated on the sand. Several pissed in the wind. The clamor made the exchanges between the people indistinct, but I could hear an order made by one of the friars: raze all the trees. The imperial military and accompanying clergy were intent on clearing land for their agricultural pursuits. Their plan was nefarious. They intended to destroy the quality of life of the Indigenous communities they came in contact with. Subsistence living involved a dependance on hunting and gathering. Razing forests and encouraging livestock to trample the land meant that hardships would follow for the Indigenous communities who lived where the Spanish intruded.

Their mandate was to institute missions with the purpose of rounding up and relocating Native people to become their slaves. The overriding objective of this imperial design was to instill a Christian worldview, stripping Native people of their language, culture, and land. Violence and theft were the ways that they planned to accomplish their goals. Their grandiosity gave them great confidence. They believed they received the graces of an extraterrestrial father figure. With a clear conscience they began to apply their blueprint for a new world order.

Some of the Spaniards handed out beads and rosaries to a large group of Coastal Miwok and Ohlone leaders. At this point, my sense of everything happening on the oceanfront was vivid. I heard the name Father Palou. Then I saw the man who bore that name. He was dressed in a priest's black robe that hid his ankles under thick woolen cloth. As his name was called out a powerful image arose. Superimposed on Father Palou's face were the faces of Charles III, Pius VI, and Maria Amalia of Saxony. The holograms moved in accordance with the priest. This triad of coiffure and jewelry overlayed the visage of Father Palou. Stunned, I gasped when I noticed that the lips of Pius VI and those of Maria Amalia of Saxony were each as pouty and reddened as another. Each person milling about on the beach was a composite of many others. For several moments there was a layered quality to everyone I looked at. All were diaphanously superimposed.

The luggage had been dragged ashore and 286 head of cattle were unloaded. The mission they had established was called Mission San Francisco de Asís, named after the patron saint, Saint Francis of Assisi, protector of animals. Some of their possessions were to be transported down the Arroyo de Nuestra Señora de los Dolores, translated as Our Lady of Sorrows Creek. The bulk of their weaponry and tools followed. The last item to come out of the galleon was a massive carved image of Jesus on the cross, wearing a scanty loincloth, his forehead dripping with blood from the crown of thorns wedged into his glistening skin, his hands punctured through with hand-hewn nails.

At every mission, death rates exceeded birth rates, sometimes by a ratio of two to one. Where did this information come from? I knew so little about early Native struggles with imperial occupiers. Horrific data bubbled up and I could only equate it with a clairvoyant insight that arose in a place supercharged with consequence. The barrage of harrowing factuality caused a great disturbance within me. I vomited onto the sand. The word *reduccion* reverberated in my skull like buckshot spray pelting a wooden target. Whispering voices swept through my consciousness. Phrases in several languages drifted into a chorus with the enunciation of waves, the cries of livestock, the gritty acoustics of boots on sand and the rubbing tensions of the seismic plates. It became dark and I began to smell the fumes of whale oil burning from the lamps the Spaniards lit.

Ed was still curled on the beach next to me. I lifted myself up to be able to see how he was doing. His breathing was faint. Blood ran down his neck. The woman who had hovered around us earlier had briefly come back. She gave him CPR. Or was that before? Had I replayed the memory? She left a fragrance in her wake that smelled of mulch and flowering lupine. Sirens and flashing lights approached again confusing my sense of things. Someone was shot as they were being apprehended. The police chase culminated a ways away from us, but not far enough. The sirens sounded different, but I knew it was the police. I had seen the lights coming over the bridge toward Treasure Island. It was night. San Francisco sparkled like a distant galaxy in the night sky across the expanse of water.

Conscious again, it was just Ed and me on the beach. I cradled his head in my arms as I sat cross-legged. We had washed up ashore on the western side of the island. The psychiatric hospital was nowhere in sight, there were few landmarks that I recognized. We had drifted here by the strong currents of the bay. We had hoped we could swim or float to the Embarcadero in San Francisco. The medication the hospital administered to us altered our sense of reality. It took days to wear off and regain an equilibrium. Before an action plan crystallized, I sat there with Ed, sobbing. He was silent. Trucks coming and going flashed at us. A fleet of supply vehicles headed back and forth to the U.S. Naval Supply Center in Oakland. Some were enroute to the U.S. Naval Air Station nearby. They took the San Francisco-Oakland Bay Bridge. We had to get to the bridge and find a ride from there.

Toward noon the following day I had Ed admitted to a hospital in downtown San Francisco. There was a room available in the Castro, and I hurried to see if I could rent it. I felt beat, broken, and alive. Whatever the hospital had us hooked on wore off in stages. My senses reeled.

The only possession I had was the twine-encircled book. When I arrived at the room in the Castro, I set it on the scuffed nightstand and went back to Ed. At the hospital a doctor gave me an update on Ed's condition. In a hushed dismissive tone, I was informed that Ed was in a coma. I wasn't family. Who was I? The question, derisive in nature, was implied. Nonetheless I entered his room and sat with him, held his hand until I woke up the next morning, stiff and sticky, feeling hungover from stress and sorrow. Ed would remain in the hospital for over a month. He was finally moved to a rehab facility, where he stayed until his death, two months later. I went into a spiral. Assimilating into the racial dynamics of everyday life was jarring after naval life, where everything was regulated. The navy sent me an official notice of dishonorable discharge. A small disability benefit kept me afloat. During that time, I didn't open the book. I tucked it away until some of the pain eased. Dishonorable discharges were issued to thousands of navy and army personnel because of their homosexuality. They were let go in San Francisco. One positive outcome was that San Francisco had become a lively, gay-acceptant place faster than anywhere else in the United States. Anonymous sex in the parks overgrown with fabulous plants blooming in the dark was what gave me a hold on life. Fleeting encounters of release, connection— something approaching joy, yet temporary. Or I would space out on a dock, watching seagrass and bladder wrack undulate in the briny waters.

After my cancer diagnosis, I began to link my involvement with blast proximity and radioactive cleanup to my illness. Evidence of the dangers of radioactivity was being discussed widely. The army didn't inform townspeople living in and near the Jornada del Muerto desert in New Mexico that the Trinity bomb had been detonated. When nuclear "snow" fell, children ran outside to scoop it up, eat it, and play in a surreal winter created by a previously unknown phenomenon, an implosion-design nuclear weapon. Decades of evasion could no longer contain the facts: they had seeped into skin and bone, into rock and tree, into creek and ocean. There were numerous incidents of nuclear bomb testing, nuclear accidents, and dumping of radioactive material that had received little to no media coverage when they initially happened that were now being exposed. Nuclear energy was gaining prominence, and with it, the gnarly aspect of radioactive waste that was generated as a biproduct—where to store it, how to store it. Radioactive treatment was also becoming the primary tool used to fight cancer. It is a strange allopathic modality, to treat disease *caused* by radiation *with* radiation. In the first instance, radiation causes healthy cells to mutate and proliferate, in the second case, radiation causes the same cells to burn out, killing them and ridding them from the body.

The book stayed near me. When I moved to new apartments, I always took special measures to carefully transport it. The book was my most meaningful possession, yet every time I picked it up something deterred me from opening it. To breach the twine that encircled it would take a bit of daring as the book had taken on the mystique of a Pandora's box. There was something about the book itself as a physical presence that had an abiding effect. It emitted an energy that changed the atmosphere in a room, ushering in a sensation of timelessness, where momentary convergences worked together as complementary forces. I thought of it as a black box. It might as well have fallen out of the sky, crashed with a plane, withstood disaster, absorbed untold blows. Something about the spongy texture and weight of the book suggested moisture-seeking reconnaissance. The book had been imparted to me in the midst of trauma, when delirium crowded consciousness, fed on phantasmagoria. But there was no denying that someone gave the book to me on the beach all that time ago. And I am sure I was surrounded by actual presences, humans dressed to resemble flowers.

When I became sick and had to rest continuously, I finally brought it out and held it as if examining something excavated from within me, looking closely at stored sensibility—a lifetime's worth, ephemeral in my hands. I'd held on to it for years. The book seemed alive, a grain of sand that sought liquid crystal viability. While convalescing I continuously searched the internet for information about the navy's involvement with radioactive bombs, the decommissioning of toxic ships, nuclear fallout, the treatment of homosexuality in the navy, aversion "therapy," sex and dishonorable discharge. My list of search terms was long. Anything to do with Treasure Island was of great interest to me. My apartment was populated with memorabilia from the Magic City, the Golden Gate International Exposition, dedicated to exploration, trade, commerce, and discovery. An intoxicating dream of the industrial-military complex. Like a prismatic crystal, the book glowed on occasion as if lit from within, illuminating in jewel colors the various postcards and posters affixed to the walls. As fantastic and terrible as the exposition was, projecting brutal desires of empire onto land, sky, and sea, a flowering terminality, as it were, continued on. The aftermath of its proposition continued to exert influence. A contradiction in the moment. Terminality signals the end of something; a long, drawn-out ending was palpable. A new phase was asserting itself, wrapped in what came before. The experimental drugs I took gave me head spins. I was enrolled in several clinical trials. Cancer erupted as a proliferation of cells invading my body. I also was diagnosed with AIDS. Where fuscous colors of Kaposi's sarcoma splotched my skin, I hoped instead to see flowers erupt. The flower people who bequeathed the book to me, they were my imaginary companions. Having the book near me dissuaded negative thinking.

The day I opened up the book turned out to be the last day I left my house. After that day I didn't any longer have the strength to do so. I had friends come by and a visiting nurse checked on me daily. Unofficial hospice. One person came in, opened the blinds, the next would promptly shut them with a whoosh—differing opinions about caregiving and whether sunlight was too overwhelming or in fact necessary at a particular moment changed the atmosphere continually. Same with music. Everyone rifled through my record collection. But I adored everyone; they were trying to cheer me in ways that they could. Everyone who came in the door left with a sentimental trifle. Parts of me were scattering to the wind, crumbling, disintegrating. I had prepared a rickety painted crate in which I began stashing certain soul items that I intended for my brother and for his daughter, my niece, Aiysha. She was to receive my journal and the book I received as a gift, also a journal. She intended to be a scientist who studied deep time. The journals were meant for her. I placed an explicit note stating my intentions atop the crate. I was waiting to add the journals and close the crate. There were a few select bundles of the best vintage porn for Montel and Ambrose in the crate, a scarf collection, a collection of crystals and other stones I found along the way, and a few books I figured my dearest dears would appreciate. That was it, one crate, a life. The record collection was going to Raymond. If my mother outlived me, the crate would go to her, she would hold onto it. On her death the contents would be distributed, such were my instructions.

Peachy rays streaked the room, and I sat in a lumpy though comfortable velvety wingback upholstered chair. Raymond was scheduled to come for an hour in an hour. It was now or never. My life again was populated by people. Friends were constantly around me, fussing over me. The pain and fatigue were minimized by a charge of anticipation and drama. It was irrational that I had waited several decades to approach the journal in its totality. The waiting signified how much it meant to me, an enigmatic gesture by people unknown to me, presented to me when I was barely conscious, barely alive. In front of me, on my desk I unraveled the scarf I had been protecting it in, laid the scarf across the surface of the desk and placed the journal on top. The journal was handmade, the feel was organic. Getting the cord around it to come loose was a challenge. Cutting it was not an option—doing so would feel like sacrilege. I teased it out and at last the twine, or hairlike material, fell to the side. The journal was revealed. Time to make a cup of tea. I needed another interlude before opening it. I made some green tea and came back to the desk. Afternoon light shone directly on the journal, the sun its lodestar.

The doorbell rang and it was Raymond, early, with groceries and a bouquet of hand-picked flowers. He found some chamomile growing in the park and made a little nosegay. How did he manage to look so cute and radiant, always? My heartbeat quickened. It always does when he is around. His presence is medicine. Raymond is also an intrepid fox and noted my furtiveness immediately. I quickly wrapped the scarf around the journal and placed it into the drawer of the desk. "You are full of vigor today," he exclaimed with a questioning tone, extending his spine curvaceously while he leaned on my desk. His wink pointed to the surreptitious atmosphere in the room. I batted my eyelashes and gave him a hug when he stooped over me. "Come, have a tea with me," I distracted his attention. He sensed I was up to something that was out of his purview and let it go. A relief not to have to find a way to explain the journal and its trajectory in my life. His inclination would be to toss it away because of its weathered appearance. We had tea, he departed, after filling me with bromides that, when originating from him, rang of utmost sincerity and consideration. I had a few hours before I was expecting anyone else to arrive at my door.

Out came the journal wrapped in the scarf. I laid it again on the desk. This time I moved quickly. To the side I placed the handmade rope and got right to opening it. The pages were made of paper so smooth and thin as to be almost transparent. The ink, organic, maybe made of plant pigment mixed with ground stone of some sort. The color was a dark green. The script flowed across the page like living floral outgrowths. It took a minute to adjust my reading technique to have the capacity to decipher it. Once I got the hang of the cursive lettering, meanings rushed at me. I couldn't falter now, though an impression of having already absorbed the messaging rose within me as reflexive recall. By the fourth page, I realized I could extemporaneously recite the previous page and then realized I could recite the following page before actually reading it. The weirder aspect was that none of this felt strange. The book implanted itself as conscious awareness. My waning body supported the contents of the book. I thought I was actively dying and that my life was flashing in front of me, except the images were of this other community of people I had briefly met all those years ago on the strand at Treasure Island. The ones wearing floral garb. The ones who nurtured me momentarily when I washed up ashore with Ed, near death with exhaustion, exposure, and from the nefarious medical experimentations that were done to us at the naval hospital. With a chronology deciphered came the understanding of who they were. They had given me no explanation as to why they had imparted the book to me, but that wasn't necessary. The book was a gift of expansive consciousness from a community at the brink of time. They didn't have much time left before they were going to be reabsorbed by time itself.

Extinction. A combinatorial process of annihilation and disappearance. A death that relates to a totalized vanishing of a group, a species, a lineage of living beings. How long now have they been gone? Or was their visitation an augury that I was somehow involved with, forecasting an event that would occur sometime in the future at a time I would not be around to experience? Time buckled. Energetically I sucked in oxygen, held the journal close to me, breathed in the evidence it shared of lived reality. One brief encounter on a shore had yielded an end-of-life euphoria, because I did feel euphoric. Their struggles and insights merged with my life history. The breadth of collective memories altered the structure of my consciousness. Understandings quaked. I no longer felt solitary in a predicament with death. I swear it began to rain in the room, but the rain didn't touch the floor. After it rained there was thunder and then a clearing. I finally placed the journal along with my journal in the crate for my niece. Then I laid down on the sofa and dozed, drifting in time, various layers of time cushioning me, and I was once again in Ed's arms, or floating on a wave in the ocean with seagrass swaying around me, the sky so black it was liquid, the stars so radiant they imprinted explosions of light within me.

FLINDERS REEF, QUEENSLAND PLATEAU, MUSHROOMING DATA

What might be most notably human is the need to detail a chronology of our involvements in time and space. Perhaps it is that data, the profusion of it, that is ultimately what qualifies an entrance into a new era. The accumulation of social, political, economic, and spiritual evidence of our terrestrial existence. The itemizations of what are known or assumed to be facts. The powerful imaginary forces at play in the invention of systems, technologies, and objects that imprint themselves on the globe. The ability to imagine a monster and then actualize it. To make blueprints that allow for the replication of maligning power. The force of conceptualizations (the data) that generate the rift between humans' and other-than-humans' lives and material forms. The documentation of every move and shift. A performance of mass destruction for the future to deconstruct, evidence intact. Will the data survive? In what forms? Will the motivations of the architects of such forces of violence make any sense in future times when conceivably there are pockets of humanity that continue to eke out an existence?

The planet's biosphere is approaching a state shift. Critical thresholds have been crossed. The data overwhelmingly proves this. One scientist I spoke with called this the sledgehammer effect. My inclination is to use a word that describes how silently deafening the anthropogenic death knell sounds. Annihilation is curiously quiet and noisy at once. The sites of disaster shift. An absurd equilibrium sets in after a crisis. Disaster occurs in so many forms. How have human sensory perceptions changed in response to the now occurring and impending destruction that anthropogenic threat represents, the scale of which is impossible to fathom?

When I was a child growing up in East Germany my parents were tasked with working on science that would ameliorate the effects of heavy metal contamination and poisoning. They worked in a laboratory that sought to understand processes of ingestion and absorption of toxic heavy metals. Their research developed chelation techniques that withdrew metals from the body and also focused on how to extract heavy metals from water and soil. Their lab was filled with plants they grew and hybridized. They also worked on a synthetic chelation chemical, ethylenediaminetetraacetic acid. The human body relies on various heavy metals for metabolic and nutritious qualities such as iron, zinc, cobalt, copper, chromium, selenium, magnesium, and molybdenum. Other heavy metals cause poisoning, lead being the most well-known. In the United States lead was ubiquitous in home and industrial use. It is a common material used in manufacturing. It also persists in underlayments of paint, in home plumbing, and in the infrastructure of municipal water systems. Leaded gas wasn't banned until 1996. There is a buildup of lead in the ecosystem. Since the 1950s the quantity of heavy metals used in industry has exponentially increased though regulations have helped to cut back quantities in certain sectors. This spring cadmium, arsenic, and mercury were discovered in a well-known baby food.

After East Germany opened, we moved to the United States. My parents learned about several visual artists who were poisoned by the substances in the paints they used, most notably Jay DeFeo, who dedicated eight years of her life on one painting, *The Rose*. The lead in the paint damaged her nervous system and eventually led to her death. The painting weighs nearly a ton and contains over five thousand dollars' worth of industrial-strength paint. Such scenarios led me to investigate industrial and military residues in geological terms, to discover how toxic heavy metals build up in ecosystems, especially in waterways, lakes, and oceans and in the plants and animals living in affected habitats. My parents were quick to point out that mushrooms were bioindicators of heavy metals in the local environment. It is from my parents directing my attention to mushrooms that I realized how important it is to field insights from other forms of sentience and from the material world. They picked mushrooms not to eat but to study. We took walks in the forest together. "Jan," they called out to me whenever one of them found a specimen. "This mushroom contains a lot of information." "Jan, look at this mushroom! It is actively absorbing everything in the environment!" they would exclaim.

Now I am based in England and work at the University of Leicester. My colleague Alita is employed by the Australian Institute of Marine Science. Before involving myself with cores from coral reefs in Australia I made a study of the presence of mercury evident in places with a history of military activity related specifically to World War II munitions. Mercury shows up everywhere but is especially concentrated in areas where ammunitions were detonated. Mercury fulminate is a material used in detonation devices and is extremely volatile. Mercury moves within the ecosystem, is transported in the water, by plants and animals who absorb it and travel around. In a marine environment, sedimentary layers collect such toxins. During World War II the Baltic Sea became a convenient dump for captured German ammunition such as aerial bombs, artillery shells, and grenades. Many of the canisters are now rusting through on the ocean floor and mercury is being released.

Turning my attention to corals has been eye-opening. Coral polyps are sensitive animals that absorb whatever is in the waters where they live. They subsist on the algae that live within the exoskeletons of their ancestors; a symbiotic relationship is operative throughout their colonies. Their colonies expand over time as exoskeletons build up creating a superstructure. Algae make sugar out of sunlight and this production nourishes the coral. At night the coral extend their tentacles out of the skeletons and seek zooplankton. Some coral eat larvae and the detritus that floats in the ocean. Certain coral eat small fish. They reproduce both sexually and asexually, through fragmentation and by budding polyps that grow off their parents. Some coral species live in all-male or all-female colonies. Coral reefs create habitats for numerous other animals and plants.

We took core extractions from a stony coral colony located at an offshore reef on the Queensland Plateau. The density bands were visibly dramatic when x-rayed. The cores collect sedimented sequences from as far back as 1710 CE. Additional samples were taken at Britomart Reef. At Britomart Reef I assisted with the core extraction from an aqueous position while the boat bobbed above the water's surface. I had on a full breathing apparatus but no wetsuit, just my usual bathing suit. In a quick turnaround I accidentally brushed against a fire coral, and its neurotoxins immediately entered my bloodstream. Fire coral are actually more closely related to jellyfishes and sea anemones; their tentacles release a stinging poison. The sting was double resonant, by which I mean physically and emotionally.

When we were working in the ocean there were tremendous fires burning on the mainland. The sting I received became a symbolic register of the crisis humans, animals, and plants were experiencing because of warming oceans, a warming climate, pollution—the whole litany of factors and now, devastating fires. I took the sting as an alarm that simultaneously sounded off in every ecosystem, in every habitat. A stinging consciousness. What causes a society to avoid an alarm and what causes recognition? The sting gave me insight into these dynamics. The sting accessed a region of my consciousness not lulled by distracted thought in the regimented, financialized, time-managed system I lived in. The sting repositioned my body in time. In time with the fire coral. In time with the fires. In time with death and in time with life. It was an inoculation against forgetting the importance of interdependence.

I mentioned to my colleague that it would be meaningful to record our experiences with the coral reef, to allow emotive elements into the science. I pegged her as resistant to this sort of intervention—letting feeling into the work. I wondered if she'd think of such an effort as anthropomorphizing experience. When I approached Alita it turned out she was okay with this. Enthusiastic even. She pulled out a notebook to show me notations she made that were more like journal entries. "We are scientists, but it doesn't mean we don't feel deeply." She told me that she felt instinctually certain that other organisms understand acutely a changing climate and are doing what they can to prepare, to survive, to make their way in radically altered ecosystems. We discussed how it was a fallacy and conceited to imagine humans as the only species capable of perceiving climate disruption and the implications of disaster. Alita told me she thought that humans might in fact be one of the tardiest species when it comes to recognizing how all life is direly challenged by human-induced climate change. Humanity hardly blinked until reaching the brink of annihilation and still we aren't organizing on a mass scale to avert mutually assured destruction.

We agreed to challenge boundaries and comfort zones. We started to brainstorm together about how to negotiate the affective environment we were working in. The near total opacity of emotions in the scientific field meant we had to start at point zero. Where in the numbers were grief and pain? We decided to preface any paper we wrote going forward with a disclosure about our personal observations regarding emotional and somatic manifestations that were impactful but couldn't be described numerically or fell outside of the focus of our areas of study. A great relief overcame me. Alita and I hugged. Our first hug. Her intelligence coursed through me.

Our team moved off the bedrock island where we'd taken several ice core extractions to a neighboring site near the Weddell Sea. We needed to take an additional sample for comparison. Around us was a scene of desolate white Antarctic endlessness. I inscribed my name in the white dunes: Elizabeth. The high velocity winds erased my name in seconds.

Once we were all fully in place, we positioned the equipment and proceeded to drill. The core we drilled extends back to around 1617 CE. As soon as the sample was removed huge sea spiders crawled out of the hole. There were dozens—they had long, spindly beige legs and miniscule heads that protruded from their legs that contained the tiniest blue eyes. We weren't prepared for marine arthropods clinging to the core as we extracted it. The spiders clambered out of the hole onto the snow into the fierce winds. Nothing, it seemed, would deter them. Perhaps they nested in the ice, had constructed tunnels in the ice. The Antarctic Peninsula was once part of Gondwana until the Late Cretaceous. These creatures looked ancient, made of ancient material and ancient code inexplicably suited for the present moment. They were unfazed by strong white light and subzero temperatures. If someone would have told me the spiders had been designed in a biotech lab, I would have believed them. On noticing the spiders everyone except Daidu scrambled away into the gale force gusts. Kimmo said, "They are extremophiles," once we had regrouped. "*We* are extremophiles," I countered. "So true, so true," he crooned in harmony with the tonality of the whipping wind. With our extraneous protective layers we didn't look human. Eventually feeling more comfortable we all paused to admire the spider's developmental plasticity.

The spiders were as large as dinner plates, just like an online article said they were, once I was able to consult the internet. At dinner where we sated ourselves on rehydrated food rations, I pointed out that polar gigantism was prevalent in many faunal species. A scarcity of food in the depths of the Antarctic causes animals to become more efficient with the conversion of caloric intake to energy. There is a phenomenon called deep sea gigantism I also read up on. Theory has it that these animals are able to grow large bodies because of the prevalent availability of oxygen and a slower metabolism caused by the cold.

Kimmo mentioned the recent proliferation of king crabs in the Palmer Deep, but we didn't see any on this expedition. Because of the warming temperatures in the region an invasion by lithodids has been predicted.

Snowdrifts piled up that night. The wind became increasingly fiercer. We could barely hear each other, even though we were crammed in together in one tent. In two days we'd retreat to the Palmer Long-Term Ecological Research study area, one of three U.S. research centers in the Antarctic. It houses twenty year-round residents and additional guests who come to do studies. It feels necessary to be with other humans in the Antarctic, a bleak place. Though, for all the expansiveness, bunking here involves tight quarters, and claustrophobia can set in. Working in the Antarctic is a moody experience.

The other core we retrieved is from the Palmer Deep, just south of Anvers Island. Cores from this zone give a window into the sedimentation from the Late Pleistocene until the present, a time of massive transition. Climactic events such as the Little Ice Age, Neoglacial, Hypsithermal, and the Bølling-Allerød to Younger Dryas transition are clearly marked in the strata. The ice is blackened, thick and goopy with pollen and other material. Volcanic events guide us in determining a timeline within the core. The annual laminae show a specific line of pollen and dust that acts as a reference point for the start of the Holocene epoch that began after the last ice age ended.

The incident with the spiders during core extraction took place in 2012, well before the pandemic affected the world. Our method now of consulting with each other is through Zoom. Since the start of the pandemic, we have been working with the core individually, though recently we've rejoined in the lab.

A sudden compulsion occurred when I worked with the core for the last time before our report was due. Kimmo was in the lab with me. We wore hazmat suits and masks. Something came over me. I moved my mask to my chin and with my finger, I gouged out a small morsel of the core, somewhere near the division of the Younger Dryas. It became important to select this period. The mushy teaspoon of sediment landed on my tongue. I swished it around in my mouth as if I was a wine connoisseur testing a rare vintage. I swallowed. Here was the delicacy of deep time. I guess I could have eaten a clump of sand by the roadside from just about anywhere to experience deep geologic time. But this was neatly sedimented. A pristine core. Perhaps my one opportunity.

Out of the corner of his vision, Kimmo saw what I had done and rushed over, "What the . . . hell! Did you just do what I think you have, or have I lost a grip on reality?" He edged closer to me, analyzed my expression. "You just gulped down a section of the core!" "Oh my god, oh my god. God is not part of my belief system, but nevertheless, oh my GOD!" and then he shook me. I think he thought I'd spit it out. I didn't. It traveled down my esophagus to my stomach. Eventually it would depart from my body, but there would always be a trace. It was a giddy feeling. Maybe akin to enlightenment, maybe enlightenment, or more simply, with similar spiritual connotation: revelation. The inside of my body never felt as pronounced, receptive. A bit of nausea came on, but it passed quickly. The expression of time as actual earth in my body was as banal as anything, and I recognized everything I usually ingest is both fresh and ancient, primordial, of a never-ending history, a holism of immersion. Time has flavor that I only then awakened to. My objective was not taste as much as absorptive fascination. An opportunity to sample earth before it had been "contaminated" by humans. Human matter might have entered this core, true, but there were no industrialized elements in the piece I ingested. The combination of briny sweatiness, bone marrow, and a rancid fetidness similar to cat feces floored me. I smelled a waft of methanesulfonic acid on my breath. Kimmo got too close to me, breaking through the boundary of creature comfort, so I burped in his face. The core was now atomized as a belch from my gut that wafted in the room and no doubt found its way down the hall, out the windows and doors, dispersing into the wider atmosphere.

vienna, austria, fire desired water and there was more

Here's what Petra, Zahra, and I, Renate, tend to try and decipher when we aren't considering the characteristics of the cores we've removed from the earth: cataclysms and conspiracy theories. When life is precarious, misinformation mixes with deep distrust allowing absurd plots to gain credibility. There is a growing population who have become wrapped up in various dubious theories that involve nefarious deep state operations. The implantation of nanocomputer chips into the bloodstream of the population to control and surveil everyone's movements is one such paranoid projection that gained a foothold during the pandemic. Anti-vaxxers claim Bill Gates is behind manipulative nanotechnology added to COVID-19 vaccines. The deep state is depicted as a cabal of satanic vampires composed of government and industry that feed on the blood and sex of children. Another is that climate change is a hoax. Such suspicions are apparent in the United States, but the tendency is spreading internationally with different iterations and ideological constructs at play. Convoluted schemes circulate globally. Many conspiracy theories center on racial anxiety and are the product of white nationalist, far-right extremists. French white nationalist conspiracy writer Renaud Camus coined the term "Great Replacement" to describe a plot by the global elite to replace the white population in Europe with nonwhite, non-European immigrants. The concept of "white genocide" has gained traction in the United States and in Europe.

The rift between reality and delusion is growing wider, is more difficult to navigate, and is becoming more violent and deadly. Humans are swept up by the accelerated pace of a world transforming beyond recognition. Petra and Zahra are conspiracy experts while also being exceptional Earth scientists. There is a link between global climate change and extremism, and both are life threatening.

Dire predictions are continually broadcast, yet major alterations to system-wide industrial and municipal practices have not been enacted when it comes to climate change. Legislation has not been drastic enough to seriously effect change. Organizing a gathering of world leaders for a week of meetings is one thing, funding science to gather evidence yet another, writing up a thousand-page document another. Behind the reticence are industrial, military interests that have little intention of holistic approaches to sustained living on the planet. For thirty years oil companies have obfuscated data from their in-house research that found conclusively that greenhouse gas emissions from the burning of fossil fuels causes irreparable damage to the Earth's atmosphere. The oil companies were not alone in corporate deception. Most industrial production has deleterious effects both short-term and long-term that pose challenges. Yet, anything that adversely affects the gross domestic product is considered hazardous to the economy, and thus a risk, even though the GDP is a structural adversary to the environment. Sometimes it's not conspiracy, it is the system.

Petra and Zahra are the University of Vienna postdoc team specializing in nuclear and isotope physics. We work with Michael, a research professor also from the University of Vienna, who heads the team. He is a geologist focused on geodynamics and sedimentation. I am a research-based installation artist who works in tandem with them. I help with the physical and logistic labor. I shadow their activities while guiding my attention to various queries of my own regarding the timescale of the human geochemical footprint of the Viennese Anthropocene. Our work site is near Hypotopia, an envisioned utopian city proposed by a group of students in response to Austria's worst postwar financial scandal. A bank was bailed out to the tune of nineteen billion euros of state aid. The scandal had been investigated ongoingly as an incidence of white-collar crime involving Austrian bankers, politicians, and Balkan mafia bosses. In the 1990s the bank Hypo Alpe Adria overextended its lending in the Balkans. The bank was nationalized in 2009 to prevent its collapse. There was little public uproar though polls showed that most Austrians would have preferred that the bank went under rather than be rescued by a taxpayer bailout. Students from the Technical University of Vienna, incensed by the meaningless expenditure, imagined what if instead the bailout money had been used to build a city. They made a provisional model out of concrete of an envisioned city at the scale of 1 to 100 and erected it in Karlsplatz Square as a way to generate creative communal actions to catastrophes. Their city plan involved viable housing for a population of one hundred thousand people, healthcare, and education for all. The name they decided on combined the word "hypo" from the failed bank and utopia. The model stood for three weeks in the plaza. There is an afterimage of it in many people's minds. The youth demonstrated what they would do if they were given responsibility. What came to their minds was mutual aid in the form of communal livability.

The techno fossils the scientific team came for are procured from nineteenth-century wells. The cores contain rubble from World War I and World War II. The anthropogenic signal is also revealed in a layer from the 1950s to 1960s with plutonium 239 present. It is extremely hazardous in low quantities, unlike cesium 137 and strontium 90, low-level nuclear waste from conventional reactors. Together, these are the three most meaningful isotopes they'll look at. There's a coconut porter named Plutonium-239 brewed by the Manhattan Project Beer Company. They sell it in Vienna! Petra bought a six-pack and brought it to the core retrieval site the first time we met together as a group. We gave out a collective gasp when we saw the label, then eagerly drank the beer.

I sipped it down and soon left the formation of scientists. I didn't say anything to them about where I was headed. We'd catch up later. Following trees and shrubbery I took off into the night. In a nearby park, I met a person seated on a bench and within minutes we were scrambling through dense hedges to a little clearing that gave an open view of the sky but was obscured from every other angle. The foliage held sway. The person I met gave off a forest vibe. When I approached them, I swear I heard bats in their hair, a kestrel's vocalization emanating near them. There was a beaver movement to their stride. They told me we were in the Wienerwald Biosphere Reserve. How did we breach the boundary? I didn't notice a fence, a gate, or anything. A black woodpecker landed on my shoulder. Then, suddenly, there were several squirrels around my feet. The person led me to a beech grove, and we reclined on the ground covered in moss and dry leaves. The slight buzz I had from the beer was long gone, replaced by a more resonant sensation of light-headed reverie. I couldn't tell where my body started and where my body ended. I was no longer confined by my skin. The forest glowed, the chlorophyll almost fluorescent. I just met this person, yet we could have been intimate for a lifetime, there was no distrust or anxiety in our interaction. "Here, drink from this spring, it's very fresh water," they gestured at a trickling brook and then to a spot where the water pooled. They slurped the liquid spouting from the earth that then ran along a stream. We reclined under the largest beech I'd ever seen. On its trunk there were carvings like those that typically spelled out lovers' names. Way up on the trunk, where someone climbed, there were daunting phrases. "Watch out what you wish for" and "You only come this way once," also more elusive statements: "Dissolving in the underbrush is an understatement" and the cryptic but spacious, "The Floracene is upon us." Further up the lettering said, "Don't forget the minerality of time." I winced when I imagined the damage to the tree.

My companion grabbed me from behind and tugged me to the soft forest floor. We didn't speak a word for a while though we did make guttural sounds. Smacking, sucking, smooching. We were reconstituted by the forest, the soil underneath the leaves, the scents in the air, our mingled bodies, the sweat merging with the trickling brook. Our clothes were off and created a nest. A grayish dust settled on us. I recognized it as illite, clay minerals that are the result of the denudation of the rising Alps, a chemical weathering process. There was also a prevalence of kaolinite, causing us to look ghostly, and disappear to ourselves. Kaolinite is a material used broadly in industry, there is an array of applications. It gives a glossy coating to paper, it is an ingredient in cosmetics, ceramics, toothpaste, and is used in organic farming to ward off insects. The minerals were common ones but to notice them in abundance here in the forest was surprising. They coated the ferns and the waxy leafed plants with red berries that now looked pinkish because of the dust coating. The clay changed us. Green hues of the forest reflected off of our bleached skin.

A compressed plate crumples, the earth is lifted, minerals come to the surface, changing the contours of the land as the mountain grows. An orogeny was taking place. The uplift and exhumation of the organic interior was happening around us. Sex caused our senses to peak. The sounds of ants and other bugs were amplified as I swiveled my head against the roots of the beech tree. My nostrils took in the scat of a chamois who had wavered from the high peaks of the Rax and Schneeberg Mountains. The person I was pleasuring seemed like a salamander to me. I worried that salty sweat might damage their skin. I felt them out, vision was faulty, touch was supportive. A rhythmic thrum of their heart organ synchronized with the woodpecker we spotted earlier. They wanted my tongue in their anus and I obliged. When I moved there the cavity became a tunnel into cavernous rock, moist with the texture of dripping stone, a lithological source. My elbow collapsed into a pit of acorns, scratchy, puncturing skin, stirring sensation away from other erogenous zones. My toes dug into the fluffy loam, and as my ears grazed the forest floor the sounds of insects marching in line or scurrying under the leaf cover filled me. Many eyes were upon us, eyes darting with our movements. Chipmunks and mice had attuned to our activity as we created a sonic rumble across the forest floor. Birds viewed us from the tree branches. I saw a raptor out of the corner of my eye with its catch in its beak, dripping viscera, blood. My lover's weight on top of me suddenly was liquid fire as their shape changed. They were seemingly everywhere, internally, and externally. They transmitted fire. The presence of smectite, expandable clay. A coeval slope and basinal deposits. From here I could navigate to the other trees. From the beech tree to a grove of downy oak below, to the roots. From here I could retrieve other bodies of water. I was required to bring water to the fire. The other bodies around me communicated this to me. My lover expressed this with gravitational force. It was logical and it was the sensual response I made. Water took me through time. Fire brought me back to the present.

notes

Presence was inspired by actual relationships and processes that have occurred, are occurring, or will have had happenings . . . in mutable togetherness. Time and space are treated historically and also kaleidoscopically.

I loosely modeled the "Performance" sections of *Presence* on David Buuck's *Buried Treasure Island* tour that was performed multiple times between July 20 and October 18, 2008, as part of a multiplatform investigation conducted by BARGE (Bay Area Research Group in Enviro-aesthetics) for *Ground Scores*, curated by Valerie Imus for Yerba Buena Center for the Arts' *Bay Area Now 5* triennial festival of visual art, film, and performance. The performance was restaged to coincide with the 2013 Conference on Ecopoetics at UC Berkeley, organized by Angela Hume, Gillian Osborne, and Margaret Ronda. I experienced this performance in 2013. The identities and life stories of the performers and Randy, the tour guide, are fictionalized. Treasure Island, too, has been transformed by my imagination.

All the golden spike sites are actual locations where stratigraphic analysis is presently being conducted by Earth scientists affiliated with the Anthropocene Working Group (AWG). The scientists' names and profiles that I have ascribed have no bearing or relation to actual persons.

The philosopher is a composite of several contemporary female philosophers, all of whom have been incredibly generative and grounding in my quest of a workable philosophic premise of being-in-worlds.

The sources I engaged with were numerous. I referred to white papers, academic journal articles, interviews, intergovernmental panel reports, online video lectures, books, and informal discussions with peers. It isn't possible to retrace the trajectory that my research took. This book represents communal intelligence and collaborative world-making. I was open to maximal influence and absorption.

The following books, articles, and talks were important in the writing of *Presence.*

Akins, Damon B., and William J. Bauer Jr. *We Are the Land: A History of Native California.* Oakland: University of California Press, 2021.

Anderson, M. Kat. *Tending the Wild: Native American Knowledge and the Management of California's Natural Resources.* Berkeley: University of California Press, 2005.

Armstrong, A. Elizabeth. *Forging Gay Identities: Organizing Sexuality in San Francisco, 1950–1994.* Chicago: University of Chicago Press, 2002.

Barad, Karen. *Meeting the Universe Halfway: Quantum Physics and the Entanglement of Matter and Meaning.* Durham, N.C.: Duke University Press, 2007.

Chakrabarty, Dipesh. *The Climate of History in a Planetary Age.* Chicago: University of Chicago Press, 2021.

City and County of San Francisco Civil Grand Jury. "Buried Problems and a Buried Process: The Hunters Point Naval Shipyard in a Time of Climate Change." June 14, 2022.

Colebrook, Claire. *Death of the PostHuman: Essays on Extinction.* Ann Arbor: Open Humanities Press, 2015.

Estes, Nick. *Our History Is the Future: Standing Rock Versus the Dakota Access Pipeline, and the Long Traditions of Indigenous Struggle.* London: Verso, 2019.

Gagliano, Monica, John C. Ryan, and Patrícia Vieira, eds. *The Language of Plants, Science, Philosophy, Literature.* Minneapolis: University of Minnesota Press, 2019.

Haraway, Donna J. *Staying with the Trouble: Making Kin in the Chthulucene.* Durham, N.C.: Duke University Press, 2016.

LaDuke, Winona. *Recovering the Sacred: The Power of Naming and Claiming.* Chicago: Haymarket, 2005.

Irigaray, Luce, and Michael Marder. *Through Vegetal Being: Two Philosophical Perspectives.* New York: Columbia University Press, 2016.

Mbembe, Achille. *Out of the Dark Night: Essays on Decolonization.* New York: Columbia University Press, 2021.

McKittrick, Katherine, ed. *Sylvia Wynter: On Being Human as Praxis.* Durham, N.C.: Duke University Press, 2015.

Merchant, Carolyn. *The Death of Nature: Women, Ecology, and the Scientific Revolution.* San Francisco: HarperOne, 1980.

Mithen, Steve. *After the Ice: A Global Human History 20,000–5,000 BC.* London: Phoenix, 2003.

M. Parsons, Keith, and Robert Zaballa. *Bombing the Marshall Islands: A Cold War Tragedy.* Cambridge: Cambridge University Press, 2017.

Rory, Carroll. "Treasure Island Radiation Discovery Casts Shadow over Expansion Plans." *The Guardian.* August 17, 2012. https://www.the guardian.com/environment/2012/aug/17/treasure-island-radiation-us -navy.

Smith, M., and K. Mieszkowski. "Treasure Island Cleanup Exposes Navy's Mishandling of Its Nuclear Past." *Bulletin of the Atomic Scientists* 70, no. 3 (2014): 65–78. https://doi.org/10.1177/0096340214531186.

Stengers, Isabelle, "On the Urgencies of Our Times." Talk delivered at the Driving the Human Festival: Section 5, Knowledge. November 20–22, 2022. https://www.youtube.com/watch?v=yMil7UDSGOE.

Stryker, Susan, and Jim Van Buskirk. *Gay by the Bay: A History of Queer Culture in the San Francisco Bay Area.* San Francisco: Chronicle, 1996.

Tudge, Colin. *The Time before History: Five Million Years of Human Impact.* New York: Touchstone, 1996.

White, M. Monica. *Freedom Farmers: Agricultural Resistance and the Black Freedom Movement (Justice, Power, and Politics).* Chapel Hill: University of North Carolina Press, 2018.

Yusoff, Katheryn. *A Billion Black Anthropocenes or None.* Minneapolis: University of Minnesota Press, 2018.

The italicized poetic fragments in the prologue are from the following sources; if not attributed they are by the author:

"My father said." Athena Farrokhzad. Trans. Jennifer Hayashida. Excerpt from the poem "Vitsvit." Pen America. https://pen.org/vitsvit/.

"A life of spare parts, bucolic." Stacy Doris. *Kildare.* New York: Roof, 1994.

"We are the singing remnants." Leanne Betasamosake Simpson. Excerpt from the poem "i am graffiti." The Walrus. July–August 2015. https:// thewalrus.ca/i-am-graffiti/.

"Two forms of fabrication." M. Mara-Ann. *Containment Scenario.* Oakland: O Books, 2009.

Additional quotes are as follows:

"Attention is an important resource." bell hooks. *All About Love: New Visions.* New York: Harper Perennial, 2001.

"dew of the sea." Juliette de Baïracli Levy. *Juliette of the Herbs.* Directed by Tish Streeten. Produced by Mabinogion Films, 1998.

"good versus evil, being versus nothingness." Jacques Derrida. *Dissemination.* Trans. Barbara Johnson. Chicago: University of Chicago Press, 2021.

"collateral damage or units of exchange." Kelly Oliver. *Carceral Humanitarianism: Logics of Refugee Detention*. Minneapolis: University of Minnesota Press, 2017.

"A tree teaches us in silence." Luce Irigaray. "What the Vegetal World Says to Us," in *The Language of Plants: Science, Philosophy, Literature*, ed. Monica Gagliano, John C. Ryan, and Patrícia Veira. Minneapolis: University of Minnesota Press, 2019.

"your own madness is what you see as nature turning against you." E. Tracy Grinnell. "The Birds." The Poetry Project. https://www.2009-2019 .poetryproject.org/birds-e-tracy-grinnell/.

"Iroquois peoples *remind* nation-states . . ." Audra Simpson. *Mohawk Interruptus: Political Life Across the Borders of Settler States*. Durham: Duke University Press, 2014.

"the ghost of oppositionality." Diana Taylor. *The Archive and the Repertoire: Performing Cultural Meaning in the Americas*. Durham, Duke University Press, 2003.

Dispatch. Raven Chacon and Candice Hopkins. Performed at Amant, with Laura Ortman and Marshall Trammel. Brooklyn, N.Y. April 2, 2022.

"One woman plus one woman plus one woman will never add up to some generic entity: woman." Luce Irigaray. *Speculum of the Other Woman*. Trans. Gillian C. Gill. Ithaca, N.Y.: Cornell University Press, 1985.

"I have watched as convenience, profit, and inertia excused greater and more dangerous environmental degradation." Octavia E. Butler. *Parable of the Talents*. New York: Warner Books, 1998.

"The oldness of new things." Ericka Huggins. *If They Come in the Morning . . . Voices of Resistance*. Ed. Angela Davis. London: Verso, 2016.

Grateful acknowledgment is made for the permission to include song lyrics from "La Vita" by Beverly-Glenn Copeland: "And the body says 'remember you gotta breathe,' the body says 'take the time to grieve,' the mind says 'let the silence flow.'"

acKnowLeDGmenTs

I am appreciative of Earth's magnitude, and the cosmos's vast intelligence. I would like to acknowledge every ocean, lake, and river, all forests, jungles, meadows, mountains, deserts, the sky, star formations, the atmosphere, rainstorms, droughts, fires, forcefields, dumps, wastelands, sacrifice zones, and occluded sites I've encountered or learned about, and the atoms whose attributes are attraction and repulsion in transformation, aiding me to mature somatically and psychically as a terrestrial being among a vast ecosystem of beings, earthly and cosmic, floral, faunal, and mineral, all finding ways to be together in spacetime. Creature familiars whom I love include Rainbow (RIP, garden spirit), Mumes (RIP, my feline mother), Tina, and Topaz.

Toshi Iijima, Laura Woltag, and Geoff Olsen engaged me continually throughout the making of this book—they were my most steadfast confidantes. They accomplished the soul work of giving me the confidence to create this labyrinth in spacetime. They are practitioners of the deepest attunement. I first met Laura at the Conference on Ecopoetics at UC Berkeley, what a lucky confluence of energies. Her book of poems *Serviceable Clothes for Life in the Open* found fruition while I worked on *Presence*, offering impactful mutual exchange. Geoff's manuscript *Nerves between Song* shapeshifted into being during this time. Hearing him read his poems at twilight in the garden was scintillating.

Thanks to my sister, Elka, who knows her way around the obstacle course we share.

Janice Lee's friendship (and her timely gift of 팅크제 약물, medicinal tinctures) gave me the inspiration necessary to see my way into cacophonies of being. During the writing of this book, her novel *Imagine a Death* was published. Being privy to her thinking and life processes is friendship holism.

Zack Finch has proved to me over and again that deep connections are what make life as a citizen of this planet meaningful. His developing collection of essays, *The Village Beautiful*, shimmers.

Tammy Fortin helped ground me when serious life challenges threated with terminating energy. Also, she read from her emergent novel at my mom's kitchen table and laugher was generated; that mirth was tantamount to liberation.

Marianne Shaneen was an important interlocutor during the editing phase of this project. We reunited at a key moment. To witness her novel, *Homing*, in the making has been monumental. Prepare yourselves, world!

Delirious thanks to Christine Shan Shan Hou for her collage.

At the first reading I gave of this work in insipient form, at a small gallery in Cambridge, Massachusetts, Christine Wertheim commented that the voicing reminded her of Riddley Walker, Russell Hoban's enigmatic character. I rode on the fumes of that compliment throughout the duration of the book's coming-into-being.

Friendships budded during the time of writing this book. Thank you, Miki Katagiri and Johann Diedrick.

Thanks to Samuel John Lim-Kimberg for his generous, detailed account of all the time he spent on Treasure Island as a child.

My wider friend network, you know who you are. Continual thanks and love.

I'm deeply thankful to Doug Carlson, Gerald Maa, Soham Patel, and everyone at Georgia Review Books who provided a hospitable, welcoming space for this book to flourish.

Sequences of this book were published in earlier form in:

The Map Is Not the Territory, mercury firs, No, Dear, Fence, and *Sobotka Literary Magazine.*

Printed in the USA
CPSIA information can be obtained
at www.ICGtesting.com
LVHW051553141223
766375LV00004B/345